Rise Above

Peg Willis

Cover art by Kelly Hudgens, Sofi Smith
Front cover background photo: The morning after, Courtesy Christopher Sigsbee George.
Front cover photos: the children: Selah Coller and Liam Coller, photo by Sarah Coller
     the father: Jeremy Moore, photo by the author

Edited by Karen Taylor

Printed in the United States of America

Willis, Peg, 1946 -
Rise Above / Peg Willis-1st edition
ISBN 978-0-578-17000-8
America-Northwest-Oregon-Disasters-History-20th Century-Fiction
Parent and child-Fiction
Child Abduction-Fiction

*To the many hurting children
of the world,
both young and adult*

*May your true Father find you
and hold you in His loving arms!*

- Also by Peg Willis:
  Building the Columbia River Highway:
  They Said It Couldn't Be Done

Table of Contents

Acknowledgments

A book is never the work of only one person.
I would like to thank:

The many people of Heppner and throughout the Northwest who told me stories of their families' experiences during the flood.

The many wonderful people at the Morrow County Heritage Museum in Heppner.

Kari Kandoll at the Wahkiakum County Museum in Cathlamet.

Kayrene and Gary Gilbertsen who shared with me about the early days on Puget Island.

The many critical readers who helped me hone the story to sharpness: Laurie Bradford, Patty Case, Terri Clay, Sally Daley, Linda Harcomb, Helen Heavirland, Marie Martin-Lake, Tammy McCullough, Rebecca Olmstead, Laurie Shafer, Nancy Stroud, Libby Swenson, Shirley Waite, Dolores Walker, and Katelyn Willis.

Marv and Rindy Ross and The Trail Band of Portland, Oregon. The theme of rising up to overcome adversity is universal and compelling. Rindy sings Marv's song, Rise Above, which inspired the title of this book. (rossproductions.com).

And most special thanks to:

Selah Coller, who allowed herself to be photographed looking terrible. She's actually a lovely and delightful young lady.

Karen Taylor, my absolutely wonderful (and sometimes very insistent) editor.

Joann Green Byrd, author of *Calamity: the Heppner Flood of 1903*, who kept insisting that I *could* write this book. She has been a huge encourager and filler-in of details I missed in my own research.

Jim Willis, my husband of almost 50 years, who (now that the book is finished) will be able to see my face more often and remember what I look like.

Real places in Heppner (1903):

1. Fred Krug's Laundry
2. Heppner Gazette
3. Red Front Livery Stable
4. Simmons, blacksmith
5. Mike Galloway, photographer
6. First National Bank
7. Palace Hotel
8. Gilliam & Bisbee Farm Implements
9. Gilliam & Bisbee Hardware
10. McAtee & Swaggert's Saloon
11. Mollie Reid's *Chateau de Joie*
12. Roberts Building
13. Yeager's furniture store/funeral parlor
14. Episcopal Church
15. The Fair (general store)
16. Tommie Brennan, farrier

Other places in Rise Above:

a. Harmony Saddle & Bridle Shop
b. McCheyne home
c. Collins home
d. Burke home
e. Harmon home

Many residences were located along the creek, and Main Street was populated by a variety of businesses ~

a bakery, two tailors, two jewelry stores, a jewelry & repair shop, boots & shoes, shoe repair shop, two restaurants, two Chinese restaurants, several livery stables, a bicycle shop, a lumber yard, six saloons, three blacksmith shops, a stage barn, four barber shops, several law offices, three grocery stores, three drug stores, a confectionary, a millinery shop, a meat market, and the Opera House.

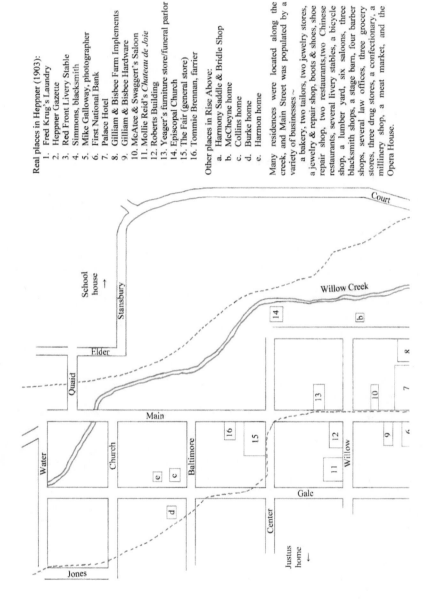

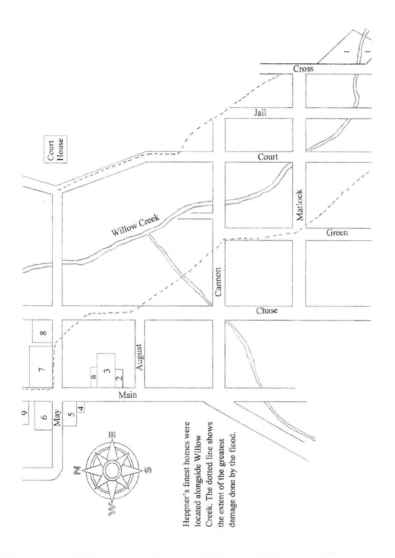

Heppner's finest homes were located alongside Willow Creek. The dotted line shows the extent of the greatest damage done by the flood.

Prologue

Twelve miles above Heppner, in the hills south of town, Air, Earth and Water struggled amongst themselves, jostling for dominance. They taunted one another, elbowing, shoving. These actors were preparing for Opening Night—a drama more powerful than any Morrow County had ever known.

Though it was not a human drama, it would become that in the end. The actors knew their lines; the lighting and sound effects were ready. Air was filled with electricity. Water groaned in the attempt to gather itself into droplets. Earth continued to grow harder, more unforgiving as it baked in the already hot morning sun.

Even this early in the day, the audience seemed to know something was about to happen. Each blade of grass drooped like the tail of a frightened puppy. The wooden boards of houses, barns, and fences stretched—creaking, groaning, as the torment of the environment spilled over into their very being. Roosters strutted, but tentatively; dogs circled and paced; horses nodded their big heads up and down, up and down. People watched the sky and shook their heads. Something was wrong, and they all knew it. They all felt it.

The actors awaited only the lifting of the curtain.

Book One

The Day that Divided History

Chapter One

L ilyann sat at the kitchen table gripping her pencil tightly. "A," she wrote on the paper before her. She was good at "A." She was also good at "Y" and "N"—all the tricky letters in her name. "A"—up and down like a Christmas tree, with ...

A piercing scream interrupted her focus. The house moved, tilted. The walls began to shake.

"Mama?"

Ella *jerked* Lilyann from her chair at the kitchen table and ran toward the front door.

Just as she reached the door, the porch, with a mighty squeal, pulled away from the house, tumbled on its side into rolling mud, and collapsed into splinters. Though the flood was not deep, the house—what was left of it—heaved and buckled, spinning away toward the center of the flow. Ella, Lilyann in her arms, jumped as far as she could toward the hillside only a block away. The depth of the flowing muck was only a foot or two, but she fell, and was rolled over and over by the muddy torrent. Only moments later, the level of the flood had doubled. Ella came to the surface and struggled forward with the heavy mud soaking her dress and pulling her down with tentacles of iron.

They went under again. Thick mud rolled and tumbled them once more, but Ella pushed against the earth below and they came to the top—for a moment. Lilyann gasped for air. The world around her—so dark, so wet, so changed! What was happening? Trees and barns and houses were rolling by, Mama and Lilyann rolling with them. Mama reached out trying to grasp something—anything. Lilyann frantically stretched her arms in every direction seeking something to hang on to. She screamed; Mama screamed!

Under the muddy water again. No air to breathe. Lilyann arched her back and frantically thrashed her legs and arms reaching for air. Back at the top. The loudest sound ever—people and animals screaming, things crashing, tearing apart.

Then ... Lilyann flew through the air, she knew not how, and landed head-first near the edge of the flood in a crumpled heap. She knew no more.

*　　　*　　　*

That Sunday morning had been about as common as they come in the tiny town of Heppner, Oregon. Roosters crowed, birds twittered, and cows announced they wanted to be milked. It could have been most any spring morning in the early 1900s. But it wasn't. This was Sunday, June 14, 1903. Soon, all of life would be divided into *before* and *after* this day.

Lilyann hummed to herself as she knocked at the Burke's back door. Not waiting for an answer, she pushed the door open and called, "Mrs. Burke! Are you ... Oh, there you are. Sorry I hollered." She skipped into the kitchen where Dacia Burke was patting out biscuits for breakfast.

"Good morning, Miss Lily! And how's the fairy princess this fine day?"

"I'm *very* well, thank you, and I'm almost grown up! I'll be five in only *two more weeks*, Mrs. Burke. Did you know?" Lilyann twirled and danced across the floor.

Dacia Burke stifled a laugh and brushed her dark hair out of her eyes. "Yes, I know, and I'm very excited about it. Are you?"

"You *bet* I am! I can just hardly wait at all! I may *die* from excitement!"

At this, Dacia laughed aloud. "Well, I certainly hope not! You're quite the chatterbox this morning. Does your mama know you're over here?"

"Oh yes, she knows. She sent me." Lilyann plopped onto a kitchen chair and began humming again as she swung her legs in time to the song.

Dacia waited, but Lilyann offered no further explanation.

"Okay, *why* did she send you?"

"Oh! I almost forgot! I'm supposed to ask if we could borrow ... um ..." Lilyann tapped a finger against her chin and gazed at the ceiling.

"Eggs?" asked Dacia.

"Eggs! Yes. How did you know?"

Dacia laughed. "Your mama was telling me she needs to raise up a couple more laying hens, so I just guessed." Dacia slid the pan of biscuits into the oven and reached for the egg basket. "Did she say how many?"

"A couple. That's two, you know."

"Is it now? Thanks for explaining it." Dacia laughed quietly and handed two brown eggs to Lilyann. "There you go, my dear. Two eggs for Princess Lily's breakfast." Lilyann thanked her and vanished out the back door as abruptly as she'd arrived.

She dashed back across the street. Then, remembering that eggs were fragile, she slowed and moved gently, carefully up the board sidewalk, a precious egg clutched in each hand.

"I'm being careful, Mama," she called out, as Ella Harmon appeared in the doorway.

"Good job, Lily Girl! I knew you could do it." Ella was glad enough to have Lilyann fetch the eggs from across the street. Being only a month away from bringing a new little Harmon into the family, she was happy for every bit of help she could get! But in truth, Ella was surprised to see her daughter walking so carefully with the fragile eggs.

Lilyann had been named in honor of her grandmother, Lillian Harmon, a lady in every sense of the word. But Lilyann was *not* a lady! She was, in truth, a disaster waiting to happen. Her freckles, cavorting across her nose, were as wild and fun-loving as the child herself.

By age four, Lilyann had already collected some fine scars—one just last month when she raced her older brother, Charlie, to the front porch and, arriving rather abruptly, took a chunk out of her right eyebrow. And Charlie had chipped a tooth as he came in for a landing.

Ella took the eggs to the kitchen, broke them into the bowl of batter, and handed a half slice of crisp bacon to little Gilbert in his high chair. "Bacon," she said, turning to the mixing bowl on the table.

"Bay—con," repeated Gilbert dutifully.

"Mama, can I help?" Lilyann asked.

"Gil—bert," Ella said to the toddler.

"Gib—bie," her son responded.

"Can I?" Lilyann repeated. She interjected her body between Mama and the bowl and tried to take the spoon to stir the pancake batter.

Ella let her have it. She tickled the baby under his greasy chin. "Mama," she coaxed.

Gilbert kicked his feet against the chair's footrest, as he recited the names of his family members. "Mama, Papa, Ye-ann, Sharlie, Gibbie!"

5

Ella laughed. "That's right, Gilbert!" *And it won't be long till you'll have another name to learn*, she thought. *Brother, sister? Who knows? Another girl would be nice.* She turned from his high chair to place more bacon strips in the cast iron skillet. "Careful, Lily! Don't splash it all over the place!" She pushed a damp strand of hair out of her face with the back of her wrist and took the bowl from her daughter.

"You know what, Lily?" Ella said, pouring the first griddle cake. "It's downright *hot* today!"

"It's sticky too, Mama. Can we go to the creek to play after church? We could cool off in the water."

"Gib—bie, bay—con! Gib—bie, bay—con!" little Gilbert crowed in delight, banging his hands on the wooden tray of his high chair. "Gibbie hab cookie? Hab canny?"

Ella laughed. "No Gilbert. No cookies for breakfast. No candy."

"Hab d'ink o' syrup?" he asked hopefully.

Even Lilyann laughed this time. "No, Gibbie!" she said. "No drink of syrup!"

Then she asked again, "Mama, the creek. Can we go play after church?"

"Lily, it's Sunday—not a day for playing in the creek. But don't worry, this heat will break before long. Did you see the clouds coming in? That means we'll probably get rain before the day's over."

There had been a good thunder storm with plenty of rain—hot rain—on Thursday, but Friday and Saturday had been just plain miserable.

Ella scooped up the bacon that had already drained and placed it on the plate in the warming oven. She placed her hands in the small of her back, stretching to relieve the ache of pregnancy, then turned back to Gilbert, who was now demanding to be let down. She dampened the corner of her apron and attempted to wipe his hands and face while he squirmed away from her and patted his hands back in the mess on the high chair tray. Mama kissed the top of his sweaty blond head and lifted him out of the chair. "Lily, would you take Gilbert to the bathroom, please? And as soon as you're finished there, go find Papa and Charlie. Tell them if they don't get in here, I'm going to feed their breakfast to the pig."

"Mama! You wouldn't do that." Lilyann wrinkled her nose. "Would you?"

Ella winked at her and said, "Just go, Lily. Time's a wastin'." She shook her head and laughed to herself.

What a precious, sweet, funny bundle of energy. What a privilege to be her Mama. And what a responsibility! Ella loved it all.

Heppner's Main Street in May, 1903
Note the many wooden buildings.
Courtesy Morrow County Museum

Chapter Two

Mac and Ella Harmon sat in their usual place at All Saints' Episcopal Church. Little Gilbert was on his Mama's lap—what was left of her lap. Eight-year-old Charlie sat between Mama and Papa, stuck to the back of the pew by his sweaty white shirt. Lilyann sat on the other side of Papa, her legs swinging rhythmically back and forth as she hummed her silent accompaniment to the dramatic cadence of the sermon.

*　　*　　*

At the back of the sanctuary a tall, slender man slid noiselessly into the last pew. He was dressed in dark pants and a brown shirt. Neither had been washed in some time. The couple to the man's right inched away from him, a little at a time, until there was a good two feet between the wife and the newcomer. She put her handkerchief to her nose every so often, but the stranger appeared not to notice.

His jet black hair and a full beard of the same color framed a well-shaped nose and dull, smoky-gray eyes—eyes that appeared to retain only a smoldering remnant of their original fire. Except for the eyes, he was a handsome enough man. After he looked around taking in the wainscoted walls, the arched windows, the wooden cross on the white wall behind the preacher, the man's eyes roamed methodically through the sanctuary until they came to rest, finally, on the back of a head several rows in front of him.

Yes. There she was, just as he'd remembered her. It was good he had come back. It was good he was here today. Good to be in the same room. She would see the truth now and want him, and all would be well.

The eyes in the back pew traced the outline of the auburn-haired figure. Left shoulder, up the graceful neck, lingering over the shape of the delicate ear, over the head and down to the right shoulder. He imagined the face on the other side of the head. Oval face, pixie nose with freckles scattered across it, warm brown eyes full of sweetness and passion. Not scorn. No, not scorn. Full, rounded lips begging for kisses. *Beautiful. Absolutely beautiful.*

He glanced away for a moment, then back at the vision before him. *You're mine,* he thought. *You should have been mine.*

*   *   *

The Reverend John Warren droned on. "...And so you see, my friends, God's love is without question. It's true, tragedy may come; hard times are inevitable; we don't always receive the good we pray for ..."

Lilyann's legs swung harder, higher. Papa quietly placed a hand on her knee and the swinging stopped. He shook her knee gently and patted it as if to say, *Yes, I know you're ready to be finished. Just a bit more patience, little one.* Lilyann understood, even though Papa used no words. She heaved a sigh, then reached for Papa's hand and held it in both of hers, smiling up at his warm face with its big, brown tickly moustache. He smiled back and winked an eye at her. She wrinkled her nose and blinked both eyes in reply.

"But remember, ultimately," the rector's words continued to flow without pause. "God's will—his pleasure—is to give us life abundant." His voice had changed in that subtle way even children recognize, indicating the approaching end of the service. "Will you all please rise and join me in singing 'On the Other Side,' number thirty-five in your hymnals."

As the congregation reached for their hymn books, Lilyann stirred and stood to her feet. She liked the singing. She did *not* like long sermons, but oh how she loved to sing!

> *On the other side is a land of wonder*
> *Watered by unfailing streams*
> *There the parted meet, torn by death asunder*
> *Oh how near it sometimes seems*

Although Lilyann had not the least idea what the words meant, she could read them easily, divided as they were into convenient syllables. She had learned to read almost without knowing it by looking over

Mama's shoulder as she helped Charlie practice in the evenings. But it wasn't the reading of the words that mattered anyway. It was the music. Mama had told her that God loved to listen to her sing. So she would sing for him.

On the other side of the rolling tide
We shall meet and sing with the glorified
We shall see the Lord and be satisfied!
Everything will be all right on the other side!

The last notes of the closing hymn died out, and the dark, brooding man slipped out quietly as the benediction was spoken. Members of the congregation began gathering their things and moving toward the back of the sanctuary. Outside, the man moved to the far side of a willow tree and stood with his back to the church, watching the small creek flow by. He waited to hear *her* voice.

*   *   *

Ella was miserable as she shook Reverend Warren's hand and stepped out the church door. *This much heat should be against the law when a body's in the family way,* she thought. *And it's only noon!* She relished the feel of Mac's arm around her shoulder, but at the same time wished he would take it away. It only made another damp sweaty spot on her dress—to match the ones in the center of her back and under each arm. As she and Mac stopped to talk with Robert McCheyne for a moment, Ella managed to maintain her politeness, but really, all she wanted was to get home.

"We'll have rain before the day's over," McCheyne said. "You can feel it in the air."

"We sure do need it," Mac agreed. "Our garden's about to dry up and blow away!"

At that moment, Ella turned and saw that both Charlie and Lilyann had climbed the nearby poplar tree and were swinging from its branches. "Oh! Lily *ANN!* Whatever will I do with you!"

Ella reached up to help her daughter down. "Lily! You *know* it's not ladylike to swing from trees. What were you doing?" She brushed her daughter's skirt back into place.

Lilyann bit her lip and hung her head. "Sorry, Mama."

Charlie dropped to the ground and gazed at the creek. Several boys—heathens who were not forced to attend church with their parents—were splashing and throwing water all over each other. "Can I go play in the creek?" he asked.

"Me too!" Lilyann said, as the family started for home.

Mac glanced toward the creek. "We'll see. Maybe after dinner," was all he said. But Charlie and Lilyann knew that "we'll see" was as good as "yes."

Ella would have just told them no. *What is it about the heat that makes people so cranky?* she wondered, as she continued putting one foot in front of the other. Thankfully it was only a few short blocks to home. At least she would be able to put up her feet, sit still and fan herself ... after she got dinner on the table, that is.

* * *

The air was still hot and oppressive when Dacia Burke set out fresh bread and the pot roast she had cooked yesterday for today's cold noontime dinner. Twelve-year-old Josie set the table. Eight plates— Johnny and Dacia, their five children, and Pappy, Johnny's Irish grandfather.

Josie gave little Walter his own plate to carry to the table, then yelled at him when he dropped it. "Walter, you're just plain clumsy! Look at what you've done now!"

Walter screwed up his face and cried.

"Josie!" Dacia scolded. "He's just a little boy doing the best he can." She stooped to pick up the larger pieces of the plate.

"Well he should be careful, that's all," Josie grumped as she went for the broom and dust pan.

Dacia sighed as the family sat at the table. She was on edge and it was obvious everyone else felt the same. Must be the weather, she thought. Little Sarah fussed continuously; Walter, Will, and Martin griped that the food tasted awful, that they were hot, that in general, they were miserable.

When Martin whined that he wasn't hungry and didn't feel like eating, Pappy took exception to his grumbling.

"You'd better be gettin' that inside o' ya," Pappy said, his voice croaky with age. "You don't know a good thing when you got it. I remember, back in '43 when the potato crop failed ..."

Martin immediately closed his ears and picked up his fork. He did *not* want to hear again about the great Irish potato famine.

Finally, Will asked permission to go play in the creek to cool off.

"No," Dacia said. "It's Sunday."

11

Johnny looked at Dacia and said, "It *is* pretty hot." Johnny, a big, friendly bear of a man, was usually easy to agree with.

"But ... it's the Lord's Day."

Pappy made a harrumphing sound. Once he had everyone's attention, he said, "The Sabbath is Saturday," and immediately went back to eating.

Johnny grinned at Pappy and looked questioningly at Dacia.

Dacia sighed quietly. How she loved this old man with his tousled hair and twinkling eyes! Yes, he repeated himself a good deal of the time; yes, he often spoke nonsense; but still—he had a lot of wisdom to share with those who would hear it. She relented. "Okay, Martin and Will, you two may go. For a while. Will, you stay right with Martin, you hear? And I'll send Josie for you when it's time for supper."

"Me too!" Walter insisted.

"You're not old enough, Walter," Johnny said. "Maybe next year."

"But Mama said—"

Pappy tapped his fork on the side of his plate and glared at Walter. Walter closed his mouth—and then opened it again to continue eating the dinner he didn't want.

Chapter Three

Mollie Reid's *Chateau de Joie* is the dark house at the center of the photo.
Beyond it is the light colored, stone Roberts Building. The building to the left of Roberts
Hall (it has windows; Roberts Hall does not) is the IOOF building,
also constructed of stone.
Photo taken from the hill on the west side of town.
Courtesy Morrow County Museum

Across town from All Saints, in a big house behind the new Roberts Building, the girl's eyes blinked open, then shut again instantly as they were stabbed by a piercing sliver of light. She stretched and rolled to the other side, laying one arm across her eyes to protect them from the glare. She had to get out of bed. She knew she had to get out of bed. It would be a way to escape the horrors which had chased her through the night. Or was it several nights? Or a whole lifetime?

She turned her head to peer at the room through tightly squinted brown eyes. Tiny room, plain in every way. But this was not a working room, just a bedroom. The paint was dark. Green maybe, or brown. But definitely dark. Adjusting to the light, she propped herself on one elbow, opened her eyes carefully, and looked around her. The other bed in the room was empty, but it had been slept in. A crooked pull shade partially covered the small window. The light that had awakened her forced its way into the room around the edges of the shade and pulled her from her tormented dreaming. She shuddered and fell back on the cot, a wavering moan escaping unbidden from her throat.

She pulled her knees tightly to her chest and pressed her face into them. She would not cry. She would not! She would get out of bed, put on her clothes—her younger brother's clothes, actually, his overalls and shirt in which she'd arrived. And she would go find Mollie. Mollie would tell her what to do.

*   *   *

Now dressed in overalls, the girl sat at the wooden kitchen table, her dark hair tumbled in a frightening disarray over her head, her eyes red and swollen.

Mollie poured two cups of coffee and sat herself down, the wooden chair groaning beneath her ample figure. She crossed her ankles, draped her silk dressing gown gracefully over her legs, and leaned back in the chair to give the girl a good looking over. She nodded slowly.

"So," she began in a husky voice. She held a match to the end of her cigarette and inhaled. As she blew the smoke from her lungs, it formed a wreath around her too blond head. "First, we need to get you some decent clothes." She blew out the match and dropped it in an elegant ashtray.

The girl tried to blink away the smoke in her eyes.

"I think you'll clean up just fine. The men'll like you. You have good ..." she held out her cupped hands in front of her chest.

The girl winced.

"... for one so young," Mollie finished. She took a long draw on her cigarette. "Fifteen, did you say?"

"Sixteen ... tomorrow."

"Hmm. Well, the men like that. And ..." Mollie waved her hands in the air describing a female figure. "You'll look fine once we get you out of those overalls and dressed up in something to show off your attributes."

The girl inhaled a shaky breath. She knew the dressing up was just for show. It was the *un*dressing that mattered in a place like this. It hadn't taken her long this morning to figure out what kind of house this was. Her mama had told her about such places. The man who had picked her up last night along the road and brought her into town had dropped her here with confidence Mollie would take her in. And Mollie did.

And she—a scrappy looking remnant of humanity found wandering a country road in the middle of the night—had had nothing to say about it. She had entered the house, collapsed onto the cot, and sought oblivion.

Now, after a long nap, she was having second thoughts. Surely there was something else in town she could do to earn her keep. Maybe she could be a mother's helper. After all, she had practically raised all those brothers on her own, in the years since Mama died.

Mollie took a drink of the thick black liquid she called coffee and squinted her eyes. "What did you do to your hair? It looks like a hay stack."

The girl's hair did, indeed, look like a hay stack. Short stiff pieces sticking out in every direction. She didn't respond to Mollie's question. How could she possibly explain? The pulling at it, sawing it with a dull knife, the ugly outcome ... she had hoped the pain and torment in her heart might be masked by the pain of what she'd done to her hair. But it hadn't worked.

"Never mind. If you've got what it takes, they won't care what your hair looks like."

Mollie sucked once more on the end of her cigarette. "That yellow dress Esmerelda has. That would work. Look nice with your dark eyes. Never looked any good on her anyway. And what did you say your name is? Never mind. I think I'll call you ..." Mollie tilted her head and gazed thoughtfully at her new employee, then at the ceiling. "Lorena! That's good. I hereby christen thee 'Lorena!'"

The girl grimaced, but held her peace. After all, beggars couldn't afford to be picky.

"But ... can you please the men?" Mollie sat up, took a long drink from her cup and leaned forward. She fixed a serious gaze on the girl as she banged the cup back onto the table. "That's what waits to be seen. No experience, huh?"

Mollie's hard look almost froze the girl's blood in spite of the heat. She shrugged one shoulder and gazed at the floor.

"So ... you're a virgin?" Mollie frowned and looked puzzled.

The girl clenched her lips and barely shook her head.

"Hmm." Mollie nodded, her voice softening. "You're not telling the whole story." She drew a deep breath. "Well, maybe you're not ready to talk yet. That's okay, honey." She reached across the table and patted "Lorena's" small hand with her large, bejeweled one. "We all have a story. This is a mean old world, make no mistake. And some folks are luckier than others. It's a shame. A royal shame, that's what it is."

Mollie rose to refill her cup, and offered a refill to the girl, but seeing that the first cup was untouched, she returned the pot to the back of the stove. "Well, I'll do the best I can for you. At least you can earn yourself a place to stay and three decent meals a day. It's better than starvin' I guess!" She leaned back in her chair again and took a drink of her dark brew.

It had been the better part of a week since the girl had eaten, and she wasn't hungry now. The thought of three decent meals a day held no temptation for her.

"Maybe there's something else ...?" the girl suggested timidly.

"Maybe there is, Sweetie. But I'm not the one to find it for you. You're welcome to go looking! Goodness knows, I wish all my girls could find something else! I'd do anything in the world to help you. But when a girl wants to leave this place, usually the best thing I can do is pretend I don't know her. I'm sure you understand."

The girl nodded slightly.

"But first," Mollie leaned forward again and assumed her most business-like voice. "First, you need a bath and some clean clothes." She pointed to the back door. "Tub's on the porch. Help yourself. I'll see if Esmerelda has a dress you can borrow. It's too late to go to church. They're probably getting out about now. But maybe you can walk around town some this afternoon and talk to people. You might find something. But if you don't ... you can come back here."

*   *   *

Shan's horse plodded one step, then another, and flicked at flies with her black tail. Pretty Girl, an old plug at best, had been given to Shan in payment for the porch he had built on Ole Swenson's house back in April. Shan was more than happy with the arrangement. Pretty Girl might not look like much, and her level of energy left a lot to be desired, but she could pull the buggy. And at this point, it was the buggy that mattered—not the horse pulling it.

After Shan's father had died a little over two years ago in Indiana, his mother had begun taking in boarders to make ends meet. But it wasn't long before she accepted the invitation of her brother, Robert

McCheyne, in Heppner to move her family west. The sheep market had been good to Robert. He was doing very well financially and had been able to provide train tickets for his sister and her eight children. In addition to their ranch house, Robert and his wife lived part time in town, in one of the large stately houses that comprised Heppner's upper class neighborhood along Willow Creek. Robert had been able to purchase a less imposing but still adequate house for his sister and her family near the edge of the west hills.

Mac Harmon, when he heard that his new next-door neighbor had worked with a saddle maker in Illinois, hired seventeen-year-old Shan Collins on the spot. Mac's business, making bridles and harnesses, had been growing to the point where he could not handle all the work himself. Shan was a quick learner. His hands were good; but his eye, even better. He could see beauty where none existed and bring it to life. He had ideas that Mac had never thought of and the diligence to pursue them. The two men made a strong team.

Little puffs of dust rose from the road as Pretty Girl plodded lazily along Cannon Street. Step, *puff*, step, *puff*. The dust drifted back toward the buggy, but Shan didn't notice.

His heart was beating a steady tattoo inside his ribs, causing him to work all the harder to maintain an aloof appearance as he rolled down the street where Ginnie lived.

In a bold move, he planned on driving right in front of her house. She would be impressed with the new buggy. Shan didn't expect her to be outside, of course, but he couldn't be sure. He was unable to turn his head to look in that direction. He gazed studiously straight in front of himself. He even turned his head to the left once to make himself appear less rigid. But he did not look to the right. He did not *dare* look to the right—except from the corner of his eye.

Well, she wasn't there. Maybe he would go around the block and drive by again. No, what if she had seen him from the house? She would realize what he was doing. He couldn't do that!

Maybe he would drive around several blocks and come back the opposite direction. It would appear that he'd been somewhere and was returning. That would be better.

He turned Pretty Girl right onto Court, then over to Balm. He circled all the way around by Krug's new Steam Laundry. He paused in the shade of a poplar tree to admire the building. Fred Krug had cantilevered his new home and laundry right over the creek. The wheel was below the building, rather than beside it. It was one of the newest and finest buildings in Heppner, much admired by everyone. Shan barely noticed, although he did appreciate his few moments in the shade.

Finally, he plucked up his courage and determination, and turned back to the horse. "Git up there, Little Lady," he said with a shake of the reins. Then he headed back to Ginnie's house on Cannon again, going the opposite direction.

Still not there. Wait! There she was, walking with her mother from the back yard. Shan swallowed. He stared straight ahead, so intent on his charade, he failed to even notice when Mrs. Hammond called his name.

She called louder, and Shan snapped out of his trance. He reined in Pretty Girl, and looking up, he nodded pleasantly, touching the edge of his hat as he'd seen older men do. "Hello, Mrs. Hammond. Nice weather we're having," he said.

"Do you think so, Shan? It's too hot for me!"

Gulp. Yes, of course! It was way too hot. How could he have said such a stupid thing? "Yes, you're right. But at least it's not raining." Saved by quick thinking.

Mrs. Hammond laughed and said, "Well, you're quite the optimist, Shan!"

Shan chuckled uneasily.

Then Ginnie spoke. "Where are you going on such a hot day, Shan?"

She spoke to him!

"Ah, just out doing a couple of errands. Well, it's been nice seeing you." Shan nodded to Mrs. Hammond and her daughter and blew out a shaky breath as he turned back to Pretty Girl and clicked her into motion with a shake of the reins.

He had survived! She was there! He got to see her! She spoke to him! And now his mind was completely full of her.

And before he realized it, he was back home again—with absolutely no idea how he got there.

Chapter Four

Once dinner was finished at the Harmon house, Mac went outside in search of a cool breeze—and to visit with Shan Collins about his new buggy. Shan, at a bit over six feet, made a striking figure. He had what Mac called an "honest Irish face" and clear eyes that could hide nothing. He was well-muscled, amiable, and handsome.

Lilyann finished eating and cleared her place, then came flying outside to join Papa. She was off the porch and well on her way across the yard before the screen door banged behind her. "Oh, Shan! I like your new buggy!" she called.

"Yup," The young man patted the wheel of his new pride and joy and grinned at Mac. "Alvin Giger had it in the *Gazette* last week, and now, as of nine o'clock last night, it's mine!"

Mac nodded approvingly and looked up at Shan. "Very nice!" He knew Shan had been wanting a buggy ever since he'd arrived in Heppner a year ago.

Charlie ran from the house and joined the others at the buggy. He crawled under it and took up a station behind one of the wheels to watch for wild Indians or coyotes, while Lilyann hoisted herself up to the running board to peer inside.

Shan leaned down to look at Charlie. "Watch out there, Charlie. Don't ya spook my horse!"

Lilyann giggled. Even she knew it would take more than a boy at play to spook Pretty Girl.

"Well," Mac said to Shan. "I don't think you'll be sorry. Giger's a fair man." He ran his hand down one of the wheel spokes. "So ... I heard he was asking ninety dollars for it."

"I gave him forty-five." Shan grinned.

"Forty-five? He settled for half price?"

"Forty-five ... and the saddle." Shan beamed with pride. The saddle *was* beautiful. Lilyann had watched sometimes while Shan worked on it early in the mornings before the shop was open. He had showed her how the parts would go together to make a whole saddle. Papa said Shan was an artist, and Lilyann believed it.

"Uh *huh!*" Mac said. He took a step back and looked the buggy over again. "I get it. I will admit that saddle is a beautiful piece of work. I think maybe Giger got the better end of the bargain."

Shan grinned. "I'm happy anyway. Got what I wanted. And I can make another saddle anytime."

"Whoa! What have we here?" Johnny Burke strode across the street to join Shan and Mac, as Charlie fired an imaginary gun in his direction from behind one of the buggy wheels. Johnny, farm implement manager for Gilliam and Bisbee's large and reputable business, flashed his ever-ready smile and patted the top of the buggy's door. "I like it. I like it a lot! Shan, is this yours?"

"You betcha," Shan responded with an upward tilt of his chin. "It's mine, all mine. Got it last night."

Johnny whistled. "Yes sir!" he said. "Very nice, indeed!" He ran his hand along the top of the door, feeling the smoothness of the finish. "Well, Shan, you'll put 'er to good use, I'm sure. You got somebody special in mind you're planning on taking out for a drive?" Johnny glanced in Mac's direction, anticipating Shan's discomfort.

"*Pshew, pshew!*" Charlie continued his shooting from beneath the buggy.

"Whatcha doing down there, Charlie?" Shan called, avoiding Johnny's question.

Lilyann jumped down from the running board and asked, "Hey, Shan. Are you taking a girl out driving? Papa said you need to get a girl."

Mac cleared his throat and suddenly discovered an itch on the back of his neck that needed rubbing. He chuckled, embarrassed by Lilyann's comment, but not willing to let the subject drop. "Well, what about it, Shan ... some nice young lady?"

The color rose to Shan's cheeks, and he ducked his head. He shrugged and spoke quietly. "Well, I dunno." He tried to wipe the grin off his face by rubbing at the corners of his mouth. "I guess maybe I got me a couple ideas." He quickly changed the subject. "Look at this." He reached to raise the top of the buggy into place.

"Huh, uh, uh, uh. Not so fast there, Mr. Collins!" Johnny pushed the buggy top back down and slapped Shan on the shoulder. "Oh, that was slick! You're pretty good at changing the subject. So who are these 'couple ideas' you have in mind? Maybe Mac and me have some advice we could give you about women." Johnny elbowed Mac and grinned.

Lilyann watched for Shan's reaction. Papa had said that Shan was so shy around ladies, he could barely look at one without blushing. And sure enough—his neck and face were bright pink! And there wasn't even a lady anywhere near!

Mac joined in the fun. "Yeah, maybe we could give you some suggestions. Like ... have you thought about Lou Lundquist?" He winked at Johnny.

Johnny nodded seriously. "They say fat people are jolly, you know." At this, both Mac and Johnny burst out laughing, and Shan clamped his jaws together.

Lilyann thought Papa and Mr. Burke should be nicer to Shan. Shan didn't even have a papa of his own. There was just Mrs. Collins and her eight children. Libby, the next-to-youngest, was Lilyann's playmate.

Lilyann reached out and took Shan's hand. "I'll be your girl, Shan. I'll go riding with you."

Shan smiled at Lilyann and patted her on the head. "Sure, Lily. I'd love it if you were my girl."

Mac spoke again. "Well, okay then Shan. But if you ever change your mind about needing some advice—"

"—be sure to let us know," Johnny finished for him. And they burst out laughing again.

*   *   *

The girl—the one Mollie had decided to call Lorena—sat on the edge of the cot where she'd slept last night. The shade was open now, and the room seemed less frightening in the light of day. The sun had moved in the sky and was no longer shining directly in the window. She could see now that the room was painted a navy blue and had faded, flowered wallpaper on one wall. Across from her, Esmerelda held up the yellow dress. How old was Esmerelda? Twenty-five? With this kind of woman, it was hard to tell. When Mollie had mentioned it, the yellow dress had sounded nice. But now, the girl was quite sure—she did *not* want it! It was too ... well, too sparse! She felt half naked just looking at it.

"I was thinking I'd go out and check around town a bit this afternoon," she said. "I was kind of hoping for something not so ... revealing."

"You're new here, honey." Esmerelda stated the obvious, one hand on her hip. "If you're going to get any business, you'll have to catch a few eyes."

"Actually ... I was kind of hoping I could find some other, um ... line of work." The girl rubbed her knotted fists together in her overall-clad lap.

"Ohhhh! I see." Esmerelda sat on the edge of her bed and let the dress fall into her lap. "Okay. Yeah. I used to wish that, too. Didn't work out for me." She shrugged. "At least here I have steady work. And you get used to it after a while. Actually," she lowered her voice. "I'm pretty good. I get lots of business. I worked in Baker City before I came here. I save up my money and go up to The Dalles or Pendleton every once in a while for some time out. Maybe even earn a little extra on the side." She smiled. "And once, I got to ride on a river boat with one of my customers, from The Dalles all the way down to Portland and back." She tilted her head, raised one eyebrow and smiled. "We stayed at a really *fine* hotel and he passed me off as his wife." She giggled, and her eyes took on a dreamy expression. "The butlers and waiters treated me just like Mrs. La-dee-da." She struck a Gibson girl pose and wiggled everything that would wiggle. "Life could be worse."

But the girl in overalls couldn't think of anything worse and couldn't bring herself to smile back. She inhaled a shaky breath. "I do need to earn some money." She ran her thumbnail up and down the outside of her thigh along the seam of the overalls. "Do you have any ideas?"

"Sure honey." Esmerelda's voice changed as she recognized the girl's seriousness. "I got a nice, boring, dark green dress you can have. And a hat to cover up that hair. You go out and check around for a job this afternoon, and if you don't find anything, come on back and I'll help you get started here. Mollie told me to be a big sister to you and I'll do the best I can. You can trust me."

The Fair in 1902
Courtesy Morrow County Heritage Museum

Heppner's First National Bank 1902
Courtesy Morrow County Heritage Museum

Chapter Five

Mac Harmon came down the porch steps holding Lilyann's hand in his. "We'll go to the shop, okay?" he said. "I need to pick up some thread to fix Mama's chair.

Lilyann sniffed away her tears and nodded. She really wanted to go to the creek with the boys, but going to Papa's shop was pretty good too. She loved playing with the leather scraps there.

Normally when Lilyann walked with Papa to his saddle and harness shop, they came down Main Street. But Lilyann had been thinking lately. "Papa, can we go down Gale Street instead of Main? We could still get to the shop that way, couldn't we?"

Mac smiled to himself and nodded. "Well, you know, you just might be right about that. Let's try it and see what happens." When they reached Willow Street, they turned to go over to Main where the shop was located. Lilyann's adventuresome spirit was rewarded by the sight of someone she'd never seen before.

Heppner was not a large town. Everyone knew everyone else, at least by sight. And Lilyann, young as she was, was no exception. Papa said she made friends, both young and old, about as easily as popcorn popped in a hot kettle. And in about the same style!

So when Lilyann saw the young lady in the pretty green dress walk down the porch steps, she smiled her best smile and said, "Hi!"

Mac winced. Why hadn't he thought about this possibility? He did not want his daughter making friends with the inmates of the local house of prostitution!

The young woman smiled at Lilyann and said, "Hello."

Mac tugged on his daughter's hand, but she held back. "Are you new here?" Lilyann asked. "I never saw you before."

Mac said, "Come along, Lily," and tugged harder, and Lilyann moved—barely.

The young lady glanced nervously at Mac. "Yes, I'm new. What's your name?"

Mac bent and picked up his daughter and carried her across the street. "Lilyann," the child called to her new friend. "But you can call me Lily."

Mac said, "That's enough now, Lily. Are you going to help me find the thread for Mama's chair? If you find it before I do, I'll give you a penny." They reached the shop and Mac lowered Lilyann to the sidewalk. He turned the key in the lock, and opened the shop door.

The sound of a banjo accompanied the opening of the door. Mac had mounted the banjo high on the door jamb a year ago. For some reason, the quirky idea had appealed to him, and now, every time the door opened, the stiff piece of leather screwed to the edge of the door strummed the instrument, announcing the entrance of one of Heppner's citizens.

"It sounds crooked again, Papa," Lilyann said. "You need to tune it!" Mac smiled at his daughter, and agreed it was definitely time to get the banjo tuned again.

The shop smelled of leather and oil and sweat. Lilyann inhaled deeply. She loved the shop. She would spend all her days here if Mama would let her. She liked to listen to the men when they came in to talk to Papa and Shan. And she liked the leather scraps Papa gave her to play with. When she grew up, she wanted to be a leather worker just like Papa. Or maybe a mama—like Mama.

Mac found the thread before Lilyann did, but gave her the penny anyway. As they started for home, he purposely turned his steps toward Main Street, to avoid the ill-reputed *Chateau de Joie.*

*   *   *

The five boys crouched in a circle as Martin Burke held the magnifying glass only a couple of inches above the grass. All five were sopping wet from the free-for-all water war they'd had in the creek.

"Whatcha doin'?" asked Bobby Tomlin. Bobby was in Charlie and Will's second grade class at school. "Hey, guys, c'mere! Looka what Martin's doin'."

Smoke rose slowly from the tiny dot where Martin held the magnifying glass. Aiden and Dennis Collins, two of Shan's brothers, had joined the Harmon and Burke boys while their mother visited her brother only a few houses away. Aiden rose suddenly and dashed to the creek. He came back with a tablespoon of water cupped in his hands. Martin rose in anticipation, torn between seeing the full effect of the magnified rays of the sun and his fear of the consequences. Just as the smoldering grass burst into flame, Aiden dumped his drops of water into the center of the tiny blaze. It sizzled and went out, and Will released the breath he didn't know he'd been holding.

"Me next!"

"Me! I want to try it."

"No, ME!"

"No!" Charlie said, and the bickering stopped. Charlie Harmon was like that. When he spoke, people listened. "Will gets to go next. It was his idea. The rest of us need to be ready to bring water—just in case."

Will was proud of his idea, but he also felt uneasy. Martin had threatened to tell on him for taking Mama's magnifying glass. He had also told Will he might burn down the whole town! But Will planned on putting the glass back after the "experiment." And he determined to be *very* careful about fire. So maybe it was okay.

One by one, the boys burned their initials into the dry grass. There was one moment of near panic as Dennis was working on his "D," but the ever-ready fire crew performed admirably, splashing water directly on the flame.

Other boys playing at the creek wanted a turn with the glass, but Charlie decided another water fight was in order first. After all, the reason they were at the creek was because of the heat, and it hadn't become any cooler as they crouched in the dry grass, proclaiming themselves rulers of their territory.

With one accord the boys left the glass where it lay and took to the water. It was deeper now than it had been—well up past the boys' knees. And it felt great.

*　　*　　*

Halfway up the hill overlooking Heppner, a horse stood in the shade of one of the few trees. His head low, his breathing nothing more than a series of rattling sighs, he was a perfect picture of despair. The saddle and bridle were both still in place, but no rider could be seen. The lone horse drew no attention from the town below.

Squatting in the shade of the tree, all but invisible from below, was the man. He didn't smell any better than he had in church that morning, but the horse didn't seem to mind. The man kept his eyes focused on the front porch of one of the houses on Gale Street. He took off his hat, wiped the sweat from his forehead and eyes on an already sweaty sleeve, and turned his gaze back again to the house.

*   *   *

Les Matlock   Bruce Kelley
Courtesy Morrow County Heritage Museum

Young Les Matlock, dressed in a three piece suit, joined his friend Bruce Kelley at his usual table near the back of McAtee & Swaggart's Saloon. He had already visited two other Heppner saloons before arriving here. After all, a man in Matlock's line of work needed to keep his finger on the pulse of the town.

He removed the bowler from his head, flicked at an invisible dust particle, and set the hat on the table. His gaze moved slowly around the room, noticing at the bar the home remedies salesman he had helped to part with his money only last night. The man might do okay as a salesman, but he was not a good gambler.

Matlock smoothed his well-waxed moustache and leaned back in his chair. He yawned. "That was a good game last night," he said to his friend.

Kelley nodded his agreement. "Good for *you*, anyway! You probably won that poor salesman's whole life savings!"

"Yeah. Like I said, it was a good game!" Matlock laughed and took a drink of his beer.

Les and Bruce, both former range riders, relaxed in the comfort of a time-worn friendship. They listened to James Yeager, standing at the bar, while he told for the eighth or tenth time the story of retrieving the body of a recently deceased Irishman from Sand Hollow, up north. After all, the salesman had never heard the story before, and it made good telling.

Yeager, Heppner's furniture dealer and recent graduate of the Myers College for Morticians and Undertakers, was also a master story-teller. "Well, that was my very first time to have to go and fetch someone back to town. I'll tell you, those Irish really know how to wake their dead! I thought I'd *never* get the job done. They went on and on, and it was nearly dark by the time I left. And even then I durn near had to drag the body away from 'em."

By the time Yeager got to the part about the sudden braying of Paddy's donkey in the middle of the moonless night, everyone in the tavern was listening. And everyone's heart raced, though most of them had heard the story before.

"I'm here to tell you," Yeager continued, "When that mountain canary let loose, I jumped off that wagon and run back to town faster than I ever run in my life! Had to go back the next day and fetch ol' Paddy the rest o' the way into town."

The men at the bar laughed, though this part was not true. Yeager had arrived in town around two a.m., still in possession of the wagon and his wits—although, according to what Matlock had heard, the wits were farther removed from him than the wagon.

Chapter Six

Ella Harmon sat on the porch swing, a pair of Charlie's trousers in her lap as she worked at applying a patch to the seat. She wiped her face with the wet washrag Mac had brought her, then draped it around the back of her neck. She leaned her head back, closed her eyes and let the coolness soak into her neck and dribble down her back.

Mac paced to the far end of the porch and back—then turned to pace again.

"Sit down, Mac." Ella's voice was gentle. "Pacing won't make you feel any better!"

"Can't. I'm all wound up inside." He strode over to where Ella sat, gave her a quick kiss, then sat back against the porch rail.

He pulled a quarter from his pocket and tossed it up and down, gazing absently toward the south. "Storm's coming. It's gonna be a doozie! I could sure use a good stiff breeze along about now!"

They sat in silence as Ella once again took up her sewing.

Mac finally slipped the quarter back into his pocket and said, "I think Charlie should come home. It's going to pour rain before long anyway, and it's making me nervous."

Nodding, Ella looked up at the heavy, yellow-brown light in the sky to the south. "I've felt uneasy about it ever since they left."

Mac's jaw tightened. "I'll go get them," he said. He took one long step down off the porch and began jogging in the direction of the creek.

Ella tied off her thread and bit it loose from the patch she'd just completed. Then she rose and entered the house.

*   *   *

The grass alongside Willow Creek, straw colored even now in June, showed the initials of the five boys. "MB" "WB" "CH" "DC" and "AC." Martin Burke, Will Burke, Charlie Harmon, Dennis Collins and Aiden Collins. It looked mighty fine. And, much to Will's relief, they had not burned down the whole town in the process.

But unbeknownst to Will and the others now splashing in the creek, the smoldering from Aiden's "C" was slowly spreading. It followed the path of least resistance, up the hill away from the creek. By the time an actual flame took shape, the boys were involved in an all out water war, and much too busy to notice. In only moments, a patch of dry grass nearly a foot in diameter was burning.

"Fire! Get water! Help! FIRE!" Charlie shouted the alarm as he dashed up the hill in pursuit of the flames.

Instantly, the creek became a frothing sea as every boy within hearing distance scrambled to bring water to the flames. The patch of fire was spreading rapidly—first a foot wide, then three feet, then six. And it was spreading faster than the boys could put it out.

The sound of approaching rain tickled Will's ears. Glancing up, he felt the first drops of rain hit his face and shouted "Whoa! Here it comes!" Within seconds the few drops had increased to hundreds, thousands! Will watched the fire sputter and die. His heart pounded as he realized Martin had been right. The fire *could* have burned the whole town to the ground. He very abruptly developed a new respect for his brother's wisdom.

*   *   *

Ella poked the needle into the fabric of the trousers and returned them to her sewing basket at the end of the sofa, where a sleeping Gilbert stirred but didn't waken. She turned to the kitchen and tied her apron over the bulge of the next little Harmon as she set about preparing a light evening meal. Lilyann sat at the kitchen table with her chin balanced on her small fist, a pencil in hand and piece of paper in front of her.

"I'm writing a story, Mama," she said. "It's about fairies. And the mama fairy won't let the little girl fairy go and play in the creek because she's too little."

Ella raised her eyebrows and smiled. "Sounds interesting! I hope you'll let me read it when you're finished. Does the little girl fairy still love the mama fairy?"

"Of course, Mama! Sometimes the mama has to tell the child no, and if she's naughty, the mama has to scold her, so she will turn out okay when she's a grown up. Papa told me that."

Ella smiled. What a precious child! What a precious husband!

She thought back to the time only months ago when Lilyann decided she would learn to write. She could do the "L, I, L" with no problem at all. But how many times had she practiced those tricky slanted letters, "Y, A, N, N?" Way too many to count, Ella decided. Lilyann lacked nothing in determination!

"Mama, sometimes when I go over to the Burke's house, Pappy talks to me. He says funny things. He says I am a fairy girl, not a real girl."

"Well, Pappy is from the old country. He has a good imagination."

"Am I a real girl, Mama?" Lilyann's face showed no concern—only curiosity.

"Yes, you are, Lily. As real as they get. Pappy's mistaken about that part."

Ella kissed Lilyann's hair, then reached for the bread and a sharp knife. She was interrupted by a loud knock, followed by Dacia Burke's "Yoo hoo!" and the squeak of the screen door hinges.

Dacia poked her head inside, then entered with her two youngest children. *How can she still look so beautiful, even in this heat?* Ella wondered. Pappy said she was one of the black Irish. But Johnny insisted she was full blooded gypsy—except for the eyes. Whatever it was, Dacia's black curly hair and cornflower blue eyes drew appreciative looks everywhere she went. And in today's heat, her rosy cheeks were pinker than ever against her fair skin.

"Just checking to see how you're holding up in this heat," Dacia said. "It's simmering out there—about to break into a boil!"

"I'll live. But I wouldn't mind a cool breeze if I could get one!" Ella said.

"I sent Josie for the boys a few minutes ago," Dacia said. "They should be back any time now." She shifted baby Sarah to the other hip while five-year-old Walter hung on her skirt looking like a bedraggled kitten. "Looks like it's going to turn nasty! Have you seen the sky? And the wind's coming up."

"Mmm. It's getting darker, alright. Mac just went to get them too," Ella said as she continued slicing the bread.

"Ella, I declare, I don't think I've ever felt a storm like this one coming on. The chickens have gone to roost. The birds are silent as

31

death. Josie's puppy has been pacing up and down, turning in circles, whining and pacing again all afternoon. It's like the animals can sense it coming. And the children are all miserable. I'll be glad when this is over!" Ella shuddered. "Any minute now. It's coming in fast!"

*　　*　　*

Twelve miles above Heppner in the valleys of Willow Creek and Balm Fork, clouds roiled, darkening the skies. Lightning struck; thunder rolled. By four o'clock, the clouds overflowed, dumping more than an inch and a half of water over a twenty-square-mile area in the steep canyons. Water poured in thick sheets off the farmland and into the streams, carrying loose boards, tree limbs, and hapless chickens and dogs, as the water began its headlong rush toward lower ground. At first, the thirsty earth drank up the drops eagerly, then it choked, unable to take any more. In only minutes, the gentle trickle of these two happy streams had become a raging torrent, no longer flowing, but now hurling itself downward toward Heppner with amazing force. As the streams overflowed their banks, they began to spread to nearby farms, snatching up bales of hay, terrified animals, and large boulders. Barbed wire, still attached to the fence posts, tore through the mass like a dull saw through cord wood. The muddy stew rolled relentlessly downward, adding farm wagons, outhouses, cows, and horses to the ammunition. Ducks and geese found it impossible to stay afloat in the roiling muck.

Balm Fork, in rebellion against its designation as "tributary" to Willow Creek, blasted into the larger stream with such force, such violence, that it crossed the descending waters of Willow and gorged out a huge gully on the opposite bank. Then the muddy flow from the two streams continued as one, relentlessly responding to the pull of gravity, their combined power greater than the sum of them both.

Finally, the vile fluid mass reached the south edge of Heppner and the new steam laundry—the building and its thousands of pounds of new equipment, built to straddle Willow Creek. At first, water pressed its way under the building filling Willow Creek to capacity as it flowed through town. Then it over-ran its banks and spread out to cover the streets. Only a moment later, Fred Krug, his wife, and their four children were thrown to the floor as the main body of the flood slammed into the laundry and stopped. For the moment.

*　　*　　*

Mrs. Collins arrived at the group of boys just as the rain poured down, putting a soggy end to the danger of fire. She looked nearly panic-stricken as she grabbed Dennis and Aiden by their wrists and hurried back in the direction of her brother Robert's house. Both boys objected, trying to pull away from her.

"But *Ma!* We were having *fun!*"

Mrs. Collins just gripped the boys all the more as she ran, head down, to get out of the downpour.

With the rain cascading down as if all the mop buckets in heaven had been overturned at once, most of the other boys at the creek had made the quick dash for home. But not Charlie. Not Will or Martin. The three boys, along with just a few others, jumped back into the creek, now flowing above the knees of even the tallest boys. Rarely had the creek flowed so high. What a great gift on this miserably hot day!

The first water appears in Heppner, just ahead of the rain,
the hail, and the flood, itself. Palace Hotel on the left.
Courtesy Christopher Sigsbee George

"Martin! Will!" Josie shouted above the pounding of the rain. She could barely see her brothers, so thick was the curtain of water pouring down. "Come home right now! Mama says!" Her hands fluttered at her sides and her shoulders hunched up to her ears against the downpour.

The last few boys in the creek began scattering, heading for their homes. Martin scrambled to the edge of the creek and up the bank, but Charlie and Will held their ground. The creek was rising higher by the moment. This was too good to leave.

Mac arrived just behind Josie and plunged right into the stream bed to grab Charlie. He swung the boy up to the bank and reached for Will.

"But Papa, we're already wet!" Charlie pleaded, as the huge drops ran down his face and poured off his chin.

"No matter!" Mac shouted, pulling Will out of the stream and sending him up the incline. "You boys head for home as fast as you can!" He scooted Charlie along with a swat on the backside, then took Josie by the hand to climb up the stream bank. "Let's *go!*" he shouted.

A moment later, the rain turned to hail. The frozen balls were perfectly clear and had increased to the size of chestnuts before Mac and the children were even a block from the creek.

A crack of lightning, louder than any Mac had ever heard, was followed immediately by a tremendous roll of thunder. Mac pulled the children into the closest shelter he could find—the outhouse at the back of Mrs. Elder's property. As the five of them crowded inside, Josie began crying. Charlie was still whooping with delight, even while holding his hands over his head and hollering, "Ow! Owie! Owie!" Martin had turned silent and white; Will was shaking.

*　　*　　*

The sound of the approaching flood was enough to strike terror into the bravest of hearts—if anyone had been able to hear it. But the crack of lightning, deep roll of thunder, and sound of the pounding hail masked the voice of the flood itself. As the ice balls bounced off roofs, clattered against windows, and pounded on wooden awnings and sidewalks, the deadly flood came closer and closer to breaking through the temporary dam Fred Krug had unwittingly constructed. The flood built up behind the laundry, and finally the building heaved drunkenly, shuddered for a moment, and gave way before the force of the muddy flow.

And in that moment, Heppner's fate was sealed. The steam laundry, along with its thousands of pounds of machinery, the remains of barns, animals, barbed wire, farm equipment, and muck collected from twelve miles of stream valley exploded onto the village of Heppner.

The twenty foot wall of mud pushed both the remains of the building and its equipment toward the center of Heppner. Fred Krug and his family were tossed like rag dolls into the flood before they had time to even understand what was happening. The torrent continued to blast through the defenseless town.

In the first hundred yards, houses belonging to the Abrahamsicks, the Salings, the Dawsons, the Waltrenbergers, Sheriff Shutt, and the Howards were crunched into oblivion. It picked up the Ashbaugh house, reduced it to a skeleton, and added its bones to the arsenal. Cora May Ashbaugh and her seven children never even knew what hit them. Building after building was toppled as the mud and debris rolled on with fierce, relentless determination. All of this, while most of the people in town didn't yet realize that a flood was upon them.

Chapter Seven

The men at Swaggart & McAtee's Saloon stood sheltered by the wooden porch awning, enjoying the amazing hail storm. None of them had ever seen hail like this before! The men had to shout to be heard above the sound.

"Whoa Nellie! This is *some* storm!"

"This might just be as bad as that one back in eighty-eight. Remember that one?"

"I sure hope Hazel made it home before this hit!"

The sound of Bruce Kelley's glass smashing on the wooden porch floor vanished into the sound of the hail. Bruce pointed, bolted over the porch rail, and began running. "Flood!" he yelled. The men scrambled from the porch, some of them grabbing their horse's reins from the hitching rail, and ran up May Street toward the hill to the west of town. Kelley turned back. Almost knocking his friend off his feet, he grabbed Matlock by his lapels and hollered, "Lexington—Ione! People there will die unless we warn them! You get wire cutters—I'll get horses. Meet me." He pointed up the hill only a block and a half away.

Les understood immediately what his friend had in mind and ran back to Gilliam and Bisbee's Hardware store. He made it safely to the building, where he kicked in the locked door and looked around frantically in the dark interior for wire cutters. Finding none, he grabbed a pair of pruning shears and started back toward the street, the mud churning its way through the town only feet from his path.

Bruce Kelley ran to The Red Front livery stable—the only stable in town not in the direct path of the flood. He tried to grab Matlock's horse in the first stall, but the animal had gone wild with the fury of the storm. Kelley gave up and moved to an old plug across the barn—Shan

Collins' Pretty Girl. He saddled the animal—fast—and slipped the bridle into place, dropped the reins to the floor, then quickly saddled his own mare, Dancer, and mounted in one smooth move.

Grabbing Pretty Girl's loose reins, he charged out of the barn and back toward Willow Street. Les Matlock was just coming around the corner with the pruning shears in hand. Kelley tossed the reins of the spare horse to his friend. Accompanied by the terrible moaning cry of the flood itself, the two men kicked their mounts into an instant and frantic gallop up the steep hill to the west of town and then north, along the Willow Creek valley.

*　　*　　*

As the flood blasted through the bottleneck at Krug's Laundry, it spread to three blocks wide and its height gradually lessened from twenty feet to a mere ten or twelve—still plenty to knock large buildings to smithereens, deposit the Opera House piano in the middle of what had been Main Street, and swallow one after another after another of Heppner's citizens and their substantial homes.

At the McCheyne house—still a half block ahead of the flood— Robert and his wife, along with Shan's mother Kitty Collins, her two oldest girls, and the two boys, Dennis and Aiden, were standing on the porch watching the storm as the accumulating rainwater rose to six inches, then seven.

"Maybe we should go upstairs—" McCheyne began. In another instant, just as they first heard the roar of the flood, the house and all seven of them were swept away.

*　　*　　*

Mac Harmon held the children tightly to himself. Martin and Josie were still crying, whether from the sting of hailstones, or from fear, Mac didn't know. But Will held tight to his sister's hand. "We'll be okay, Josie. Don't cry. We'll be okay, won't we Mr. Harmon?"

Mac pulled his arm tighter around Will's shoulder. "Sure, we'll be fine. This is just a little hail storm. It's pretty exciting, really. Just listen to it!" He reached to open the door so they could better appreciate the violence of the storm.

At that moment the wall of mud hit the outhouse, swallowing it instantly. Mac tried to hold them all together, but Charlie was pulled from his grasp first, followed by young Will.

*   *   *

The Episcopal Church, on the bank of the creek, was lifted and floated down stream like a toy boat. It crumbled to bits, the steeple remaining intact even after the rest of the building was nothing more than toothpicks. But in the end, it too, vanished from sight.

*   *   *

Johnny Burke sat on his front porch, marveling at the storm with Pappy. Johnny had always loved storms—especially if they involved lightning, thunder, or snow. And this storm ranked as one of the finest he'd ever experienced. As he struggled to hear Pappy speak over the clatter of the hail, he glanced up. His face drained of color, and he abruptly scooped Pappy from the wooden rocker as if he were a small child and raced with him up the hill behind the house.

*   *   *

Shan Collins finished pinning a fresh diaper on little Danny and picked him up. Danny chortled happily, not seeming to mind the pounding of the hail and rain. Shan blew horsey noises on Danny's belly and the baby squealed in delight.

The house jerked, then trembled. Shan looked up, nearly thrown off balance, and grabbed the back of a chair. He glanced out the window. It looked like the world was floating around him! Water and mud poured in through the open windows and front door. Shan turned with the baby in his arms and ran to the stairs. Taking the steps two at a time, he clattered to the top where a crying, four-year-old Libby met him.

"I want Ma!" she sobbed.

Swallowing his own fear, Shan answered, "She went over to visit Uncle Robert, remember? She'll be back before long."

The house continued to quiver as Shan rose and pulled Libby with him to the window.

*   *   *

Ella screamed as the rolling wave of mud lifted the Harmon house from its cornerstones and swirled it away like a leaf on a river. She lost her footing, scrambling to grab Lilyann.

With a baby already on one hip, Dacia scooped little Gilbert from the sofa with her other arm. "I have Gilbert" she screamed at Ella and ran to the front door.

As the house swirled nearer the edge of the flowing muck, Dacia pushed six-year-old Walter from the porch with her knee and yelled, "Run, Walter! Run for the hill!" She half waded, half ran through the roaring mud, only about two feet deep here, but rising rapidly. Walter, clinging to her skirt, was dragged through the mud behind her.

Holding Lilyann tightly against herself, Ella jumped into the flood only a moment after Dacia. She struggled forward and made a bit of progress before being forced under the muddy water by the branches of a huge tree. She came up for a moment—long enough to catch a breath—but then was plunged back into the depths of the flow.

Coming up once more, she reached with her legs and one free hand toward the hillside, only yards away. Sometimes her feet touched bottom, but mostly not. She stumbled forward and fell to her knees in the muddy torrent, tried to stand, and fell again. But she was closer to the edge than before. Lilyann's scream was muffled as both of them plunged below the surface yet again.

As Ella's head sank beneath the flood, she forced her body forward and up one more time. Closer now—nearly to the edge. With her last bit of strength, she planted her feet in the mud and heaved with all her might, throwing Lilyann toward the hillside beyond the torrent.

Dacia turned back just in time to see Ella dragged to her knees and swept away in only a couple feet of water. So near the edge! A form came hurtling through the air toward the hillside—muddy calico, muddy braids. Just above the reach of the rolling muck, it tumbled into a miserable pile of humanity—with no sign of life.

Chapter Eight

Shan's view from the window completely overwhelmed him. The whole town was coming toward them. Houses floated at crazy angles. Trees swept past—slowly, but with incredible fury. He braced himself against the window frame and gasped as his own floating house came to an abrupt stop and shuddered.

"Shan, pick me up. I want to see!" Libby had stopped crying and now pulled at his hand.

"It's nothing, Sweetie," Shan lied. "It's just loud because it's raining hard and there's hail." He saw a huge poplar tilt and slowly become a part of the flood.

Oh God! Shan's stomach was tied in knots; his whole body was shaking. *What do I do? The kids! God HELP!*

He stood, scooped up Danny, grabbed Libby by the arm and dragged her along to the boys' room where six-year-old Michael still slept.

How can he sleep? The world is coming to an end and Michael's sleeping!

*   *   *

"Johnny! Josie! Johnny, help!" Dacia screamed as she plunged up the hill. Johnny sat Pappy abruptly on the ground and raced back to grab Walter.

Dacia dumped baby Sarah and Gilbert unceremoniously on the ground next to Pappy. "Don't move!" she commanded, and flew back down the hill, where the water was rising rapidly, higher—and still higher. Walter and Sarah Burke and Gilbert Harmon added their howls to the unearthly screams curdling the air. But their loud wails were absorbed by the sound of the mighty waters, the hail, and the cries and moans of others. Pappy scooped little Sarah into his ancient arms and huddled over her, trying to protect her tender head from the hailstones. Gazing at the flood in disbelief, Pappy shook his head in wonder and asked, "God, are you there?"

Dacia turned to look below. The Harmon's house had disappeared entirely. "Lily!" she screamed. "Ella, where are you! Oh! Josie! Martin! Will! Oh, Jesus!"

Dacia turned and ran alongside the flood. She plunged into the flood, reaching out to a woman and child who clung frantically to a broken piece of roof. Their hands almost touched, but at the last moment, the roof spun away, putting the two out of her reach. Dacia lost her footing and fell deep into the muddy torrent. She scrambled frantically to regain higher ground.

*   *   *

Through the pouring rain and hail and premature dusk, people appeared as shadows moving frantically on the hillside. As one of the shadows plodded deliberately up the hill, a child in its arms, Gilbert tore himself away from Pappy and ran after the ghostly apparition. "Ye-ann!" he screamed. "Ye-ann!" Pappy reached out to pull Gilbert back, but the boy was already gone. The old man continued to gaze after the child, his arm out—reaching, grasping, his mind thinking hard. Trying to comprehend what was happening. Trying to stop it.

*   *   *

Johnny ran back to the edge of the flood, frantically searching the flow for the rest of his family. *The children. Think, Johnny! Where are they?* Josie had gone to the creek for the two older boys. Johnny peered through the hail and early darkness, trying to see as far as the creek. It was hopeless. He couldn't see at all. There was no way to get to them. Johnny opened his mouth and collapsed to his knees, a savage howl erupting from deep within.

"My children! Oh, God! My children!" His scream was deep, guttural, from the very depth of his being.

Unclenching his fists, he plunged into the roiling mud and reached out his hand, trying to grasp anything human that came within his reach. As a man appeared with several lengths of rope, Johnny grabbed one, tied a knot in the end and flung it out into the muck as far as it would reach.

41

*   *   *

"Michael!" Shan bellowed at his brother, shaking his shoulder. "Michael! Wake up!"

Michael woke immediately. Shan stood by his bed with Danny in his arms. Libby was clinging to one of Shan's long legs, thumb in her mouth, crying.

"What?" Michael asked sitting up abruptly, pretending he hadn't really been asleep at all.

"Michael, get up. I need you," Shan commanded.

Michael closed his eyes and stretched his neck.

"Michael!" Shan pulled the boy from his bed. "Michael, there's a flood. You take Danny. I'll take care of Libby. I don't know what's going to happen, but we need to be ready. You understand?"

Six-year-old Michael blinked in confusion and took the baby from his brother.

*   *   *

"Johnny!" Dacia screamed, but her cry was buried in the rumble of the flood and the thunder. "Martin!" she screamed. "Will! Josie!" She lay sobbing for a moment. "Johnny, where are you?" Her body shook and heaved as groans escaped her lips. "Jesus, help!"

She lay in the mud alongside the violent flood, drawing deep breaths.

Then she rose and squared her shoulders. *The children. I have to take care of the children.*

Lilyann was not where Dacia had last seen her. Someone must have pulled her to safety.

Dacia turned and stumbled up the hill, gasping for breath and sobbing. "Jesus!" she cried. "Help! Where are you? Oh God! Please make it stop!"

But it didn't stop. The flood rolled on. And on.

*   *   *

The twenty-foot wall of water and debris that had first hit Heppner now flowed only a third that high as it continued to roll through the town and out again, headed toward Lexington, nine miles away. The depth of the flood diminished further as it dissipated in the wider valley below Heppner, but it was still high enough to sweep away homes and farm buildings. Houses were lifted as the flood rushed under them and then sent them drifting, spinning, crashing.

Though the roar created by the rushing flood was terrible, the loudest sound in Les Matlock's ears was the pounding of his own heart as he urged Shan's horse on. He could barely see the ground in front of him. He and Bruce Kelly held their mounts to a steady run, straining to see ahead, watching for telltale fence posts. They both knew first-hand the threat to a horse from a barbed wire fence. Wishing he had the Stetson of his range-riding days rather than the ridiculous bowler, Matlock crammed the hat farther onto his head. It was partial protection against the vicious hail. Pretty Girl resisted Matlock's attempts to urge her on, but he refused to yield. *You may drop dead before we get there, old girl, but I'll have every—last—ounce—of strength—you have.* He kicked at the mare's sides with each word, wishing he had spurs. The pounding of his heart could at least match that of his mount, even though she was the one doing the running.

"Comin' up!" Kelley yelled. Both men hit the ground at the same time, still alongside the flood, but above it on the hillside.

Matlock frantically chopped at the wires with the pruning shears. *And if lightning strikes this fence,* he thought, *I'm dead!*

As the last wire broke free, the men remounted their soaking wet saddles and galloped on to meet the next fence. Approaching the Gunderson sheep ranch, they dismounted twice more to hack their way through fences.

As they rode past the ranch house, both men shouted "Head for the hills! Flood! Heppner's washed away!" then rode on. They still had not caught up with the front edge of the flood, but maybe they could outdistance it before reaching Lexington.

They rode hard, yelling, "Flood coming! Flood! Get to the hill!" at every farm home along the way. Sweat poured off both men's faces, mixing with the rain. They were soaked to the skin, battered by hail, and exhausted physically and emotionally. But still, they rode on.

*   *   *

Over half an hour passed before the flood began to subside. But even at a lesser depth, it continued to pour its filthy, deadly flow through the center of Heppner. It rolled like thick pudding, moving so slowly that a running man could keep up with it.

An hour after the sudden destruction of the steam laundry, the main body of the flood had passed completely through town and on down the valley toward Lexington and Ione. The entire central section of the town was nothing but mud, slime, and debris. Houses were gone—

businesses, large trees—everything. Almost nothing remained intact in the two-block-wide swath from the former location of the steam laundry to the railroad station, a mile north.

Most of the men in town had already left to follow the path of destruction in the hope of saving some of the victims. Silence, interspersed with bouts of moaning, dotted the hillside. The entire scene was chaos.

Dacia made her way to Pappy and noticed that little Gilbert was no longer there. She asked, "Where's Gilbert?"

The old man, battered by hail, drenched and shaking, looked back with blank eyes, then lifted his arm to point a quivering finger up the hill. He muttered something Dacia couldn't understand. People were beginning to rise and move in the direction of the few houses perched on the hillside. Dacia could only assume someone must have taken Gilbert and Lilyann to safety there.

Dacia took little Sarah from Pappy as she and Ralph Justus helped the old man to his feet. They slowly began walking toward the Justus home. Walter hung on Dacia's skirt, crying, sopping wet, and shaking.

After the first few steps, Pappy pulled his arms away and stormed, "You think I can't walk by meself?" He pushed away Dacia's hand. "Leave me be! I know how to walk!"

Dacia inhaled a shaky breath. Here was a 74-year-old man who struggled to walk, even on the level floor of the Burke home, and used his shillelagh more often than not to steady himself—and he refused to be babied! She had no time to be exasperated with him.

"It's okay, Pappy. We're all just holding onto each other for safety. Here, take my hand and help me."

Pappy harrumphed, but reluctantly took Dacia's hand to walk up the hill.

After seeing Pappy and the children to the Justus home, Dacia continued to move mechanically, gathering children and stricken parents, helping them to safety in the few homes located above the flood line on the hillside. A number of the women helped. Some merely sat, staring into space.

*   *   *

Even the horrendous downpour had not emptied the heavy skies of their load. The evening was still overcast, black; the only light was from the feeble oil lamps or tallow candles the men carried. The land in the path of the flood was desolate, dead, empty. Farm implements and the remains of buildings hung high in the branches of the few sturdy trees which had withstood the flood's mighty power. The bodies of men, women, and children, as well as farm animals, littered the swath through the middle of town. Along the edges, piles of debris—the remnants of Heppner's finest homes and businesses—created a natural fence, setting off the hallowed ground and hiding even more bodies. A recognizable bit of house might be spotted here, a part of a farm wagon there, but for the most part, the scene greeting the sad eyes of the searchers was one of havoc, devastation, and horror.

Johnny saw several men helping George Conser, Heppner's most prominent banker, and his wife from what had been the upstairs of their house. George Conser—substantial, is the word that came to Johnny's mind. If a man like Conser wasn't safe from the ravages of the flood, who could be?

The mansard roof of the Conser home and the hole that was cut
allowing George Conser and his wife to escape
Courtesy Christopher Sigsbee George

Johnny joined a number of others as they set out on foot to follow the path of the flood, in search of survivors. As they chased the feeble light of their oil lamps, they found piles of rubble, dead horses and cows, bodies of Heppner's human population—but no survivors.

Until they reached Phil Cohn.

Responding to the shouts of Sheriff Shutt, Johnny came upon the remains of Mr. Cohn's house. It was nearly unrecognizable. But Cohn himself had struggled out an upstairs window and was attempting to escape over the pile of rubble in an alfalfa field a mile below town.

"I'll take him back to town," Johnny offered. "And I'll bring more rope and tools."

Sheriff Shutt just nodded and turned back to the devastation.

*　　　*　　　*

Shan's body shook badly. He had wavered between trying to calm the three children and wondering if the house was going to break apart with them in it. He watched as over the minutes of an hour, the flood gradually subsided, but he didn't know what to expect next. Should he try to leave the house? Could he get all three children to safety on the hillside? Or should he sit tight until tomorrow morning? No, he had to get out. The house was still creaking, settling. Who could tell how long it would hold together?

"Michael," Shan took the boy's shoulders in his hands. "I'm going to need your help. Do you understand?" Michael nodded, his eyes huge, staring.

"We are going to leave the house and go someplace else. Someplace where we will be safe from the storm. Let's trade. I'll take care of Danny, and I need you to help Libby. She can walk better than Danny, so it will be easier for you."

Michael nodded again and reached out to take Libby's hand.

"This is going to be hard," Shan warned his brother. "Whatever you do, don't let go of Libby. Understand?"

Michael nodded again, but seemed dazed, almost as if a spirit other than his own had taken hold of him. Shan wondered if the boy was in a trance.

"Michael, tell me what you're going to do," Shan said.

"I'm going to not let go of Libby."

"Good." That's all he needed to know. "Let's go then."

Shan lifted Danny in one arm, took Libby's free hand, and moved to the stairway. It vanished into slimy muck at the bottom. When Shan reached the mud he stepped cautiously, his feet sinking in as he stepped. As they reached floor level, the watery mud came halfway to his knees. "How you doing, Little Girl?" he asked Libby, his voice expressing a carefree confidence he did *not* feel. Libby shuddered, but did not cry. As he moved forward, one step at a time, he gently lifted her by the arm and placed her one giant step forward in the mud. Michael tried to help, but was not tall enough to make much difference.

Shan headed for the front door, which was standing open. The screen door had vanished.

As he stepped off the porch, Shan warned Michael and Libby, "It's still raining. We're going to get wet. Michael, what are you going to do?"

"I'm going to not let go of Libby."

"Okay, here we go." Shan stepped off the porch and into the yard, where the mud was even deeper than in the house. After only a few feet, Libby fell, taking Michael down with her. Shan turned to lift them, one at a time, and saw that Michael still clutched Libby's wrist with a death grip.

"Shan! Coming! Just wait there!" Shan heard the voice and breathed a prayer of thanks. Looking up, he saw two men wading slowly toward him.

"Come on, boy. Let's get you out of here." A husky man lifted Michael, but was jerked back. "Let go," he said, seeing that Michael's hand was gripping his sister's wrist.

"No."

Another man, so covered with mud he was unidentifiable, lifted little Libby into his arms, and still, Michael refused to let go of his sister's arm. The men began wading, linked together by Michael's and Libby's arms, through the muck, toward the hillside only a block and a half away. Shan followed, with little Danny in his arms, breathing deep, ragged breaths. They were safe.

*   *   *

Will Burke rocked gently, the arms that held him cradling his head as if shushing him to sleep. He didn't know where he was or what was happening. He was sleepy—so sleepy. He lay in the gentle arms that rocked him, eyes closed, waiting for sleep to come. He felt cool for the first time in a week. And he was rocking so gently.

Then he heard voices, shouting, a loud rumbling. Will was jolted from his half sleep as the sound of crashing timber accompanied the breakup of his bed of dreams. He wished they would stop and leave him in peace.

Instead, he began to sink and drew in a breath of muddy water. He jerked and lunged up choking and coughing, reaching frantically for something solid. He splashed in water and muck, clawing his way toward safety. Then he heard a shout.

"Over here!"

The light of a lantern bobbed into view and a strong hand reached out to grasp Will's arm. As he was pulled to safety, Will cried out, then drifted once again into a quiet dreamland.

"Who is it?" One of the men held a lantern aloft to better see the child's face.

"Dunno. A kid."

"Take him up to the schoolhouse. That's high and dry."

"Better be careful. He might be hurt bad."

"Here, this'll work." One of the men dragged up a broken door. They gently placed young Will on the makeshift stretcher, and the two men started back toward town. Will knew nothing.

*   *   *

The mud-covered forms streaming into the Justus home defied recognition. Finding the kitchen faucet out of order, Dacia sent an older child out to the well for water and laid out a pile of rags she found. At least people could wash their faces.

She looked around, trying to spot Lilyann or Gilbert in the crowd, but didn't see them. They must be at one of the other houses.

Tears, which had dried in response to the need to help others, returned to Dacia's eyes as she saw Johnny approach. "What?" she asked. "What did you find?"

"Not good. Only one found alive so far. Phil Cohn." He drew a deep breath. "Bodies. Lots of bodies. We can't get over to the other side of town at all. Probably won't be able to 'til morning. But it can't be good."

"Our children?" Dacia's voice shook, but she persisted, looking Johnny square in the eye. "Johnny, tell me."

Johnny took her shoulders in his hands. He shook his head and said, "Dacia. Dacia listen to me. They're gone."

Dacia gripped his wrists and nearly collapsed against him.

"They were at the creek, Dacia—the very center of the flood. Josie and Martin and Will ... are gone." Johnny choked and tilted his head back. "Ella is gone. Mac is gone. Their children. The Collins boys. They're all gone, Dacia. All gone." He cried silently.

Dacia sobbed in her husband's arms. "No!" she cried. "God, no! That can't be!" She pounded her fists on Johnny's chest. "God wouldn't do that! What kind of a loving God would kill all these people? No, Johnny! No!"

But Johnny had no answer. He just held his wife and wondered for himself about God's supposed goodness. He couldn't speak. He looked up for a moment as if searching for an answer, then buried his face in Dacia's beautiful Gypsy hair, now sodden, filled with mud. He had no answer. There was no answer. They were gone. And it was over. Only one question resounded in his heart and mind: *God, why?*

Chapter Nine

Monday morning – courthouse just r. of center, school on the hill, right
Courtesy Christopher Sigsbee George

The sun should not have risen Monday morning. But it did. Reluctantly—as if the gray light of dawn was ashamed to reveal nature's bad behavior. A heavily overcast sky threatened more storm, and it seemed the true light would never shine again.

The Burke home appeared to be only slightly damaged by the flood, but the mud on the floor would have to be shoveled out and everything cleaned before it could be used again. Dacia stepped out the back door carrying eggs, buckwheat, and rice. Putting one foot in front of the other, she dragged herself with desperate determination back to the Justus home where two of her five children were bedded down in the front room like a couple of puppies in a very large litter. Every room in the house was filled with refugees. The children had slept during the night. At least the younger ones had. But for the adults, sleep was a luxury they could ill-afford.

David and Margaret Justus had gone to visit her brother at his farm yesterday afternoon and weren't home yet. Their two nearly-grown sons, Nelson and Ralph, had opened up the home to refugees. Blankets and quilts carpeted the floor, strewn with sleeping bodies. Children slept end-to-end and side-by-side, tumbled over each other, on every spare inch of flooring. It was still hot. Even in the early morning. Even after the storm.

On the front porch, Dacia paused to steel herself before entering the house. She leaned heavily against the post supporting the porch roof as she summoned courage to enter. The children were beginning to wake, some crying for mothers, some wanting breakfast, and some, amazingly, wanting to play. Play? Was life so normal that children could play?

"Mama!" little Sarah cried, running to Dacia as she entered. "Where you was at? I miss you!"

Placing her load of food on the floor, Dacia knelt to hug her daughter and began sobbing. She couldn't stop. Precious, precious Sarah! She clutched the child to herself with arms of steel. No one would take this treasured child from her. Not even God.

"Mama?" Walter said. "Me, too." She reached out to include him and held him tight, her tears watering his dark blond hair. Walter patted her gently on the shoulder. She realized once again that she was not allowed the luxury of tears. Not now.

Pappy dozed in a chair, snoring gently. Dacia gave the children an extra hug and sent them across the room to the old man. They would be comforted in his presence.

She started to stand, then noticed the Collins children. Michael's hand still held little Libby's wrist. His fingers were relaxed in sleep, but when Dacia reached to release Libby's arm, Michael's fingers clamped down and he whimpered.

How old was Michael? Six, Dacia thought. A year younger than Will. How would the flood affect these little ones—her own children, the Collinses, the other children scattered all over the house—all over town? What would they remember? The sound? That was the thing in the forefront of Dacia's mind. The horrible, horrible sound. The beating of the rain, followed by the even heavier hammering of the hailstones— a literal pounding! The sound still boomed in her memory, as if she could hear it at this very moment. She would never forget that sound. And the screaming on the hillside. She had nothing in her experience she could compare it to. The loud, loud sound of ... of what? The flood itself? Maybe that's what it was—the flood moaning. As the thick semi-liquid rolled over and over on itself in its race toward lower ground, the broken buildings, the screaming of animals and people had created their own cry, the cry of anguish and death.

Katie Currin, a young woman who lived nearby, came through the kitchen door. Dacia handed Katie the egg basket and said "I brought some food for breakfast. And some other things." She rose to her feet. "Do we have any meat? And has anyone heard from the other side of town?"

"Nothing yet. Guess we'll hear soon enough." Katie turned back toward the kitchen while Dacia picked up the rest of food she'd brought and followed. "Shan Collins is down rummaging through his house. He'll bring anything he can find. I guess we'll need to feed the men first so they can get going again," she said. "The children will have to wait. Except the babies."

Dacia found an apron hanging on the back of the kitchen door and tied it over her muddy dress. Katie gave her an odd look, but said nothing. Dacia had not slept—really, no one had except the children— but it was nearly morning and people must be fed. Dacia's chest shuddered as she inhaled deeply, and turned to the stove. A young lady she couldn't place bent over the fire, nursing it to life. The girl's dark hair was chopped short and she was covered with mud from head to toe. She looked terrible. But then, so did everyone this morning. Dacia found a large bowl and began mixing the buckwheat into batter for hotcakes.

Where were her other children? Josie, Martin, Will? No matter what Johnny had said, Dacia refused to believe they were dead. Not yet. Had Johnny found them? Where was he now? Where were *they*? She set the bowl of batter on the table near the stove and prepared to mix another.

Where were Gilbert and Lilyann? They must be at one of the houses on the hill. No time to look for them now. She would find them as soon as she could.

Katie returned from the pantry with her arms full of canning jars. "Peach and strawberry preserves and some apple butter," she said. "And there's more when this runs out. I'm sure Margaret won't mind us raiding her pantry." She bent and awkwardly placed the jars on the table.

Dacia nodded in thanks, but didn't respond.

The girl who had built the fire poured batter into two large cast iron skillets and a griddle. Katie was slicing the last of Margaret's small supply of bacon when Shan came in the back door with his haul of food and supplies. He set a basket of eggs carefully on the table, then bent forward, letting a sack of flour slide from his shoulder. Dacia nodded grimly to him.

As the girl at the stove used the last of the batter, she handed the bowl to Dacia in exchange for another full one, and Dacia began mixing flour, buckwheat, eggs, and milk for yet another batch.

"Bacon, Shan," she said. "Can you find us a side of bacon? Or some sausage, or any kind of meat? And you can get beans and potatoes from my house. I just couldn't carry any more."

"I'll try. I thought we had some meat at home, but I guess it washed away. I'll try some other places."

Shan looked over at Danny, who was just waking up. "I guess we'll be needing diapers too. How many babies do we have here?"

"I don't know. Lots. Check with the Johnstons. Their youngest is just out of diapers. She should have some."

Shan took three of the older boys along with him to help carry whatever he could find—food, diapers—*anything* useful.

Dacia glanced again at the girl at the stove. Her face was grim and unfamiliar. Her dark green dress was muddy, but not soaked through. "Have I met you?" Dacia asked as she mixed the batter.

"Maybe not. I'm kind of new here." The muscles in the girl's jaw tightened. Dacia could see she didn't want to talk.

"Could you take over for a minute?" The young lady eased out the back door—in search of an outhouse?—while Dacia looked after her, puzzled. *I certainly hope there's a mirror in that "powder room".* Dacia thought. *I wonder if she knows what her hair looks like.* But Dacia gave not a single thought to her own appearance.

She looked out the kitchen window to where a group of men stood around the yard eating from the plates they held in their hands. There was a complete absence of friendly bantering that would usually accompany such a picnic. Faces were somber, mystified, determined. Conversation was limited to the work of the day. Plates were returned for more, or passed on to the next hungry worker with no time for washing. No water for washing either.

No running water. No telephones. No electricity. The flood had plunged the town back twenty years. The people would have to make do with the methods their parents and grandparents had used. It had been done before. It could be done again.

Left: Palace Hotel,
Center: flood debris and the Courthouse in the background on the hill.
Courtesy Morrow County Heritage Museum

Chapter Ten

J ohnny Burke's head hung low as he trudged back toward town. He was caked with mud, and his lantern, now empty of oil, swung uselessly at his side. The night had been long—the longest Johnny had known in his thirty-four years. He had seen enough death to last a lifetime and more as he traveled from one pile of rubble to another, searching for survivors. There had been a few. Precious few. But in the bed of the wagon he followed lay the body of his son, Martin. Five other bodies lay in the wagon as well—another child, three women, one man.

Daylight had just begun to break as the sad group entered Heppner on the west side of the flood's path. The town had been effectively split in two by the wide swath of mud and wreckage left by last night's torrent. In the dim light, Johnny tried to see across to the east hill, beyond the muddy center of town. There was no movement. Everything looked dead.

Johnny dreaded facing his wife. He had managed to save Pappy, his 74-year-old grandfather, but he'd lost his own children! Had he really thought it would be a good idea for the boys to cool off in the creek that afternoon? How could he have allowed himself to think that? Could he ever forgive himself for allowing Josie to go to the creek for the boys? Could Dacia forgive him? Why, oh why had he not gone himself?

Sheriff Ed Shutt and George Conser met Johnny as he re-entered what had been, until last night, one of the finest young towns in Eastern Oregon. Even in the dim light, Johnny could see that Shutt's eyes were glazed. He figured the sheriff's home was a loss. It had been right next to the creek. He wondered about Mrs. Shutt and their children. Had they died in the flood?

"Sheriff," Johnny nodded his head at Shutt in greeting.

"What do you have?" Shutt asked.

"Six dead—no live bodies. What are we going to use for a morgue?"

"Well, Jim Yeager's shop is gone. All the furniture lost, all the caskets he had. Although I saw him working a drift just a few minutes ago. At least *he's* alive." Shutt took a deep breath. "But we have no coffins—none at all—and no morgue."

"We've been taking bodies to the bank," George Conser told Johnny. As head teller at the First National Bank, he had offered the one place that seemed most reasonable at the moment. At least it was still standing. A number of bodies lined the floor of the lobby already.

Shutt nodded slowly. "Maybe we can use the new Roberts Hall above the Belvedere, once we get things organized. It's a lot bigger. I think we're going to need plenty of room."

One of the men asked, "Where's Gilliam, anyway? We need somebody to take charge—coordinate everything and get some order going."

"The mayor and his wife are in Portland. Some kind of convention or something. I'm sure he'll be back as soon as he can get here."

"Not by train!" Johnny said. "You should see where the track used to be. It's all washed out. Even the steel rails are gone—wrapped around the biggest trees as if they were barbed wire."

"Well, he'll get here one way or another. For now, let's take the bodies to the bank. Johnny, maybe you could get some men to help you start setting up Roberts Hall."

Johnny nodded. "I'll need to see Dacia first," he said. "I've got Martin's body here."

Shutt shook his head. "Sorry," he said in a choked voice. He couldn't go on.

"Well, we'd better get moving," Conser said, reaching for his watch in the pocket of his vest. He pulled it out, but it was useless. Dead. It had stopped at 5:45—the time George Conser and his wife were clinging to life and to each other in their attic as the water crept up to their chins before finally beginning to recede. Conser looked around the group of men. "Let's meet back here in an hour to get started. Tonight, when it's too dark to work, we can meet again to get a little better organized."

Sheriff Shutt nodded and addressed the other men who had gathered, "You others, check on your families, get something to eat, and be back here as soon as you can. Bring teams and wagons. Tools if you can find any. We need to cover every square inch of ground." The sheriff rubbed his hand across his eyes and turned away.

Johnny went with the wagon and carried the body of his oldest son into the bank as Conser opened the door of the temporary morgue. Laying Martin's body gently on the floor, Johnny stood looking down on his son. Unthinkable. He closed his eyes and took a deep breath. He turned and started up the hill toward the Justus home, then stopped and turned back to gaze again at the awful bare strip through the center of town. Abruptly, he walked toward the devastation. He had to cross to the other side. Before he talked to Dacia, he had to see if anyone had news of Josie or Will. It was more likely that the children would be found on the east side—closer to the creek itself.

He walked, sliding in the muck, until he came to the creek. He hesitated for a moment, looking in amazement and anger at the tiny stream. There it was, pretending to be a pleasant little brook flowing gently within its banks. Johnny's body shook with built up tension and anger. He exhaled loudly, cursed the creek, and jumped across to the other side, almost slipping back in as he landed. He could see activity at the courthouse and climbed the hill to the new bluestone building.

As he approached a group of men near the courthouse lawn, Johnny interrupted without ceremony.

"Has anyone heard anything about my Will or Josie?" he asked. "They were at the creek."

Heads shook apologetically. Johnny only nodded.

"We're taking the dead to the bank for now. I'm going to set up Roberts Hall as a morgue and have it ready as soon as I can. I'll need some help."

"We could use bathtubs to wash the bodies." One of the men suggested. "Gibson has some for sale at his place. I saw his ad in the *Gazette*. Maybe he'll let us use them."

"Great, Tom. Can you find Gibson and arrange that?"

"Sure thing. I'll meet you down there."

"Good. Bring a couple other men to help carry."

Johnny looked at the other men in the group. "We're meeting at the bank at six to organize into groups for searching. Bring teams and wagons and tools. I'll be at Dave Justus's to check on my wife. And if anyone hears anything about my children ..."

The men all nodded solemnly, and Johnny turned to retrace his steps to the west side of the creek, hoping for a moment with Dacia before continuing this endless day. How he hated to face her and tell her of Martin's death!

The second story and cupola of the Thomas Ayers home
Courtesy Christopher Sigsbee George

Chapter Eleven

The flood beat Matlock and Kelly to Lexington. A number of homes were seriously damaged, and the Baptist Church had washed off its foundation and slammed into the Methodist Church. Both buildings were damaged considerably, but there were no deaths.

Poor old Pretty Girl, Shan Collins' mare, had given out just below Lexington, and Matlock had found a new mount at Andrew Rainey's farm. With the fresh horse, Les caught up easily with Kelly's Dancer. Pretty Girl was still alive, the last Matlock saw her, but she was in need of much tender loving care.

The two men had finally overtaken the flood and beat it to Ione, shouting out the warning to farm homes along the way. By the time they reached Ione, the people had already taken to the hills. It seemed Heppner's railroad agent had telegraphed both Lexington and Ione just before he, himself, was swept away. Ione's Mayor, J. A. Woolery, had sent teams of young men down to retrieve blankets from homes. He intended to keep his people on the hills until morning. He figured spending the night under a soggy blanket in the pouring rain and pounding hail was a far sight better than dying in a flood.

After a short rest in Ione, Matlock and Kelly had started for home around midnight. Their mounts dragged into Heppner just after six in the morning.

At the north entrance to the town, both men stopped and stared. The sight that met their tired eyes was beyond anything they could have imagined. The entire center section of the town was missing. Gone. A tragic, barren strip, a hundred yards wide and a mile long— nothing but mud and debris—broken parts of homes, farm wagons, torn lumber, buggies. Portions of a few of the fine homes could be recognized, but most of it was nothing more than rubble and muck.

Neither man could think of a word to say.

Finally Les nudged his horse and the two rode up to where Sheriff Shutt was talking with Johnny Burke and several other men.

"We warned Lexington and Ione," Matlock told them. "Don't think anyone died there."

The sheriff nodded. "Guy Boyer left about dawn for Echo," he told the men. "He's going to send word to Pendleton asking for help. And Dave McAtee and Frank Spaulding are on their way to Arlington. Left last night." He looked at Matlock. "Dave took your horse. Within a day, all of Oregon will know what's happened. They'll stand ready to help us."

"He took *my* horse?" repeated Matlock. "Why didn't he take his own?"

"How will they get here?" Kelley asked, ignoring his friend. He dismounted stiffly, grabbing at the stirrup as his feet slipped in the mud. "The road's gone, the railroad is nothing but twisted rails and splinters. The valley's all mud—every inch between here and Ione—probably all the way out to the Columbia!"

"Well, it ain't going to be easy. But they'll come." Shutt's tone of voice indicated that he didn't need an argument. He needed help and encouragement.

Matlock shifted in his saddle, anxious to get into town. "So you're in charge, Sheriff?"

"For now. Gilliam will be here as soon as he can. And in the meantime, we'll just have to make do." He closed his eyes, then looked back at Matlock. "Your uncle, James Matlock, was the first body brought in, Les. Sorry to have to tell you."

Matlock nodded solemnly. He had guessed as much. And he knew his uncle would not be his only family member lost to the flood.

*   *   *

Will awoke slowly. He lay with his eyes closed, the world he couldn't see rocking and spinning beneath him. He grasped for something to hang on to, but the floor beneath him was the only thing available, and it wouldn't hold still. He tried to think. It all seemed unreal—and yet the *most* real thing in his life right now. *Be still!* His hands reached out in search of something solid. If only he could stop this floating feeling. His head hurt so badly. He cracked his eyes open. It hurt too much. He let them drift shut as sleep once again overpowered him.

*   *   *

"Hold up there," Johnny said, as he and Shan carried a bathtub to the door of the Roberts Hall stairway. He paused as Shan opened the door behind him, then, grunting with the effort, they carried the heavy tub up the stairway to the room above. This was the last of eight, brought for the purpose of washing the dead—preparing the bodies for burial. Entering the room most recently used for the high school graduation ceremony, Johnny and Shan placed the tub's legs on large wooden boxes, elevating it for ease of access. The other tubs in the large room all had wooden slats laid across them to support the bodies. As Shan returned to the street below, Johnny picked up a pile of two-by-fours from the floor and laid them in place on the last tub. He looked around at the women already at work.

Seeing Dacia, grief washed over him afresh. She looked up at him, sorrow lining the face he loved so well. Dacia worked with a young lady Johnny didn't know. They used sheep shears to remove the muddy, torn clothing from the body of a child—a young boy about seven or eight, the age of his Will. He walked to Dacia, took her head in his hand, and pressed his lips against her forehead.

"Josie? Will?" Dacia looked intently at Johnny.

He shook his head. "Nothing yet." He closed his eyes and took a deep breath, despising the smell around him.

Martin's coffin had been one of the first, earlier this morning, to be loaded onto the wagon and driven up the hill to the cemetery. Pappy rode up front with the driver. Johnny and Dacia walked behind, Johnny carrying Walter—little Sarah in Dacia's arms—to see the remains of their oldest son lowered into the ground. Brother Mount, the Baptist pastor, looked as if his heart had been broken as he tearfully spoke the words committing Martin's soul back into the hands of his Maker.

Now, in the morgue, as Martin's parents stood in their sad embrace, they grieved for their loss, and at the same time, wondered about their two other children.

"Doing okay?" Johnny asked Dacia. She nodded, but looked down and pulled away from him to continue her task.

"Be careful when you go out," she said. "The floor's slippery."

The floor was indeed slippery. A number of teenage boys with buckets were busy hauling in water drawn from nearby wells. The women dipped the water out of the buckets as needed for their task; then the muddy water was drained from the tubs back into empty buckets to be carried downstairs. Quite a bit of it ended up on the floor.

"Coming up!" Johnny heard a voice below and went to the stairs to see if they were bringing bodies or caskets. Bodies. Always, more bodies. Shan entered the room again carrying one end of a door, serving as a stretcher, and carried the body to a tub that had just been vacated. It was 10:30 in the morning. Twenty-eight bodies had been prepared for burial already. Twenty-three of them were in coffins—coffins made of random boards salvaged from the edges of the flood. Four wagonloads of the rough-built caskets, filled with the remnants of human dreams, had already been taken up to the cemetery.

*   *   *

Across town, sixty-three homeless people were housed temporarily at the courthouse. At the schoolhouse, ninety-eight more had taken up residence, including Will Burke, lying on a blanket where he'd been deposited earlier that morning. He had wakened once and complained of his head hurting. Little wonder, considering the huge gash extending from his forehead down across his left cheek. The whole side of his face was badly bruised and swollen. When he was first found, the gash was barely noticeable, hidden as it was by a thick layer of mud. Every time the child began to wake, he squinted his eyes against the bright light of day. Then he immediately turned his head away from the windows and drifted back to sleep.

When Lou Lundquist took charge of the schoolhouse, she sent for Dr. McSwords, but the good doctor could not be found. His house had vanished as if it had never existed, and most people felt it was only Dr. McSwords' body they would find, rather than the man himself. Lou sent several of the older children in search of the other three doctors in town. "Find a doctor—any doctor—and bring him back here," she instructed.

Several people had expressed surprise to find that Lou had stepped up to take responsibility for Will. And while watching over him, she was helping others in every way she could. Normally, she would expect others to cater to *her* desires. Now, she only wanted to know how she could help. In a crisis of this magnitude, anyone willing to help was pressed immediately into service. No one seemed to care anymore who had the most money, the nicest figure, the best personality, the fanciest house—indeed, it was the finest houses in town, those right by Willow Creek, that had suffered the greatest indignity at the hands of the flood.

Lou knelt awkwardly beside young Will and looked at him with concern. His face had been washed of the muck that had encrusted it, but he probably needed stitches. And she was worried by the fact that the child couldn't seem to stay awake. She pulled up a small chair and sat uncomfortably. She wished she knew what to do. Hopefully, there would be at least one doctor still alive in town.

Chapter Twelve

Bath tubs used for cleaning bodies in the morgue, upstairs in Roberts Hall
Courtesy Morrow County Heritage Museum

Dacia dipped her rag in the bucket at her feet and gave it a good squeeze. As she resumed washing the shoulder and arm of the child she couldn't identify, she glanced again at the young lady working opposite her. She was the same one who had walked out on her hotcake flipping job earlier this morning. Her face was plain—but might be pretty if she had something to smile about. And if she had more hair. Dacia wondered briefly what had happened to it. The girl's hands were rough. It was plain to see she was used to working. Dacia didn't recall ever seeing her before.

"So you're new around here?" Dacia asked. "Where'd you come from?"

"South aways."

Dacia nodded and rinsed her rag. "Been here long?"

"Huh-uh. Just a couple days."

"Some welcome, huh?" Dacia's voice sounded bitter. "Sorry. We didn't plan this, you know." They worked silently for a while longer, then Dacia broke the silence. "My name's Dacia."

The girl nodded but said nothing.

Dacia rinsed her rag again. "You got a name?"

The girl clenched her jaws. She swallowed hard. "You can call me Grace," she said.

"I can *call* you Grace? Is that your name?"

But Dacia received no answer.

*   *   *

Jim Yeager
Courtesy Morrow County Heritage Museum

James Yeager had set up sawhorses in the street outside the Roberts Building. Between him and his two oldest sons, Ora and Harvey, coffins were being turned out as fast as possible. He swung his hammer again and again, pounding nail, after nail, after nail into the box he was making. It was constructed from scrap lumber retrieved from the drifts along the periphery of the flood. Seven feet long, two and a half feet wide, two feet deep. Yeager's sons sorted the boards into piles of similar sizes, then sawed them to lengths as needed. Yeager had already sent several tiny coffins up to the morgue. Harvey had just come back with a report that eight more full size boxes and eleven smaller ones were needed. He handed his father a scrap of paper with the measurements for the smaller coffins.

When Yeager had received his degree in undertaking only two months ago, he could never have envisioned this horror he now faced. Nothing in his education had prepared him for *this!*

He pulled another nail from his mouth and continued hammering, the sound of the hammer beating a steady cadence to the dirge playing in his head. Death. Too ... too ... much ... death!

*   *   *

Johnny loped across the heavy board which had been placed over the creek and hurried up the hill on the opposite side. Word had come that Will was alive and at the schoolhouse. He had asked the bearer of the news not to mention it to Dacia yet. He needed to be sure. As he hurried past the yard of the courthouse, one of the men called out to him, "Johnny! Did you find Will yet? I heard he's at the schoolhouse."

Johnny just waved his thanks and continued up the hill. Now that he was above the flood line, the ground was not so slippery. He broke into a run.

Ignoring the people in the schoolyard, Johnny took the steps two at a time. "Third grade room," he heard someone call after him. As he entered the classroom, Lou Lundquist rushed to him with her finger to her lips. "Carefully, Mr. Burke. He's sleeping."

As Johnny bent over his son, his body shook with sobs. Alive! Will was alive! That's all that mattered for now. *Oh God, thank you!* Johnny's eyes traced the outline of Will's small face, now badly bruised and swollen, with a horrible gaping wound.

"Tell me ..." Johnny looked up at Lou. "Tell me how he got here. What happened to him?"

"I don't know." She shook her head. "They found him down by Cunnington's place—more dead than alive, they said. He's woken up a few times since they brought him here, but just barely. He hasn't said much of anything since early this morning when they first brought him in. He was complaining that his head hurt. But that was about the last word out of him."

Johnny nodded.

"I've cleaned him up a bit and sent for a doctor, but so far, we haven't found any of them."

"Dr. McSwords is dead," Johnny said.

Lou sighed. "We figured. His house was so close to the creek."

Will's eyelids fluttered.

"Will? Will, can you hear me?" Johnny's hand rested gently on Will's shoulder.

The child showed no response at all.

"Lou," Johnny said. "Would you send someone to get Dacia? She's in the morgue—in Roberts Hall."

*   *   *

Mac Harmon's head pounded. He was alive, but covered with mud, his clothing torn half off, and he was lying on the sofa at Frank and Effie Gilliam's house on the hill. He could see Ona, Frank and Effie's nineteen-year-old daughter, sitting in the chair opposite him.

He took a painful, shallow breath. "Where's Ella?" His voice sounded raspy. "I need to tell her." Ona rose and moved to his side. "The children ..." He hesitated as his chest shook and throat choked up. "The children. I think they're lost. I tried. I tried to hold them!" Mac struggled to sit up.

"Mr. Harmon, don't worry. Just rest." Ona pushed gently on Mac's shoulder, pressing him back into the couch. She had opened the home to anyone needing a place to eat and sleep. She knew it was what her parents would want.

Mac had no strength to resist. But as the memory returned even stronger than before, he sat up again, ignoring the pain in his side.

"No! Where's Ella? I need to find her!" His eyes were wide, frantic.

"I'm not sure where she is right now, Mister Harmon." Ona hadn't the heart to tell him what she knew—that Ella's body had been recovered just a short time before. "Just rest, and we'll try to find out. You've been through a lot." Ona tried to comfort him, but Mac rose and stormed awkwardly toward the door of the house. *Don't know where she is ... are you trying to tell me ...?* He stumbled, clutching the door knob and the frame on his way out.

The sight that met Mac's eyes was beyond description. Nothing. Yesterday there had been a town—now nothing. He looked down on Gale street. It was gone. His house was *gone!* The Collins's house was still there, though it sat at an odd angle in the wrong place, but the Harmon's house was nowhere to be seen.

His face blanched and he fell to his knees in the yard. *"Ella!"* he whispered.

*   *   *

"Comin' up!" Shan's voice from below elicited little response from the ladies working in the makeshift morgue.

67

"We have room for two," Dacia called down the stairs. "And we have three more ready to go out as soon as we get more caskets."

Shan carried in the body of a toddler and laid her gently on the slats of Dacia's tub. "Six more coffins ready," he said. "We'll get 'em up here as quick as we can." His voice seemed to echo in the large room with its high ceiling. Even with the women working, the bodies being prepared for burial, and the tubs perched on wooden boxes, the room seemed empty, hollow.

Two men entered carrying a man's body on an improvised stretcher. "How many have we sent up to the cemetery already?" Shan asked Dacia.

"Forty-two," she said, checking the bank ledger the women were using to record the names of the dead. "And with these here, that'll make fifty-three."

Shan took the ledger from Dacia and glanced down the list of names. Number seven—A. C. Geiger. The man who had sold him his new buggy. Well, the buggy was gone. Geiger was gone. The saddle Shan had lovingly crafted as a part of the purchase price was probably gone too. Shan looked at the other names and shook his head in wonder. He knew most of them. Real people. Men he'd passed the time of day with at the shop. People he sat next to in church. His mother's friends. And now they were dead. His face was grim, and his mind struggled to believe it all as he handed the list back to Dacia.

Although none of their bodies had been found yet, Shan suspected that his mother, two sisters, and two brothers had all died. His mother and sisters were at the McCheyne's house right by the creek, while the boys were playing nearby. But Shan wasn't ready to think about it yet.

"Look at this beautiful child! But who is she?" One of the women workers looked down on the face of a little girl, probably six or seven years old. "I wish the school teachers were still here. I read in the *Gazette* they've all left town for the summer."

"Mmm," Dacia nodded in agreement, as she laid aside the ledger of names and returned to helping Grace. She looked up as she heard a loud clatter on the stairs.

"Mrs. Burke!" the young woman nearly shouted. "Will is alive! Your husband sent me to get you."

"Will? Will is alive?" Every nerve in Dacia's body stood at attention as warmth flooded her chest. She dropped her rag in the bucket at her feet. "Where is he?"

She ran to the door, pushing Grace out of her way, but stopped as the men from below entered, carrying between them a wide board—and on the board, the body of a girl.

Her heart-rending cry filled the air, and Dacia collapsed to the floor. "NO!" she screamed. On the wooden slab suspended between two men lay the mangled body of Josie, sweet Josie, recognizable only by her torn and muddy dress.

*   *   *

Johnny Burke shook his head in wonder. Was this still Monday? His day had been too full. The worst he'd ever known in his life. In the course of twenty-four hours, he had survived a flood, saved several others from its malicious grasp, walked over fifteen miles in search of survivors or the remains of the dead, buried one son, discovered another son alive but injured, and helped prepare the body of his daughter for burial.

Hope no longer existed for finding live victims. It was now assumed that all missing persons from the town of Heppner were dead, and only needed to be found and buried. No one wanted to mention it, but the burials needed to take place quickly, lest illness overtake the whole of Willow Creek Valley and the death toll increase.

Now as the light began to fade from the Monday sky, Johnny stood next to Dacia on Cemetery Hill for the second time that day. They gazed in silence at the two fresh mounds guarding the remains of their two oldest children. No words were spoken. There remained no strength for words. They would sleep, or try to sleep until dawn tomorrow, which would come far too soon.

*   *   *

Grace staggered down the stairs at the end of her first day in the morgue. She had never been so exhausted in her life. She felt as if she, herself, had died. Perhaps she had. She stood, undecided, for a moment, then walked slowly, deliberately in the direction of the creek. Bile rose to her throat as she looked at the small stream. So tiny. So ... gentle. There was still enough light in the sky to see the devastation left in the wake of last night's storm. Amazing. Amazing that such destruction should also become a means of grace. Gritting her teeth, she turned back and strode purposefully past Mollie Reid's *Chateau de Joie* and on up the hill. She would sleep at the Justus home again tonight.

*   *   *

The first news report: *East Oregonian* (Pendleton)

Pendleton, Umatilla County, Oregon, Monday, June 15, 1903

HUNDREDS OF PEOPLE DEAD AT HEPPNER
Awful Cloudburst Came Down
Without a Moment's Warning

Two Hundred and Fifty People Are Known to be Drowned and 400 to 500
Still Missing--Ione a Total Wreck, Lexington Devastated, Heppner a Waste of
Ruins, People Had No Time to Flee, Heavens Opened Without Warning,
Flooding the Narrow Valley, Darkness and the Crash of the Deluge Render
the Night Awful to the Survivors in the Stricken Cities.

The men of Heppner are hard at work pulling apart drifts in the search for bodies.
Courtesy Morrow County Heritage Museum

Chapter Thirteen

On Tuesday morning, Dacia sat on the schoolhouse floor with little Sarah in her lap and Walter beside her. She placed her hand on Will's forehead, gently pushing his tawny hair back from his face. Dr. Kistner had sewn up the huge cut that ran from his left temple down across his cheek. It was now swathed in white. The doctor hadn't wanted Will moved yesterday, but after his examination this morning, he had told Dacia she could take the boy home to care for him. She would wait for Johnny to come with the wagon.

Lou Lundquist came into the room and sat on a child-sized chair on the other side of Will. The chair was small for her, but she seemed not to mind. She took one of Will's hands in her own and looked up at Dacia. "Are your other children all okay?"

Dacia didn't answer. She didn't want Lou to be here. She had never liked the woman much, but somehow the tragedy of the flood seemed to have leveled the ground. Dacia guessed it didn't matter what she thought of Lou. What mattered was that Lou was willing to be here. Willing to do a job that needed doing.

"You doing okay?" Lou pressed.

Dacia nodded slightly. "Uh-huh. You?"

"They just found my mother's body." Lou said. "I need to go now." She pulled both lips between her teeth and took a deep breath, then stood.

Dacia rose and embraced her. Yes, in the face of death, the ground was level. "I'm so sorry! Your father?"

"Nothing yet." She turned to go, then stopped and looked back at Dacia. "I'll be back to help out here as soon as I can."

"Don't worry about it. I'll be here 'til Johnny comes with the wagon to fetch Will home."

"There's just so much need," Lou said. "I wish I could do more."

Dacia watched as Lou walked out of the room and down the hall, feeling a sudden admiration for this woman. Lou was the one who had held and fretted over Will when he was first brought in. She had given as much as anyone in town—more than many—and she wished she could do more! Maybe there was more to the woman than Dacia had realized.

*　　*　　*

The ride from the schoolhouse to the Burke's home was tediously slow, Johnny trying to make the trip as easy for Will as possible. Will lay in the wagon bed on a pile of quilts, with Dacia's hand shielding his eyes from the brightness of the sun. Walter and Sarah sat up front with their father.

"Mama," Will said softly.

"I'm right here, Sweetie."

"Mama," Will said again. Tears formed at the corners of his eyes, and Dacia brushed them away.

"Shhhh," she said. "It's alright. Everything will be alright now." She knew she was lying. Josie was dead. Martin was dead. Things would never be the same again. Dacia ran her finger down the uninjured side of his face and under his chin. Precious Will—now her oldest child.

Johnny carried the boy from the wagon to the house, where Pappy stepped forward and placed his ancient, gnarled hand on Will's brow. "Thank you, Jesus." He sobbed quietly. "Thank you for this one, Lord." His hand hovered over Will's head, as if in benediction, then he turned back to his chair and painfully lowered himself into it, nodding. "Thank you, thank you, thank you, Jesus!"

Will drifted off to sleep almost as soon as Johnny laid him gently on his bed. Dacia brushed his hair back from his eyes, kissed his forehead, and followed Johnny down the stairs.

Johnny left to check on the morgue, and then the feeding program for the workers and the homeless. Dacia got tea from the ice box for herself and Pappy. She needed to sit. Even with the floor still covered with mud, she just needed to sit and breathe. She needed to *not* be surrounded by death for just a few moments. She lowered herself stiffly to Johnny's overstuffed chair and gazed at Pappy. He had survived. He was confused—perhaps even more than before the flood, but he had survived. And Josie and Martin were gone. Her children. Ella was gone. Her best friend.

"They're alive," Pappy said.

"What?" Dacia lifted her head. What was the old man talking about?

"They're alive. Those two children. They didn't die." Pappy turned to gaze off to his left. His wrinkled fingers reached out to grab something, but came up empty. He turned his hand over and frowned at his palm. Nothing there.

"Are you talking about Josie and Martin, Pappy? They *did* die." Her voice shook, choked. "We took their bodies up to the cemetery and buried them. Remember?"

"No." Pappy shook his head. "No."

Dacia frowned as she looked at the old man. She loved him, but ... well, this wasn't making things any easier. *God, why? He's old. He doesn't even know what's going on! Why Josie? Why Martin? They were so young, and he's so ...* Dacia stopped, ashamed of herself. She knew better than to question God. At least in her mind she knew. But her heart didn't know. Her heart was bruised and angry. And at this moment, she felt more righteous than God himself.

*　　*　　*

Johnny was furious. He kicked the door, and when it didn't give at all, grabbed the handle and rattled it fiercely. The only meat market left in town was locked, and its owner had taken flight. That, in itself, was completely understandable. Of the two owners, one, George Kinzley, had died along with his wife, and the other, Guy Boyd, had lost his wife and children to the flood. Declaring that he could not stand the strain of trying to function in a town cursed by death, Boyd had packed his bags, locked the door, and taken the train to Portland. Well, he had to get a wagon to haul him past Lexington before he could catch the train. But he did it.

Johnny's anger was directed not at Boyd, who had lost his entire family, but at the door itself. He needed for things to work. The town needed meat; this door should open!

Johnny kicked at the door one final time. "Get this door open," he growled. "By now Sam's on his way back to town with some of Criswell's beef cattle. We need to be ready." He left the men to open the butcher's door and strode up the hill to the encampment above the

Christian Church where the Portland men were staying. The leader of the recovery team came to meet him.

"Mr. Teal?" Johnny asked.

The man nodded. "Johnny Burke, right? What can I do for you?"

"A butcher. We need someone to cut up a bunch of beeves."

Teal turned to face the camp where about half the men were just arriving for their turn at the breakfast tables. "Hey, men! We need a butcher. Anybody here know how to cut up a cow or a pig?

"Me." An older man stepped forward. "I'm a butcher."

"Good. You go with Johnny here. He's your new commanding officer."

Tents donated by the National Guard housed the Portland volunteers.
Courtesy Christopher Sigsbee George

By the time Johnny and the conscripted butcher returned to the shop, the men had broken open the door and pulled some of the larger equipment out into the area in front of the shop. He looked up to see Criswell and two others riding down Main Street—or the place that used to be Main Street—driving before them five steers.

"Okay, all the rest of you are going to need to clear out now. It's going to get very messy here in a very short time." He looked at Heppner's newest butcher and asked, "Do you find everything you need? I assume you'll want some helpers. Take your pick." He nodded at the three men still standing, hands in pockets, watching. They dispersed immediately.

The new butcher tried, but didn't fully succeed in hiding his smile. He looked over the equipment standing in the street and nodded. "Can you ask at the Portland camp for a man or two to help? Experienced would be good. That ought to do it for now anyway."

Johnny nodded. "Hey Shan," he called the young man away from a group of workers just heading out of town to continue searching. "Go up to the leader of the Portland Camp. Tell him his butcher needs a helper."

Shan nodded and headed for the hill.

Johnny called after him. "And then, go to the courthouse, the school, the Palace, and to any homes on the hills where they are feeding people. Tell them we'll have meat available by four o'clock this afternoon. If they are feeding workers or people who've lost their homes, they're welcome to as much meat as they can use. Just send someone to fetch it. Understand?"

Shan nodded again and waved his hand.

"And kind of check around to be sure we're not missing anyone," Johnny called. "See what the needs are, and let me know. Shan, you're in charge." He knew that even though Shan was young, he would do the job.

Chapter Fourteen

A drab expanse of sand will be their only sepulcher and
the murmur of a dying flood their only dirge.

Portland Oregonian, June 16, 1903

*   *   *

Temperatures continued to soar in the Willow Creek Valley as day
followed miserable day. Carl Klein sat under a scrubby pine
somewhere to the west of Heppner. It cast only a little shade. He
looked at the children on the ground beside him. The boy was sleeping.
The girl had her eyes open, but was just staring into space. He decided
he should probably go someplace, since both his meager provisions and
his water, not to mention his attitude were all wearing thin. But where?
He tore off a chunk of jerky with his teeth and chewed slowly. The horse
reached its head into to the edge of the shade, but Klein refused to give
the animal another inch.

He sighed, looking toward the west. What should he do next?
The horse was about worthless, but the children were too slow on foot.
Too bad there wasn't a train in this wilderness. Not that he had any
money for train tickets. And even if he did, he'd have to buy three of
them.

His sister lived around here somewhere, if only he could remember where. Out in a place called Valby. But where was that? He
could see no sign of civilization in any direction.

Heaving a sigh, he lay back next to the tree and drifted off to
sleep.

*   *   *

Fred Warnock, publisher of the weekly *Heppner Gazette*, groaned in despair as he considered the front page for Thursday, June 18. It was 7:00 p.m.—well past time to be getting home. The rest of the paper, including the list of those known dead, was already written and typeset, ready to print first thing in the morning. It was three days after the flood, and he had nothing but bad news to publish. The town's population of just over eleven hundred appeared to have been reduced by nearly a fourth. Over one hundred fifty bodies had already been recovered and buried. No, not just one hundred fifty bodies, thought Warnock. One hundred fifty *people*. Friends, neighbors, husbands, wives, children. Real people who had been alive only last Sunday. And the names of the missing were many. The expectation was that there would be at least a hundred more confirmed dead before it was over.

A pall hung over the town even though the stormy sky had finally cleared. Dr. C. J. Smith, the new State Medical Examiner, had ordered by way of the newly reconnected phone line that all animal carcasses be burned as soon as possible. The smoke from the fires was pungent. It did help to mask the unmistakable odor of death, but still, it made breathing hard. The men sorting through piles of wreckage below town wore grim faces. The relatives of the dead mourned as one. And Warnock, a man who made his living using words to paint pictures for his readers, could think of nothing to say. No words could describe what the men and women of Heppner had experienced in the past few days. But tomorrow they would demand a newspaper.

Write he must. So he wrote.

The Heppner Gazette 6/18

Days of Sorrow

From the best information available at this time, the dead and missing—and for the missing all hopes have been abandoned—will not be far from 250 people.

While only about 150 bodies have been recovered, there are many that never will be found. Already bodies have been found 10 miles away and it is thought that many have been carried as far as the Columbia River, a distance of 45 miles.

About 141 residence buildings were wrecked and carried away. With a great many of these buildings, not a board remains to indicate that they had ever been built.

Words cannot express the horror, the awful destruction. Entirely helpless, from the hillsides, the survivors watched the terrible waters take their course. To attempt to battle the great waves meant only suicide without being able to accomplish anything. The first warning that the people in the business portion had was when the large two story residence building of T. W. Ayers left its foundation and swung around into May street and crashed into and lodged on some wooden buildings just back of the Palace Hotel.

The town is now in a deplorable condition, debris, slime and mud is piled up in great quantities, and it must be cleared away or the health of the people will be in great danger. The homeless and orphan children are being taken care of as well as possible under the existing conditions.

The Light and Water Company is doing good work, and the city is pretty well supplied with water.

Heppner's greatest need now is money. The people of the town and surrounding country are worn out under the awful strain and we need money to pay laborers to continue the work.

Warnock pushed away from his typewriter. Done. His typesetter could finish up in the morning. He squinted his eyes against the sting of the smoky air and walked home.

*   *   *

Smoke from the fires intended to prevent disease
Courtesy Morrow County Heritage Museum

(l. to r.) Sheriff Shutt, George Conser,
and Mayor Gilliam; unidentified deputy in the rear
Courtesy Morrow County Museum

*   *   *

Johnny sat hunched on a wooden chair with his elbows on his knees and his hat in his hands. George Conser and Sheriff Shutt sat nearby. Shutt heaved a long, loud sigh, but no one spoke. Mayor Gilliam walked into the room. His gentle, oval face sat atop shoulders stooped by the terrible weight of death—the deaths of so many people—*his* people, in *his* town. How could this have happened? This man bore little resemblance to the fatherly mayor the townspeople knew and loved.

Gilliam's mouth was a tight, grim line as he pulled his desk chair into the circle with the others. He nodded at the men. "Thanks," he said. "Thanks for coming." He patted his pockets, then rose and returned to his desk for a pencil. He settled back into his chair, notepad in hand.

Each evening, these men of the recovery committee had met to update each other on the progress being made. Of the four men in the room, only Johnny had lost family members in the flood, but the others bore the unmistakable sorrow of an entire town devastated. The Shutt home was a total loss. Conser and his wife had also lost their home, and nearly their lives as well.

The remains of Sheriff Shutt's house—nearly 500 yards from its original location
Benjamin Gifford photo, Library of Congress

Gilliam spoke. "Okay, men, as I see it, we're doing well—moving forward. But we're still a long way from having this thing under control. Sheriff, let's hear what you've got first—both the good and the bad."

Shutt took a deep breath before beginning. He was a slender man, clean shaven. Well, except that he'd not shaved since the flood on Sunday. He looked exhausted, angry. "Okay, first the good. I've closed anything even resembling a saloon and made it known that the consumption of alcohol will not be tolerated. We can't be dealing with drunks along with all the rest of this."

He looked at his notes and went on. "I've deputized 30 men. They're doing a good job of keeping order. No looting to speak of, even though there's a lot of stuff just layin' around. I think just having the deputies so visible has helped."

Conser interrupted. "I heard there was a guy found this morning, trying to take jewelry from a corpse. What about that?"

Shutt nodded. "Turned out he was the lady's brother. Just wanted to get the brooch that had been passed down from their grandmother. Not only did he lose his sister, he was almost arrested without cause.

"As you know, I've established a curfew," Shutt continued. "Pretty much the only ones allowed out at night are the deputies. They're keeping tight control.

"And then, the things I'm still working on. We were starting to have a problem with pigs running loose—you know, rooting around, and uh ... disfiguring bodies we hadn't found yet." He looked disgusted. "I had signs posted and warned owners to pen their animals or they would be shot—the pigs, not the owners." His attempt at humor was met with only tired half-smiles and weary eyes. "We can always use the extra meat to feed the workers."

The others nodded.

"We've started to accumulate a few sightseers. I offered them a choice—told 'em they could clear out, go to work, or go to jail. So far, none of them have liked the shovel I offered them or the prospect of living on bread and water. They've decided to leave."

"Good." Gilliam nodded.

Shutt looked over the paper in his hand. "And ... I guess that's about all I've got."

"Thanks Sheriff." Gilliam turned to Conser. "George, what do you have?"

Conser looked as he'd had the stuffing knocked out of him. The banker's normally well-padded body hadn't actually changed, but somehow, he just looked deflated. He shifted in his chair and began. "Well, the bank opened this afternoon. We have a number of deposits from around the area. For now, it's all going into a general fund—each donation carefully recorded, of course. Portland has sent money to pay their workers. So has Milton. We also have donations from Pendleton, Baker City ... quite a few towns around the Northwest. Pendleton has sent blankets from the Woolen Mill and a lot of other stuff. Several towns have cancelled their Fourth of July celebrations and sent us all the money they had set aside for that. We'll present workers with vouchers to receive their pay when they're ready to leave town. We're offering two dollars a day for a man and three-fifty for a man with a team. Quite a few of them have said they don't want to be paid. But we're ready if they change their minds. Locals too—if they ask to be paid, we'll pay them. 'Course most of 'em wouldn't think of asking."

He checked his notes. "Meals are being served at the courthouse, the Palace, the school, and also the Portland Camp between the Crawford place and the Christian Church. Anyone who works eats free.

"The National Guard is sending more tents. They should be here tomorrow. We can put a bunch at the courthouse and at the school. We're also expecting small stoves for cooking, pots and pans, utensils, bedding—that kind of stuff."

Conser rubbed his eyes and continued. "Every business in town—well, every business still standing—has offered all they have, no charge. Hopefully, we'll be able to reimburse them when this is all over. The women—those who aren't in the process of burying the dead—are preparing food all day long, making sure people are fed. And a lot of the homes on the hills are serving extra people too."

He glanced up at the others. "At least we have plenty of food. We've had I don't know how many wagonloads of food that's been coming in from wherever the train tracks end. The rails should reach Heppner by tomorrow. That'll make things a lot easier."

"The rails will be here tomorrow?" Johnny was surprised.

Conser smiled at him and nodded. "Over sixteen miles in only three days—including bridges. They were almost to Minor's place by dusk tonight. I bet that's the fastest track they've ever laid! I don't know how many men are working on it. Let's see ... what else?"

"Sanitation?" asked Gilliam.

Conser looked again at his notes. "Yeah. We've got disinfectant coming in by barrels every day. And we're using it as fast as it comes in. The waterworks is up and running again. Thank God they're up on the hill and didn't get hit. Their water is pure and good. Oh—Sheriff, we need to stop the use of well water—at least for drinking. Issue a notice or something."

Shutt nodded, jotting himself a note.

"Maybe Bill Cooley could take care of that," Johnny said.

Shutt shook his head. "Cooley's dead."

Johnny dropped his eyes to the floor.

Conser cleared his throat and went on. "People who don't have pipes into their homes yet can get water at the Palace or the courthouse—any place that's close to where they live. The state has appointed Dr. Smith, the new State Medical Examiner, to take over the health aspect of recovery. He's from Pendleton. He'll arrive tomorrow, but he connected with Doc Kistner by phone yesterday and gave him some instruction on getting things headed in the right direction.

"Sewage—that's a serious problem." Conser tightened the muscles in his jaw. "Flush toilets are fine—for those who have them. But there aren't enough privies in town for the rest of the folks, and even the ones we do have are overflowing with contaminated mud. So are the basements. I've arranged for getting all the ... um, slop ... scooped into wagons and hauled away. Dr. Smith also has men bringing in wagonloads of alkali soil from up north. They're spreading it in the cesspools and cellars—anywhere sewage may have accumulated. And the Portland men have dug some new temporary privies near their camp. That's helping some."

He flipped the page in his notebook and continued. "Almost all the light poles have been reset, and tomorrow the men will be stringing new wires, so we'll have electric lights again in most places. Oh, and the phone lines in town are working.

"Another thing—maybe not so important, but important enough—we still have farm machinery and other stuff hung up in trees. There's a perfectly good plough about fifteen feet up a big poplar that's still standing. We're trying to salvage things without cutting trees if possible." Conser checked his notes one last time. "That's it." He snapped the notebook shut.

Gilliam nodded and rubbed his hand over his face. "I think when this is all over, it would be a good idea to publish a list of donations and expenses. Put it in the paper or something, so people will have no cause to make accusations."

"Right," Conser answered and scrawled a note on his pad. "I'll make sure to get a full accounting of every penny to the *Gazette* when it's all over."

"When it's all over," Johnny echoed. The others nodded.

"Johnny, how are you doing with burials?" Gilliam asked.

"We've buried 164 so far. Quite a few of them are in a large common grave. All our local pastors and also a Reverend Lake from Portland have been up there almost non-stop since Monday morning. Some of the women have been taking meals up to them. I have twenty-four or twenty-five older boys and young men detailed to dig graves. Some of them have been there digging since Monday. The ground is pretty hard once they get about three feet down. They're having to use picks to break it up." Johnny stretched his back and took a deep breath. He was getting stiff just sitting still for so long.

"What about Roberts Hall?" Gilliam asked.

"We have eight washing stations. Monday and Tuesday, it was just women working up there. This morning I brought in three men to prepare male victims for burial."

"What's the feeling like up there?" Shutt asked. "How are they holding up?"

"I don't know." Johnny sighed. "It's a terrible job! Dacia told me they had to take three ladies out on Monday. They just fell apart!" Johnny shut his eyes and shook his head. "Several of them up there have lost family members themselves, but they keep on working. Frankly, I'm amazed."

"Who are these ladies?" Shutt asked. "Just ladies from town, or were they sent in from somewhere?"

"From here. Even some of Mollie Reed's girls have been helping."

Mollie Reed's girls—from Heppner's bordello, the *Chateau de Joie.*

Conser raised an eyebrow, while Shutt chose to pretend he hadn't heard.

Gilliam nodded. "That's fine," he said quietly. "They're as welcome as anyone."

Johnny continued his report. "Yeager and his boys were making up coffins from whatever wood they could get their hands on, but yesterday afternoon we got our first couple wagonloads of real caskets. Got several more loads today and we'll keep on getting more until ... well, until we don't need any more."

As the meeting broke up, Johnny took a huge breath and exhaled both exhaustion and a determination he didn't realize he had. One more day—done.

The Fair at the left
Courtesy Morrow County Heritage Museum

The second story of Oscar Minor's house
Methodist Episcopal Church at the right
Benjamin Gifford Photo, Library of Congress

Chapter Fifteen

B y Thursday, Heppner's condition defined the word "tired." The people were worn out, of course, but even the land looked tired. The grass—where there was any. The sky. The piles of debris. The entire environment reeked of exhaustion as bodies were pulled from their muddy shrouds. But still, the men retrieving bodies, the women in the morgue, those cooking and serving meals—they all worked on. Not because they had the strength to do it, but because it needed to be done.

"So we meet again," Grace said quietly. She glanced around to see if anyone was listening.

Esmerelda stood on the other side of the tub, clutching her hands together awkwardly. She nodded. "That was less than a week ago, but it seems like a month."

"I want to thank you again for your kindness to me," Grace said. She dipped her rag back in the bucket at her feet and continued gently washing the face and head of the woman's body before her. "This is how we do it. We cut off the clothes, get the bodies as clean as we can, then wrap them before they go in the coffins," she said.

"What do we wrap them in?" Esmerelda asked, her hands still clutched uncomfortably before her.

"Table cloths and sheets mostly, from the Palace Hotel. But I heard we'll be getting a shipment of muslin soon, as soon as the tracks are finished. Maybe by later today." Grace looked pointedly at Esmerelda who was still standing, doing nothing. "It's a mighty hard job, but somebody has to do it."

"I know." Esmerelda took a shaky breath, then bent to get the rag from the bucket on her side of the tub and went to work. "I wish it had never happened!" she said softly. "These people didn't deserve this.

At least most of them didn't. Think of all these children!"

"Life ain't fair," Grace said. "But I guess we knew that already."

The two worked in silence for a few minutes.

"Will you be coming back?" asked Esmerelda.

"No."

"How will you live?"

"I don't know. But I'm not coming back." Grace's words were spoken with finality.

Esmerelda nodded. "Lorena, I've been thinking ..."

Grace shook her head and spoke firmly. "Lorena's dead. She died in the flood."

Esmerelda stopped her washing and stood, just staring at Grace. After a minute, she said, "Yeah. I get it." She smiled. "Good. Good for you!"

"You can call me Grace."

"Grace?"

"Mm hm. It's my middle name. I got it from my mama."

At this, Esmerelda smiled. "I'm really happy for you. Truly, I am! And it's a beautiful name."

Grace smiled. "It's something I really treasure. My mama's dead now."

"I'm sorry."

The two worked in silence for a few minutes.

"So ... *Grace*, I've been thinking." Both young ladies smiled in spite of their surroundings. Esmerelda looked around and saw that all the others in the room were busy with their own jobs. She continued speaking quietly. "I can't figure out why Mollie's place wasn't destroyed by the flood. I mean, if anyone in town is wicked, evil sinners, it would be the whores, wouldn't you think? At least that's the way some people see it."

"Or maybe it would be the men who buy their favors," Grace said.

Esmerelda looked up sharply. "Maybe."

*   *   *

Late Friday morning, Shan's steps thudded in his ears like the pounding of nails in coffins as he walked down the hill from the cemetery. He had stomped off in anger and despair, leaving Mac and the Burkes behind. He also left behind the fresh mounds covering the graves of his mother, his sisters Kathleen and Margaret, and his brother, Dennis. Aiden's body had not been found yet. But he was nowhere among the living. Shan wasn't sure that he, himself, was among the living.

Shan had served most of the week with a group of men from Pendleton. They had worked their way down the valley as they pulled apart piles of debris, searching for bodies. Even five days after the flood, a few of the bodies had been found buried in hailstones, still completely frozen. Every horse, mule, and half-able animal in the Willow Creek Valley had been dragged from retirement to help in the distasteful task of pulling apart the rubble which had covered the mauled bodies scattered throughout valley.

Half-way down the hill, Shan slowed and glanced across town at the tents, visible on the hillside above the Christian Church. The National Guard had sent tents not only for the workers converging on Heppner from cities around the Northwest, but also for displaced families to live in. The courthouse lawn and schoolyard had blossomed into small tent cities.

Shan finally stopped and waited for Mac, Johnny, and Dacia to catch up with him. He gazed down where Cannon Street had been ... where Ginnie Hammond had lived. It was gone. The street ... her house. *She* was gone. And he'd only spoken to her once. Shan crossed his arms and glared down on the place where her house had been. Had he actually spoken to her on Sunday afternoon? Yes, he told himself. It had really happened. But no more. Never again.

It had been rude, walking off and leaving the others at the cemetery. Somehow, rudeness didn't seem to matter anymore. Nothing seemed to matter anymore.

He swallowed hard, a groaning sigh escaping unnoticed.

"Well," Johnny said solemnly as he, Dacia, and Mac caught up with Shan. "We're nearly home."

"What do you mean?"

"Nearly all our dead are buried." He hesitated, then counted them off on his fingers as he named them. "In the Harmon family—Ella and Charlie. My family—Josie and Martin. And your family—your mother, your sisters, Kathleen, Margaret, your brother Dennis ... Eight among our three families buried already." He shook his head in sorrow. "Only Lilyann, Gilbert, and your brother Aiden are unaccounted for."

Shan spoke with a wooden face. "They're saying they may never find all the bodies. They say some are buried in the mud along the valley." Bodies woven into the fabric of the debris. He shook his head to clear it of the image.

"Well, if they are, then it's sacred ground," said Dacia. "I hope we find them, but if we don't, it will be because the Lord has buried them well enough." She glanced meaningfully at Mac, but he didn't notice. The group continued in silence down the hill toward home.

*   *   *

After checking on Will and a eating a quick supper, Johnny and Dacia headed toward the Palace Hotel, where Mac was staying. Johnny knocked on the door of room 212 and called out, "Mac, it's Johnny and Dacia."

"Come in," Mac grunted, wondering which hurt his broken ribs more, talking loud enough to be heard or getting up to answer the door. He nodded to the sofa, and Johnny and Dacia took a seat.

"How ya doin'?" Johnny asked.

Mac shrugged. "So so."

Johnny nodded. He took a deep breath and reached out to hold Dacia's hand. He gave it a squeeze, trying to give her some needed courage.

"Mac," Dacia began. "I need to tell you how it happened."

He just nodded. He had been waiting for this moment—both dreading and welcoming it.

Dacia took a deep breath. "I was at your house. When it hit, the house lifted off its foundation and began floating. I jumped and Walter just hung onto my dress while I waded out carrying Sarah and Gilbert. As soon as we were up out of the flood, I turned back. The house was way out in the middle by then and breaking up. I could see Ella. She had already jumped and was getting close to the edge with Lily, but the water was getting deeper *really* fast. She was only a moment or two behind me. She just couldn't make it. I saw them both go under ..."

Dacia's voice broke; Johnny put his arm around her shoulder.

When she could speak again, Dacia continued. "When they came up, Ella threw Lily toward the edge. She *threw* her! Lily made it. I saw her land, Mac. But Ella—"

Here Dacia stopped again as her body shook with sobs.

Mac sat silent, waiting.

"But Mac, I need to tell you. I saw Lily at the edge of the flood. I don't know if she was dead or alive. She was right at the very edge. She was probably washed away. But I carried Gilbert out myself. I *know* he was safe. I put him down right beside Pappy. When I couldn't find him later, I assumed someone had taken him to one of the other houses on the hill. It was just chaos up there—people running everywhere, screaming, half-dark. Nobody knew what was happening or who was going to which house. We were all just trying to get to safety.

"You know how it is with young children on a hillside, they always wander *down*hill. I guess he just wandered back down there and somehow ..."

Johnny's teeth were clamped together. He spoke not a word, but his arm tightened around Dacia's shoulders.

"I'm sorry I lost them, Mac. I'm so sorry!" Again, Dacia's body shook as she sobbed.

*   *   *

East Oregonian **Daily Newspaper (Pendleton)**
Friday, June 19, 1903

> **Dead Body Eighty Miles Below.**
> The Dalles. June 19.—The body of a boy about 10 years old was found yesterday evening in the Columbia, near Stevenson, 80 miles from Heppner. It is thought to be one of the victims of the flood.

Book Two

In the Wake of Disaster

Chapter Sixteen

"Etta, listen to this." Elisabeth read to her sister from the *Morning Oregonian*, one of Portland's two daily newspapers. "This is about that awful flood they had at Heppner."

> ### Identified by Her Boy.
>
> Mrs. A. M. Gunn's 10-year-old son identified her body today by an engagement ring which the woman wore. On the ring was inscribed, "Libbie, from Marcus; June 30, 1887." Mrs. Gunn's four children escaped. The husband warned the family of danger. All ran from the house, the children first, the father next, the mother last. Gunn looked back as he went out of the yard. He saw his wife fall in a faint. He returned to save her, and both perished. Gunn's body was found Monday.

"Just imagine!" Etta said. "That poor boy having to identify his mother's body. My heart just aches for those people!"

Each morning when breakfast was cleaned up, the two ladies took a break—on the porch in good weather, at the dining room table when it was cold. Today, they sat in their chairs on the porch. And today was Elisabeth's turn to read the newspaper highlights aloud.

"It says most of the cleanup is now being done by bands of men from other towns, with a man from Pendleton in charge. Let's see ..." Elisabeth's eyes scanned down the page. "They've received about twenty two thousand dollars so far from many towns, and even more money is needed."

"What are they using the money for? Seems like they would need help more than money."

"For food for the workers, to pay workers, more caskets, embalming fluid maybe? All sorts of things."

"Guess you're right. It's sure a pity!"

Ivar Petersen, square of frame with bright blue eyes and graying hair, stepped out onto the porch. Ivar was the Norwegian husband of the Snowburg ladies' youngest sister, Jane. "Vell, are you ladies all ready for da big party?" He let the screen door swing shut and took a chair near them on the porch.

"No, we're not ready, and now that you mention it, I guess it's time for us to get busy again." Etta rose and stretched her back. "There's still lots to be done!"

Although they were only a day under the age of seventy, Etta and Elisabeth were as excited as a couple of children on Christmas Eve. The entire Snowburg clan had not been together since 1895. Eight years.

The ladies' birthday would be on Saturday. They had been born on June 20, 1833, and were the first two of eleven girls born into the Oregon branch of the Snowburg family. They were the only two of the brood who had not married. Fortunately, they had each other and their boarding house in Oregon City. While the nine younger sisters had all married and raised their flocks of children—fifty-seven in all—Etta and Elisabeth had worked at building the reputation of their boarding house. With six rooms to rent, they kept busy most of the time. And most of their boarders were fine, upstanding citizens. Not the upper crust of Oregon City perhaps, but good people all the same. There was very little turnover. The sisters divided the work evenly, with Etta, older by almost ten minutes, in charge of the cooking, and Elizabeth taking care of the cleaning and washing. Over the years, the two had refined their operation into a smooth-running machine.

Elisabeth handed the newspaper to Ivar as she and Etta rose and returned to the chores awaiting them in the house. Six inches taller than her pleasantly plump sister, Elisabeth tilted her head to gaze critically at the flower arrangement on the sideboard. "I think it needs a few more daisies," she said. Her voice cracked a bit with age, but her enthusiasm more than made up for it. "With nice long stems."

The two ladies were fussing like a couple of mother hens. After all, it wasn't every day a body got to enjoy so many sisters and their families all at the same time. Most of them would be arriving tomorrow morning, and the house had to be spotless before the thundering herd set foot in it.

Everyone was contributing something for the party. Jane and her husband, Ivar, who lived farthest away, had arrived from their home on Puget Island last night and were staying in a room which had been conveniently vacated just last week. Jane was in the kitchen already, making and baking pies with the fruit she'd put up last summer. She'd started work even before breakfast and was still going strong.

Edith had offered to bring six chickens, dressed and ready—some for the oven, some for frying. Esther and Eula were each bringing a ham.

Jane was not only the last child born into the family, but she was also different in so many other ways. While all of the other girls had been destined to grow either tall and thin like their father or short and plump like their mother, Jane was just plain Jane—average height and average build. She was the only dark haired one of the flock—until her hair had begun to turn gray—and she was the only one whose name did not begin with the letter "E." It seemed that mother and father Snowburg had run out of "E" names by the time Jane came along. The older girls all teased her about it, but Jane was proud of her name. In fact, she planned on cutting a "J" in the crust of at least one of the pies for tomorrow!

*   *   *

Carl Klein woke up Friday morning to find that his horse was gone. Nowhere to be found. The farm wagon he'd stolen in Hardman and driven into town in the middle of the night had washed away in the flood. Well, probably. He didn't really know. And now, here he was with no horse—in the middle of nowhere—miles from the nearest town. He called. He whistled. Finally, leaving the children under the scraggly tree where they'd spent the night, he hiked to the top of the nearest hill where his lackluster eyes searched in every direction. Nothing. His eyes grew even darker, matching the look on his face. He threw his hat to the ground, gave it a good kick, and cussed his luck. Finally he gave up and went back to the children. He'd have to carry them the rest of the way to Sadie's.

*   *   *

In a small farm house about eighteen miles west of Heppner, Sadie looked out the kitchen window toward the late afternoon sun. The light hugged the dust in the air, holding it in place. Eastern Oregon. Beautiful in its own way. Barren, some folks called it. But Sadie loved it.

Not everything in her life was good, but this—this land, this place—was very good. Wide open spaces for miles in any direction. Occasional juniper trees or pines. Lots of sagebrush. Also, lots of sky. This was nothing like the western side of the state, where it rained so much the people were said to grow webs between their toes! No, this was God's country, caressed by sunshine and warmed by the living of life itself.

Yes, it was a good land. The view was free, and Sadie, like most Westerners, had an independent streak. She willingly wrested a living from her own little corner of this paradise, and loved every minute of it.

Valby is what they called this place. Not a town, but a cluster of farms snuggled around the Valby Lutheran Church. Most of the people here were Swedes. The church services were in Swedish, a language Sadie understood only a little. But she fit in anyway. This was her land. These were her adopted people. Her husband's people. Even though he had turned out to be a rotten egg—gone these nine years—she still loved his people. This was home.

Bang, bang, bang! The back door rattled, making Sadie jump. *Well, who on earth could that be?*

Klein stood on the back porch of the old farm house, holding a child in each arm. He kicked at the door a second time, and finally heard steps coming to open it. He pushed his way into the kitchen and deposited the largest child, a little girl, on one of the chairs at the table.

"Here, here! What is this?" the woman demanded in a coarse voice. "What do you think you're—" She stopped abruptly as the man turned to face her.

"Carl! What are you doing here? I haven't seen you in years!" Her voice conveyed surprise, but no welcome.

"I ain't been here in years, and you never poke your nose outa this house. Course you ain't seen me." He dumped the little boy on another chair and whined, "I'm hungry, Sadie. You got anything to eat around here?"

Recovering from her shock, the woman scurried out to the well house and brought back a ham. She stirred up the fire and tossed another piece of wood on it, then took the large knife from the table top and began slicing the meat. "I see you got kids with you," she said, but was immediately sorry she'd spoken. When would she learn? Just don't stir him up. She knew better.

"That's right. I got kids with me." Surprisingly, the man's voice softened as he looked over at the children—the girl staring vacantly into space, the boy beginning to cry. "Good grief!" he said, disgusted. "What's wrong now?"

"Maybe he's hungry. I'll feed 'em. I'll feed you all." Anything to keep her brother from becoming angry. Sadie began laying slices of ham in the cast iron skillet on the stove. "Where'd you get 'em?"

"Huh?"

"The kids. Where'd you get 'em?" *No! Just keep quiet!* She winced and bit her tongue. But surprisingly, Klein didn't seem upset. Sadie looked at the little boy. Cute with his curly dark blond hair—but he looked pretty bedraggled.

"They're mine. Mine and Ella's. I told you we'd get married and have kids some day. Well, we did."

"Ella married you?" Sadie didn't believe it. "I heard she married a man from Heppner named Harmon."

"Well, you heard wrong. Take a look. Them's her kids. Hers and mine."

"Where is *she* then?"

"Dead." He paused for a moment. "Died in childbirth. You know?" He nodded his head and repeated. "Died in childbirth."

This time Sadie did hold her tongue.

"'Member when we was kids growing up on the farm? All those years I loved her. And she always pretended she didn't love me. But she really did. 'Member how I used to tell you I'd get Ella for my wife? Well, now they're mine. Ella's kids." An empty grin spread across Klein's face, revealing yellowed teeth. The dreamy quality in his voice disappeared, and he snapped, "What's taking so long, woman? I told you I was hungry!"

Sadie flinched slightly and cracked a half dozen eggs into a second skillet.

"And don't break the yolks. You know I can't stand to have my eggs broke. Cook 'em real easy like."

She gritted her teeth, but said nothing, looking again at the little girl. Something was wrong with her. Except for the fact that she was sitting up under her own power, she looked like she was dead.

Klein scratched at his beard and yawned. "Where's that no-good husband of yours anyhow? He run off and desert you?"

Sadie said nothing.

"He did, didn't he? I always knew he would. He weren't good for nothing. You're better off without him. What about the boy? He go off with his pa?"

Sadie turned the eggs carefully. "No," she said. "He's living with a family out in Eight Mile, working for them."

"Ha! I thought as much. Just like our pa—ran off and left Ma and us kids behind. Left us to figure out how to live on our own." Klein's eyes clouded for a moment. His pa, his and Sadie's, had been no good. Well, no one would be able to say that about him! He had Ella's two children. He would treat them right and take care of them.

"The children don't look too good," Sadie said as she set the plate of food in front of her brother. "I didn't see a horse. You been walking a long time?"

The sound of Klein chewing was the only response she got. She brought two more plates to the table for the children. The little boy could barely reach his, but he climbed up on his knees and plunged in with real enthusiasm. It was obvious he hadn't eaten for some time.

"What are their names?" Sadie asked.

"Ann," Klein said, nodding at the girl.

"Ann. Pretty name." Sadie looked at the girl. She had braids, but it was impossible to tell what color they might be. Her hair was matted and filled with dirt. "And the little one?"

"He can tell you his own name—can't you, boy?" Klein's voice had turned silky. "Tell my sister, Sadie, what your name is, son."

"Gibbie!" He spoke around the large chunk of ham in his mouth and shoved in another bite as if he were starving.

Grubby was the word that came to Sadie's mind. She carried the skillet to the sink and began washing it. "So where did you come from and where are you going?" she ventured to ask.

"Come from Wildhorse, up past Pendleton. Goin' to San Francisco."

"You come through Heppner? I heard they had a terrible flood over there."

"I dunno. I ain't been to Heppner."

"What's in San Francisco?"

"I heard there's jobs there for willing hands."

Sadie turned her back on Klein and muttered under her breath, "You must have changed. I don't remember you being a willing hand."

Klein stood so fast he knocked his chair over and was across the kitchen in two strides. He grabbed Sadie's arm and spun her around to face him. "What's that you said?"

Sadie gulped. "I thought you always wanted to work as a manager, not a common laborer."

Klein returned to the table, righted his chair, and sat back in it. "That's better."

Sadie blew out her breath in relief and said, "So, how're you going to get all the way to San Francisco without a horse? That's quite a ways off, ain't it?"

"Yeah, I reckon I'll need a horse. Or a mule. You got one I could borrow?"

Sadie didn't respond. Yes, she had a mule. And no, her brother couldn't "borrow" her. Daisy Belle was Sadie's only way to get into town, the only animal to pull her plow. The mule worked hard and demanded nothing in return except a little hay through the winters, but she was a good animal. So far, at least, Sadie had always been able to exchange sewing or washing for hay. She grew a good garden—enough to feed herself through the winter. She raised chickens and pigs and was able to exchange eggs and meat, and sometimes sewing, for some of the things she couldn't produce on her tiny farm. But if she lost her mule ...

Klein finished his meal and shoved back his chair. He took a deep breath and stood up taller, straighter than he'd stood before. Even the sound of his voice was different. "Sadie, you just don't realize what I've become." He looked confident, like a man who knew his way in the world. "I'm an educated man now. A man of refinement. My life is completely different."

She looked at him suspiciously. He certainly looked different than he had a minute ago. This was not the Carl Klein she had grown up with. Even in his tattered, dirty clothes, this man suddenly appeared dignified, gentlemanly ... everything that Carl was not. Sadie was confused.

"I've learned how to fit in, Sadie." He cleared his throat politely. "I'm like one of them now. I know how to speak correctly, how to act. I'm somebody. Or at least I can act like somebody when I need to. I have the children to care for. I need to be responsible—to be a good father to them." He suddenly threw off the refined appearance as abruptly as he had taken it on and laughed. "Bet you didn't know I could do that, huh?"

Sadie didn't know what to say. Her mind was filled with suspicion, but she kept her mouth shut. She noticed that the girl had not touched her food. Sitting, Sadie scooped some egg onto a spoon, and held it to the child's mouth. The mouth opened slightly, and Sadie inserted the egg. She waited patiently until she saw the girl swallow and started again. She watched the child closely, looking for some sign of awareness, but found none. Finally she waved her hand in front of the girl's face. There was no response at all. Nothing.

That's it—she's blind! No wonder she just sits there. Sadie scooped up another bite of eggs. It was the only thing she knew to do.

* * *

Aiden's body, retrieved from the Columbia River near Steven-

99

son on Thursday evening, was returned to Heppner on the Friday train. They buried him that evening. As Shan stood with Johnny and Dacia on Cemetery Hill, he felt—along with his grief—a sense of peace that all his family was accounted for.

Chapter Seventeen

The Snowburg twins could not have been happier with their party. It was everything a seventieth birthday party could possibly be. Etta fussed with the food, and Elisabeth fussed with everything else. And each was happy in her fussing—the sort of thing that made a family celebration so special. No one had counted, but there were enough sisters, husbands, nieces, nephews, grandchildren, and even great-grandchildren present, in addition to the regular boarders, to pretty much fill the parlor, dining room, and kitchen of the house, as well as the wide front porch and most of the yard.

At fifty three, Jane was the youngest of the Snowburg girls. Her first three children, all sons, had grown, married, and moved to Denver, Seattle, and San Francisco, respectively. Jane and her husband, Ivar, had recently given their only daughter in marriage to her now grown playmate and next-door neighbor, a young man who had decided to move to Kansas. *Kansas* of all places!

Each of the sisters had, in turn, commiserated with Jane and Ivar. A home with no children. Sad indeed. Of course there were the grandchildren ... if only they lived closer!

As late afternoon approached, pie was served from the long table in the side yard. The conversation slowed and nearly came to a stop, replaced by the sound of forks against plates and murmurs of appreciation. Soon, a few of the sisters and other relatives began making noises about how it was getting late, and they needed to start for home if they were to arrive before tomorrow dawned. No one actually made a move toward a wagon or buggy. It was just time to start talking about it, not time to actually do it.

"You heard about da big flood in Heppner?" Ivar asked the crowd in general. Yes, they had all heard. Both the *Oregonian* and the *Journal* had run front page stories every day since Monday. Tragic. Unthinkably tragic!

"Portland has sent a t'ousand men already, and people are sending workers and money from all over da place to help out."

"I offered to go," said Esther. "But they say they don't really need more nurses. I guess most people were either killed outright or got to higher ground in time. There are only a few who were injured, and they have enough doctors and nurses there already."

"I have some blankets and quilts I could send," offered Ellen. "Could they use those? And flour maybe? What kinds of things do they need?"

"What about tools—shovels and the like?" Edith's husband, Jack asked.

"I know—clothing. Most of those people lost everything they own. Can you imagine? And cooking utensils," Edith said. "Just think! Those poor people probably have to cook over an open fire in the back yard!"

"If they *have* a back yard," Etta said. "I hear most of them don't even have houses anymore!"

Ivar nodded as family members named the items. "Yah sure. Dat's gut. Anyt'ing you can get together. You yust take it down to dat big bank on da corner of Front and Ankeny tomorrow afternoon. Dey'll make sure it gets on da train."

With several of the relatives making plans to take things into Portland tomorrow afternoon, the last sliver of summer sun was about to sink below the horizon. And now, it really *was* time to be getting home.

Wives began packing up picnic baskets and rounding up children, husbands shook each other's hands and promised to keep in touch, and children, frantic to use up every moment of semi-light in the sky, called, "coming, Mama!" and chased each other one last time around the house. Then they took to their wagons and buggies.

Except for Jane and Ivar who would be staying over one more night. "We *have* to stay," Jane explained. "It will probably take us all week just to get these dishes washed!"

They all laughed.

*   *   *

Block by block, building by building, inch by precious inch, Heppner struggled back to life. Shan and Jim Carr finished hitching the mixed team of horses and mules to the cables attached to the Collins house.

Jim Carr and his wife had lost their youngest child, Lilias, in the flood, and her body had not been found. The Carrs, along with so many others in Heppner, grieved their loss. But now Jim was back at work. As the foremost construction man in town, his skill was desperately needed in rebuilding Heppner.

His first job was to move salvageable buildings back into place. Already, Carr and his men had moved nine houses and the Methodist Church. "I'd rather build something from scratch," Jim had told Shan. "But this job needs to be done, so I guess that's what we'll do." Shan had no idea how to go about getting the house back where it belonged. Thirty feet. Just thirty feet, but *how* to move something as big as a house? Shan was glad for the help.

He had shoveled out the small cellar under the back corner of the house and helped Carr check the placement of the cornerstones upon which the house would rest. He glanced up at Dacia watching from the street with Michael, Libby, and Danny by her side along with her own three children. Her presence and interest gave him a bit of comfort.

Shan stood by the lead mule on his side of the team and patted it on the rump. The animal quivered, but didn't move. These mules and every other animal left in town were half dead. They, along with the many more animals sent to the stricken town from all over the Northwest had worked hard—harder in the last week than they'd ever worked in their lives.

Jim Carr pulled on his leather gloves and checked with his men. "Ready?" he called.

"Ready," Shan answered with the others.

He moved the mules to tighten the traces, and at Carr's "Let's go! Git up there!" he urged the animals forward. The team of twelve animals pulled with all the strength they had, and the house moved forward on its log rollers.

Shan's front porch was still intact, although its relationship to the main house was severely compromised. The back porch had vanished altogether. Carr had decided to keep the front porch attached as the house was moved, hoping it would remain in place.

"Whoa up there!" Jim hollered. "Whoa!" He took out a handkerchief and mopped his face. Even though the animals were doing most of the work, the men felt the heat of the day as well.

Jim looked critically at the porch, while some of the men carried the logs that had been left behind to place them at the front edge of the building. He suspected the porch wasn't going to make it, but decided to go ahead and hope for the best. When all was in place, Carr called to the others, "Okay, this time is it. Shan, you holler when your corner's in place. When Shan gives the sign, the rest of you on that side, hold up, and we'll keep pulling over here 'til—Albert, you tell us when to stop your corner. Everybody got it?"

Jim hollered, "Go!" and immediately, as the house moved, the front porch began to tear away from the rest of the building. "Go!" Carr shouted. "Keep on pulling! Let it go! Just keep on moving!" The movement of the house, foot by precious foot, was now accompanied by the squeal of tearing lumber, as the porch floor, then the railing, the supports, and the roof were wrenched away from the house and fell into a heap of lumber and nails like so many other heaps around town.

In less than a minute, Shan gave the sign for his side to hold up, followed almost immediately by Albert.

"Hooray!" Dacia applauded the men from the road in front of the house. Shan looked up and smiled. At least someone besides himself cared about his family—his future. He smiled his thanks, then turned to help separate the mules so they could travel on to the next job.

*   *   *

Johnny surveyed the bare land behind the Palace Hotel. This had been the location of Gilliam & Bisbee's farm machine storage shed. The main store building was fine—or would be once the broken door was repaired. But it was on the other side of Main. This large building, along with all the farm implements it had housed, was completely destroyed. Gone. Nothing here would even suggest that a substantial building had once rested on this piece of real estate.

Without this building, Johnny had no job. He'd been foreman of the shop and overseer of the sales department for six years. Now there was no shop and nothing to sell even if someone wanted to buy. But this was summer. Farmers were well into the growing season. Many had already put up their first cutting of hay. And those who had lost crops and gardens to the flood were replanting in hopes of a late harvest.

Jim Carr appeared from the May Street side of the lot with his pencil and notebook in hand.

"Hey Jim. Thanks for coming." Johnny showed him the sketch he had made for the new building. It would be similar to the original, but with an extended open area on the south side for summer forge work and for the larger implements. The open area would be covered with a high wooden roof.

Carr looked over the sketch and nodded his head. "Yup. We can do it," he said. "I've got plenty of lumber coming in on every train load now, so we should be able to start it in no time. You want a foundation?"

"Absolutely. Frank Gilliam was positive about that. It has to be on a rock or cement foundation."

"Okay, I can have some men lay the lines and start that this afternoon."

"I'd like to be one of the men," Johnny said. "Until it's built, I don't have enough of a job to keep me occupied. It'll be better once the new machinery gets here."

"When will that be?"

"It's on order," Johnny said. "I've ordered replacements for everything we had plus a lot of extra stuff. Farmers all down the valley lost equipment and are looking to replace it. Some of them see it as an opportunity to move up to better quality. They'll be needing cutters, binders, balers, loaders—just about everything. Cook shacks too."

"Speaking of better equipment," Carr said. "What about putting a line in for electricity? The main store's had electricity for years now. You could use some electric lights in here when it's dark and overcast. And anyway, before long, there will be electric tools for just about any job needs doing. You may as well bring this place up to the new standard."

Johnny's eyes lit up. "That sounds really good! Let me check with Gilliam to be sure he approves. I'll get back to you on that, but you can start on the foundation right away."

*   *   *

Shan drew a deep breath and looked at the three children sitting in a row on Dacia's sofa. He stood with his hands in his pockets and his heart in his throat.

"Well," he said, and swallowed hard. "This is Grace." He paused and glanced in the general direction of the young lady standing beside him. Dacia had trimmed her hair, and she looked fairly respectable, but Shan didn't notice. Even this small acknowledgement of her presence was enough to cause his face to turn beet-red and his stomach to knot even tighter. "She is not our ma, but she knows how to take care of children. So ... she will take care of you."

"Why can't Ma take care of us?" asked Libby.

Michael snapped at her. "Because Ma is gone. Ma went to heaven. Remember?"

"I wanted to go with her!" Libby wailed. Even after a week, three-year-old Libby didn't seem to understand that Ma would not be coming back—ever.

Shan ran his hand over his face. He could feel the soft stubble where he'd not shaved in the last week. Before all this had happened, he'd been proud of his need to shave every few days. Now he didn't care. Not one bit.

Before. He'd had Ma before. Now he was the head of what was left of his family. Seventeen years old ... and he had to figure out how to raise Michael and Libby and Danny. How to care for them. Who would cook? Who would wash the clothes? Who would comfort the children, hold them when they were afraid or hurt? Who would plan for their future and help them grow up well? Shan would. He would have to. The job had to be done, and there was no one to do it but himself. And Grace. But *she* had not been his idea.

"Why can't Will's mama take care of us?" Michael asked.

"Just ... because she can't." Shan glared at him. He felt like he was betraying his family. Actually, he'd prefer that Dacia care for the children, but she had insisted that the children needed to be raised in their own home. In truth, he wasn't convinced at all, but he didn't have the strength to think. He needed Grace, at least according to Dacia. But he hated her for it—for not being Ma. For intruding on his family. And he hated having to convince the children that having her was a good thing. But he would do what Dacia suggested. He had no strength to argue.

Grace hoped she didn't look as uncertain as she felt. It was an awkward situation at best. Michael glared at her with thinly veiled distrust. Libby just looked down at her lap, twiddled her fingers, and whimpered. Danny, however, squirmed off the sofa and lifted his arms to her to be picked up.

Grace leaned down to lift the baby and nuzzle his face. She knelt to the floor and sat back on her heels in front of the other children, sitting Danny on her lap. "Hello," she said softly, and smiled. "You don't know me yet, but I hope we can be good friends. I will cook for you and wash your clothes. If you get hurt I will try to make it better. I'll do the very best I can for you." She cleared her throat, waiting for some response. But no one spoke. She patted Danny on the knee and then tickled his ribs. He giggled and squirmed away. She looked up at the other two children. What was she supposed to do? She knew how to work.

She knew how to laugh with children when they were good and how to make them behave when they weren't. But she didn't know how to get them to accept her. She didn't even know where to start.

Michael gazed out the window, a grim look on his face and said nothing

Grace took a deep breath. "And I will need lots of help," she continued. "Michael, you're the oldest. Maybe you can help me. I'll need someone strong around when Shan is gone at work. You look like you have very good muscles."

Michael turned his eyes in the direction of the kitchen door, a blank look on his face. He didn't respond. Grace looked up at Shan, who was studiously avoiding eye contact with her.

"Well, then," he said. "I guess it's time for me to get to work." He turned and walked out the door with no further comment.

Tears burned Grace's eyes and the muscle in her jaw tightened. Shan hated her. Michael hated her. Libby just missed her ma. Only Danny seemed to welcome her. And now he began to stink. She scooped him up and headed off to find a clean diaper.

Chapter Eighteen

The door to the Harmony Saddle and Harness shop was already unlocked when Mac came to work on Tuesday morning. It had been over a week since the flood, but Mac had been laid up in his hotel room at the Palace Hotel. This morning he decided, broken ribs or no, he was going to work. He grimaced as the banjo twanged its out-of-tune welcome. The last time he'd heard this sound, Lilyann had said it needed to be tuned.

"Hey Shan." Mac's voice was weary, flat.

"Hey, yourself. Doin' okay?"

"Yeah. You?"

"Okay," Shan said. Each knew the other was lying. It was just a formality—greeting each other pleasantly. Somehow, it brought a sense of normalcy to their meeting.

"I had to open up shop last week." Shan nodded to the jumbled pile of leather straps awaiting repair. "We've got all kinds of broken stuff here and collars that need new padding. There's no one else in town to do it now. It's all us."

"Okay," Mac said, pulling on his leather apron. "Thanks for keeping things going." He picked up a bridle and examined it. "Any word yet on Aiden?"

"Mm-hm. We buried him Friday."

"Sorry. I hadn't heard."

"What about Lilyann and Gilbert?"

"Huh-uh, nothing yet."

There was nothing more to be said. The two men worked in silence, each grieving in his own way.

*   *   *

After lunch on Thursday, Grace put Danny and Libby down for a nap at the Burke's house. Michael refused to go. He had refused to nap ever since the flood—perhaps remembering what happened the last time he fell asleep in the middle of the afternoon. He hadn't slept well at night either.

Pappy agreed to listen for waking children, so Grace and Dacia walked across the street with Michael to continue the work on Shan's house.

They entered at the back door, climbing first on an inverted bucket, since the back porch was still missing. Shan had plans to replace both the front and back porches, but it would take time. Grace walked to the door leading to the front room. It was awful! A week and a half after the flood, and still, the sight of the dried mud and slime made Grace's skin crawl. Shan had shoveled out the worst of the muck, but more shoveling was needed before the cleaning in the front room could even begin. The sofa and parlor chairs would need new stuffing and uphol-stery, but the wooden frames seemed to be intact. All of the downstairs rooms were mud-soaked two feet high or more on the walls.

Turning back to the kitchen, both women heaved a sigh of relief as they encountered the fresh smell of soda. They'd started on this room yesterday, and their progress was encouraging.

After the third hard scrubbing of the floor by hand, Dacia rose from her knees and dropped her rag back into the bucket at her feet. "Done! And that was the dirtiest floor I ever scrubbed in my whole, long, entire life!" The water in the bucket was nearly clear now, and both agreed it was high time to move on to some more needy part of the house. Yesterday they had emptied all the kitchen shelves, washed each item carefully, scrubbed the shelves, lined them with new paper, and returned the cooking utensils and dishes to their places. This morning Grace had washed the lower part of the kitchen walls while Dacia watched the children. Now, with the floor done, this one room, at least, was livable. It had taken two days of hard, hard work.

Michael banged through the back door. "Can I have some wa-ter?" he asked.

"Sure, go ahead," Grace said, and Michael disappeared with one of the buckets.

"Let's do the bathroom next," Grace said. "With the upstairs bedrooms still okay and a clean kitchen and bathroom in the house,

Shan and the children can actually begin to live here again. Not just sleep here and take meals at your house."

"I agree. It will be good for them—make it feel like home again. At least a little. But let's sit a minute first. I think I'm getting old!" Dacia said, rubbing her back.

Grace smiled. Yes, Dacia did seem old to her. After all, she'd had a child almost Grace's age—only four years younger.

At a loud yell from Michael, both women dashed for the back door.

"Watch out! Here comes more!" Michael hollered, sloshing the rest of the water from the pail onto the pile of sticks on the ground.

"Michael! What are you doing?" Grace called.

"I'm making a flood! See, it crashed my houses I made. No houses anymore. Just sticks and mud!"

Grace's stomach lurched. How *could* he?

Dacia swallowed hard and said, "Well, Michael, looks like you have a lot of cleanup to do, just like the men in Heppner!"

"Yup. Now I have to get a shovel and clean up." He ran for the shovel leaning against the house and took it back to begin salvage operations on his stick town.

"Well done," Grace said to Dacia. "I wonder if every boy in town will be playing the same kind of games. I guess it's only natural, considering ..."

"Yeah ... natural. Who knows? Maybe it's their way of healing. At least he's not harming anyone." She chuckled. "Kitty—his mama—always said he was her 'frisky' one. He still needs a bit of taming, I guess."

"Iced tea?" Grace asked, and took down two sparkling glasses from one of the immaculate shelves. She took the pitcher of tea from the icebox and chipped some ice off the block—just delivered this morning—for their drinks.

Dacia accepted the glass of tea and sank onto one of the kitchen chairs. She gazed thoughtfully at the young lady opposite her. Plain to look at, yet there was a beauty that went much deeper than mere physical appearance—a depth, a story. Dacia hoped it was a story that would be told in time. For now, she focused on just getting to know this new friend a little better. "Did you say you're only sixteen, Grace?"

Grace nodded.

"In some ways you seem very mature ..."

Grace seemed to be considering her response. Finally she said, "I had to raise my brothers after my mama died."

"Mmmm." Dacia's facial expression and the single syllable spoke of her sympathy.

"I've watched you with the children and you're pretty good with them. Your mama must have taught you well."

Dacia waited, but no explanation was forthcoming.

"Okay then. How about the future? Are you willing to talk about that?"

Grace laughed and nodded. Yes, Dacia was being nosy, but Grace didn't mind. Actually, she enjoyed Dacia's company—was maybe even beginning to trust her a little.

"I don't know," she finally responded. "It seems like I have more than enough to do right now. No time to think about what might be next."

In an earlier life, Grace had entertained ideas of love, marriage, a family, grandchildren gathered at her knee. Now? Love was not for the likes of her. Love was a mirage, a fairy tale for beautiful women. No, Grace could not hope to find love. Marriage—maybe. To some desperate man who needed a woman to wash his socks and slave away at household chores day after day. To provide for *all* his physical needs. Right now, she was not ready to consider such a thing.

She gazed at her tea for a moment, then said to Dacia, "I really appreciate what you've done for me—letting me stay with you and setting it up with Shan so I could care for the children. Michael is a bit of a handful, I admit. But we'll get it worked out in time. And the others— they are pure joy."

"Grace—I'm not just *letting* you stay with me," Dacia said. "I need you. I guess, in a way, I'm using you. I miss Martin and Josie so much!" Dacia pressed her lips together and took a deep breath. "Josie was more than just a daughter to me. More than just a helper. She was a companion. She was twelve, you know. Beginning to grow up. In some ways it was harder. The child she had been and the woman she was becoming struggled sometimes."

Dacia couldn't go on. Grace reached across the table and laid her hand over Dacia's. "I'm so sorry." she said.

"You're not a replacement for her," Dacia said after a moment. "Such a thing could never be. But having you around to call on for help has blessed me—more than I can say. Just having another person to fill the void. You make the house seem less empty. And I thank you for it."

"You're welcome." Grace's face brightened. She drained the last of the tea from her glass and took it to the sink to rinse it. "So what about the garden?" she asked Dacia. "You said you had extra seeds?"

Dacia nodded. "Yes, and I don't know if you noticed, but the beets at my house seem to be thriving again. They are farthest back in the garden—where it begins to rise up the hill. It looked like they were a total loss after the flood, but the leaves are coming back strong and healthy. It's funny though. The stuff isn't in very good rows anymore."

"I'd like to do some canning in the fall." Grace smiled. "I love seeing the jars filled—all the bright colors lined up on dish towels on the table. But this year ... can we plant a garden this late and expect to get much from it?"

"We can sure try!"

"I think I'll start the bathroom next—till the children wake up. And then—if Shan can tolerate my presence—I'll get a kitchen garden started this evening when it's cooler." She opened the back door to check on Michael.

Dacia shook her head. Shan was a puzzle for sure. He was a handsome young man, nearly marrying age. And here was this lovely girl caring for his brothers and sister while he worked in the saddle shop all day—and Shan could barely stand to look at her! Of course his whole world had been turned upside down. He had lost half his family. Who wouldn't be struggling with life under these circumstances?

Dacia only hoped Shan would come around in time.

Chapter Nineteen

Methodist Episcopal Church at left and smoke from the fires
Courtesy Morrow County Historical Museum

Sunday, June 28, the two week anniversary of the flood

Mac Harmon left his room on the third floor of the Palace Hotel, descended stiffly to street level, and began walking up Main Street, in the direction of his former home. He hadn't seen it yet—except for that first day; he didn't want to see it now. But he felt he must. He walked slowly. His broken ribs hurt no matter how he moved, but somehow walking slowly seemed wiser. He was in no hurry to see where his house had been.

The Baptist church was still standing, although the flood had destroyed nearly everything around it. Mac stood in the shadow of the church and gazed around him. Across Baltimore from the church stood Shan's house. It was back in the right place now, but it looked awful. No front porch. An overturned pail had been placed in front of the door as a step, and a neat pile of used lumber rested on the ground nearby.

Mac gazed at it for some time, then looked at the Burke's house across Gale Street. It was set higher than many of the houses around it, and had a good stone foundation. The mud line on the house was only a few inches above the porch level. When he had looked at both houses long enough to gather his courage, he finally crossed Baltimore and walked toward his own place.

Nothing there. No grass, no garden, no chickens, no trellis for children to climb. No children, no wife. Nothing. He stepped into the place where his yard had been and just stood there for a moment, the silent emptiness of loss alternating with the screaming anguish within him. Then, with his hands in his pockets, he walked to the place where the porch had been. This porch. This place—the last place he'd been with his precious Ella. *Ella, I love you. I always will.*

In the lot behind his, facing Main Street, the roof of the Telephone Stables rested on the ground where it had been deposited by the flood. It now served as a temporary shelter for a bevy of volunteers. A number of bedrolls were laid out in fairly straight rows under the roof, but they were empty now. The few volunteers left in town were busy searching drifts down the valley. Heppner itself had already been thoroughly searched.

Mac didn't want to rebuild his home and start over. He wasn't ready to build a new life. He wanted to bring back his wife and children. He wanted the life he'd had before.

They told him his whole family was gone. He didn't believe it. There were others, of course, besides Lilyann and Gilbert whose bodies had not been found. They were presumed dead. Most people assumed Lilyann and Gilbert had died, too. Their names appeared on the official death list.

But Mac knew better. Even before Dacia had told him about that night, hadn't he felt the children were still alive?

In a sudden awareness of their need for him, he understood what he had to do. He would search for them. And he would *not* give up until they were safe with him once again. He drew a deep breath and let it out slowly.

He looked once again at the forlorn place he had once called home. He pictured Charlie's face—his eyes, lashes, hair. How long had his hair been that day—that auburn hair so like his mother's? When had he had his last haircut?

"Charlie." Mac whispered the name. The boy's freckles had begun to multiply as they did every summer. What about his teeth? How many baby teeth had Charlie lost all together? Mac knew it had been a while since he'd grown his new front teeth. The chipped tooth ... Lily had raced Charlie to the flower bed and back. Charlie won, but barely. Lilyann had put a miserable gash in one eyebrow when she crashed into the top step face first, and Charlie had slammed so hard into the porch, a front tooth was chipped. Not too bad—a small chip. And it didn't hurt, after the initial shock and the blood had been dealt with. Yes, Mac remembered that chipped tooth, the scarred eyebrow. He wanted never to forget. Never to forget any of it. Could the wound to the soul of an entire town be any worse than the wound to the soul of one man?

He heard the screen door bang at the Burkes', but Mac didn't turn. Then he heard Johnny's voice behind him.

"I'm sorry, Mac."

Mac nodded. "Thanks."

Johnny stepped forward. "Dacia sent me to ask you to supper."

Mac gritted his teeth and swallowed, then shook his head.

Johnny just stood looking down at the ground. Finally he asked, "Doin' okay?"

Mac nodded. What could he say? That he was thinking about his son's chipped tooth?

"You want to come over and just sit on the porch for a bit?"

Mac looked up at the Burke's porch, but shook his head. "Nah. I just wanted to come by and see it. Guess there's no reason to stay." He nodded to Johnny, turned, and walked out of the yard.

*   *   *

The next morning, Mac went to see Sheriff Shutt.

"Thanks Sheriff, for taking the time. I know you're about worn out."

Shutt nodded and rubbed his eyes. "What can I do for you, Mac?"

"My children. The bodies of two of my children have not been found. They won't be found, because the children didn't die."

Shutt shook his head. "Well, now, Mac. You've got to realize that we have a number of bodies that have not been found. We just have to accept that they died, because they are nowhere among the living."

"Yes, I understand. But this is different. These children didn't die. They vanished." Mac's eyes pled with Shutt to understand.

Shutt crossed his arms and narrowed his eyes. "How do you know that, Mac? What makes you think so?"

"Dacia Burke—she carried Gilbert up to the hillside, and she saw Lilyann on the ground at the side of the flood."

Shutt nodded, encouraging Mac to go on. Mac started to speak, then paused, wiping a hand over his face.

Finally he spoke. "Have you ever known something—been absolutely sure of it—only you can't explain *how* you know it?"

"Well, no, I can't say as I have. And I guess in my job as sheriff, I have to have evidence to go on. I can't be making decisions based on how I feel, or on what I think I know."

"Right." Mac nodded his understanding. "I realize that. But this is … Well, you know my wife and oldest son died."

Shutt nodded, even though he couldn't actually remember. There were just too many to remember them all.

"My oldest son was with me, near the creek, and I know he died. And the next morning, when I saw the house—or where the house used to be—I realized that it had been washed away. And I knew, even before I was told, that Ella had died. But I also knew, even then, I *knew* that my two younger children had not died. The searchers found Ella's body, and Charlie's. But they did not find Lilyann or Gilbert. Their bodies have not been found. And the reason is—they are still alive."

Shutt rocked his chair back on two legs, his arms still crossed over his chest. "Okay … where are they?"

"I don't know. That's why I'm coming to you. I'm hoping you can find them."

"Mac!" The chair went back down on all four legs. "Think about what you're asking! I have here a town devastated by a horrible flash flood. Probably two hundred and fifty people have died. We are trying our best to get people buried and get the town back on its feet. I'm needed here about twenty-five hours a day. And you want me to go find your children? Who, by the way, were in the direct path of the flood and were probably killed by it? That hillside was in total chaos! Think how easy it would be for a child to get too close and be swept away before anyone could notice and stop them."

"No." Mac spoke softly as he leaned forward and gazed into Shutt's eyes. "They weren't killed by it. They are alive."

Shutt clamped his teeth together, flexing the muscle in the side of his jaw as he shook his head.

"It's okay," Mac told him. "I understand. I'll be searching on my own, but I thought maybe, if you heard anything …"

"Okay, Mac." Shutt softened. "I don't quite understand how you can be so positive about this. To tell you the truth, I'm wondering if you're all right. But I also have a responsibility to you. And I'll do the best I can. I'll keep in mind what you've told me and keep my eyes and ears open." He took a deep breath and blew it out.

Mac merely nodded. "I do thank you, Sheriff. Thank you very much."

*   *   *

Johnny once again found himself on one end of a bathtub navigating the steep stairs at the Roberts building. He was at the top with two men below. The tubs were being scrubbed thoroughly before being returned to Gibson's tonsorial shop. In fact Lou Lundquist was upstairs working on the last one now.

"Careful!" Johnny cautioned as the men neared the bottom. They passed through the open door and angled across the street. Depositing the tub at the rear of Gibson's shop, they started back for the last tub.

"I can't believe Lou is up there cleaning that place all by herself," one of the men said.

"Somebody has to do it," said Johnny.

"Is she getting paid?"

"Of course not!"

"Yeah. I just find it strange that nobody else is there helping her."

"They're tired. They're through. They need to heal."

"And Lou doesn't need that? She lost both her mother and father, didn't she? I just think it's pretty impressive what she's doing. There's no glory in it."

"Maybe she's not looking for glory," Johnny said.

"No," one of the men snickered. "She'll be looking for glory soon enough. You know Lou. Everything has to be about her."

"She's the one took care of Will at first," Johnny looked up sharply. He felt a surprising fondness for this lady who had held and prayed for his son. "I sure thank her for that! She was serving meals at the Palace for a while. Then, when the others gave out, she came over here and helped prepare bodies for burial. She was working with one of Mollie's 'wayward girls.'"

Suddenly, Johnny remembered a conversation with Shan on the Sunday afternoon of the flood. He and Mac had teased Shan about Lou being a possible object of his affection. Both men had laughed. He felt ashamed of himself. Lou was a fine person. At least she might be.

Johnny pushed open the door and the three men clomped up the stairs one last time.

117

Chapter Twenty

D r. Kistner patted Will on the knee and rose from the chair at the boy's bedside. "Well, you seem to be doing fine, young man." He banged his head on the slanted ceiling, then ducked and grinned at Will. "You're healing up real well. That head is about as good as new, now that the stitches are out. And the scar's not going to look too bad. It'll still show enough to give you bragging rights. But it won't be horrible."

He offered Will the small mirror he carried in his bag, and Will admired his scar. It looked better already with the stitches out.

"What about his leg?" Johnny asked. "Will he be able to walk soon?"

Will had been back on his feet only a few days after the flood—as soon as Dr. Kistner had given him permission. But he was having trouble walking. He dragged his left leg along as if it refused to cooperate.

The doctor nodded in answer to Johnny's question and said, "Oh yes, I imagine he'll be up runnin' around any minute now." He cocked his head in the direction of the stairs and looked meaningfully at Johnny. He picked up his bag from the floor by the bed and ruffled the boy's hair. "You take care to eat all the food your mama fixes you so you can grow big and strong, you hear?"

Will nodded solemnly as he handed the mirror back to Dr. Kistner.

Downstairs, the doctor dropped into a kitchen chair while Dacia poured him a glass of lemonade.

"What's the real story, Doc?" Johnny asked him.

"I don't know. And that's the truth." Johnny and Dacia glanced at each other.

"That cut is healing up nicely. I'm very pleased with how it looks. I was afraid it would leave a bad scar, but ... Well, you can see. It's looking pretty good. About his leg—he seems to be fine, but it may be that his body is just taking a long time to get back to normal. As far as I can tell, there's no reason in the world why he can't walk yet. Sure, the leg was injured. But it wasn't broken—the bone is fine. The muscles seem to be okay too, although they'll get pretty flabby from disuse if we don't get him moving soon. He can bear his weight on it when I ask him to, and he can move it fine. He just can't seem to walk on it."

Dacia rose from her chair and went to stand next to Johnny.

The doctor turned his glass on the table—around and around. "Yes, his head was injured, and I suppose there could be something there." He took a long drink of his lemonade and wiped his forehead on his handkerchief. He set his glass on the table and gazed at it thoughtfully. "Maybe something else got hurt that day. Maybe Will's spirit just needs time to heal."

*   *   *

Sheriff Til Taylor
Photo by Lee Morehouse

119

Mac Harmon and Sheriff Til Taylor of Pendleton sat across from each other in Taylor's office. The sheriff's sturdy frame of over six feet could have appeared almost overwhelming, but instead Taylor projected an air of comfortable confidence, which Mac appreciated. He'd never met Taylor before, but had heard he was one of the best sheriffs around.

Mac held out his picture to Taylor. "It's old," he apologized, "but it's all I have. This is Lilyann, and here is Gilbert in his mama's arms. They're older now, of course."

"I don't know," Taylor said. "The little girl maybe. But the baby—he would have changed so much. Two years, you say?"

"Only a year since the picture was taken. But he looks the same … only … older," Mac finished, lamely. "You know—more hair, bigger …"

Taylor was known for never forgetting a face. "It's all in the eyes," he often said. "Focus on the eyes." But he looked at Mac now with pity. "Well, I'll certainly show this picture around everywhere I go, but I can't promise you anything. Even if the children were brought here, it will be hard to identify them from this picture. And like I said, as far as I know, we haven't had any stray children turn up in town lately."

Mac winced. His children were *not* strays! He had already sent prints of the photo to every major city in the Northwest—The Dalles, Portland, Seattle, Spokane, Baker City, Boise, Walla Walla—and most of the smaller towns, as well. He'd had no response and couldn't stand waiting any longer. He would travel to every town in Oregon and Washington—and beyond, if he had to—searching, until his children were found.

"I know it must be hard for you folks in Heppner." Sheriff Taylor's face showed his sincerity. "It made a big impact on Pendleton as well. I guess you know that almost half of the people who died were related to someone here in Pendleton."

Mac nodded.

"I sure wish it had never happened!" Taylor said.

Mac quietly thanked him and turned to go. His children were alive somewhere. Mac knew it, beyond a shadow of a doubt.

*   *   *

Little Sarah Burke climbed into Pappy's lap and leaned her head against his bony chest as Dacia and Pappy sat watching Walter jump from the porch rail.

"Pappy, look at me! I can fly!" Walter jumped, flapping his arms with all the energy of a five-year-old. He landed and rolled over to his back, spread eagle, then hopped up to try again.

Pappy sat nodding in Johnny's rocker, which was surprisingly found still on the porch—tangled in the railing—when the flood subsided.

"That little lassie ..." Pappy murmered. "That little lassie with the fairy smile and the look of Ireland about her ..."

"What, Pappy? What are you talking about?" Dacia asked.

"Leprechauns, the both of 'em. Leprechauns they are." He stretched his arm out to the side, reaching, grasping at something invisible, then stared intently at his hand, but it was empty. "Where are they?"

"The leprechauns, Pappy?" Walter giggled. Even at five years old, he knew leprechauns were imaginary. At least he was pretty sure.

"That little wisp of a fairy. Where is she? And her brother." Pappy peered up toward the sky. "Jesus, do you know?"

Walter just looked at him and shrugged. Dacia narrowed her eyes and stared intently at Pappy's face with its faraway look. She remembered hearing Pappy call Lilyann a 'fairy girl.' Did he *know* something? One thing Dacia had come to understand—if Pappy did have some knowledge about the missing children, it would only come out in his random musings. She had already tried—several times—to get Pappy to respond to her questions about Lilyann and Gilbert. He seemed to know nothing. Until moments like this.

Chapter Twenty One

Etta Snowburg hurried to the front door of her Oregon City boarding house as she heard knocking for the second time. "Coming!" she called. Her hands and apron were covered with flour. She brushed at her hair, then stopped, as she realized she was probably not straightening it at all—just flouring it. Where was Elisabeth, anyway? It was her job to take care of visitors.

Etta, complete with a smudge of flour at her right temple, opened the door wide to reveal a tramp, hungry looking and miserable. On either side of him stood two scraggly children, one only a toddler. What on earth? The Snowburg sisters' boarding house wasn't in the very finest section of town to be sure, but still, these people were of an entirely different class of humanity than Etta was in the habit of looking on.

The man snatched his bedraggled hat from his head and held it clamped in one slender, dirty hand; the other hand grasped a limp pillow case, apparently containing his possessions. "'Scuse me, Ma'am," he said, and nodded his head slightly. "I saw your sign on the fence that you have a room to let?"

Oh my! Where is Elisabeth, anyway? "Elisabeth?" Etta's voice wavered as she called back over shoulder. She turned back to look up at the stranger.

"Well, yes, we ... um, might have a room. My sister usually makes these arrangements. Would you mind telling me a little about yourself?"

"Oh yes, ma'am. Of course." Suddenly the man looked more weary than disreputable. He spoke with a refinement Etta had not expected, considering his appearance. "You see, ma'am, the children and I ... well ... their mother died, you see. In childbirth." The man's face was somber, grieved. "It was ... well, I decided I just couldn't stay in Seattle." He bit his lip and took a deep breath. "Too many memories. I'm sure you understand."

Etta nodded slightly. She couldn't really understand, never having had a husband or children of her own, but just imagining such a thing was overwhelming.

The visitor, despite his ragged clothing, appeared to be a man of good upbringing and character. "Well, we've just arrived here in the area you see, and noticed your sign. We need a place to stay."

"I see. And um ..." *Drat! Where's Elisabeth? I'm no good at this sort of thing!* "Well, you have work here? A job?"

"Well, no ma'am, not just yet. I thought it was important to get settled with the children first. As soon as we have a place to stay, I'll be looking for work. Providing for the children must come first, you know."

"Yes, well ..." She paused to glance over her shoulder. "Why don't you step in. I'll, um, I'll go get my sister. She's the one who usually handles new boarders." Etta nodded nervously. "Just ... well ... just make yourselves at home for a moment." She turned and made her escape as quickly as possible. *I'll kill her! Where is that woman?* "Elisabeth! Where *are* you?"

"I'm right here, dear. There's no need to shout so." Elisabeth came through the kitchen door and laid an armful of flowers on the dining room table. "Aren't they lovely? I thought I'd make up a vase for each room. The hollyhocks are so nice this year, and just look at these lovely roses!"

"Elisabeth! You are needed!" Etta's eyes were wide. "There are some ... *people* ... in the parlor. *You* need to go take care of them!"

Etta scurried back to her kitchen, leaving Elisabeth to deal with the strange man and his dirty children.

Elisabeth pulled out one especially fine rose and started toward the parlor, humming. *People* indeed! Elisabeth loved people. They couldn't possibly be as bad as Etta's attitude had seemed to indicate. She opened the parlor door and entered. The smile froze on her face. *Hmmm. Maybe they are that bad. And they smell too!* She lifted the rose to her face and inhaled deeply.

Quickly regaining her composure, she asked the man, "How can I help you?"

"A room, ma'am. We are looking for a room."

"Well, we don't usually take children." *But that room's been empty for over a month, and we need to fill it!* "But perhaps ... Our rooms alone are three dollars a week, or five dollars a week with board as well. I would charge only half board for the children, of course, as I'm sure they couldn't eat much. Seven dollars a week for all three of you." She assumed the figure named would serve as an adequate deterrent to this man, who obviously couldn't afford decent clothing or a bath, much less room and board.

But he surprised her. "Yes, well, that sounds quite fair." He nodded.

"Payable *in advance* on the first day of each week."

"Yes." He nodded again "Um ... we've just arrived from Seattle. Perhaps your sister told you."

"No, she told me nothing."

The man smiled a tight little grin. "I need a place to stay first. Then I'll be able to go out and find work. I do have one dollar I could give you now, and the rest later. Would that be all right? You see my wife ..." He screwed up his face as if he was about to cry, and Elisabeth got the point.

Oh my! A man alone with two small children. His wife dead. My goodness, but life can be hard sometimes!

"I see. Well, it's rather unusual, but I understand it must be difficult for you." She twirled the stem of the rose in her hands, then offered it to the little girl. "Be careful," she said gently. "It has thorns."

But the child neither took the rose, nor looked up when Elisabeth spoke. She merely gazed at the floor. Elisabeth smiled and drew the flower back.

"All right. You may stay for one week, but if, by the end of the week, you have not found work, you'll have to move on. I'm sure you understand, my sister and I must have paying tenants in order to support ourselves."

"That's most generous of you, ma'am. I do understand." He pulled a crumpled dollar bill from his pocket and presented it to Elisabeth.

She nodded curtly and led the way to the stairs to show her new tenants to their room. The man picked up his grimy pillow case from the floor and followed, with the children tagging along behind.

*　　*　　*

Heppner Mayor Frank Gilliam dropped the letter onto his desk and put his face in his hands. *Oh God! Thank you! You knew I needed this, didn't you? Something to tell me you're really there—that you understand.* He picked up the letter and read it again.

Colfax, Wash.
June 25, 1903
Honorary Frank Gilliam
Mayor of Heppner, Or.

Dear Sir:
We are some little girls who wanted to do something for the poor people of your city who lost so much, so we started a little candy stand and sold home-made candy, lemonade, gum, etc. for two days and have made eleven dollars which we send you to give to some poor person. One of our playmates lost her grandpa, Mr. Jas. Matlock, in the flood and we all feel so sorry. Hoping this little sum will do somebody some good we are

Yours very truly,
Grace Stafford, age 11 years
Jennie Miller, age 8 years
Agnes Gillespie, age 10 years

The mayor lifted his head to look out the window of his office. *What am I going to say? You know, God. You know. I don't. Just, please, help me find the words!*
He picked up his pen and began his response to the girls.

Heppner, Ore.
June 29, 1903
To Grace Stafford, Jennie Miller, and Agnes
Gillespie
Colfax, Wash.

My dear little girls:

I am just in receipt of your kind letter of June 25th, with money order for $11.00 enclosed.

Your letter, dear children, above all those received by myself and the relief committee in charge of moneys subscribed by the generous and kind-hearted people throughout this great country, has touched my heart, in the fullness of which, I say to you in reply: God bless you.

Two weeks ago yesterday morning, Heppner was a happy little town. Our church bells rang and our little ones sang songs of praise and worshipped by their mother's side. Evening came, and with it the storm, and many of our precious little children were carried away to worship at the throne of God. Those who have gone before are happy now, while those of us who remain are sad. Sad because of the little ones who are no more—who cannot be with us to cheer our weary way.

I might say, while writing you, that many good people all over this land, both rich and poor, contributed most liberally toward the relief of our suffering ones. They have sent us mercy and supplies of all kinds and also sent us their strong men to aid us and give kind words of cheer and heartfelt sympathy. But of all that we have received, the gem which has been contributed by the three little girls in Colfax will hold the hearts and love of our men and women as only the sentiments of a little child can do.

Very lovingly yours,
Frank Gilliam, Mayor

Mayor Gilliam laid his pen aside, blotted the paper, and slid it into an envelope. It would go out in the morning mail.

Chapter Twenty Two

By the end of the first week, Klein had indeed found work. He took a job at the lumber yard sweeping up and moving things. He didn't like it, but he was able to pay the Snowburgs what he owed them. Elisabeth hoped he would begin to settle in and make a new home for his children. But a week later, the children were still dressed in the same dirty clothes in which they had arrived. They had nothing. No extra clothing, no toys, no books. They came to breakfast and supper with their father, but apparently spent the rest of the time in their room.

Elisabeth finally asked Klein if she might have the children's clothes after they undressed for bed one night so she could wash them. He looked confused at the request, but later that evening, he brought her the clothes. Even though it was late, Elisabeth first laid the clothes on old newspapers and drew around them. She could make patterns and sew them some new things.

Then she took the smelly, filthy clothes to the kitchen sink and scrubbed them thoroughly. Fortunately, the night was warm and they dried quickly on the line outside. Early in the morning, she folded the clothes and set them on the floor outside Klein's door. When the children came down for breakfast, they looked almost human. Elisabeth determined to bathe the children and wash their hair as soon as she and Etta finished the dishes.

"You're just going to spoil him," Etta insisted, as they cleaned up after the meal.

"Well, it's not him I'm interested in. It's the children. After all, it isn't their fault. They're only children."

Etta nodded. "We've never had anyone even half as bad as Mr. Klein living here before! We just need to get rid of him before he gives our lovely home a bad name." Etta washed the last plate and began on the silverware. "I think we should give him a month to get on his feet, and then ask him to leave. I don't think the other boarders like him very much either. He doesn't even bathe, Elisabeth! He's just not nice to have around."

"Maybe his wife always took care of things like that. The poor man is in shock! After I bathe the children, maybe he'll notice, and things will begin falling in place for him."

"Humph." Etta rinsed the silverware and began on the pots and pans. "I wouldn't count on it."

Elisabeth said nothing, but she got the washtub from the back porch and fetched a clean towel from the hall cabinet. When the children had finished eating, she brought them to the kitchen.

She washed the girl first, the child sitting perfectly still in the tub. After Elisabeth had changed the muddy water, she put the girl back in. This time, the child ran her hands gently over the top of the water as if feeling it. She picked her hands up and looked at them, then pushed them all the way to the bottom of the tub.

Elisabeth and Etta smiled at each other. "Looks like she enjoys it," Etta said.

When the girl was dried off and dressed, Elisabeth braided her beautiful clean hair. Then she stripped the toddler and lowered him into the water. She asked him gently, "What is your name?"

"Gibbie!"

"Gibbie? That's a very nice name." Elisabeth soaped him up and began rinsing. "What about your sister? What's her name?"

"Ye-ann!" Gibbie responded.

"Ann?"

"Ye-ann," Gibbie repeated, and began splashing his hands in the water—hard—causing a huge rainstorm in the kitchen. Elisabeth grabbed the towel and scooped him out of the tub laughing. "Oh, you're just quite the young man, aren't you, now?"

*　　　*　　　*

The clock on the wall said nearly 4:00. The work load had been heavy the past months, especially at first when Mac and Shan had the only intact saddle and harness shop left in town. But gradually, they had been catching up. They were almost to the point where they could count on a little breathing space.

Mac spoke without looking up. "That saddle you made?"

"Which one?"

"The one that Al Geiger got as part of your payment for the buggy—what happened to it?"

"Gone. Like Mister Geiger, himself. *And* the buggy. All gone."

"Hm. Kind of sad. All that work! It was a right fine piece of work, Shan."

Shan nodded in silence. Yes, he'd been proud of it, but it didn't matter now. Not in the face of so much death. Death mattered. Saddles didn't.

"Are you going to make another one?"

"Maybe. Hadn't thought about it really. I don't need a saddle. Pretty Girl is beyond carrying a rider. And we have plenty of work here without taking on anything extra." Shan hammered another rivet into the strap he was working on and turned to look at Mac. "You got a reason for asking?"

"Maybe. Just thinking of young Will. He's still not walking right, you know. It's been over two months. Doc says there's nothing wrong that he can see. I'm just wondering if riding might help him. You know ... make him feel more confident. Or maybe even feeling his hips move like that would help."

Shan put down the strap he was holding and looked intently at Mac.

"Huh. Kind of makes sense. I hadn't thought about it. Yeah! Maybe that would help. I'll do it! I'll make him a saddle just the right size for him. And he can ride Pretty Girl. I bet she could carry a kid that size without any problem."

"Okay. Tell you what. I'll donate the materials. You do the work. Okay?"

"Okay!" Shan said, and he began designing the small saddle in his mind even while he continued splicing the broken tug line before him. For the first time since the flood, he was looking forward to the future.

*   *   *

"Ouch!" Grace stuck her thumb in her mouth and tasted blood.

"Did you poke yourself?" little Sarah Burke asked.

"I *did* poke myself, and I'm *not* happy about it!"

"Then why you did it?" Sarah asked.

Grace laughed. "I guess because my fingers are clumsy. That's why. I should be more careful!" She rearranged the heavy fabric on her lap and forced the large needle through the edges. She had done most of the work on Dacia's sewing machine, but was finishing up the details by hand. One more stitch. One at a time. Not easy work on such heavy fabric, but she was determined to succeed.

"I can sew too," Sarah said, eyeing Grace's work. "When I'm big, I'm going to sew. Mama will teach me."

"That's right, I'll teach you," Dacia said. "When you are four, you can have your first sewing project. You still have a few months to wait." Grace smiled to herself. Technically, Dacia was right—ten months was "a few" even if it was actually closer to a year.

The fabric Grace struggled with was a deep brown brocade. Beautiful! The only reason it was available so soon after the flood was that Dacia had bought it last January, intending to make a new cover for her own sofa, which was very worn. But now, it didn't matter. Worn was nothing compared to the sofa at the Collins house.

Shan's sofa had been thoroughly mud-soaked in the flood. Shan and Grace had carried it out into the yard and removed the cushions so it could dry. A week later, Grace brushed it as clean as she could with a scrub brush and had Shan help her carry it back inside. Shan had cooperated—barely. He had carried his end of the sofa, and put it down on command. But he spoke not a word during the entire process, and did not look at Grace at all.

Once the sofa was back in the Collins' front room, Grace had covered it temporarily with a blanket. She had set aside material for the stuffing, and now she was working every evening on the new covering from Dacia's fabric. She had never upholstered a piece of furniture before, but Dacia had. So Dacia guided; Grace cut and sewed.

She was hoping to surprise Shan. She hoped he would like what she had done and appreciate her efforts.

"So, how was Shan when he came home today?" Dacia asked.

"The same. Nothing."

"Nothing at all? Didn't he even say hello?"

"Well, he said 'I'm home.' 'Bout the longest sentence I've ever heard him say!"

Dacia sighed. "Yeah, he's sure hurting. I wish I knew how to bring him around."

"Well, maybe he'll actually be pleased with the new sofa." Grace poked the needle through the fabric one more time. "Maybe he'll actually smile or something. But I'm not going to count on it." Grace had about had it with Shan. Taking care of his brothers and sister was one thing. Putting up with his sullen ways was another. She had not signed on to raise Shan, after all.

"Oh Grace, try not to be too hard on him. You know, besides losing most of his family, Johnny says he's really shy around women."

"Well, for goodness sake, it's not like I'm trying to court him or anything! I just think it would be nice if he'd treat me like a human being."

"Yes," Dacia agreed. "That would be very nice, indeed. Maybe he just needs a little ... grace." Dacia laughed.

Grace moaned and rolled her eyes.

Chapter Twenty Three

B y mid-summer, life was beginning once again to take on a rhythm. The frantic recovery efforts were gradually giving way to a more normal, familiar pace of life. Grace hoped other things would be changing as well.

Day after day, Shan came home, nodded in her general direction, and went to wash up for supper. The first few days, Grace had waited around to see if he had any instructions for her or wanted to comment on anything, but he'd been silent as a tomb and just about as friendly. Finally she had settled into a pattern of just leaving when Shan got home. It made things easier.

She heard Shan come in the back door and quickly rinsed her hands in the sink. Supper was ready, and she was free to leave. Even though she felt quite sure that Shan hated her, she was determined to be kind to him. To give him time, as Dacia said.

Tonight she would stay. At least for a few minutes, just to see if Shan would tolerate her presence.

She had finished the new covers for the sofa, and Dacia had helped her put the whole thing together today. Grace was mighty proud of the good job she'd done. The sofa looked beautiful—at least she and Dacia thought so. She hoped Shan would be pleased.

She set the fresh bread out on the table and called the children. "Michael, Libby, Danny, come get washed up for supper!" The two younger children appeared instantly from the front room, and Grace went to the foot of the stairs to call Michael again.

She smiled tentatively at Shan. But he wasn't looking. "I got the sofa finished," she said.

Shan glanced up, though not directly at her. "Did you say some-thing?" he asked.

"The sofa. I reupholstered it."

Shan looked at it and nodded.

"Is it okay?"

"Yeah. It's okay."

Grace clamped her lips together as her face turned red and her heart sank. Without another word, she marched out the front door, slammed it behind her, and crossed the street to the Burkes' house.

*   *   *

Shan lifted Will Burke into the saddle on Pretty Girl's back. Will settled into place and grinned down at Shan. The saddle felt wonderful! It was not fancy, but it was Will's own, and it fit him perfectly. He had never had his own saddle before.

Pretty Girl heaved a sigh and snorted, tossing her big head, and Will laughed out loud. Shan laughed along with him.

"What do you think, Will? Can you ride her alone?" The boy looked mighty fine, Shan thought, sitting tall in the saddle. And the scar over his eye—although it had faded some—gave him quite an air of dis-tinction.

Will looked uncertain. He'd ridden double, of course, with Mar-tin. But that was before. Now Martin was gone, and Will couldn't even walk right by himself.

Shan mounted Jack, Johnny's gelding, and took the reins from Will. "Come on then. We'll go together for a little bit."

Will's smile lit up the whole street as he and Shan started south on Gale. It felt so good to be riding. To be up high and moving along smoothly without a crippled leg to slow him down—wonderful! Not only that, but he was sitting in one of the finest saddles in Heppner—maybe in all of Oregon. Shan had even used a fine chamois skin to cover the padded seat. The fittings were of nickel silver—not real silver, but to Will the saddle was perfect.

"Hey, what's this?" Les Matlock rode up on Gold Dust, the palo-mino mare he'd bought to replace the horse Dave McAtee had ridden to exhaustion only two months ago.

Will quickly let go of the pommel and tried to look sharp.

"Look at you sitting up there, just as big as you please! And that's a mighty fine saddle you've got there, young man!"

Will blushed. Yes, it was a mighty fine saddle, but he felt small in the presence of Les Matlock, who had become one of Heppner's heroes. He knew that both Matlock and Kelley were held in great esteem by everyone along the Willow Creek valley.

"Thank you," Will said, and grinned at Shan. "I think I can take the reins now."

Shan dismounted for a moment to loop the reins on either side of Pretty Girl's neck, then handed them to Will. "Off you go then. Do you want me to stay alongside you a little longer?"

Will glanced at Matlock, then nodded quickly. "Yes please."

*   *   *

By the beginning of September, the town was well on its way to recovery, and the people were slowly showing signs of healing. The dead had been buried. Damaged structures were on the mend and new buildings were going up. Gilliam and Bisbee's Farm Implement building was completed and Johnny was kept busier than ever replacing machinery for the farmers up and down the valley. Jim Yeager rebuilt his furniture store and funeral parlor. All three of the saddle and harness men who had been wiped out by the flood rebuilt and rejoined Mac and Shan in offering much needed services. The Gazette published an account of every penny that had been donated for relief and how the money was disbursed.

The most obvious effect of the flood, aside from the empty places where buildings should be, was the people's lack of interest in discussing it. The repeat discussions about nothing in general seemed to be a way to avoid all that had been left unsaid.

In spite of this, Grace had settled into her new life living with the Burkes, and spending her days caring for the Collins children. This prompted speculation and knowing smiles around town about a possible wedding in the future. Only Grace and Dacia knew the real story. And Shan.

Mac and Shan both looked up at the sound of the banjo. Scott Brown had come and tuned it this morning. It was one small thing that would make life more bearable. Mabel Dupont entered the shop, followed closely by Bruce Kelley.

"Thank you very much," Mabel said to Kelley who held the door for her as she entered. "And hello, Mr. Harmon," She ignored Shan and walked directly to Mac.

Kelley entered and placed his bridle on the end of the workbench near Shan. He held up a section of strap that was worn nearly through and raised his eyebrows in question. Shan nodded and said, "Okay. This afternoon by closing time."

Kelley, always a man of few words, nodded and left. But Mabel wasn't ready to leave yet. Mabel Dupont was Heppner's most available spinster. Well, no. Actually, she was just a lady in search of a husband. Not yet thirty, she was a widow—twice over. She'd buried her first husband only three months into their marriage after he died as a result of a farming accident. Exactly one year later, she had married again, but this marriage too, was destined to be short-lived. Henry Dupont had died less than two years after the wedding, from what the doctor called "a case of appendicitis gone bad." Mabel had spent several years in mourning this second husband. Not that she loved him more than the first, but rather to give herself time to figure out if she was jinxed in marriage.

Mabel's feelings and musings were the property of the entire town of Heppner. She was more than glad to share her heart with anyone who would listen. She lifted her chin and graced Mac with a refined smile.

Mac nodded politely and greeted her.

Mabel closed her large, blue eyes, tilted her head a bit, and nodded just slightly. She placed one delicate hand on the counter in front of her—a hand bearing no wedding ring—and gestured with the other as she spoke. "I've been thinking of coming to see you for quite some time, Mr. Harmon. I surely do admire your work!" She turned her head, touching her neatly coiffed hair just behind her ear. Then she smiled again. "Now I *do* realize your business is saddles and harnesses, but I have a leather chair seat that is just in *desperate* need of repair. And I'm wondering if you could *possibly* be talked into doing something of this nature."

Mac just looked at her and rubbed his hand over his face. Then taking a deep breath, he said, "I'm sure it's something we could do, but what about Noble's shop? Really, he's more interested in that sort of thing than I am."

"Oh yes, I know, but I really like *your* work. I'd *prefer* to have you do it ... if you're willing." She smiled sweetly.

Mac nodded. "Well, we have just about all we can handle right now. I'm sure you understand—the horses are needed for the continued work around town, and for the farms—you know, getting ready for harvest. Quite a few people lost all the tack they had. The horses are pretty much unusable 'til they have saddles and bridles and harnesses. Maybe in a few more months." He glanced over at Shan, who chose not to look at him.

Mabel's face clouded over and her lips took on a delicate pout. But Mac could do nothing about it. Turning back to Mabel, he said, "Why don't you come back in October or November. I think we'll be caught up by then."

She nodded and thanked him, but her disappointment was obvious.

Huh! What's so all-fired important about a chair seat? Mac wondered.

Chapter Twenty Four

A s the lightness of dawn began to creep into the Heppner skies, Dacia curled her body behind Johnny's, slipped one arm beneath her head and the other around her husband's mid-section, to hug him close.

She walked her fingers up his chest, his neck, over his chin.

"Mmm!" Johnny shook his head to escape the tickling.

"Hellooo? Anybody home?" Dacia teased.

"Hm-mm!" Johnny shook his head.

"Johnny, guess what?" Dacia flipped her finger back and forth on the tip of his nose. "Jo-o-ohn-ny."

He rolled to his back, grabbed her finger and kissed it. "Mmm."

"All right, if you won't talk to me, then I won't tell you." She turned to her other side and scrunched far away from him, to her own side of the bed.

Johnny lunged up after her, rolled her to her back and anchored her wrists to the mattress. "Uncle!" he said, his eyes laughing. "Say uncle!"

She laughed and tried to squirm away, but he held her tight. "Uncle—come on. Say it!"

"Uncle!" she finally gasped through her laughter, and he let her go.

"Just for that, I'm not going to tell you anything," she said.

"Okay. I'll go back to sleep." Johnny turned to his side and produced a good imitation of a snore.

"Johnny! You're impossible! Wake up!"

"Mm-hm," Johnny muttered.

"Don't you want to hear?"

"Mm-hm." Johnny nodded.

"Then you have to wake up."

"Mmm ..." Johnny opened one eye and turned to look at his wife. She smiled into his rumpled face. "You're going to be a father again."

"I'm going to ..." Johnny's face broke into a huge, if somewhat sleepy smile. He smoothed back Dacia's beautiful, sleep-mussed hair and kissed her on her forehead, her cheeks, her lips. "Mm!" he said yet again.

She laughed at him. "Your vocabulary is pretty limited first thing in the morning. You know that?"

"Mm-hm." Johnny nodded and smoothed her hair again, running his fingers through it. "That's not a problem, is it?"

"Hm-mm," she responded and they both began laughing.

"When?" Johnny asked as he pried his body from the bed and reached for his shirt.

"Mmmm," Dacia responded, shrugging.

"Hey, stop that! I'm awake now. Talk to me!"

"Mm-hm."

"*When?*" Johnny repeated.

"I'm not sure. Things have been pretty ... confusing lately." She sobered. "You know. Maybe March?

"Maybe March. That'll work. I'll write it on the calendar."

Dacia giggled. "We don't even have a 1904 calendar yet."

"I'll write it on the wall then, behind the 1903 calendar. And where's my breakfast, Woman? I hope you're not going to lie around and fan yourself just because you're carrying a baby! Outa bed! You got work to do!"

"Hm-mm." Dacia shook her head in an emphatic *NO!* "Going to lie here all day and pamper myself!"

"Oh, Dacia!" Johnny dropped back onto the bed, put his arm around her, and drew her close. "I sure do love you! You know that? A baby—how about that! A new baby!"

*　　*　　*

September 12, 1903
Dear Mr. Harmon,

I just happened to think of a family who moved here to Spokane only a couple of months ago. They have two children near the ages of the children you told me about when you visited early in July. The girl is five, I believe, and the boy is about two or three. It's difficult to tell if the children resemble those in the picture you left me, as the picture is an old one. Perhaps these are not the children you are seeking, but I thought it would be good to at least mention them to you. The little girl's hair is light red, like you described. The family appears to be a good one, but, as I'm sure you well know, appearances can be deceiving.

Please inform me if you plan to travel this way, and I can arrange a meeting between yourself and the family I have mentioned.

Sincerely,
John F. Reddy
Chief of Police
Spokane, Washington

*   *   *

Mac laid coins on the counter to pay for the telegram he had just sent.

DOMESTIC SERVICE		WESTERN UNION		INTERNATIONAL SERVICE

WESTERN UNION
W. P. MARSHALL, CHAIRMAN OF THE BOARD   **TELEGRAM**   R. W. McFALL, PRESIDENT

NO. WDS.-CL. OF SVC.	PD OR COLL	CASH NO.	CHARGE TO THE ACCOUNT OF	TIME FILED
	Pd			

To_ John Reddy, Chief of Police, Spokane   Sept. 14, 19 03

Destination Spokane

Will arrive 10:40 train tomorrow morning.

MacKennon Harmon

He gathered up his coat and small carpet bag and walked toward the passenger car of the waiting train.

*   *   *

Mac stood at the door, waiting for the train to stop. He looked around the platform as the train pulled slowly into the station, hoping the police chief would be there to meet him, but he couldn't spot the man. It appeared Mac was on his own.

His foot hit the ground almost the same moment the doors swung open. He ignored the porter and strode through the door of the station. Still not seeing the man he sought, he continued out the front door and straight to the nearest waiting taxi buggy. He flung his carpet bag inside and settled himself onto the seat in one smooth motion.

"Police station," he said to the driver and folded his arms across his chest. He closed his eyes and tried to relax. He didn't try very hard. He knew it was hopeless. As the rig slowed and stopped at the station, Mac handed the driver enough money for his fare plus a generous tip and waved away the man's attempt to give him change. He was inside the station almost before the driver had time to blink.

Mac strode across the lobby to the Police Chief's office. The door was open. Mac walked in, shook Reddy's hand and took a seat. "Well?" he asked.

"Well, now, I don't want you to get your hopes up, Mr. Harmon." The man spoke slowly, carefully. "I could be completely wrong on this, you know. I just thought it was worth a look ..."

"I know," Mac interrupted. "I understand. When can we see the children?"

Reddy picked up the telephone on his desk and spoke to the operator. Mac tapped a hand on his right knee as he waited for the connection to go through.

"Mrs. Jamison? This is Police Chief John Reddy calling from the station. Maybe you remember, we met a few days ago at the county fair." Silence. Then, "That's right, we were talking about our favorite breeds of chickens." Silence again. Then Reddy laughed a bit. "Well, you might be right, after all. I'm not convinced yet, though. Say, if you and your husband are going to be home this evening, I thought I'd drop by for a couple of minutes. I have a friend here who would like to meet your family." He nodded to Mac. "Fine. That'll work just fine. The children will be there too?" He nodded again. "Okay. We'll see you in a little bit, then."

Mac wanted to get out and push the horse pulling the buggy. But Reddy was taking his time, pointing out various landmarks and telling stories of Spokane's early days.

Finally, they arrived at a neat bungalow with a picket fence. As the men stepped through the front gate, two children came running around the side of the house into the front yard. A girl with strawberry blond hair, a younger boy—dark blond curls bouncing as he chased his sister.

Mac's heart sank. Lovely children, but not his. Not Lilyann and Gilbert. True, they were about the right size, had the right color hair. But that was all. It was over. The hope and excitement of the past 24 hours came crashing down on Mac, dumping back on him all the despair, loss, and emptiness that had been his constant companions since that awful day three months ago.

Chapter Twenty Five

S chools in Morrow County opened this week to fewer students than last year. While the enrollment in most of the county remained the same or a bit higher, Heppner's student count was down by nearly a quarter. Excepting the beginners, only 3 new students entered the school this year, while non-returning students numbered forty-seven.
Heppner Gazette, September 17, 1903

* * *

Will Burke limped into the third grade classroom with his lunch pail, which he put on the floor by the coat hooks. The first day of school was usually an exciting day, but today, it didn't feel right. Charlie Harmon wasn't here. Aiden Collins wasn't here. Neither was Bobby Tomlin. The class room seemed almost empty.

He looked around. A bunch of the girls were missing too. Emma Krug—Will used to pull Emma's long blond braids. They were really long—almost long enough for her to sit on. But Emma wasn't here. He knew why. She had died in the flood too.

So many people! All dead.

Will took a seat on the boys' side near the back of the room and balanced his chin on his hands. He didn't feel like talking to the other boys. He didn't feel like running in the play yard, even though Michael Collins and some of the others had called to him on his way in.

* * *

When school had been in session for almost a month Will limped into the house after school on a Monday afternoon and dropped his books on the sofa. He plopped down beside them with a sigh.

Dacia knew it was going to be hard. Everyone in town knew it was going to be hard. With just one class room for each grade, it would be quite obvious who was missing.

Dacia tried to put herself in Will's place. Eight years old. Third grade. How must it feel to walk into class, only to find that a quarter of his friends were missing? Not just missing—dead! Even her adult mind struggled to get around such a thought.

She sat by Will on the sofa. "So how was school today?" she asked, running her fingers through his hair.

"Okay I guess."

"That's all? Just, 'okay I guess?'"

Will said nothing.

"Would you like a something to eat?"

"Mm-hm."

Dacia gave Will's shoulder a squeeze. "There are apples in the kitchen."

"How's Pretty Girl doing?" she asked, as Will reentered the front room with an apple.

"Okay."

Dacia tilted her head and looked at Will critically. If only she could figure out how to help him!

A knock sounded at the door and she opened it to see Eva Joseph, Will's teacher.

"Hello Mrs. Burke. I wonder if you have a moment? I'd like to visit with you about Will."

Dacia looked over at her shoulder at the child in question. He didn't seem to be worried about his teacher making a house call.

"Certainly, Come in!" Dacia said. "Will just got home a couple of minutes ago, himself. Would you like to visit in the kitchen? Or here in the front room?"

"Hello, Will. Anywhere will be fine, Mrs. Burke." Miss Joseph smiled. "And it would be good to have Will join us."

"Let me just get you a cup of tea and we'll stay here in the front room then." Dacia pointed to the best chair and went to the kitchen for tea.

"Would you like sugar?" she called through the kitchen door.

"Yes, please! That sounds wonderful!"

Miss Joseph turned to Will. "You must have been pretty fast to beat me here. I came as soon as school was out."

"I rode Pretty Girl," he said.

"Is Pretty Girl your horse?"

"No. Shan's. But Shan lets me ride her. Because I can't walk very well."

"That's really nice of him. Is that Shan Collins you're talking about? I've met him, but I don't know him well."

Little wonder, Dacia thought as she reentered the room with two cups of tea. *There's probably not a single female between the ages of twelve and ninety who knows Shan Collins well.*

"Are things settling into a routine at school?" Dacia asked.

"Most things. It always takes a while at the beginning of the year. But this year is ...." She shrugged, knowing Dacia would understand. This year she was not only dealing with a room full of youngsters who needed teaching and encouraging. These children were traumatized. They had lived through an incredible experience and were struggling now in ways no one had even considered before. A mere school teacher could never make up to them what had been lost. All she could hope to do was provide a stable environment in which the children could work through their feelings—and hopefully learn the third grade material as well.

Miss Joseph took a sip of tea. "Mm—good. Thank you. This is my fourth year teaching, so in some ways I feel like I'm doing okay. But in other ways ... I'm not so sure."

"That's a feeling I can recognize," Dacia said laughing.

"Well, one of the things I'm concerned about right now is Will." Will looked up at the mention of his name. He had just taken a huge bite of the apple, so it was hard to look at all dignified—which he assumed was how he should look when the teacher came to call and mentioned his name.

"Will hasn't been doing his work. I know he's an intelligent boy—I looked at his marks from last year. But he seems not to be interested. Now, please don't misunderstand. I certainly did not come to complain about him! He has been well behaved—*very* well behaved! He is courteous, thoughtful—a fine young man in most every way. It's just that he doesn't do his work. I wanted to let you know now, rather than waiting, because I don't want him to fall behind the class."

Dacia nodded. "Will?" She looked at him. "Is this true, what Miss Joseph is saying?"

Will nodded.

"Can you explain why you aren't doing your work?"

Will shrugged, swallowed most of the huge bite of apple in his mouth, and shoved the remainder into one cheek. "I dunno."

Dacia leaned forward, elbows on her knees and her hands together. She turned her head to look at Will. "Do you understand why Miss Joseph is concerned about that?"

Will nodded, swallowed the last of the apple, and replied. "She doesn't want me to fall behind."

"That's right. What would happen if you fall behind?"

Will rubbed at the scar on his forehead and thought for a moment. "Um ... maybe I would have to do third grade again next year?"

"Well, I guess I hadn't even thought that far ahead yet," Dacia said. "I was thinking how it would be harder and harder for you to catch up. If you start doing your work now, it would be kind of hard. But if you wait and start doing your work in November, or December, or January it would be even harder! And yes. If you keep it up, you would have to do third grade again next year."

Will sighed.

Dacia looked at him through narrowed eyes and nodded slightly. "Miss Joseph, thank you so much for taking the time to come and let me know what's happening! I don't know the answer to this problem. But you can be sure Mr. Burke and I will talk with Will about it. Maybe the three of us together can figure out what's going on."

*   *   *

That evening, Will set the table for supper. It used to be Josie's job. Now it was his. Grace came in from the Collins' house, just as the meal started.

Sure enough, after supper, Mama and Papa wanted to talk with Will about school. But he didn't really have any answers for them. He'd never been an A student. He'd received mostly C's with an occasional B thrown in. They said his grades were fine—they weren't asking him to be best in the class. They weren't asking him to become something he never was before. But he really should do his school work.

No, he didn't want to repeat third grade next year, but he just had bigger things on his mind right now. He just couldn't manage to think about school work.

*   *   *

Johnny put his arm over Dacia's shoulder as they sat on the porch swing. The Indian summer day had been warm, and the evening air was just about perfect.

"Okay," Johnny said with a huge sigh. "My day is over, my tummy's full, I am sitting beside the most beautiful woman in the entire world ..." he stopped to kiss Dacia's hair, "and I'm finally ready to think. Except it's hard to think of anything except you, Dacia. I love you. Have I mentioned that recently?" He bent to scratch her cheek with his stubbly whiskers.

"Stop, Johnny!" She giggled as he stuck his nose down into her neck. "This is serious. We have to talk."

"I know." He patted the place where the new baby was growing inside Dacia's body. "Feels like your tummy's full too."

Dacia smiled and put her hand over her husband's.

"But we need to talk about Will. What are we going to do about him?"

"Maybe we won't have to do anything about him. Maybe just having Miss Joseph come to the house and tattle on him will be enough to get him moving. After all, he's been through a lot."

"Yes," Dacia agreed. "But we can't just let him flunk third grade!"

"Why can't we? What would be so bad about flunking third grade?"

"Johnny! What are you saying? You know as well as I do, we just can't let that happen!"

"Seriously, Dacia, why not? Is it a moral issue? Is there some unfailing eternal law that says he has to pass third grade this year?"

"Well ...."

"Well ... so, think about it. What if he fails this year? Couldn't he do third grade again next year?"

"No, Johnny!"

"Yes, he could, couldn't he? Let's say he keeps on not doing his work. Maybe he's so overwhelmed he doesn't care about the capital of Alabama or how to do long division. Maybe his brain isn't ready to tackle those things yet."

Dacia stood up from the porch swing and glared at Johnny, tears in her eyes. "Johnny Burke, I thought you cared about your children! *What* are you saying? That it doesn't matter what happens? That it doesn't matter if Will is left back this year? Don't you want him to grow up to be successful? Don't you ..." Dacia stopped, the tears finally spilling from her eyes and down her cheeks. She turned away from Johnny and crossed her arms over her chest.

Johnny rose and took her shoulders in his hands. He kissed the back of her head, then turned her around to engulf her in his strong arms. "It's okay," he said softly into her ear. "Shhh, Dacia. It's okay." "Oh Johnny, I don't know what's happening to me!" she said. "Everything is just so hard!"

Johnny held the back of Dacia's head in his big hand and kissed her tenderly, rocking gently back and forth.

"It was so much easier that first week." Dacia wiped tears from her cheeks and hiccupped. "We were all so numb. We just did what had to be done. But now ...." Her voice trailed off. "The children—we don't know how to help them. Michael is becoming really naughty, and Grace doesn't know what to do with him. Will can't walk and doesn't do his school work. Poor little Libby still cries all the time for her ma. Every child in town, Johnny."

"I know, Dacia. I know." Johnny released her and held her shoulders in his hands. "I don't know how to fix it. It just ... *is*. But time will make a difference, Dacia. Let's give it time. Will needs for us to just love him and let him work through this in his own way. We need that too."

Dacia nodded and let herself be drawn once more against Johnny's chest and into his heart. He held her as she sobbed out the ache of the past four months.

Chapter Twenty Six

The day before Thanksgiving, Shan sat on the fence watching Will Burke as he finished caring for Pretty Girl. "How's school going?" he asked the boy.

"Okay, I guess."

"You guess?"

Will shrugged.

"You don't like school?"

"I like it okay."

"What then? Too hard for you?" Shan hadn't liked school. He didn't care to learn arithmetic and poetry. He would rather work with his hands. And he was good at it. He'd gone through 8th grade, and that was more than enough, as far as he was concerned. But Will wasn't anywhere near eighth grade. "You need to go to school—at least for a few more years. You don't want to be a dummy when you grow up."

"Maybe. I don't care. I'm no good at anything." Will tossed hay down from the loft and slithered back down the ladder. He limped over to the pump. As he worked the handle, filling the trough, he muttered, "and besides it's all my fault about ..."

Shan waited in silence, watching Will as he pumped.

"It's all your fault about what?"

"Oh nothing. It was just a dumb ol' magnifying glass." This was spoken under his breath, but Shan heard it.

Will finished pumping and said, "Guess I'll be going." He limped away in the direction of home.

Shan looked after him, first in confusion, then with a growing suspicion. Will felt guilty about something. And what was that bit about a magnifying glass? He would talk to Johnny about it.

*   *   *

The following week, one day after school, Will sat astride Pretty Girl, while his brother, Walter, and Michael Collins rested on the bank of Willow Creek. This was Walter's first year in school, Michael's second, Will's third. The boys had stopped on the way home from school and were tossing pebbles into the stream. It was flowing fairly high for September—probably a foot or more deep. The farmers were happy with the amount of rain so far this year. It had been pretty sparse before the flood, but since then, the weather seemed to have settled into a more normal routine.

"Is this where you were when the flood happened?" Michael asked Will.

"No."

"Where were you?"

"I don't know."

"You don't know? How come you don't know?"

"See that little branch down there?" Walter interrupted. "I'm going to hit it. Watch." He skipped one of the flat rocks he had picked up, and it sailed right over the branch on the second bounce.

"Ha, ha. You missed. Here, let me try." Michael jumped to his feet and snatched one of Walter's rocks from his hand.

"Huh uh! It was right on." Walter grabbed to retrieve his rock, but Michael held it tight.

"You didn't hit it."

"I skipped right over it. That counts."

"Don't neither. Watch this." Michael tried, but his rock didn't skip even once. It hit the water and sank directly to the bottom.

"Shoulda had a better rock," he complained. He turned back to look up at Will. "So where were you in the flood?"

"He said he don't know," Walter said to Michael. "So he don't know."

"Aw, I bet he does know. It was right here, wasn't it, Will?"

"I really *don't* know 'cause everything's different now. The houses and everything. And anyway, I don't want to talk about it." He turned Pretty Girl's head toward home and said, "Come on! Last one home's a nanny goat!" He took off without even looking back.

"Hey, wait!" Michael yelled at Will's retreating back. "No fair! You got a head start!" Pretty Girl was walking fast—the best she could do.

When Michael saw that Will had no intention of waiting, he raced after him. He soon caught up and passed Will, with Walter tagging along behind. Leaving the Burke boys behind, he slammed through the gate of the Collins's new picket fence, took the new front steps in one leap, and barreled through the front door—right into Grace. She put a foot back to catch herself, but fell anyway, the plate of cinnamon rolls in her hands smashing first onto her face and the front of her dress, then to the floor, where the plate broke and scattered glass shards in every direction.

Michael sat on the floor gazing stupidly at Grace, his eyes huge, his mouth closed.

Danny toddled in from the kitchen, and Libby bumped down the stairs to look with horror on the mess all over the front room.

Grace sat up and wiped at a patch of frosting on her left cheek. She smeared it on her skirt and sat gazing at Michael, through slits where her eyes should have been.

"Libby and Danny, I want you to go upstairs and play, both of you please. Michael, I am going across the street to change my clothes." She looked around her and saw that the rolls and shards of glass had flown clear across the room. "While I am gone—and it won't take me very long—" she glared at him, "you will collect all the pieces of glass. Use the broom and dustpan. Do. Not. Cut yourself. Put the glass into the mop bucket. After you pick up the ruined cinnamon rolls you'll need to get a rag. Get it wet and begin cleaning up all the sticky places. *All.* It will be a hard job and you may not be done in time to have any supper tonight."

She rose and walked regally out the door.

Little Danny tip-toed to the stairs and joined Libby in silently climbing them.

And Michael burst out laughing.

*   *   *

Grace held Libby by one hand and Danny by the other. Michael walked along beside them. Michael had not actually apologized for the cinnamon roll incident—in fact there were a number of things he had not apologized for. But his demeanor had been somewhat improved in the past two weeks. Or, if not improved, at least less outwardly disagreeable.

Grace had decided taking the children for a treat might help Michael get his feet under him again. He just seemed so scattered—in his thinking, in his feelings, in his behavior—even in his whereabouts.

There was just no telling where he would turn up or what he would be into next. Stability. That's what the boy needed.

Maybe a bowl of ice cream at the Pastime would be a good thing. Maybe Michael would feel appreciative and *maybe* he would even begin to calm down.

It was too cold for ice cream to Grace's way of thinking, but offered their choice between candy and ice cream, all three children had opted for ice cream—in November, no less.

As they entered the Pastime, Grace noted Esmerelda and two of the other girls from the *Chateau de Joie* at a table drinking coffee and visiting. She shot Esmerelda a quick smile. Esmerelda smiled back, but didn't speak. She turned back to her friends. She had made it clear that if Grace was planning on living a life outside of the bordello, the two could not be friends in public. "It would destroy you," she had said. "You don't want to be known as a friend of prostitutes!" In spite of the wisdom of this, Grace felt bad about it.

She paid for the children's ice cream and led them to a small table to eat it. With the soft sound of a billiards game going on in the next room, she could easily hear the conversation of the only other visitors to the ice cream shop.

"I'll be going over to Redmond next month," Esmerelda said to the room in general. And she said it louder than Grace thought was necessary. Redmond? What would she do in Redmond? *Oh,* Grace thought. *The same thing she does here.*

"Oh, I'll probably be back in a year or so. You know how it is in this business." Again Esmerelda spoke louder than was necessary. *She wants me to know,* Grace realized. *She's saying good bye.*

As the three got up to leave, Grace caught Esmerelda's eye and mouthed the words, *good bye.* She felt empty.

*   *   *

Shan was late getting home. The late November evening was chilly, and near darkness made the whole neighborhood look different. Lights were lit in the houses, and Shan could see families as they finished up their supper, washed dishes, or relaxed together. Grace might be upset with him for being late, but she seemed to be upset with him all the time anyway, so what difference did it make? Last night when he came in, she'd left without saying a word. *Why won't she talk to me? She must really hate me.* Sometimes she spoke to him, but only to tell him something he needed to know about the supper in the warming oven or something that had happened during the day. *I wish ... she's so beautiful! I wish she'd just look at me. I wish I was brave enough to look at* her! In a way, he didn't want to go home at all.

But, he decided, the children *did* need him. He would do what needed to be done for their sake and ignore Grace. And ignore his feelings.

Michael came tearing out of the house and vaulted over the picket fence as Shan came into view. "Hey Shan! You're late!"

"How was school today?" Shan asked him.

Michael quieted as he said, "Okay."

"Okay. That's all?"

"Pretty much. Nothing bad happened." Michael grinned hopefully at Shan.

"Well, that's good, anyway." Shan opened the gate and pulled a small round of leather from his pocket. It was tooled with an intricate, interlocking knot design with leather lacing around the edge. He held it out to Michael.

"What is it?" Michael asked.

"It's to put under hot stuff so the table won't get burned."

"We don't need it. We have those cloth things that Ma made."

"I want to save those. I don't want them to wear out." He hesitated, thinking of Ma. "It's something we can remember her by. Maybe hang them up on the wall or something so we can still see them."

Michael didn't respond, and Shan sensed his sadness—shared it.

The door swung open and Libby bounced out onto the porch, reaching her arms up to Shan. "Pick me up, Shan! I missed you! And Grace made baked apples—yum, yum, yum!"

Shan scooped his little sister into his arms and knelt to hug Danny as well.

Grace swept by Shan and the children on her way out. "Hi Shan. Supper's on the stove." And she was gone.

Shan felt empty. He set Libby down and watched Grace cross the street. Libby and Danny still clung to his legs begging to be picked up, but he had completely forgotten them. The door closed behind Grace as she entered the Burke home. Shan stood looking after her and swallowed hard. Finally he turned to get supper on the table for his family.

*   *   *

As November shivered its way toward December, Will Burke's school performance had not improved a bit. Shan, remembering Will's odd comments from the week before, left the shop one day at dinner time and took his noon meal over to The Gilliam and Bisbee Farm and Machine Shop. Johnny was more than happy to see him. He had developed a sincere admiration for this young man. A talented artist, a hard worker, a great sense of humor, and mighty good-looking, besides. He was probably the best catch in Heppner for some young lady—if only he would quit turning red at the mere mention of one!

"How are things goin'?" Johnny asked.

"Some good, some not so good," Shan replied. "But mostly good. You?"

Johnny nodded and swept his hand to encompass the shop filled with new machinery. "Getting settled back into normal I guess. And the new building is great."

"How's Will doing?"

Johnny shook his head. "I don't know, and that's the truth. I just don't know."

Shan shared Will's odd comments with his father. Both men were puzzled, but they agreed on one thing. Will needed help of some kind.

That night, Johnny sat on the edge of Will's bed. Walter was in the other bed snoring softly. Will was pretending to be asleep, but Johnny knew better.

"Will?" Johnny whispered.

"Mmmmm."

Johnny pushed Will over and lay on his back beside him. "Will, I've been thinking."

Silence. Johnny reached over and tickled Will in the ribs, whispering, *shhh!* in his ear at the same time. The boy laughed quietly as Johnny had known he would. Will had always been ticklish, and he was not very good at feigning sleep.

Johnny laughed along with his son. "Hey Will." He spoke softly. "I need your help with something. I need to ask you a question."

"Why? Am I in trouble?"

"Nope. At least I don't think so ..."

"Then I wanna sleep."

"Later. Right now, we need to talk."

Will sighed and opened his eyes. "Okay. I'm awake."

Johnny smiled into the darkness. "Well," he began, "I need your help in solving a mystery."

"What kind of mystery?" Will propped his head up on one arm.

"A missing item. You remember that little magnifying glass of Mama's?"

Silence.

"Well, ever since the flood, Mama hasn't been able to find it. The Harmons lost everything—even their house. And Shan's family lost lots of things, too. But the flood hardly touched our house. Our yard, yes. But not the house. It didn't get inside the house except a couple of inches."

Johnny heard a quiet sniffle. "So the flood didn't take the magnifying glass ..."

The tiny sniffle became a cry, then full-blown sobbing.

"Hey, hey, hey there." Johnny turned on his side and wrapped an arm around Will. "What's the matter there, Will? I'm just asking if you might have some idea where it went to."

"It's all my fault!" Will sobbed. "The fire and the storm and the flood and all those people died and I killed them because I stole the glass and I'm so, *so* sorry, but God can never forgive me, and oh Papa, I'm going to go to Hell! What can I do!"

Johnny sat up and scooped Will onto his lap, hugging him tightly. "Whoa there, Will. What's all this about? What are you even talking about?"

Will tried to answer, but the words were nothing but gasps and moans coming from his tortured mouth. Johnny shushed him and rocked him, held him close. He waited, his lips pressed against Will's hair. And he prayed. *Oh God, what do I do now?*

Johnny cradled Will in his arms until the sobs gradually subsided. Eventually, Will hiccupped and drifted into a troubled sleep, and Johnny laid him back in his bed and rose quietly to go downstairs. Dacia was already asleep. They would have to wait until morning to get to the bottom of it.

*   *   *

In the morning, Johnny called Frank Gilliam to say he'd be late for work. He had something more pressing to take care of.

Dacia, of course, was surprised. Johnny asked her to please wait until the children were fed and busy for the day to ask questions. When breakfast was cleared, she tried to shove Will out the door for school, but Johnny put his hand on her shoulder.

"I think school can wait this morning," he said. "Will has something he needs to take care of first. He can be a little late this once."

Dacia looked confused, but she nodded her head and turned to send Walter off by himself to pick up Michael for school. She sent Sarah across the street to play with the Collins children, watched her cross and waved to Grace before joining Johnny and Will at the kitchen table.

"Pappy?" Johnny called to his grandfather in the front room. "Why don't you join us in the kitchen for a little bit?"

Pappy slowly made his way to the kitchen, leaning on the stick he'd used ever since his shillelagh had gone missing in the flood.

Dacia poured him a glass of apple juice and set it on the table at his place. She took a drink of her coffee and looked from Will to Johnny and back at Will again. Maybe Will was ready to make a commitment to his school work. She certainly hoped so. "Well, I'm ready," she said. "Is anybody going to tell me what all this is about?"

"I'll tell you," said Will. He spoke quickly, almost frantically. "I did something really bad. I took your magnifying glass." He ran his thumbnail along the crack where the table opened to add a leaf. "Borrowed it really," he said, looking up at Dacia. "'Cause I was going to put it back. Martin told me I shouldn't do it, and I knew that too. I knew I shouldn't." Will paused and looked down at the table again, as the words refused to come. Dacia looked up at Johnny, but said nothing.

Will swallowed and continued. "But Charlie said it wasn't really stealing, if I was going to put it back. So, anyway, I took it. And we went to the creek and used it to make fire. We burned our initials in the dry grass along the creek. And then the grass caught fire, and ..."

Will's voice caught. He gulped, but continued. "And then we couldn't put the fire out, and God had to send the rain." Here he broke down completely.

Dacia moved to the chair next to Will and pulled him into her lap. She looked over his head at Johnny. How on earth was she supposed to handle this?

She held Will, rocking him, not unlike the way she'd swaddled and held him as a tiny infant when he cried. She wrapped her arms tightly around his small body, tortured with sobs, and rocked him back and forth.

Dacia closed her eyes as she began to understand the depth of Will's anguish. The child held himself responsible for all the deaths resulting from the flood! All of them.

"Shhh," she crooned into his hair. "There, there, Will. Shhh. It wasn't your fault!"

"Well, God sent the rain to put out the fire, and all ... all those people ..." His voice trailed off as once again Will took the sin of the whole world on his shoulders.

"No Laddie! No!" Pappy spoke sharply. Sharply enough that Will stopped his crying and inhaled a shaky breath.

Pappy spoke more gently now. "Tell me now, do ya think ya have the power to make God kill people? You don't, ya know. Even if you were a grown man. Nobody has power like that! *Nobody!*"

Will looked up through his tears in wonder.

"Truly, Lad!" Pappy said. "You couldn't get God to kill someone, even if you tried!"

"But ..." Will hesitated. "If he didn't send the flood on account of me, why *did* he send it?"

"He didn't. Not every question has an answer, lad. The flood happened. That's all. It just happened. Bad things happen all the time. In Ireland, in Heppner. And sometimes bad things happen to good people. That's just the way it is. The flood was *not* your fault! It was *not* Charlie's or Martin's fault! It was nobody's fault! We live in a broken world, Lad. And sometimes, things just happen."

Dacia glanced at Johnny. Such wisdom! Where was this coming from? Was this the same confused old man she knew yesterday? Last week? *This* Pappy was a force to be reckoned with!

Will sat thinking for a moment. "But the rain put out the fire."

Pappy nodded.

"And the rain caused the flood, and the flood killed people."

The old man nodded again. "Aye, and I'm really sad about that. Martin and Josie—I miss 'em. And Charlie and the others. But it's *not* your fault. And it's *not* God's fault. It just happened. Believe me, Will. Believe me."

Will looked over at Papa. Johnny nodded his head. "Pappy's right, Will. It couldn't possibly be your fault, because God doesn't let *you* decide what happens in the world. Only in your own life."

Pappy set his glass of juice loudly back on the table and glared at Will with his piercing, blue eyes. The old man's face cracked into a grin and he raised his wonderful eyebrows at Will.

Somehow, because Pappy said it, that made it right.

Will wiped at his nose and gave Pappy a hint of a smile—his first all morning.

"And don't ya be takin' things that don't belong to ya anymore, now. Ya hear?" Pappy reached over a bony finger and thumped Will on the head.

Will nodded, and turned back to Dacia. "I'm really, truly sorry, Mama. But I feel a *lot* better now that I told you."

"It's always a lot better to tell the truth and get it over with, Will. Always. And I forgive you." Dacia gave him one last squeeze and set him on the floor.

"So, what do you think, young man? Is it time for me to go to work and you to go to school?" Johnny asked.

Will smiled, wiped at his nose one last time, and nodded. "I'm ready." He took Johnny's hand and the two of them headed for the front door.

Pappy continued sitting at the kitchen table. Dacia offered to help him back to his easy chair, but he declined. "That Will," he said. "That Will is a fine boy altogether now, he is." And having made this pronouncement, he nodded, rose, and walked slowly back to the front room.

Dacia silently thanked God once again for Johnny's grandfather. Even though his mind wandered from time to time, he certainly did have a way with children!

Chapter Twenty Seven

Christmas time came to Oregon City. The Snowburg sisters' boarding house was more quiet than usual. Boarders from four of the six rooms went to visit family out of town, leaving only old Mr. Hollaman and the Kleins. Meals were small; activity was muted. Even Elisabeth and Etta slowed down. Cooking and cleaning took very little time with so few people in the house.

Elisabeth had asked Klein about his Christmas plans, but he'd seemed almost offended that she brought it up. No, he had no special plans to speak of. He hoped he would get the day off was about all he had to say.

"Etta, I've been thinking," Elisabeth said as she put away the last of the supper dishes.

"Hmmm ..." Etta gave her sister a suspicious look. "That could be dangerous. What do you have up your sleeve now?"

"It's the children. Mr. Klein says they're staying here for Christmas. When I asked him about it, he acted like he didn't even know Christmas was coming, or that he should do something special for the children. I'm sure he hasn't planned anything for them." She poured two cups of coffee and sat at the kitchen table with her sister.

"He hasn't done *anything* for them, *ever!* I agree, he's not going to treat them special on Christmas."

"So let's *us* do something!"

Etta looked up at her sister. "What? Do what?"

"Sew? They both need new clothes."

"We already made them each a new set of clothes."

"But if they had one more, we could throw away those old rags they came in."

"Elisabeth, this is Wednesday evening. Christmas is on Friday! How much sewing can we get done in only one day?"

"A lot! We can take turns with the machine. I can be cutting while you sew, then I'll sew and you can hem by hand. Or the other way around. I don't care. I'll go shopping first thing in the morning. I'll get goods for a dress, a pair of trousers and a shirt. And I'll buy some new under things. We can do it, Etta! It will take no time at all!"

"Yellow," Etta said finally. "That sweet little girl would look like a beam of sunshine in yellow. She is so beautiful with her hair freshly washed—shiny looking. Somehow it kind of makes up for the smile that's missing."

"Maybe a pinafore too." Elisabeth's eyes shone.

Etta rose and went to the hall closet. She pulled out the patterns they had used in August. One day. They could do a lot in only one day!

*　　*　　*

Three weeks had passed since Will's confession. Dacia finished changing the beds and threw the last rolled bundle of sheets down the stairs. She gathered up a few remaining dirty clothes and sat on the top step for a moment to gather strength before finishing her work.

It felt good to sit. Being in the family way had always agreed with Dacia. But she was tired, all the same. It wouldn't hurt to rest for just a minute before resuming her morning chores. She turned sideways on the top step and leaned against the wall, closing her eyes. She opened them again when she heard a sound in the front room below her. Will. He had come in from the kitchen and now stood completely still near the kitchen door. Dacia watched through the banister with curiosity.

Will took a deliberate step with his right foot. Then, slowly, carefully with his left. Right, left. One foot at a time he walked perfectly, half way across the front room.

Dacia put a hand to her mouth and leaned forward to see better.

Then Will faltered. He took a step dragging his left leg, as he'd been doing ever since the flood. He stopped himself immediately, backed up, and stepped correctly, sharing his weight evenly between his two legs. "I can do it," he muttered softly to himself. "I *can*."

Dacia leaned forward farther, gazing between the spindles, but said nothing.

Will continued, right foot, left foot. "God is not punishing me," he said to himself softly. "He knows it's not my fault. The flood just happened. Sometimes things just happen." He spoke softly, but Dacia could hear. He reached the bottom of the stairs.

Dacia's face broke into a beautiful smile. "Will!" she said. "I'm so proud of you! Look what you can do!" Her voice shook as she felt tears choking her.

He looked up toward his mother with a huge grin. "Did you see me, Mama? I can walk right!"

Dacia ran down the stairs, shoving the loose sheets out of the way with her foot and reached out to hug Will. "Yes, I saw you! That was wonderful! Papa is going to be so happy too!"

"Me too!" Will said. "Me too! I can walk again!

*   *   *

On this first day of the new year, 1904, the dining room of the Snowburgs boarding house was quiet. Dinner was over, and supper was still several hours away. Crisp winter sunshine pierced the boarding house window. At the table sat the girl in her new yellow calico dress. Her upper arms were laid on the table with her hands on top of her head. Her eyes seemed to gaze out the window, although she showed no response at all as two riders tore by at a full gallop. On the table before her lay a pencil and a ragged piece of paper. She'd found the pencil yesterday on the floor under the far back corner of the bed—along with some rolls of dust and a large brown sock with a hole in it. The paper had been left on the table after dinner, and one side of it was blank. Removing her hands from her head, the girl picked up the pencil and sat gazing at the paper, pencil clutched tightly in her left hand.

She leaned her head on her free hand and, beginning at the top left of the paper, she made a mark—first a squiggle, then a straight line. Next she made a circle. Then, scratching out the marks, she started again and formed a letter—D. "D," she whispered. "Dog." She sat and looked at the letter, chewing on the end of the pencil, then added an "O" and a very large "G."

Elizabeth Snowburg walked into the room carrying clean plates to put away in the sideboard and was surprised to see the child at the table. Elizabeth glanced over the girl's shoulder at the paper. Her hand flew to her mouth in surprise. *The child can write! She's not stupid after all!*

The pencil moved again. Slowly, a line of writing took shape. "The ... cat ... is ... afrad ... of ... dog."

"My goodness, child! That's marvelous!" said Elisabeth. "I had no idea you could write!"

The girl dropped the pencil to the table and gripped the seat of the chair with both hands. She swung her legs wildly. Her head tilted to one side and her eyes gazed blankly at the paper before her.

"Can you write more?" asked Elisabeth gently. She pulled out a chair and sat next to the girl, setting the plates on the table. "Can you write your name for me?"

The child swung her legs and did nothing. Finally she picked up the pencil, chewed on it for a moment, and then made the letter G.

"No, you don't want a 'G,'" said Elisabeth. "You want an 'A.'" But by this time, the letters I and N followed the G. Elisabeth fell silent, watching.

Gingum dog and the caleco cat

The writing was cramped, irregular, but quite legible.

"Well, I'll be!" Elisabeth exclaimed, her hand patting her chest in amazement. "Wonders never cease!" She called to her sister in the kitchen. "Etta, come here and look at this, if you will. Look what this child has done! How can she do this?" She looked back at the girl. "How old are you, dear?"

The girl just laid the pencil down and gazed into space. She drew a deep ragged breath and turned finally to look at Elisabeth But she gave no indication that she had heard the question. Her eyes searched Elisabeth's face as if looking for the way out of a maze. Turning back to the paper, she slowly wrote, "Y-A-N-N."

"Yann," read Elisabeth. "Is this your name? It's close. Would you like a little help?" She took the pencil and wrote, A-n-n. "Ann," she said.

The girl retrieved the pencil, tapped it several times on the paper, and wrote, "Y ... Y-A-N-N." She left a space and made another "Y," then laid the pencil down and sighed, her legs hanging absolutely still for once.

Elisabeth took the pencil and wrote, A-N-N-Y. "Anny," she said. "Is this your name? Anny?"

The girl looked puzzled. *What is she talking about? My name, Anny? What IS my name?*

*   *   *

The spring in Elisabeth Snowburg's step matched the smile on her face as she turned the corner and entered the white picket gate. It was a lovely day—only late January, but the sunshine spread a wonderful warmth over her shoulders. These last three days of sunshine were enough to clear away the winter blues and make a person feel young again! Entering the yard, she stepped around little Gibbie, who was playing at something involving twigs and rocks on the board sidewalk. She climbed the five steps to the large front porch where Anny sat in the porch swing, gazing without expression at the railing. An old sweater of Elisabeth's was draped around the child's shoulders.

"Hello Gibbie," Elisabeth said. "Hello Anny." Neither child responded.

Elisabeth set her shopping bag on the porch rail and hunted around in it until she found a small notebook. She took it out and sat on the porch swing next to Anny. Setting the swing gently in motion, she said nothing for a few minutes.

Anny appeared to like the motion of the swing. She seemed to relax a little and closed her eyes.

Finally, Elisabeth reached over and patted Anny on the knee. The child opened her eyes.

"I brought you something," Elisabeth said. "Would you like to see?"

Anny said nothing, but did turn her head slightly in Elisabeth's direction.

Elisabeth held out the notebook to her. "It's a book for you to write in," she said. "See? Here's the first page ... and the next ... and there's nothing written on them. The pages are all empty so you can write whatever you want."

Anny's eyes came into focus. She looked at the book as Elisabeth flipped through the pages. "See? *Lots* of pages. These are pages for *you* to write on." She took Anny's hand, pressed the book into it, and closed the child's fingers over it.

Anny gazed at the notebook and drew a deep, shaky breath. Slowly she opened the book and turned a few pages. Finally her eyes focused on Elisabeth.

Was that a smile on the child's face? Not really, but it was close. It was a real expression—not the vacant stare Elisabeth had come to know so well. She smiled, but said nothing. This child was like a doe in the forest—quiet, gentle, large beautiful eyes, but easily frightened.

As Anny ran her fingers over the cover of the book, front and back, Elisabeth retrieved her bag and hunted once again, until she came up with a bright yellow wooden pencil. She extended it to Anny. "This is for you too. I'll tell you what," Elisabeth said, picking up her shopping bag and pocketbook from the porch rail. "I'll go see if Etta needs me to help her in the house. And after dinner we can write something."

As she entered the front door, Elisabeth looked back over her shoulder. Anny was clutching the notebook and pencil tightly in her hands—and gazing at the world as if she were blind.

Chapter Twenty Eight

The front of the Roberts Building where the dance was held.
The stone building on the left is the IOOF hall.
The *Chateau de Joie* would be off the left side of the photo.
Courtesy Morrow County Heritage Museum

Dacia put her hands on her hips and stretched her back. It wasn't that the work was so hard, it was just awkward, being so very pregnant. She had only a month and a half to wait now, by her calculations. The middle of March. She was ready to kick this baby out into the world *now!* Waiting had never been easy. But this time, still struggling with the after effects of the flood, it was downright *hard!*

The men had come early and set up several long tables at one end of Roberts Hall. Now Dacia, along with Grace, Lou Lundquist and Mabel Dupont were decorating—trying to make the place festive enough that everyone would forget the last time this hall had been used—in the days following the flood.

Dacia looked around the room trying hard to *not see* the places where the tubs had been set up to wash bodies for burial. Hopefully, Roberts Hall would never again be called into service as a morgue. It was now a place to have fun. A place where the young ladies could adorn themselves in their most flattering dresses and parade in front of the young men, feigning disinterest. Where young men could nudge each other in delight as the girls swooshed by, and bid their hard earned dollars on box suppers to win the privilege of eating the meal with one of them. Where men could dance with their wives or sweethearts—and papas with their little girls. When the night grew too long, the children would be wrapped in quilts and put to sleep around the edges of the hall, but the music, the dancing would go on until morning.

Jim Carr and several other musicians had brought their instruments early and were busy warming up. Eliza Martin sat at the piano, running through a couple of new tunes she wanted to try out tonight. One of them was a cakewalk—"At a Georgia Camp Meeting." She loved it, but the rhythm was tricky.

Lou Lundquist had brought along the two children she had taken into her home after the flood. Little Claire and Tommy Jackson had lost both parents to the disaster. Although a search had been conducted, no relatives could be found. The family had lived in Heppner only a short time, and apparently no one knew them well. Actually, many people had chosen not to know them well. They appeared to be less than desirable in terms of social stature, not to mention cleanliness or astuteness. Young Tommy appeared to be retarded, and the parents had seemed not to care about him at all.

Lou seated the two children where she could keep an eye on them and spoke to them occasionally as she worked with Mabel to set up the refreshments.

Claire was a delight. Dressed in clean clothes, and with someone who actually paid attention to her, the little girl had blossomed. She smiled shyly when Lou introduced her to her friends, but her eyes sparkled with happiness. Soft-spoken and gentle, she began picking up on Lou's loving attitude toward her older brother. And soon, even Tommy had begun looking like a fine little fellow. At age ten, he had not been in school for the last two years, but Lou, in the months since the flood, had encouraged him in every interest he showed, knowing that sooner or later, this child would find something that he could do. She was quite sure he would be able to support himself once he learned a trade.

"I'm glad we're having this dance," Lou said to Mabel. "I'm afraid some of us feel almost guilty about laughing and having a good time, but I think we need it!"

Mabel spread cookies on a plate, but said nothing.

"I hope you won't be offended that I can't remember, Mabel," Lou continued, "But we lost so many, and I feel like I'm just now beginning to get it all sorted out in my mind. Did you lose family?"

"Oh no, goodness no! I don't think I could have lived if that had happened! But I still feel like my life has almost come to an end. I'm so afraid at night. It's made a nervous wreck of me! I don't know if I'll ever be able to relax again."

"I'm sorry. It must be hard." Lou took the plate from Mabel and handed her two more bags of cookies. "My mother and father both died. Our house is well above the flood line, but they'd gone down to visit the Morgans. I was working in the morgue on Wednesday when they brought my father in."

"Oh!" Mabel shuddered. "How did you ever stand it? I could never live through that!"

Lou shrugged. "Sometimes you just have to do what needs to be done. That's all."

"No ... that's not right." Mabel shook her head emphatically. "You need to think about yourself. That's what I say. There's just too much talk about doing what we have to do and moving on. We can't just ignore our feelings. Why, the experiences I've had have wounded me so deeply I may never recover!"

You're right, you probably won't recover, Dacia thought as she listened to the conversation between Lou and Mabel. *In fact, you'd probably hate to recover! What on earth would you talk about then?* She looked at Grace and rolled her eyes. Grace ducked her head and giggled quietly.

Dacia handed her the end of a length of ribbon—the last one they would string from one side of the hall to the other. She tilted her head and looked sharply at Lou.

"Lou, have you lost weight? You're looking thinner than I remember."

"Maybe I have. My clothes have been getting kind of baggy." She laughed as she pulled at the side of her dress. "I need to do some sewing, but I just haven't had time yet. Having children in the house takes more time and energy than I ever imagined! I love it—but oh my goodness!"

"You look good!" Dacia said, unrolling the ribbon as Grace pulled her end across the room. She twisted it and tacked it in place. The hall was actually beginning to look festive.

*   *   *

Jim Carr set his cup of coffee on the floor beside his chair and lifted his horn into position. He tried a few random notes and glanced at the other members of the band.

The crowd had begun to gather, and the young men were clustered in the corners, slyly conferring about how the various young ladies looked in their finery. It had been seven months since the flood. Seven months was a long time for Heppner's younger set to wait.

Lou rearranged a few of the plates on the table across the end of the room. It held cookies, small sandwiches and punch, but she and Grace covered it with a clean sheet for now. The sheet would be removed during the first break in a couple of hours.

Mabel stood near the refreshments and looked over the people present at the dance. She visited with Mayor Gilliam, but kept looking in the direction of Mac Harmon.

Mac had not intended to come to the dance, but Jim Carr had pressured him. The man was too much alone, Carr said. Living in a room at the Palace Hotel by himself allowed him to hide from the rest of the world. Jim had not been the only one to express concern for Mac. A number of others in Heppner had noticed also. Oh, Mac visited with the men who came each day to the saddle and harness shop, but even then, it seemed as if his mind was someplace else. Or maybe his heart.

Carr understood Mac's anguish. His own daughter's body had never been found. It was the not knowing that made it so hard.

But Mac kept insisting his children were alive. His travel around the Pacific Northwest in search of them was becoming legendary. Every weekend, he traveled to one town or another, always with copies of the family photo. Looking for his children, he said. And always, he returned looking discouraged, but more determined than ever.

Mac needed to find a new life. He needed to move on. Jim was glad his friend had come to the dance. The obligatory year of mourning was more than half over, and maybe it was time for Mac to begin looking for a new wife—to think about starting a new family. Several couples had already married and combined families in the wake of the untimely deaths of former spouses. And no one questioned these quick marriages. After all, it was much easier to merge two partial families into one, than to sustain two separate homes—especially when there were so few houses left in town.

Jim wondered how many new matches would come out of tonight's dance.

At a nod from Carr, Scott Brown, the fiddler, took a few trial runs with his bow and then broke into "Arkansas Traveler." Men took the hands of their wives or lady friends and moved to the center of the floor to form two long lines for a Virginia reel. Scott's brother, Andrew, stepped up to call the dance.

*   *   *

Shan stood in the doorway with his arms folded across his chest. He watched Grace as she fairly flew around Johnny and the other dancers. At Dacia's insistence, Johnny had invited Grace to dance with him. Dacia was in no condition to dance. At least not a Virginal reel. A waltz maybe, but not a reel. So Johnny swung Grace on his right arm, then they both moved to the next in line with their left arms. Strip the Willow, it was called. Round and round they went. Grace in motion. Her lovely, dark hair was growing out and had a natural curl. Beautiful! Shan's face turned beet red, but he continued to stare at her slender waist as she twisted her hips and shoulders. Shan gritted his teeth, closed his eyes and turned to exit the building. He needed some fresh air.

*   *   *

Will sat on the sidelines and watched as Papa and Grace sashayed back to head position, and Andrew called, "First couple, cast off." Papa and Grace, at the top of the set, turned away from each other and lead the dancers to the other end of the line where they formed an arch with their hands for the other couples to pass under.

Will's feet tapped the floor in rhythm while many of those not dancing were clapping along. Skirts were swishing, shoes and work boots were pounding the wooden floor.

The dance continued until Johnny and Grace had moved gradually up the set and regained their position as head couple. As the music ended, the dancers and spectators applauded the musicians. Jim Carr blew the first few notes of "Susannah Gal," another well-known hoedown. This time the entire band would play. The dancers moved to form two sets as more couples joined them on the floor.

When the second dance was finished, Grace, breathing hard, came and sat next to Will. She put her arm around his shoulder and gave him a quick squeeze. "I'm worn out!" she said. She realized she felt better than she had in ... well, since her mama had died four years ago. It was a good feeling! "How is Will tonight?" she asked.

"Great!" He appeared to be having the time of his life just listening to the music. "I want to learn to play fiddle like that. The music just dances all by itself, doesn't it?"

"It does, truly," Grace answered.

"Pappy says God loves to watch us dance. It makes him smile."

"Well, I think Pappy must be right. He's a very wise old man."

"When I grow up," Will said, "I'm going to save up my money and buy me a fiddle."

"But then you couldn't dance. You'd be busy playing for the other dancers."

"Huh-uh! Look there." Will nodded at Scott Brown, who had laid his fiddle on top of the piano and was walking onto the floor with his wife. "You get to play sometimes, and dance sometimes. Grace, will you dance with me?"

Grace laughed. "Oh, Will! I'm exhausted ... *but* ... for you, I will dance again."

Will's face lit up with joy—scarred eyebrow and all—as he took Grace's hand and led her onto the floor. He could walk, and he could dance with the best of them. Will had never felt so happy in his life!

*   *   *

Mac stood near the refreshment tables, his hands clasped behind his back. His eyes roved over the dancers, but all he could see was Ella. Ella laughing, Ella swishing her skirt in time to the music, Ella's face, pink with exertion, her slender ankles, her sparkling eyes. He didn't even see Mabel Dupont approach.

"Hello, Mr. Harmon." Mabel looked up at him and smiled.

Mac started, as the sound of her voice cut into his thoughts.

"I want to thank you again, Mr. Harmon, for the *fine* job you did on my leather chair seat! It is really wonderful! The best work I've ever seen."

Mac nodded politely. "You're entirely welcome. I'm glad you're happy with it."

"Oh this is *so* wonderful!" Mabel exclaimed, looking around at the dancers. "I'm *so* glad we're doing this, aren't you, Mr. Harmon? I mean, it's been such a difficult year—for all of us, really. I ..." Her voice broke as she put her finger tips to her forehead and closed her eyes.

Mac said nothing, just pressed his lips together and nodded slightly.

Mabel looked up and continued. "I think the whole town really needs something like this—to make us feel alive again. I would just love to get out there and dance! It would make me feel so good!" She waited, but Mac offered no invitation. Mabel began to move slightly to the beat of "Golden Slippers" as the band played. "This has always been one of my favorite tunes. I can hardly keep my feet still!"

Mac nodded politely to Mabel and glanced toward the door. "If you'll excuse me," he said. He forced a polite smile and began moving toward the door.

Mabel's neck, then her face began to redden, and it wasn't from the exertion of moving with the music.

*   *   *

By midnight, the dancers were hungry. The musicians rose and returned instruments to cases. Shan stood nervously just outside the door as Mayor Gilliam stepped up to auction off the suppers. The dance committee had dedicated the take from the evening's festivities to the purchase of new band instruments, hoping to inspire more children to take up music.

Shan inched his way into the room and stood at the edge of the crowd leaning against the wall. He brushed his hair out of his eyes and put his hands back in his pockets. He straightened for a minute, then leaned against the wall again. He knew he'd be eating his supper from the sandwiches and cookies spread on the table at the rear of the hall. Why did they have these stupid auctions anyway? Why all the fuss about box dinners and who made them and who bought them? He could no more bid on a box than stand on his head. Even if he bid and won, he would never be brave enough to sit down with a young lady and eat it with her. And besides that, there was only one young lady he was interested in. And she had not brought a box. And on top of that, she hated him.

Chapter Twenty Nine

One day in the middle of February, Klein came home from work early. He shot a surly look at Elisabeth to discourage her from asking questions, stomped upstairs, and slammed his door.

Anny and Gibbie were sitting on the floor, Gibbie building something with a couple of broom straws, his shoes, and a blanket. Klein threw himself onto his bed and crossed his arms.

Gibbie jumped up and said, "See my house? I builded a house!" Klein said nothing. Gibbie began jumping around, singing about the house he was building.

Suddenly Klein jumped up from the bed. "Shut up!" he shouted. "Gimme that!" He snatched the blanket from Gibbie and threw it in the corner. "And you!" he hollered at Anny. "What's the matter with you anyway? Why don't you ever say anything? Cat got yer tongue? Are ya stupid or something?" He pulled Anny to her feet and shook her. "Huh? Are you listening to me?" He shoved her away from him.

Her face hit the iron bedstead with a crack as she fell. She didn't cry—just curled up on the floor under the bed. Klein collapsed back onto his own bed and stared at the ceiling. "Fired," he muttered. "Stupid boss. I hated that job anyway."

*　　*　　*

Elisabeth stormed into the kitchen with a pile of dirty plates from breakfast. "Etta! Have you seen Anny this morning?"

"Of course not. I've been in the kitchen, cooking."

"Her lip is swollen and her two front teeth are missing!"

"Her teeth are missing? Whenever did that happen? I didn't even know they were loose."

"I didn't either. But they're gone. She was at the table sticking her tongue through the hole. I asked her about it, but of course, she didn't answer. So I asked Mr. Klein, and he hadn't even noticed. Honestly! That man! He doesn't deserve to be a father!"

"Oh, now Elisabeth! Don't be so hard on him about a little thing like a tooth. He's their father, after all—not their mother. Mothers notice things like that. Poor little tykes with no mother!"

Elisabeth lowered her voice and whispered harshly, "I guess I'm just angry with him about so many other things, so it's convenient to blame him for everything." She shook her head. Then she remembered the exciting news she'd overheard at the breakfast table. "Oh! And guess what else! Just guess what Mr. Hollaman said at breakfast."

"What did Mr. Hollaman say at breakfast?"

"Well. Mr. Jenner, the butcher, has gotten himself one of those smelly, noisy automobiles everyone has been talking about. Mr. Hollaman saw him driving it."

"Really?" Etta stopped scraping the plate in her hand to stare at her sister. "Mr. Jenner? No. He wouldn't do that! When did this happen?"

"Yesterday, I guess. He's bound to be driving it around the neighborhood, scaring all the decent folks and their horses to death. But to tell you the truth ..." Elisabeth lifted her chin and smiled. "I'd kind of like to see it. Seems I'm always in the wrong place at the wrong time. I haven't even seen one of them yet." She turned back to the dining room for the rest of the dishes.

"Hmph," Etta muttered to her sister's retreating figure. "You're right about the noisy and smelly part! We'd be better off without them, if you ask me."

Elisabeth returned to the kitchen with more dirty dishes. "Well, I didn't ask you, and I think I'm going to like seeing one very much." Elisabeth set the dirty plates on the kitchen counter. "In fact, I'm thinking of asking Mr. Jenner if he'll take me for a ride!"

"Oh, you are not! You wouldn't do such a thing. You'd be the scandal of the neighborhood!"

"Maybe. But I'd also be having more fun than anyone else in the neighborhood!" Elisabeth laughed, but Etta only shook her head.

Elisabeth's eyes brightened as a new idea occurred to her. "But think about this, Etta. Maybe I could ask him to give Anny and Gibbie a run around the block in it. Wouldn't that be wonderful? He would do it—I know he would!"

"Hmmm ... Well, Gibbie would love it for sure. That's a fact. I don't know what Anny would think. No harm in asking him, I guess. The worst he could do is say 'no.'"

"I'll do it. As soon as we get the dishes done and put away."

* * *

Anny's journal: February, 1904

> My mouth feels
> Funny. My tung
> stiks thro my teeth.

* * *

It had rained Friday night, and the roads, by Saturday morning, were a sea of mud. *No worry*, thought Elisabeth. *A great day for an adventure!*

She knocked at the Klein's door. Klein opened it, looking like he had just tumbled out of bed.

"I've come for the children," Elisabeth said. When Klein just stared at her blankly, she prompted him, "Remember? We're going for an automobile ride. We won't be long. I'll bring them back in only a few minutes."

Klein nodded and shoved Gibbie out the door, then turned to get Anny and shoved her out too. He shut the door with no comment.

Well, I never! But at least she had the children, unkempt as they were. She took a child in each hand and started down the stairs to the waiting automobile.

"We are going for a ride in an auto," she told them.

"Notto?" Gibbie asked.

"Notto"

Elisabeth laughed. "You'll see. I think you will like it a lot!"

Waiting in front of the house, shimmering and shaking in time with the chugging noise it was emitting, stood a shiny black horseless carriage. Elisabeth's heart fluttered. She was glad she'd thought of asking Mr. Jenner if he would take the children. Of course it would have been entirely inappropriate for her to ask for a ride for herself. And also, of course, it would be expected that she would accompany the children on their ride. After all, she couldn't just send two children off in something as dangerous as an automobile without going along to take care of them.

Mr. Jenner had dressed up for the occasion. He wore a wool jacket and derby and looked mighty fine. He turned off the engine and came around the vehicle, rubbing his hands in delight. "All ready?" he inquired with a smile and gave Elisabeth a hand up into the automobile. After she was seated, he lifted each of the children up to her.

Elisabeth sat with Gibbie in her lap and Anny beside her. She held an arm around each child, just in case. In case of what, she didn't know, but she wanted to be prepared. Or maybe it just gave her confidence herself to be hanging onto someone.

After several fruitless attempts, Mr. Jenner restarted the engine and hopped into the driver's seat. His shoes were muddy, but he seemed not to notice. As he put the vehicle in gear, it lurched forward, hiccupped a time or two, and settled down to a steady clatter as it progressed down the street—all by itself. Elisabeth gasped and gripped the children tighter. Gibbie hollered, "Yay! Riding! Riding fast!"

"Oh my! How fast are we going?" Elisabeth asked Mr. Jenner.

"About ten miles an hour. It can go faster. Hang on! I'll show you!"

"Oh no! I wasn't asking to ..." Elisabeth's hand flew up to clamp her hat tight to her head as Mr. Jenner accelerated. "Oh my! Oh *my!*"

The car hit a deeper than average rut and shuddered for a moment before coughing, gagging, and coming to a complete halt, the motor dying as the auto slid sideways in the mud.

Uh oh, now I've done it, Elisabeth thought. *Etta will never let me hear the end of this!*

Mr. Jenner hopped jauntily out of the driver's seat and made his way through the mud to the front of the automobile.

"Is there anything I can do to help?" Elisabeth called to him as he tried again and again to restart the motor with the hand crank.

"No, no. Now don't you worry about it a bit, my dear. We will be underway again very shortly here." He gave the crank another good whirl, and finally the motor turned over. He removed the crank, placed it in the auto and resumed his seat—considerably muddier than he'd been a few minutes earlier.

The auto died twice more on the trip around the block, but finally, nearly half an hour after their departure, they arrived safely back at the gate of the Snowburg house. Gibbie chattered almost non-stop the entire time, adding words like notto, automobile, motor, and crank to his vocabulary. He also imitated the sound of the motor as it choked and chugged along. Elisabeth was thrilled—she didn't even mind the slipping and sliding in the mud or waiting to have the motor restarted every time it died.

But Anny—Anny sat, impassive as ever, eyes straight ahead through the entire experience.

When the automobile finally chugged back to the Snowburg sisters' boarding house, Etta was just emerging from the front door. She narrowed her eyes and glared suspiciously at the nasty, huffing machine. Elisabeth still held Gibbie tightly in one arm. The other hand was clamped firmly on top of her head, holding her hat in place. As Mr. Jenner reined in the vehicle, it came to an abrupt halt, causing its occupants to jerk forward, nearly slamming into the wind screen.

"How was it?" Etta asked.

"Marvelous! It was simply wonderful! Etta, just wait 'til I tell you about it!" Elisabeth tried to hand Gibbie out the door to Mr. Jenner, but the boy objected vehemently.

"More!" he squealed, kicking his feet in mid-air as Mr. Jenner lifted him over the side. "Gibbie wanna go more!"

Mr. Jenner just laughed and put him down on the wooden sidewalk at the side of the street. He patted Gibbie on the head. "Maybe we'll go again some other day," he said.

While Gibbie continued to wail his displeasure, Mr. Jenner lifted Anny out of the vehicle. But as he tried to set her down at the edge of the muddy street, Anny pulled her legs up to her chest and grabbed fiercely at his arms. Surprised at the strength of her grip, Mr. Jenner lifted her back up and looked into her eyes. "What's the matter, dearie?" he asked her. "Don't want to get mud on your shoes?" She was looking down at the mud with an expression of horror on her face.

He carried her a step nearer the house and lowered her gently to the wooden sidewalk. This time, Anny allowed herself to be set down.

Mr. Jenner then extended his hand in a courtly fashion to help Elisabeth out. She took his hand, but remained seated as she spoke to him.

"I don't know how to thank you for this delightful ride, Mr. Jenner! I know a lot of people think you're crazy, but I think it's wonderful! Absolutely *wonderful!* Thank you so, *so* much."

"My pleasure, entirely, Miss Snowburg." Mr. Jenner nodded graciously and handed Elisabeth up to the walk leading to the house.

Gibbie had taken Etta's hand, and was now bouncing up and down in his excitement. "We goed for a ride in a notto! It was fast— really, really fast. Go again? We can go again?"

*   *   *

February, 1904

We went FoR a
ride in a
notomobeel.
Gibbie liked it.

176

Chapter Thirty

February 29th. Leap year. What a time to have a baby! But that's exactly what Dacia seemed intent on doing today. When she had gone into sudden, hard labor yesterday, Johnny decided it was too late to take her to the Sperry House—Heppner's birthing home. They would have the doctor come to the house. So far, however, none of the three doctors in town had put in an appearance. Johnny had already determined that Dr. Kistner was in Portland for the week and Dr. Gundlach had gone to Montana for his mother's funeral. That left Dr. Higgs. But Johnny's search for the man had been, so far, unsuccessful. He'd left word all over town that the doctor was needed. Now all he could do was wait.

And his waiting was making Grace nervous!

Dacia had assured Grace she'd already given birth to five babies in her life. All had been healthy, squalling infants—ready to take on the world. She would do fine!

Grace, however, did not share Dacia's confidence. Oh, she'd had plenty of experience—she had delivered her mother's last two babies herself, with no doctor close enough to call. And she'd helped with the one before that. All had gone according to plan. The deliveries had been easy.

But then ... then Mama had died. Only a few hours after the baby had entered the world, crying, squirming, wanting to be fed and comforted.

That was the end. The end of Mama's life. And the baby had died a day later, in spite of Grace's best efforts to keep him alive. She shared Johnny's apprehension about this birth. It was taking way too long! The baby should have been here by now. The doctor should have been here by now too. Heppner was a big enough town to have a doctor available when he was needed. So—where was he!

Grace tied the braided strips of torn sheeting to the bed posts, laying the loose ends on the bed next to Dacia. "Don't use them yet," she commanded. "We just want them ready for when the time comes."

"It won't be long," Dacia panted. "It can't be much longer. So close, so close. Agh, ah, *ah!*" She kept her voice low. She had never been a screamer. Dacia didn't know for sure if it helped. She'd never done it any other way. But by now—her sixth delivery—it had become a normal part of how she gave birth.

What wasn't normal was the time this baby was taking to arrive. Labor had started yesterday afternoon before supper. And here it was, after eleven o'clock on Sunday night. Well over twenty-four hours already, and still no baby. The children were at the Justus home. And poor Johnny was fit to be tied!

But at this point, Grace wasn't worried about Johnny. She was worried about Dacia. The water had broken early this morning. The pains had been four minutes apart, then three, then two—hour, after hour, after endless hour. Still no baby. And still no doctor.

"Johnny!" The harshness of Grace's voice startled both of them as Grace poked her head out the bedroom door and called. "Try again for a doctor."

She couldn't say more. She didn't want Johnny to worry—as if she could stop him.

"Grace!" Dacia's sharp voice pulled Grace back to the bed. Grace checked and found that the baby's head was finally entering the birth canal. "*Now,* Dacia! Yes!"

Dacia grabbed the sheets and pulled for all she was worth. "Aaugh!" Then her voice jumped two octaves, and she screamed as she never had before. "*Aaeee!*"

Grace held Dacia's head and shoulders as Dacia pushed harder, harder. Then she collapsed back onto the bed, her face as white as the sheets.

"Johnny! Johnny I love you..." Her voice faded to silence, and she was still.

"No!" Grace screamed at her, shaking her shoulder. "No! Dacia! You're going to make it! Come on ... again! Yes!"

Another contraction pulled Dacia up off the bed. Grace moved to receive the baby. "Yes, Dacia! Yes! It's coming ..."

Dacia fell back again. Her face was whiter than Grace could imagine. She appeared not to be breathing.

"Dacia!" Grace screamed. "Dacia! Come back!" She reached up and slapped Dacia's cheeks—hard! "You're almost there! You can do it!" She drew a ragged breath as she saw Dacia's chest begin to move again.

"Now *go! Push!* Let's get this baby out of there!" And then she shuddered as the baby's head emerged. She could see the cord— wrapped tightly around the baby's neck. *Oh no! No!*

She grabbed the razor knife, and the ties. She couldn't wait. Struggling to pull the cord away from the baby's neck, she quickly tied it in two places, sliced it with the knife, and unwrapped it from the baby's neck. One, two, three times. Blood everywhere. She looked at Dacia's face. So white! Was she breathing?

"Dacia!" Grace called. "Don't quit now! You're doing fine ... just fine. One more big push, that's all we need. You can do it. Come on ... *PUSH!*" She slapped at Dacia's cheeks again and pushed against the top of the womb. Suddenly, Dacia lunged up off the bed as her body was wracked with another contraction and the baby came sliding out into Grace's waiting hands.

Grace laid the baby girl gently on the bed. She rolled the baby to her side and cleared her mouth. "Breathe," she said. "Come on, baby, *breathe!*" She picked up the infant by her blue feet and smacked her soundly on the bottom. Nothing. She smacked again. Hard.

A feeble whimper rewarded her efforts. One more spank—a yell, a good healthy cry! And the baby girl turned from blue, to purple to pink as she continued to yell lustily. Grace wrapped her quickly and laid her on her mama's chest.

Looking back at Dacia, Grace realized the battle was only half over. White as the sheets upon which she lay, Dacia's breathing was shallow. Very shallow! Grace rubbed her cheeks, her hands and wrists. "Come on Dacia. Almost done. Let's finish this up, now. Then you can rest. We have to get the—" She heard the front door of the house bang open and footsteps running in the hall.

The bedroom door burst open, and Johnny ran in with Dr. Kistner.

And Grace sat down abruptly on the chair by the bed and sobbed.

*   *   *

The baby was born. And Dacia lived.

Seeing the doctor had Johnny to help him, Grace stifled her sobbing, rose silently, and left the room. Walking out the front door of the house she turned up Baltimore, and when the street ended only a block

179

away, she continued on up the hill to its crest. She sensed around her a presence—the people from that terrible night nearly nine months ago. The crying, the anguish. People running, trying to pull others from the wretched rolling current. Why? Why had it happened? And why did it come back to her now?

Grace sat under the lone tree on the hill and cried out her fear for the baby, for Dacia. She sobbed as she remembered the flood, the trauma of working in the morgue. She cried for her last night at home, her lost childhood. The fear ... running, hiding ... walking mile after mile, after mile. Getting a ride the rest of the way into Heppner, only to be left at a brothel. And she cried because Shan hated her.

Drenched in sweat, no shawl, the cold February night ... She hugged her arms to herself and breathed deep shuddering breaths. The night was still—except for a small breeze. The stars were huge and low. *Oh God! Are you there? Are you real? Because I need some help right now. I really, really need you!*

*   *   *

A half hour later, when Grace returned to the house, Dr. Kistner, newly returned from his trip to Portland, had delivered the afterbirth and was issuing instructions to Johnny, who had taken over as a very capable nurse in Grace's absence. Dacia looked weary, but her color had returned. She was able to smile at Grace and reach out her hand to invite her to come close and see the baby she'd delivered. The doctor repeated his instructions to Grace—most importantly, to make sure Dacia did *nothing* until he gave his permission. "She's had a pretty hard time here. I'm confident she'll recover, but she needs rest and care."

Johnny and Grace both nodded solemnly. Dacia would have the best care they could give, and yes, they would send for Dr. Kistner if even the tiniest little thing concerned either of them or Dacia herself.

"Promise!" Johnny assured him. He shook the doctor's hand and led him out to the front door.

As Johnny returned to the room, the tiny newborn squeaked and nuzzled, searching for her mother's breast. Dacia's face shone, even in her exhaustion.

Grace changed the bed under Dacia, then gathered up all the linen and took it to the back porch. She would have a big washing to do tomorrow.

Johnny stood at the foot of the bed, gazing lovingly on his wife and new baby. "I love you," he said. "I love you so much!"

"Mmm. Me? Or the baby?" Dacia's voice was soft as she smiled and opened her eyes.

"Mm-hm," he answered with a huge smile on his face. "Yes. The answer is yes." He moved to the side of the bed and motioned to the empty spot beside Dacia. He raised his eyebrows in question, and she nodded. "Yes, sit down. Don't worry, I'm fine."

He sat and reached out his hand to touch his daughter's fingers. "What a wonder! Dacia, we made this. We did this together, our love. Amazing!"

"Mmm ..." Dacia closed her eyes. "I love you, Johnny Burke. Did you know that?"

"I've suspected for some time."

"Hmm. Well, I do."

"Good. What'll we call her?"

"Ella? I'd like to call her Ella."

Johnny nodded. "Mm-hm. I like that. I think it's perfect. Middle name?"

"Josie's middle name—Grace. It would remind me of Josie, and ... our Grace. She's such a wonder—how God is working in her. Grace. A precious gift that's undeserved. What do you think?"

"Ella Grace Burke." Johnny nodded. "I don't think it could be any better, and that's the truth."

*   *   *

Next morning, Dacia sat propped in bed with pillows around her, snuggling the new baby. Her face was wan, but wore a smile. Will, Walter and Sarah knelt on the bed beside her, gazing in awe at their new baby sister. The boys were excited, full of bubble and bounce. Sarah, however, displayed a gentleness Dacia had not expected. She moved her small hands tenderly around the baby's face and down to the chin. Her fingers were gentle, loving. As she caressed the baby, Dacia watched in amazement. So far, each time a new child had been born into the Burke family, the next in line had displayed the usual jealousy, pouting and making it known that a new baby was *not* to his or her liking. But little Sarah seemed entirely unaware that this new sister might be perceived as a threat. She was enamored with the tiny life and seemed to want nothing more than to love and protect her new baby sister.

Grace entered the room with a steaming cup of tea. Both she and Dacia looked considerably better than they had last night. Dacia's hair was pulled back in a neat braid, and Grace's, now long enough to put up, beautifully framed the smile she bestowed on the three older Burke children. "Okay boys, Sarah," she said. "Time to hop down off the bed now so Mama can put her tea there and not worry about getting it spilled."

The boys hopped down willingly, having seen enough of the new baby to determine that it was, indeed, a new baby. They were ready to return to their play. But Sarah looked up at Grace with excitement in her eyes. "Can I hold her?" she asked. "She *wants* me to hold her!"

Grace caught Dacia's eye, and the two smiled at each other. "Yes, I think you're right, Sarah," Dacia said. "I think she *does* want you to hold her!"

"Here," said Grace. "Let's scoot you back against this pillow first." She set the tea on the dresser and scooted Sarah back so she was sitting right next to her mother. "Now hold your arms like this." Grace helped her to form her small arms into a cradle, and Dacia placed the baby in them.

Baby Ella wiggled, and Sarah's face looked like it would split in two with her smile. "She likes me!" Sarah said. A tiny arm worked its way loose from the swaddling and flopped back over the baby's head. Sarah giggled in excitement. "I have a baby! I have a baby sister! Oh, thank you, Mama. I really love her!" Sarah placed her hand on the baby's, and the infant clutched her thumb, causing an even greater giggle from Sarah. With her thumb in the grip of the baby's fist, Sarah ran her finger gently down the side of the tiny face. The baby turned her head toward the touch and opened her mouth wide. "Oooh! She likes me!" Sarah whispered. "She says she's happy I'm her sister!"

Dacia hugged her tightly. "You know, I think you're right. I think that's exactly what she's saying."

Dacia looked at the tea on the dresser and smiled at Grace. "Thanks for the tea ... but it's getting cold."

Grace laughed and said, "It's worth it! This is too good to miss!" She handed the tea to Dacia and pulled a chair close to the bed, so she could help Sarah if needed. "It really is an amazing thing, you know." Grace ran her finger over the black fuzz of the baby's head. "A baby—what an amazing thing!"

Dacia set her cup and saucer beside her on the bed and looked questioningly at Grace.

"She's starting brand new," Grace explained. Nothing has gone wrong in her life. It's so precious! Makes a person want to start all over."

"You're so right!" Dacia nodded and took a sip of her tea. "You're *so* right!"

Chapter Thirty One

The Carr window at All Saint's Memorial Episcopal Church

Late summer 1904

M ac Harmon sat at the back of the church. He closed his eyes, but the image of the stained glass window before him was still clearly visible on the inside of his eyelids.

Jim Carr had commissioned the window for the new All Saints Memorial Episcopal Church building. It complemented the window on the other side of the altar honoring all the flood victims, which had been given by George Conser and his wife.

Mac understood. The Carrs had lost their little girl, but they had this stained glass window—like a grave marker, only much more beautiful. They could gaze, every Sunday morning, at the colors, the letters, the name Lilias. And in that gazing, and the passing of time, healing would come.

Mac had no such healing. Oh, he had the gravestones—Ella's and Charlie's. The stones and the passing of time, both helped. But Lilyann—Gilbert? Where were they? Most people believed they were among the unidentified dead in the large grave up on Cemetery Hill or buried in the mud—many feet deep in places—along the Willow Creek Valley. Some even speculated that their bodies had been swept out to sea. Mac did *not* believe any of this. They *were* alive somewhere, wanting him. Were they lonely? Hurting? Needy? Waiting for him to come rescue them?

Mac put his face in his hands. *"Oh God! Help me!"* The nightmares of his time in the flood had begun to visit him, not only at night, but in the daylight hours as well. Holding four children with all the strength he had, feeling them torn from his grip, a force a hundred times stronger than anything he'd ever imagined, tossing him like a twig in its rolling waves. The children ... the children! He pressed a thumb and finger to his eyes as Reverend Warren called for the closing hymn. He couldn't sing about peace. He had no peace. *God, where are you?*

As Reverend Warren asked the congregation to stand, Mac stood and walked out of the church. Reaching the cemetery, he walked directly to Ella's grave but looked first at those beside it. Ada, his and Ella's baby who had died. Charlie—Charles MacKennon Harmon.

Mac put his hands in his pockets and gazed down at the ground for a moment. Then he lifted his eyes to Ella's stone marker. "Ella ... I'm nothing without you. Dead without you! I love you—you know that, don't you? Did I remind you that day? I hope so, but if I forgot, I'm telling you now. I love you!

"Did I tell you Dacia and Johnny had a baby? They named her after you—Ella Grace. They call her Ellie.

"I'm so worried about the children, Ella." He looked up for a moment, then back at Ella's stone. "Lilyann and Gilbert. I really believe they're alive, but I can't find them! I just wish you were here. I don't have anyone to talk to. You were always so good at making sense out of things. And it seems like nothing makes sense any more.

"You know Ella, most people think I'm going crazy—believing that Lilyann and Gilbert are alive. Pappy believes me, and maybe Dacia. But that's about it. Even Johnny doesn't believe."

Mac turned to survey the cemetery. How many of these stones, he wondered, were emblazoned with the date June 14, 1903? The surface of the ground over the large common grave, for the unidentified and those who had no family to bury them, was still uneven, nearly a year later. The whole cemetery looked raw.

Turning back to Ella's grave, Mac spoke again. "Some people think I should be looking for a new wife, Ella. I just can't bring myself to even think of it. It's you I want, you I love. I don't know what I'll do when I bring the children home. They will need a mother. But I just don't want to face it."

He pinched the top of his nose, trying to keep the tears from falling. "Good bye, Ella. I'll always love you!"

"Oh God," he sobbed silently. *"Help me! Take care of my children for me! I can't do it, and I'm not even sure if I can trust you to do it. Please ... just, please help!"*

*　　*　　*

Grace helped Dacia clean up the kitchen after supper, then went up to her room. She flopped back on the bed. She wanted to cry, but resisted, afraid that if she got started she wouldn't be able to stop. Too much. It was all just too much! Her life had been pretty good until Mama died—almost four years ago now. But now *all* of life seemed wrong. And on top of it all, she was now unfit for marriage. Why couldn't she have a chance at life? At love? Even Esmerelda was gone.

She rose from the bed and looked out the window. Shan was in his front yard with Michael, Libby, and Danny. Johnny and Dacia had crossed the street with their three and baby Ella and were sitting on the porch watching Shan play with the children. Grace hugged her arms around her waist and watched, longing in her eyes. Shan was swinging Libby on one arm, Sarah on the other. Big, strong, sweaty forearms below his rolled up shirt sleeves. He was laughing—not just his mouth, but his eyes as well. His whole being was laughing! The children loved him. He loved them. Why couldn't he love *her*?

Well, really ... who in their right mind *would* love her? No one! She should have walked into the flood when she had the chance. Grace let the tears fall.

*　　*　　*

Mabel Dupont breezed in the front door of the Harmony Saddle and Bridle Shop on a lovely April morning. Shan glanced up at her and grunted quietly, but Mabel wasn't here to see Shan.

"Good morning, Mr. Harmon." Mac looked up and smiled. What a handsome smile!

"Well, Mrs. Dupont, what can we do for you today?"

"Oh, I was just on my way past the shop and thought I'd stop in for a moment. Isn't this just the most lovely weather we've been having? A person can't help but feel good in weather like this!" She shrugged her shoulders with pleasure.

Mac nodded but looked distracted. Rushing on, Mabel said, "Mr. Harmon, did you know the social committee is planning another dance for the end of June?"

"Uh, no, I don't believe I'd heard that."

"Well, they are. And there will be a box supper as well. I'm thinking of preparing a box, but I'm not sure anyone would even bid on it. That would be so humiliating—to offer a supper that no one was willing to share with me. What do you think? Should I do it?" There. Mr. Harmon was paying attention now. At least he appeared to be paying attention.

"Well, now," he stopped to clear his throat. "A fine looking lady such as yourself should have no trouble in that department!"

"Oh, Mr. Harmon! Do you really think that? You've never said, and I wasn't sure how you felt. So you think if I prepare a box supper someone would bid on it?"

"Oh, I'm quite sure someone would, Mrs. Dupont." He looked back at the saddle he was working on.

Mabel put her fingers in front of her mouth and giggled. "You've given me courage, Mr. Harmon. A girl like me needs courage—and encouragement. Otherwise I'd never be brave enough to move forward with my life."

Shan dropped the awl he was using. Mabel looked his way to see him glaring at Mr. Harmon.

"I guess I'd better be getting back to work," Mac said. "Thanks for letting us know about the dance. Maybe I'll go."

"Maybe?" She giggled again. "If I hope for anyone to buy my box supper, you'll have to come!" She turned and swept out of the shop.

"What was *that* all about?" Shan's question sounded more like an accusation

Mac looked up at him, but didn't respond.

"Mac, she's trying to court you. Don't you get it?" Shan shook his head in disgust. "You need to run! Or are you planning on courting her back?"

Mac clamped the leather for the splice he was making into the stitching horse. He threaded both needles and began to sew. "Hmph," he said. "I'm doing okay. I'm comfortable living at the hotel. And anyway, I just don't feel I can do anything else 'til I find my children."

Shan shook his head. He didn't agree with Mac that the children would be found. Shan thought, as did most people in town, that Lilyann and Gilbert had died in the flood. The fact that their bodies had not been found was hardly evidence that they were still alive.

"Well, I noticed Mabel has been pretty interested in you. Seems every time you and her are in the same room, she's right there beside you, trying to get you into a conversation."

Mac grasped the end of the second needle and pulled it through the hole using pliers. "Huh! She tries to get every available man within ten miles into a conversation. I tell you, I'm just not interested." Mac banged the pliers back onto the bench. "And besides, I thought you told me I should run," he added.

Shan shrugged and grinned at Mac. "What would you have to lose? She's not that bad, is she?"

Mac's staring eyes challenged Shan, almost demanding to know how a young man who lived his life in fear of females dared to be giving him advice on the art of pursuing and catching one.

"You don't have much room to be advising others in matters of the fairer sex," Mac said to Shan, "seeing as how you're terrified of them yourself." Shan looked down at his work ... and turned red in the face.

"And anyway, I didn't say she was bad. I'm just not interested in beginning a courtship."

Shan tried a different tack. "So who says you have to court her? Just be nice to her. You could at least be friends—maybe visit with her once in a while, eat dinner together at the hotel, that sort of thing. Johnny thinks you should do it, too." Shan reached for a larger punch. "Johnny says—"

"Oh Johnny does, does he?" Mac interrupted, irritated.

"Yeah. We figured you wanted our help and just forgot to ask." Shan's handsome Irish face lit up with one of those irresistible grins he had, and the blush receded. "That's what friends are for. So, since you're not up to it, Johnny and me, we just thought we'd help you out." Then that tell-tale pink began to creep up Shan's neck again. "Seems like you ought to be tired of sleeping alone."

Mac jammed one of the needles into the next hole and blew out his breath. "Shan, don't talk. Just work. Okay?"

"Sorry," Shan muttered, but the grin on his pink face refused to go away.

Mac sat thinking for a moment, then put down his tools, and walked to the door. "You close up tonight," he snapped over his shoulder and slammed the door on his way out. The banjo squawked in indignation.

*   *   *

It was Monday. On Mondays, Pappy liked to walk the two blocks to the farrier, Tommie Brennan's place, on Main Street. A farrier himself for many years, Pappy enjoyed the familiar, masculine atmosphere of the forge. He had been making his weekly pilgrimage for so long that Brennan had taken to bringing an extra dinner to share with the old man on Mondays. Today, however, Pappy had wandered off his course by several blocks. Bruce Kelley had found him and, knowing the old man's routine, had brought him to Brennan's—where he, himself, was headed to have a new set of shoes made for his horse. As they waited, Bruce sat listening to Pappy tell of the old country as if he'd never heard the stories before. Some people thought of Pappy as an interesting old geezer. Others called him "crazy as a bedbug." Either way, Kelley enjoyed listening—not because the stories were new and exciting, but because he liked the Irish brogue. And besides, Kelley had always been more of a listener than a talker.

Pappy paused in the story he was telling and leaned forward to scrape the burnt tobacco from the bowl of his pipe. *Thud!* He heard the first blow of the blacksmith's hammer against the horseshoe. *Thud. Thunk, whank! Ping!* As the hammer came down again and again, forcing the shoe to take shape, the blows became higher and higher pitched, until the ringing tone told Brennan the shoe had cooled enough that it needed to be returned to the fire. If he continued to hammer past the *"ping"* sound, the iron would shatter. He reheated the shoe and returned it to the anvil.

As Pappy watched the blacksmith work, he paused mid-sentence and seemed to forget what he was talking about.

"T'was the evil of a broken world stole them. Ah yes. T'was the evil of a ..."

"What about the dances, Pappy? You were telling about the dances at the crossroads."

"Ah to be sure!" Pappy scratched just in front of one ear and nodded. 'Twas rollicking good, it was! Along the Blackwater's banks between County Cork and County Kerry. And old Cormack played his fiddle, and young Cormack the pipes, and we danced 'til the sun rose in the east." The old man's eyes sparkled as he saw once again the dancers flying round each other to the fine music of Paddy and Con Cormack.

"What kind of dances did you do?"

"Ah, well, we did the jigs and the reels, of course, like they do up north. But slides and polkas too! *Sliabh Luachra*. That's where we were. That was our music, and none so fine in all of Ireland." Pappy reached out a hand and placed it on Kelley's arm. "But have ye seen the little lassie with the sparklin' eyes? Irish eyes, they are, and set in a fairy face. Ah sweet Jesus, where is the little thing? And that leprechaun. Where are they? Do you know?"

Bruce looked sideways at the old man. Pappy looked more childlike these days. The fringe of white hair hugged the back of his head like a puffy shawl of cloud, and his wrinkles seemed softer, more gentle.

"Ah, the sweet little fairy lassie!" Pappy continued. "And that leprechaun of a brother. Did ever you see such mischief in the eye of a child? No, I think not."

Thud! Thunk! As Brennan's hammer bounced off the shoe one last time, and he prepared to nail it in place, Pappy sat muttering to himself. "That man ... that man took ..."

Just as Brennan was placing the first nail in the shoe, Will Burke and Michael Collins charged together into the blacksmith shop with such a clatter, everything stopped. Brennan lifted his head; Pappy stopped his mumbling; even Dancer, the horse, turned to look at the two young intruders.

"Pappy, look!" Will held a dirt-covered stick before him triumphantly. "Look what we found!"

A slow smile spread across Pappy's face, and he reached out his gnarled hand to embrace his equally gnarled shillelagh from the boys. Brennan dropped Dancer's foot and looked on.

"Is that what I think it is?" Kelley asked.

"It is, to be sure," Pappy said. His sparkling eyes showed no confusion at all. "A wee bit the worse for wear ..." His eyes probed the baked dirt covering the stick. But enough of the shillelagh showed through that there could be no doubt of its identity.

"How long's it been missing?" Kelley asked.

"Since the flood. I was sittin' on the porch with Johnny. We ran up the hill, and ... well, me shillelagh ..." Pappy looked up at the roof over his head. "We ran up the hill and ..." Pappy stood abruptly and pointed over his left shoulder, his arm and finger shaking. "He took them. That man took them!"

Kelley and Brennan exchanged glances, while Michael and Will did the same. It seemed Pappy was gone again, his mind wandering like a lost puppy.

At Kelley's suggestion, Pappy returned his attention to the mud-covered stick. Pappy pulled out his pocket knife and began using the back of the casing to scrape at the dried mud. "You know ..." Pappy looked again at the two boys. And his mind seemed to be as sharp as ever. "If this stick was all cleaned up nice and shiny, a man might be proud to walk in town with it. Maybe even walk to the Pastime with a boy or two and have a bowl of ice cream. He just might."

Will and Michael turned to each other with big eyes, then Michael snatched the shillelagh from Pappy. "We'll be right back," Will called as they flew down the street in the direction of home.

Brennan laughed. "Well, don't that beat all!" he said. "Don't that just beat all!"

*　　*　　*

Mac sat alone at a table in the dining room of the Palace Hotel. In fact, he sat at a corner table with his back to the room. He needed to think, and he didn't want any help in doing it.

Is there any chance—any chance at all, that Shan is right? Should I be looking for a new ... wife? What will happen when I find the children? Who will mother them? I don't even have a house. Where will we live?

No. No! I don't even want to think about this. And anyway, I'm not sure I even like *Mabel. Face it, Mac,* he said to himself. *You're so mixed up you don't know what you think!* He rose from the table, tossed his napkin on top of his unfinished dinner, and walked slowly upstairs to his room.

Chapter Thirty Two

Mabel Dupont arrived at the shop right at closing time. Shan had just left for home, and Mac was closing up. He pushed the hasp into place on the front door and hooked the padlock through it. "Hello, Mrs. Dupont. It looks like you've brought me a piece of leather." The lock clicked into place.

Mabel graced Mac with a sweet smile. "Mr. Harmon, do you remember the chair seat you replaced for me last year?"

"Well, yes, I think I do remember that. As I recall, it had a fleur-de-lis design on it."

"Yes, that's the one. I need your opinion on whether I should replace the rest of them or not. This one is the most worn." She held the leather chair seat out to Mac, who examined it closely.

"Well, it doesn't *need* replacing at all. How old are these chairs?"

"Well, we've had them since I was just a child." Mabel giggled a little and looked down as she said, "I won't tell you how many years ago that was."

She began walking away from the shop in the direction of Mac's hotel. Realizing he was supposed to walk alongside her, he hurried to catch up.

"There are six more chairs like that one. The seats are beginning to show some wear, and I was wondering if you might be willing to make new ones for me?"

They stopped on the corner to let a buggy pass.

"Well, Mrs. Dupont, with normal use, these seats should last you a couple of lifetimes."

"You're right, I suppose," Mabel said in a pouting voice. She took the leather piece from Mac and looked at it critically. "I guess I just want to have new ones because it would make me feel good to have something new and pretty in the house. My parents are getting older and they just have no enthusiasm for much of anything. I'm young! I want to enjoy life! I like seeing pretty things and thinking happy thoughts!"

"Well, it's entirely your choice," Mac told her. He wished she would go away.

"Hmmm ... so maybe I'll take this one home and think about it a bit more before I decide." Mabel offered Mac her brightest smile. "Thank you so much, Mr. Harmon! I knew I could trust you to give me a truthful answer."

Mac tuned out Mabel's cheerful babbling long enough to remember some of Shan's comments over the past year. Mac should get out more. His children would need a mama. Mac should prepare for their return.

On the other hand, what would Shan know on the subject? He was only eighteen—and afraid to come within ten feet of a female!

Well, Mac told himself, *it won't hurt to at least ... what? Pretend I'm interested?*

"Mrs. Dupont," Mac said, interrupting her mid-sentence. "Would you care to dine with me this evening at the Palace?"

"Oh! Oh my, Mr. Harmon. That would be simply lovely! I would be so honored!"

"Well, fine. That will be just fine." He nodded uncomfortably. "Um ... perhaps you could come in about an hour. You know, give me a chance to get cleaned up." He glanced down at his work clothes and the leather apron he'd forgotten to remove before leaving the shop.

"Well, that would be just wonderful! Thank you so much, Mr. Harmon! I'll see you in an hour then." She grinned, wiggled her fingers at him and turned up May Street, towards her own home, the chair seats apparently forgotten.

*   *   *

"I would love to hear more about your business, Mr. Harmon," Mabel said between bites of mashed potato.

"Uh, Mac. Please call me Mac."

"Oh then you must call me Mabel!" she replied. "Mac is such a distinguished sounding name. How did you get it?"

"Short for MacKennon. My mother's maiden name."

"I'm sure she was a lovely woman to have such a fine son as you!"

Mac felt vaguely uneasy. He wondered if he could get through this meal. He smiled—a quick, tight little smile—and nodded.

"You must please tell me more about your business, Mac. I find it fascinating!"

Before answering, Mac took a bite of green beans, chewed, and swallowed. "Well, my father back in New Hampshire was a saddle and harness man too. I learned from him." Mac took a bite of chicken.

"New Hampshire! My goodness, but you've traveled a long way from your home. When did you come here?"

Mac finished chewing and swallowed. The food went down like a lump of coal. "Well, I came across on the Emigrant Road in a wagon. A lot of people were taking the train by then, but I didn't have much money. I signed on to help a family by driving their second wagon. It was a kind of adventure for me."

"Oh my! I can't imagine! Was it frightening? The Indians? The buffaloes?"

"Not much to worry about. It wasn't really a hard trip at all. Not like in the old days. I came out in '89. I was fifteen. I met a man in Pendleton who told me about Heppner." He shrugged. "I liked the sound of it, so I came here to visit—and stayed."

Mabel nodded.

"I met Ella, my wife, at a dance down in Hardman. Couple years later, we got married. Bought us a house here in town and settled down." Mac's eyes softened at the memory of his precious Ella.

"And you and your wife had children, I believe?" Mabel smiled in seeming innocence.

Mac flinched inwardly. "Yes. Charlie, the oldest, died in the flood, along with Ella." Mac swallowed hard. "The two younger ones didn't die, but they disappeared that night. I haven't been able to find them yet."

"Oh!" Mabel's eyes grew large. "I don't want to hear that! It hurts my heart too much to even think of it! I just couldn't bear it!"

Mac was surprised by this response. Most people shied away from the subject entirely. Mrs. Dupont—Mabel—was saying she didn't want to talk about it, but at the same time, it sounded like she was enjoying the excitement of the very thought of missing children! Strange. Not knowing how to respond, he turned back to his beans.

"Mac, the whole flood experience just nearly overwhelmed me entirely! It was *so* hard to bear. They wanted me to work in the morgue—the *morgue!* Can you imagine? A sensitive woman like me. I couldn't do it. It would be too grievous. I would *not* be able to bear up under the strain! Even serving meals to those poor souls was more than I could handle! Just looking into their faces—it was heartbreaking. I was a nervous wreck! Finally, I had to just stay in my house 'til it was all over."

Mac said nothing. He couldn't even *think* of anything to say. His dinner was sitting like a rock in his stomach.

Mabel tried a different subject. "Let's talk about something more pleasant. Like maybe music. Are you fond of music, Mac?"

Mac swallowed, even though there was no food in his mouth, and finally said, "I am." He thought of the banjo hanging in the shop.

"Do you like opera? Oh, I just love *La Traviata*! It's my very favorite! About ten years ago Mother and Father and I heard it performed in New York. It was truly uplifting! The soprano—oh my! She was divine! And the theater was amazing! Truly amazing! Carved marble, mahogany, plush seats …"

"It sounds pretty impressive."

"Oh, I'm so glad you like opera too! Perhaps someday in the future, we will find ourselves attending at the same time." She smiled in delight.

Good grief! The opera? Did I say I liked opera? Mac took another bite of chicken and chewed in silence.

Chapter Thirty Three

March 1905

E lisabeth sat on the porch swing with Anny at her side. Gibbie was running around the outside of the house. He'd been around twice already and didn't show signs of stopping any time soon. Elisabeth marveled at the endurance of young children. She spoke softly to Anny. "Would you like to go for a walk with me?"

Anny said nothing.

Elisabeth reached out and patted Anny's hand resting in her lap. "We could walk out to the front gate and back," she suggested, standing. She pulled gently on Anny's hand.

Anny took a deep breath and slowly stood to her feet. Elisabeth rejoiced inwardly, and her heart beat a little faster. She moved slowly toward the porch steps, gently tugging on Anny's hand. Anny began moving with her.

They walked down the steps and along the wooden sidewalk to the gate. Anny reached out and clasped the gate with her free hand. Elisabeth stood still and waited. "It's a pretty day, isn't it?" she asked. Receiving no answer, she added, "I love to feel the gentle sun on my face. It makes me feel happy." She smiled, even though Anny was not looking at her. After a few minutes, she turned and encouraged Anny to walk with her, back toward the house. And Anny did.

Anny sat again on the porch swing, but Elisabeth hurried inside to share her excitement with Etta.

Gibbie, finally tiring of his marathon run, came and crawled up onto the swing with Anny. "I runned, Anny. I runned fast—the fastest of fastest!"

Anny turned her head to look at her brother. "I went for a walk," she said softly.

Gibbie scrunched up next to her and laid his head against her shoulder.

*   *   *

"For the first few weeks it was never—and I do mean *never*—out of her hand." Elisabeth spoke to Etta as the two sisters shared the chore of drying the supper dishes. "And I've seen her writing in it, so I know she's using it. She's been keeping it in her lap with her hand on it even at meal time! And now she keeps it in that big pocket on her pinafore. But she never lets me see it!"

"Why should she have to let you see it?" asked Etta, adding a dry plate to the stack on the kitchen table.

"Why should she have ... well, she shouldn't *have* to, but I was just thinking ..."

"You're snoopy. That's what. You just want to know what she's written," Etta said. She picked up the pile of plates and went to the dining room to put them away until tomorrow morning.

Elisabeth sighed. "You're right." She followed Etta to the door of the kitchen. "Or at least partly right. I *do* want to know what she's written. Etta, there's something going on in that child's mind. I know there is. Maybe if we could see what she writes, we could help her more."

"I think you *have* helped! You got her the notebook, didn't you?"

Elisabeth had no answer.

Etta poured two cups of coffee and sat at the small kitchen table while Elisabeth carried the clean silverware to the sideboard in the dining room.

"What are we going to do about Mr. Klein?" she asked as she reentered the kitchen. "He is still out of work. It's been over a month this time."

"How long have they been here? When did they first come?" Etta asked.

"It was July in aught three." Elisabeth named the months as she ticked her fingers. "A year and nine months, I guess. And he's not worked more than twelve months all together. He scares me—that thing he does. Remember when he first came—how refined he sounded? And he does it whenever it suits his purpose. But then, he's ... entirely different at other times. Mean and ugly and hateful! It's like he's two different people. That's not *normal!*

"Of course," she continued thoughtfully, "he has had a hard time ..." Her voice drifted off.

Etta shook her head and took a drink of her coffee.

"Fiddlesticks! We're making excuses for him," Elisabeth finally said. "And we're doing it on account of the children."

Etta rubbed her hand across her eyes. "How far behind is he?"

"Six months at least." Elisabeth stared into her coffee cup. "That little Gibbie is such a cutie! Do you know what he said to me this morning? When he came in from playing in the yard, he said 'I enjoyed myself very much and I didn't get dirty.' That whole long sentence he said! And he can't be more than three or four. He's just such a funny little guy! Of course, he *was* dirty—filthy, in fact! But I washed him up."

Etta chuckled and shook her head. "Oh my!" She turned her coffee cup round and round as she thought. "How does our budget stand?"

"Most of our bills are paid. We still owe twelve dollars to the green grocer. He seemed the most willing to carry us for a while longer, but he asked this morning when I thought we'd be able to pay. I think we need to take care of him first next week. I'm ashamed and embarrassed to have him ask!"

Etta nodded in agreement. "We've always paid on time, and in cash. That's why people trust us. And that trust won't continue if we can't come up with the money soon to pay our bills."

"Can we raise the rent for our other boarders?"

"That wouldn't be right, and you know it."

Elisabeth shrugged her shoulders. She didn't want to think about what was right. She wanted to find a way for the children to stay.

The kitchen faucet dripped in the background as they sat in silence considering their options.

"And we need to pay someone to fix that spigot before it drives me mad!" Etta said. "And the roof won't be far behind. We've had it patched what? Three times? Four times already? It won't be long before we need a whole new roof! Too bad Mr. Klein is no good at handyman chores. He could pay his rent that way."

"I hate to even mention it, but maybe we could ..."

"No!" Etta interrupted. "I know what you're thinking, and no, we can *not* dip into our savings! You know good and well we agreed we would never do that. That money is for when we get too old to keep the house open to guests. Do you want to go to the poor farm when you're old?"

The coffee on the table grew cold as the sisters searched their minds for some answer that might have eluded them.

"We have to let them go," Elisabeth finally said. "My heart breaks for the children, but we have to do it or we will eventually lose the house and everything we own. And then what?"

Etta said nothing as she drank the last of her coffee and set the cup carefully back on the table. She gritted her teeth. "I think you're right. You'll talk to him then?"

*   *   *

"I'm sorry Mister Klein, truly I am. But you must understand. We need to keep our rooms rented to paying customers. This is how we earn our living. And I do hope you find something soon."

Today was March thirtieth. Elisabeth had informed him of his need to find a new place to board two weeks ago. She'd reminded him one week ago. And tonight was his last night.

Klein scratched his head as if he didn't quite understand. "But I've been trying to find work. You know I have. Just yesterday I was down at the road department asking if they needed a supervisor. You know, a supervisor earns more than a regular laborer. If they'd just give me a chance, I'd show them what a good job I could do. And then I'd be able to pay my back rent in no time at all."

"Yes, I do understand. And I wish you well. You may have breakfast in the morning before you leave. We will need time to prepare the room for its next tenant. And please mind what I said about sending Anny to school in September. She's more than ready." Elisabeth turned on her heel and walked out the door and towards the kitchen. She needed no more argument from Mister Klein.

Elisabeth's heart was breaking for the children. And Etta, if the truth be told, was in anguish as well. The sisters had cared for the children whenever Klein was at work. They had made sure the children had clothes, and fed them a wholesome dinner in the middle of the day, even though dinner was not included in the rental agreement. Nor was child care. They also kept an open ear for the children when they saw Klein leave in the evenings without them. They knew of his condition when he returned late at night from the noise he made coming in.

Klein was the worst father they had ever seen. He seemed completely unaware of the children's needs—or even the fact that they *had* needs. He rarely spoke to either of them.

Now what would become of the children? What would become of Anny? She was intelligent; that was clear. But something was wrong.

She rarely looked either of the sisters in the face and had spoken no more than ten words since she'd arrived. Her response to most questions was nothing. Absolutely nothing. She seemed lost in a world that she couldn't escape. Whatever would become of her?

*   *   *

Klein slammed the door on his way out of the house for the last time. He stopped on the front porch, thought a moment, then took out a pocket knife and scraped a long scratch on the porch railing. At the end of the scratch, he dug the point of the knife into the wood and twisted it around and around, leaving a deep hole. Grinning and muttering, he pocketed the knife and strode down the street with the children following behind.

He used most of the coins in his pocket to catch a bus into Portland, then found a place in a cheap rooming house. He didn't even try to find work—just waited day by day, until the landlady threw them out. Then he moved himself and the children into yet another rooming house. He was offered a job with the city—road work. Not as a supervisor, but man-handling a shovel. It was hard and dirty. But he did it. And he got paid. The lady who ran the boarding house did not like Anny and Gibbie. But she put up with them, because Klein paid every week.

At the end of summer time, Klein stayed home from work one day, combed his hair, and took Anny and Gibbie on a walk. Yes, he would see that the children had a good education. He was a refined man and an upstanding citizen, and he wanted his children to bring him pride.

*   *   *

Father took me to
scool. the teacher
siad I was to little.
Father said I can
read and rite. the
tecHer made me Do
it. So I did. But she
stil said I was to little.
Father said he will
bring me munday

Chapter Thirty Four

M ac stepped out of his room at the Palace Hotel and turned to lock the door behind him. As he looked up, Les Matlock came down the hall, carrying his gold-headed cane. Matlock and Kelley had each received this memento from the grateful citizens of Ione, in commemoration of their now famous ride on the night of the flood. Matlock carried his with pride.

"Les," Mac nodded to his friend.

"Hey Mac, I was just going to stop by your room, but here you are. How you doing, anyway?" He extended his hand and Mac shook it.

"Good as can be expected." Mac pocketed his key.

"You're headed off again soon on another trip?"

"I am. Seattle. It's been over a year since I've been there, and my letters aren't getting any response. I just feel like I need to go back and try again—in person. Last week I went up through the Walla Walla valley again. " Mac didn't need to say that the trip had not been successful.

Matlock shook his head. "I know this must be hard on you, Mac. Especially since a lot of people think you're kind of ... well, they think you should just accept the fact that the children died."

The muscle in Mac's jaw twitched. "If I believed they died, I would have mourned their loss."

"Mac, are you familiar with Robert Herrick?"

Mac shook his head. "Don't think I've met him."

"Well, no." Matlock smiled and slipped his hand into his pocket. "He died a couple hundred years ago. But he was a writer. A poet. I've always liked poetry." Matlock gazed at the ceiling a moment, then quoted,

"Attempt the end, and never stand to doubt;
Nothing's so hard but search will find it out."

Matlock smiled and said, "I've…well, I've wished for some time I could do something to help you in your search. I don't know if your children are alive or not. But I can see that you don't believe for a moment those children died. It's not like you're too stubborn to believe the truth. It's more like you *know* they are alive. I guess I'd like to support you in that. Going on trips all over the country like you do has to be expensive. I want to help." Matlock pulled his hand from his pocket and pressed a folded bill into Mac's hand.

Mac found himself fighting tears as he shook Matlock's hand in thanks. "I thank you, Les. I do. It's not just the money—it's that … you believe in me. Thank you for that."

Matlock just smiled. "I wish you the best, Mac." He dropped Mac's hand and continued down the hall to his room.

*   *   *

Anny took out her journal and flipped through the many pages she had already filled with writing. Arriving at a clean page, she began a new entry.

November, 1905

> It is warm inside the
> scool when the rain
> fals and the wind blows
> the leevs. I look out the
> windows. ther are
> other children to. I
> dont no who thay are.
> I dont talk to them. Som
> of the leevs are pretty
> when they fall down but
> some are just brown and
> wet and misrbut miss
> miserbl. Gibbie isnt
> here. I miss him.

January, 1906

We live in a brown house now. Our room has 2 beds. Father sleeps in one of them. I sleep in the other one. Gibbie sleeps in my bed to but he sleeps at the other end. There is just me and Gibbie and father. Nobody else. and we live in the brown house. The lady makes brekfast and supper for the people. we all eat at the big table. The plates are green. All the big peple talk to each other but Gibbie and me we dont talk we just eat. Thats all. But I talk to Gibbie. Nobody else.

*　　*　　*

Mac Harmon had changed. At first people didn't notice much, because everyone in town looked terrible—just one more thing the flood had done. But most people gradually found their balance again and were able to move on. Not Mac. Although it had been only three years since the flood, he looked a good fifteen years older. And at least fifteen pounds thinner. Probably the thing people noticed most was the change in his personality. The old Mac was cheerful, helpful, encouraging—a great addition to the community. The new Mac was serious—far too serious, some said. He kept to himself, didn't talk much. If he suddenly vanished, most people wouldn't even have noticed.

Mac bowed his head over the stitching horse and clamped the leather strap into place. *Just do the next thing,* he told himself. *Pick up the thread, form it and wax it, sew the strap into place. Move on to the next step.* He knew, his hands knew, how to do the job. He'd done it hundreds of times. *Just do it again.*

Mac couldn't stop thinking about a conversation he'd had with Dacia Burke a few days ago. Dacia had told him how she suspected Pappy knew something about Mac's missing children, but couldn't seem to bring it to the surface. She'd also told him the more Pappy was pressed to tell the story, the less he seemed to know. The thought of it tortured Mac. If only there was a way to get through to the old man.

He drew in a breath and heaved a deep sigh. Shan looked up from his work, but said nothing.

Pappy entered the front door, accompanied by young Will and the sound of the banjo. Will walked his great-grandfather to Mac's shop most every Wednesday when he was not in school. And school was out for the summer. The third summer since the flood. Far too long for Mac to be without his children. Most people considered Mac and Pappy two of a kind. Men with slightly scrambled brains. Men who couldn't seem to tell truth from imagination.

Pappy stood bent over his shillelagh, staring at Mac. Finally Mac sensed his presence and looked up, staring back. Pappy just shook his head silently and slowly turned to sit on one of the wooden chairs in the front of the shop.

Mac sighed deeply again and poked the needle through the leather. He would head out for Bend tomorrow. And next week, Baker City.

*   *   *

April, 1906

Today teacher told us to write
something about the spring
flowers. I didn't do it because
I didnt want to. I talked to the
teacher. I told her no thank
you I was very polite. But she
didn't here me talk. I was
quiet. Now I want to write
about flowers. Here is my
writing.

The flowers of spring

Dance and sing

And bow when they are finished

But hart akes do not

Dance or sing

They ~~just~~ only bow

And cry

Chapter Thirty Five

September 1906

Today was the first day of school. This would be Anny's third year in school, and Gibbie would be coming too. Yesterday at breakfast, the lady had mentioned school to Anny. "It starts tomorrow," she said. "Didn't you know?"

No. Anny had not known. How would she know unless someone told her?

"You don't know nuthin' do ya? I don't see how a kid as dumb as you can survive!"

"Gibbie too?" Anny asked, softly.

The lady looked at Anny sharply. *Hmmm ... she can talk—when she wants to.* The woman had no idea how old Gibbie was, but he was at least as tall as Anny. And she was tired—very tired—of having these children underfoot all day every day. "Yeah. Him too," she said.

The next morning, Anny smoothed Gibbie's shirt and tucked it into his trousers. Somehow, he didn't look quite right for going to school. She looked him over carefully. The hair. That was the problem. It was way too long. Anny needed to cut it. She didn't want the other children to make fun of her brother. But where would she get scissors? She had none. Father was gone. He was at work. "Gibbie, come," she said. "Let's eat breakfast."

She took him by the hand and led him down the stairs to the dining room. They were late. The other boarders had already eaten, and the table was partly cleared. Anny didn't know what to do, so she sat on her usual chair and had Gibbie sit beside her. When the lady came back into the room for the rest of the dirty dishes, Anny looked up hopefully.

"What are you doing here?" the woman demanded. "Breakfast is over."

Anny said nothing. She didn't know what to say. But she certainly hoped the lady would give them something to eat.

"Humph. Well, I suppose I can't let you starve. I'll go get you something. But mind, you show up on time from now on, or no breakfast for you."

Anny's head made a tiny nod in response.

When the woman reappeared with two slices each of plain bread for the children, Anny patted Gibbie's blond curls and asked, "Do you have a pair of scissors I could borrow?"

It was the longest speech the woman had ever heard from the child. She glared at her for a moment, and then went to the sideboard, pulled open the silverware drawer, and extracted a pair of scissors. She banged them onto the table near Anny with the warning, "I don't want hair on the floor. Do it outside."

Anny ate one piece of bread and put the other in the large pocket of her badly worn and much too small pinafore.

She took one of Gibbie's slices of bread, folded it in half, and put it in his trousers pocket. He wanted to pull it out and eat it, but Anny told him no. "You'll need it for dinner at school," she said.

Then taking her brother by the hand, she led him outside. She stood him in the middle of the yard and began chopping long clumps of hair from his head. Soon he looked like he'd been too near an egg beater. Anny decided it looked terrible, but couldn't see how to fix it. She jumped when she heard the lady behind her.

"Well, you've made a royal mess of it, that's for sure. Give me those scissors." The lady snatched the scissors from Anny's hand, put one hand on top of Gibbie's head, and cut around the bottom edge of his hair. It wasn't good. But it was better.

"Thank you," Anny said quietly, and she took Gibbie's hand and started for the schoolhouse two blocks away.

*   *   *

September, 1906

We live in a nother wite house.
The lady is mene to me and
Gibbie. We dont like her.
Father has a job. He goes
to work. Gibbie and I go to
school but I dont do the
work. I dont want to. I dont
talk. I dont want to.

*　　*　　*

October, 1906

Father was fired again, and
now he is drunk. drunk menes
he cant walk right and he is
loud and mene. The lady tolld
me and Gibbie that. Somtimes
he is mene to Gibbie. Yester
day we moved to a nother
new house. It is gray. Dirty
gray. Our room is in the
atik. Its pretty cold at night
becaus the window wont shut
all the way. We only have 1
blanket. Father has 2. On
Munday Gibbie and I will
go to a new school.

*　　*　　*

March 1907

In Heppner, life had not returned to normal. It had, instead, settled into a *new kind* of normal. Everyone was different. Attitudes were changed, dominant traits became even stronger—or disappeared entirely. Some people struggled in ways they had never been susceptible to in the past. No one went on as if nothing had happened. Heppner was an entirely different town than it had been before the flood.

"Y'er gonna get in so much trouble!" Will Burke was on his hands and knees watching Michael Collins inch his way under The Fair. He grabbed the leg of Michael's trousers and was pulling backwards, trying to keep his friend from disappearing all the way under the store. He looked over his shoulder as he heard a sound behind him. Even in the darkness, Will didn't *think* he saw anything to be afraid of. Still, he was mighty uncomfortable with the situation.

"Michael, c'mon! We shouldn't be here."

Michael, head and body out of sight under the store building, legs quickly following, turned on his friend suddenly. "Go home if you want, scaredy cat. I'm gonna get me some peanuts. And I ain't going to share if you leave!"

Will struggled with himself. It had sounded like fun when Michael suggested crawling out of bed at night and going "to a special place I know of" to get some free peanuts. Now? It didn't seem like a good idea at all. Will was pretty sure Michael was up to no good. The brace and bit Michael had brought along only added to Will's suspicions. And ... *that's it,* he decided. *I'm leaving.*

He gave a final jerk on Michael's trousers, jumped to his feet, and ran for home.

*　　*　　*

A week later, Grace wiggled her shoulders and stretched her neck in delight as she slowly walked home carrying the groceries she'd bought at The Fair. The beautiful sunshine and gentle breeze in the air made her feel better than she had in some time. Michael had refused to come into the store with her, but that's what she had come to expect from Michael. He was uncooperative about most everything these days. The only time she saw him happy was when Shan came home from work. Dacia said he'd never been like this before the flood. But he was now. He most definitely was now!

Johnny said he might be president someday—if he didn't hang first! If only she could think of a way to help the boy.

Grace looked up to see Esmerelda coming toward her. She had been so glad when Esmerelda returned to Heppner a little over a year ago. They had even found a way to visit with each other—on the far side of the cemetery. Grace had gone up to the cemetery one Sunday for some time by herself. After wandering through the graves for a while, she saw Esmerelda just arriving at the top of the hill. Esmerelda walked close enough to be heard and said, "Come with me." Grace followed, as Esmerelda led her to a big poplar tree about halfway down the hill at the back of the cemetery. They had sat and visited for over an hour, and it had been wonderful! Grace felt so much less alone, adrift. Esmerelda—no matter what her profession—was good for her.

Now, as she saw Esmerelda coming her way, she started to speak, then remembered not to, as she saw the warning look on Esmerelda's face—the look that said, *you don't know me. Remember?*

As they passed each other, Esmerelda spoke softly. "I'm going to Baker City soon, but I'll probably be back in a year or two."

Grace looked over her shoulder but Esmerelda continued walking as if she had not spoken. Grace could only wonder.

She carried the groceries into the house and put them away, then checked the stew and mixed up some biscuits. Hearing Shan's step on the porch, she slid the biscuits into the oven and closed the door.

"Hi Shan," she said to the air. "Biscuits are in the oven. There's pie on the counter." And she walked past him and out the door.

*   *   *

The wind was cold as Anny and Gibbie walked behind Father. "I need to go take care of some business," Father said. "You children stay here 'til I come back for you."

"Where are you going?" Gibbie asked.

"Just down the street a bit."

"Are you going to the saloon?"

"What does it matter to you where I'm going!" Father drew back his hand as if to smack Gibbie, but Gibbie ducked. He'd had experience.

Anny turned and walked away. Yes, Father was going to a saloon. That's what he did whenever he got fired. Actually, it's what he did even when he didn't get fired. Fired meant he didn't go to work anymore. Until he found another job, that is. He was always angry when he got fired, but going to a saloon would make him feel better, he said.

"Gibbie," Anny called softly. "Come!"

Gibbie came, and Father turned and walked away from the children. Anny took Gibbie's hand and walked to a bench near what might have been a flower bed at one time. There were bushes also, and other benches. *A park,* Anny thought. *But it's not a very nice one.*

As the children sat staring at their surroundings, Anny thought about going home, but she couldn't remember where it was. They'd moved into this new house only a few days ago. Not the gray one. Another white one, with dark green shutters. They had not started school yet. In fact, this was the first time Anny and Gibbie had been out of the house. She looked around her, but saw nothing she recognized. Nothing at all.

Anny put her arm around Gibbie's shoulders and pulled him close to her. Her bare legs swung gently as she looked beyond the park to the buildings across the street. "Bakery," she said softly. She smelled it before she saw the sign. Her grip on Gibbie tightened as she gazed across the street and lifted her nose to better smell the aroma.

Making up her mind, she scooted off the bench, pulled Gibbie by the hand, and crossed the street. The two children stood in front of the bakery, gazing through the window at the bread and rolls within.

Before long, the lady behind the counter put her head out the door and said, "Get along now, you two ragamuffins. You've no business here unless you have money to spend."

Anny stood her ground, just looking at the lady.

"Go on! You heard me! Clear out now! Off with you!"

Anny looked down at the sidewalk and turned to walk away. But she walked only to the edge of the building, pulling Gibbie the last foot to get him out of sight of the window.

The fattest woman Anny had ever seen came out of the bakery, her arms full of packages. She turned away from the hungry children and waddled down the street.

Next out the door was a boy who looked to be not much older than Anny herself. He turned toward Anny and Gibbie, then stopped short to look directly at them. "Hi. I heard her tell you to get lost. How come? You do something wrong?"

Anny just shook her head.

"Why are you standing there?"

"Hungry!" Gibbie said. "We're hungry. It sure smells good here!"

The boy cocked his head. "How come you're hungry? Don't you have any supper at your house?"

"We're lost," Gibbie explained, almost proudly. Anny looked sharply at him and jerked his hand. "Well, we're sort of lost." He looked hopefully at the bag the boy was carrying.

"It's okay," Anny said hurriedly and pulled Gibbie off the side-walk to cross the street back to the park.

But the boy said, "Wait! C'mere a minute. You really don't have any food?"

Anny stopped and faced the boy. "Not right now, we don't. But our father will be coming back for us soon, and he'll bring us something."

The boy looked as if he didn't believe her. "Here." He took a large roll from the bag and tossed it to Gibbie, who caught it neatly. "Mom will scold me for not getting enough, but I don't mind going without."

"Hey thanks!" Gibbie's face shone. "What's your name?"

But the boy had turned and was running down the street.

*   *   *

Anny woke up the next morning when Gibbie crawled out of her coat and left her to feel the cold air against her chest where he had huddled all night. She sat up and pulled the coat around her. Gibbie looked funny. He had twigs in his hair. And wrinkles on his face. Anny brushed his head off, but didn't think to brush her own as well.

"Anny, I'm hungry," Gibbie whined. "And I have to pee."

Anny looked around, but couldn't see anyone. "Pee in the bushes," she said. And Gibbie did.

Breakfast. She should think of something to feed her brother. The only thing she could think of was to go back to the bakery. She took Gibbie by the hand and began walking there. It smelled good, but it was locked. Everything on the street was locked up. And no people were around. The children walked back and sat on a bench in the cold sunshine, which was just beginning to creep into the park. Anny pulled Gibbie close to her and put her arm around his shoulder. They sat and swung their legs. There was nothing else to do.

Anny looked all around her. The park looked different in the morning light. Nothing looked familiar. Which direction had Father gone when he left them? And where was he now?

Anny took out her journal and pencil. Soon Gibbie began to grow drowsy as the sun rose higher in the sky. He slipped down into Anny's lap and fell asleep.

Anny opened her journal and balanced it on Gibbie's shoulder, pencil in hand—but she could think of nothing to write. Finally she wrote:

> muffins eggs bacon soup
> potatos. I like food. I like
> a warm bed. Gibbie is a
> sleep and we are lost
> and a lone.

*   *   *

Klein was *not* happy when he showed up late that morning to get the children. After all, wasn't a man entitled to a little drink when he lost his job? Stupid boss anyway. Fired for a little thing like being a couple of minutes late. Eight o'clock, eight-thirty—what difference would a few minutes make? And the boss said it was the fourth time. Klein didn't think so. Might have been the second. Certainly not something to get fired over! Anyway, now he'd gone and lost the kids. He sat on a park bench, laid his arms on the backrest, propped his left ankle on his right knee, and sulked. Some days it just wasn't worth getting up. He let his eyes drift shut.

Having the children had lost its shine. At first they had been his connection to Ella. Having them proved his worth—at least to himself. Now, he wasn't so sure. Ella was only a faint memory. The children were a nuisance. He needed to figure out something to do with them.

He hadn't even noticed last night when he staggered home that he didn't have the children with him. Whatever time that was. Kids shouldn't be out that late anyhow. But this morning when he'd gone down for breakfast, Mrs.—oh whatever-her-name-was—he couldn't remember. Anyway, she wanted to know where the children were, and he couldn't remember. Couldn't remember until he'd thought long and hard about it.

He remembered going to the saloon. Before that? The park! That's right, the park. He'd told the kids to wait for him there. Hmmm. He wondered where they were now. Well, he supposed he'd have to go back to the park and look. It was six blocks away. And chilly out this morning, in spite of the bright sunshine. Also, his head hurt from last night. But he'd have to go. Mrs. Whatever-her-name-was would give him no rest until he did.

And now here he was. No kids. Just a big empty park. Did he have to search the whole thing or could he just say he'd looked and they weren't here? No. He'd better look.

He opened his eyes—and there were Anny and Gibbie standing right in front of him. He blinked. Yes. There they were.

"Well," he said. "I guess it's time for us to go home now. Come along." And he stood and walked out of the park, never once checking to see if the children followed.

*   *   *

Grace had left the minute Shan set foot in the door. No surprise there. She did every night. Shan wished he could understand why she hated him so much. Well, actually, she probably didn't hate him. She just despised him—which was even worse. Didn't even consider him worthy of notice. Except for when he came home at the end of the day. She noticed then, and left.

Shan picked up the dirty dishes from supper, rinsed them and stacked them by the sink. Grace would wash them in the morning. Michael had gone outside to roll his hoop with a stick. Mr. Marquardson, owner of The Fair—since Alvin Giger died in the flood—had given Michael the hoop, broken and useless, and Shan had repaired it for his brother. "That boy needs something to keep him occupied," Mr. Marquardson had told Shan. "He's trouble, just lookin' for a place to happen!"

Shan wasn't sure what was happening to Michael. He didn't used to be like this—did he? Shan reached back in his memory to the days before the flood. Yes, Michael was always full of beans, but Ma had made him behave. He had respected Ma and obeyed her. But Ma wasn't here anymore to raise these children. And Shan sure didn't know how to go about it. He was their brother, for goodness sake, not their pa! Grace should do it. She was the one who was with them all day. She should be able to make Michael behave.

Shan wiped the table and tossed the rag in the sink. A knock sounded at the door, and he went to answer it. Mrs. Neal—grumpy old Mrs. Neal—stood there with a very unhappy looking Michael. Shan groaned inwardly.

"Hello, Mrs. Neal," he said, knowing immediately she had not come for a friendly visit. He knew without asking, Michael was in trouble. Again. What had he done now?

"Shan, you need to know. Michael here chased his hoop through my flower beds. He just went stomping through there as if he owned the place. Broken flowers layin' everywhere! Not only that, but he wouldn't apologize to me! He told me he didn't do it on purpose and so he didn't have to apologize."

Shan gritted his teeth and glared at Michael. "He *does* have to apologize. Michael, when you do something wrong, even if it's by accident, you apologize for it. That's just how it is. Apologize to Mrs. Neal, please."

Michael hung his head and grumbled, "Sorry."

"And I really am sorry, Mrs. Neal. Michael is having a hard time adjusting to life without a mother."

"And don't you go making excuses for him, Shan Collins!" Mrs. Neal shook her finger in the direction of Shan's face.

"Yes, well ... thank you very much for coming to tell me about this. I'm doing the best I can." He pulled Michael inside and nodded, as politely as he was able, to Mrs. Neal before shutting the door in her face.

Shan blew out his breath through clenched teeth, and shook his head. "Michael, what am I going to do with you?"

Michael just shrugged.

"You really need to start behaving. Mrs. Neal is not the first person in Heppner to complain to me about your behavior."

"Who else?" Michael looked out of the corner of his eyes at Shan.

"Well, your teacher at school, for one. And Mr. Marquardson at The Fair. And Mrs. Jacobson—she said you scared her chickens on purpose. Michael, you know chickens don't lay when they're upset. And the Jacobson family needs those eggs!"

"Is that all?"

"Isn't that enough? And no, that's not all. Michael, this has got to stop!"

Michael stood with his hands in his pockets and his eyes on the floor. "Can I go now?" he asked.

Shan just stared at him for a moment, then nodded. "Yeah. Go. And behave yourself!"

*   *   *

Anny stood before a brown mare in a field of tall grass. The horse put her nose right up to Anny's face. Anny felt the warm rubbery lips and the bristles on the nose. She petted the nose tentatively. *Soft.* She liked it. She reached up and moved her small hand down the length of the horse's long face—so much face! The horse blew gently against Anny's chest, and she giggled. "Horse," she said. "You're beautiful, horse!"

The animal lowered its head, and Anny took one ear in each hand. "Oh!" she breathed. "So soft! I love your ears, horse!" She leaned her cheek against the horse's forehead and rubbed the ears. What a wonderful silky feeling!

"Hey Girl!" Father's voice. "What do you think you're doing? Trying to get yourself killed? Git over here! Right now!" Even in the blast of angry words, the horse stood completely still. And Anny stood still—she didn't budge.

"Anny! Git over here!" Father climbed through the fence and stormed across the field to retrieve her. Grabbing her arm, he dragged her back toward the house he'd come from.

The landlady came quickly down the porch steps. "What's wrong?" she called. "Is the child all right?"

"She's fine," Father shouted back. "She's deef. Don't hear much, so I had to go get her." Anny's arm hurt as Father dragged her from the field. She struggled to keep her legs moving fast enough to keep up with him, hoping he'd let go of her arm. But he didn't.

Stupid kid, he thought as he dragged Anny out of the field. *Both of 'em. Don't know why I have 'em at all. There are ways to get rid of kids. Yeah, there are ways.*

Book Three

A New Dawn

Chapter Thirty Six

March 1907

Klein's clothing hung on him like laundry on a clothesline, flapping in the wind as he walked. He was as tall and thin as he ever was and encrusted with grime. He held in each of his large hands a small grubby fist. The one in his left belonged to Gibbie, now six. Gibbie twisted and jerked, trying to escape from the powerful grip. He whined loudly and kicked at anything and everything in his path.

In the other hand was Anny, who seemed not at all perturbed to be dragged along by this human scarecrow. She shivered as she walked with measured steps, deliberately, almost as if she were walking to her death. She knew neither where they were going, nor why. Nor did she care.

Father had not felt it important to explain himself to the children. They were going. That was all.

Eventually, they arrived at a large building set amidst other large buildings. Father told the children to wait. He vanished, then returned with a stocky, dark-haired man who proceeded to hitch a horse to his wagon. The man—Father called him Robinson—gave his horse an apple, and though he didn't speak to them, he gave each of the children one as well. Then they all got into the wagon with the man and rode for a long time. After Anny and Gibbie finished their apples, they fell asleep in the wagon bed.

The children woke when the wagon stopped at a store alongside a huge river. The man and Father went into the store and came out with some smoked fish and bread. They gave some to the children. When evening came, the wagon stopped at a place that served food at tables. They had hot soup and bread. The hot soup was wonderful!

Then they all climbed the stairs to a room with beds and slept for the night. The next morning they left without taking time for breakfast. In the back of the wagon, Anny clutched Gibbie close to her, pulling him into her coat the best she could. They were both cold, but being close together helped. Anny had no stockings to warm her legs, so she pulled her feet up next to her and pulled her too-short dress down as far as she could. It didn't reach the tops of her shoes.

Around noon, they came to a village and a boat landing, and the wagon stopped.

"Get out," Father said, and Anny and Gibbie did. They stood by the wagon while Father talked with a tall yellow-haired man on the dock and gave him some money. "Come on," Father said, grabbing Gibbie under his arms and swinging him, after the man, into a small boat.

Gibbie kicked and yelled, but the blond man took him from Father and sat him down on the bottom of the vessel. He smiled at Gibbie. *"Ikke gjør det være redd for. Jeg vil ta godt vare på du!"*

Though Gibbie had no idea what the man had just said, his voice was gentle. Gibbie stopped yelling and stared at the man who spoke with such strange words.

"Gut boy!" The man nodded. "Is okay, ja? Ve go in da boat." He reached up to grab Anny, and set her by her brother. Then Father climbed aboard.

"I am Nils," the man said to Father as he rowed along the small slough, and then out into the big river. By this time, Gibbie had decided the boat was wonderful and was up on his feet trying to look everywhere at once.

"*Sitte!*" the man said. "Sit. You fall ... oferboard! Not gut!" But Gibbie didn't sit. Not by himself. He took several uneven steps toward the bow, and suddenly plopped to his bottom as the boat rocked. He tried to get up again, but the man pulled one of the oars back into the boat and pushed Gibbie down with his hand. "*Nei,*" he said. "Sit." This time, Gibbie sat still.

Eventually, the boat pulled up alongside a small dock, and Nils threw a rope over one of the pilings. He handed the children up to Father, who said to him, "Wait here. Understand? Wait." Nils nodded.

"Hurry, ja?" he responded. "Da tide comes. Big rough water. Hurry."

Father took the children by their hands and began walking up the road. Eventually, they reached a small white house with a white fence and crocuses beginning to poke their heads above the darkness of the damp earth. Letting go of Anny's hand, Father consulted a wrinkled paper he took from his shirt pocket and turned in at the gate, where a lady met them on the stoop.

"Good afternoon, ma'am," Klein said with a slight nod of his head. "I hope I'm at the right place."

The lady's face was filled with sunshine as if this was the best day in the world. She beamed at Father. "Yes, we've been expecting you. You're the man who's going to see about a job at the salmon cannery, right?" Then she smiled at Anny and Gibbie. She reached out and patted Anny's thin shoulder, then cupped Gibbie's chin in her hand and said "Ah! Aren't you just a fine little man, now?" But Gibbie didn't like being cooed over.

"I'm hungry," he demanded, pulling his face away from her hand.

"I know what," said the lady. "I have some gingerbread in the house. Shall we have some?" She seemed not the least put off by Gibbie's demanding tone.

Gibbie looked at her with interest at the mention of gingerbread. His eyes began to sparkle and he nodded his head.

The lady took Gibbie by his hand and turned to lead the children into the house.

"Well," Father cleared his throat. "Now, if I understand correctly, I just take the road down here to the left to get over to Cathlamet?"

"That's right. It's not far." The lady nodded. "There will probably be a boat there that can take you over."

"Thank you, Ma'am, very much. I'll be going, then." He ducked his head slightly, touching the edge of his worn cap, and without a backward glance he passed through the gate and down the road.

*   *   *

The children seemed not at all concerned about being left with a stranger and ate their gingerbread as if they hadn't eaten in a week. Mama Jane—she told them that was her name—took note of the children's hunger and wondered if they had enough to eat at home.

Oh well, she thought. *I've just forgotten how young ones eat. It's been so long.*

When Anny finished, Mama Jane encouraged her to make something with the pretty colored beads she kept in a special box. Anny said "thank you" quietly, politely, but sat and did nothing. Her face looked pleasant enough, but she responded not at all to Mama Jane's friendliness.

When Gibbie's second piece of gingerbread was gone, Mama Jane pushed him out the back door and told him to go find Granddaddy. Then she watched out the window.

Sure enough, Gibbie started walking around the yard, attempting to discover not only where Granddaddy was but *who* he was. Gibbie found him working in the yard behind the house. A stocky man with short, thick hair and a ruddy face, Granddaddy had the look of a friendly over-sized elf about him. He used a rake and sometimes his fingers as he scraped up the dead grass and leaves. He spaded the soil to loosen it for the new growth of spring. Gibbie followed Granddaddy around like a baby duck, wanting to know what he was doing and why, and could Gibbie help? Mama Jane chuckled. What a joy to have children in the house, even if it was only for a day!

She turned to find Anny had moved to the sofa. Oslo, the Petersen's very old dog, was sitting at Anny's knee with his head in her lap. Anny placed a tentative hand on the dog's head. She moved her hands slowly over the coarse hair of his head, his neck, his back. He made a pleasant whimpering sound and scooted himself even closer to Anny. She bent down and rubbed her face on the dog's head while burying her fingers deep into the dog's shaggy coat around his neck. Mama Jane smiled. Happy to see the girl would respond to something, she began her preparations for supper.

The meal Mama Jane gave the children was yummy and plentiful. Mama Jane and Granddaddy seemed puzzled as supper time came and went with no sign of Father returning. When darkness came, they put the two children to bed on the sofa, one at each end. The blanket Mama Jane gave them was soft and old ... and warm.

By the next morning, when she made biscuits and gravy for breakfast, the children seemed to have forgotten about Father entirely.

Chapter Thirty Seven

B y Saturday—four days after they arrived—Mama Jane decided it was time to do something about the children in her care. She took them down the road to the home of her friend, Birgitta Svensen. "I was hoping you might have some clothes left from when your children were young," she explained, while Gibbie stared openly at the woman's head with its braided golden crown.

"You haf children? Oh, what darlings! Ven did dis happen? Come in, come in! I yust made coffee! Are dese some of your grandchildren?" Birgitta's English was easy to understand when she spoke slowly and carefully. Like many of the settlers on Puget Island, Birgitta and her husband had come from Norway. They spoke Norwegian amongst themselves, but insisted that their children be schooled in English. And most of them could speak English—at least a bit.

"Well, they are staying with us for a few days." Mama Jane frowned. "Actually, it's a bit of a mystery. Their father brought them on Tuesday. And ..."

"And vat? He forgets to come back?"

Mama Jane shrugged. "We're not sure what happened. But I have no other clothes for them. I can make them some, of course, but that would take time. Do you ...?"

"Oh, of course! Of course I have t'ings. Come! Let's see what we can find for dem. Poor little ... oh! What is dat word? Poor little ... tykes? Yes?" Mrs. Svensen, a woman "built to last" according to her husband, huffed and puffed up the steep stairs, Mama Jane and the children following behind.

In only a matter of minutes, Anny had two new dresses. Well, not new, but quite nice. One fit perfectly. The other was too large, but only a bit. Mrs. Svensen found a pair of trousers and two shirts for Gibbie, and even under things for both of them.

"But I have trousers," argued Gibbie. "At home in a box under the bed. And Anny has another dress too."

"Well, this is just for now," Mama Jane assured him. "Don't worry about it."

"Let me get da children some cookies before you leaf," Mrs. Svensen said, heading for the stairs.

"Cookies! Yum!" Gibbie smiled in anticipation and completely forgot about the new clothes and the clothes at home under the bed.

The children took their cookies outside to the front porch while Mama Jane and her friend sat at the kitchen table with their coffee.

"Oh ja, so now you can tell me da real story," Birgitta said. She leaned in close. "Tell me, how dis is possible! Two children yust show up on da Island, boom—like dat? Very strange!"

Mama Jane blew on her coffee before beginning. "Well, you know Ole Bergstrom from the north side of the Island?"

Birgitta nodded. "Ja, ja. I know Ole."

"Well, Ivar was talking to him about a week ago, and Ole asked him if we might be able to keep a couple of children someday soon while the father went to apply for a job at the cannery. Ivar told him yes, that would be fine." She stopped to blow again on her coffee and take a small sip. "So on Tuesday morning, a man showed up with Anny and Gibbie. He left them and started over toward Cathlamet. At least that's where he *said* he was going. We just assumed that he would come back for the children in a little while. But he didn't."

"He didn't?" Brigitta's face showed her amazement. "He yust didn't come back?"

Mama Jane nodded. "That's about it. We don't know what happened. Maybe they needed him right away and he just hasn't had time to come back. Or maybe he's injured, or sick. We just don't know what to think. If we don't hear anything by next week, Ivar will go over there and see what he can find out."

"Who is dis fadder? How does Ole know him?"

"Ivar says a cousin of Ole's from Portland wrote Ole about it. Said he heard of a man was planning on going to work in the area and would need to leave the children just while he went to find a job. He didn't say anything about where the children would stay when he actually went to work. Ole wrote back after he talked to Ivar and gave him directions to our house." She shrugged in a gesture of uncertainty. "He found the house all right. Maybe we can track down Ole's cousin if nothing else turns up."

Gibbie charged back into the house and stopped at the kitchen threshold. He smiled and asked hopefully, "Are there more cookies?"

Mrs. Svensen laughed aloud and gave him two more cookies. He ran back to the porch to share with Anny.

"Gibbie told me their last name is Klein. He says his father's first name is 'Mister.'"

Birgitta smiled. "And da girl?"

"She doesn't talk."

"She doesn't talk?" Birgitta repeated with concern.

"Well, barely. I've heard her say 'thank you' a couple times. That's about it. And she doesn't look at me. She just kind of gazes off into space mostly."

"Hm ... Dat's not gut. Will you send dem to school?"

"Well, if they stay here—yes, I should."

"Send dem to da Sunny Sands School. At da Welcome Slough School, sometimes dey can't get to da outhouse during high tide. Dey haf to vait."

"Yes, I remember!" Mama Jane laughed aloud at the memory of the children having to time their bladders to the tide. Of the two schools on Puget Island, Sunny Sands was her definite choice for the children. "Our four all went to Welcome Slough before Sunny Sands was built. But it's about the same distance." She put her empty cup in the sink. "*If* they stay." She smiled at Birgitta and shrugged again.

"Thanks for the coffee, and thank you very much for the clothes, too! I'll return them when I can, but for now, I think it's time for us to get going. Anny, Gibbie!" she said as she walked out on the porch. "Time for us to go home now."

Anny tucked her lower lip between her teeth and started walking. Gibbie glared at Mama Jane and said, "I don't live with you. I'm just visiting."

*   *   *

On Monday, Ivar Petersen caught a ride in a small fishing boat over to Cathlamet, on the Washington side of the river. He went to the Warren Cannery, but they had never heard of a Mr. Klein, and no one had applied for work for over two weeks. Next, Ivar borrowed a horse and rode out to three different lumber camps, but still he met with no success. At Benson's operation, they said they weren't hiring, and no one had recently asked for work. At a little gyppo camp near Steamboat

Slough at Skamokawa, Klein's name was unknown. Ivar's questions met with a similar response at the Elochoman camp. So where was the man? He couldn't have gone all that far. But apparently he *had* gone a lot farther than one day's journey in search of a job. And who could guess when or if he would return for the children?

When he got back to Puget Island, Ivar stopped at the Bergstrom place. Ole Bergstrom was surprised to hear that the children's father had not come back for them, and promised to write a letter to his cousin in Portland.

On Tuesday, Mama Jane took the children to school. She entered the one-room schoolhouse with the children in tow and spoke to Mr. Marshall, the schoolmaster. She couldn't tell him where the children had come from or how long they would be staying.

He grumbled, but allowed as how he'd just have to make the best of it.

Before she left, Mama Jane took the schoolmaster aside and told him, "I'm not sure about Anny. I don't think she's quite right if you know what I mean." She tapped her finger to her head. "But she won't cause you any trouble, I don't think."

The master looked at Anny and rubbed his hand over his face with a sigh.

Gibbie was already making his presence known to the other boys coming into the schoolhouse. "My name is Gibbie," he stated proudly, "and I just come in from the California gold fields. Yes sir! My mamma and my daddy, they're plumb rich."

"I got a agate," stated a young man named Francis. "You wanna hold it?"

"Aw, that ain't nuthin'!" Gibbie tossed the rock up and down in his hand. "I got gold nuggets bigger than that at home."

"I betcha don't," said Francis, and snatching the rock mid-air, he stuffed it back in his pocket.

"Frances is a girl's name! Whacha doin' with a name like that anyway?" Gibbie puffed out his chest and cocked his head.

"It's Fran*cis* with a 'i,' and you can call me Frank. And if you don't … you'll just see what this can do!" The boy waved a small fist threateningly in Gibbie's face.

Gibbie, delighted to accept the invitation, shoved Frank backwards and leaped on top of him with both fists flying.

The schoolmaster turned from Mama Jane to see the two boys rolling top over teakettle in the center of a crowd of students, the girls horrified, the boys cheering with determination, some for Gibbie, some for Frank.

"Here, here!" the master scolded, shoving his way through the ring of spectators. "Stop that right now! Francis, you should be ashamed of yourself! And you, young man," he held Gibbie by the back of his shirt. "I certainly hope this is not an example of what we may expect from you here at Sunny Sands!"

Gibbie hung his head as was expected, but then turned it to the side and grinned at Frank.

"Take your places. Everyone! Right now!" The master released Gibbie's shirt and pointed to an empty seat. "Six years old, you're in the first grade. And you," he said turning to Anny. "Eight years old. Third grade. There." He pointed to an empty seat next to a girl with blond curly hair.

The children in the room began moving to the wooden seats, but Anny stood rooted to the spot she had assumed when she first entered the building. Aside from watching Gibbie during his encounter with Frank, she had shown no sign of even being in the room.

Gibbie was supremely happy. He was accepted by his peers. Anny, however, was miserable.

*   *   *

Eventually, Anny moved to the seat the teacher had indicated and sat beside the girl with loose golden curls tumbling down her back. Anny gazed at the desk top and made no attempt to listen to the teacher or do any work. When Mr. Marshall moved on to the fourth grade class, the girl spoke to Anny.

"My name is Mary Jolene Hendersen, but you can call me Mary Jo," she said. She waited for Anny to answer. When she didn't, Mary Jo went on. "My parents wanted to give me an American sounding name, because we're Americans now. Do you think Mary Jo sounds American?"

Anny didn't answer.

Mary Jo continued, unperturbed. "I live up on the north side of the Island in the white house, just across from Little Island. I don't have any brothers or sisters. There's just me. That makes it hard sometimes, because if I do something wrong, my parents *know* it was me and not my brother or sister." Mary Jo waited, but still, Anny did not respond.

She went on. "My mama can't have any more babies. She almost died having me. But I don't mind being an only child. I have lots of friends. Would you like to be my friend?"

Anny remained silent, but she did glance up at Mary Jo's face. Mary Jo accepted this as encouragement and began asking Anny questions.

"How old are you? Where did you come from?"

Anny moved her eyes from the desk top to gaze out the window.

"Where do you live?" Mary Jo asked. "Do you speak English? *Gjør du snakke engelsk?* It's okay if you don't. We all speak Norwegian at home, but at school we speak English. I'll help you learn."

Anny still spoke not a word, but she did turn her eyes and look at Mary Jo with a confused expression on her face.

Mary Jo, not at all discouraged, continued. "I saw Mrs. Petersen bring you this morning. Is she your grandma? *Far Mor? Mor Mor?* I know her. The Petersens are good friends of my family. I remember when their daughter got married. That was two years ago, but I still remember. She was a *beautiful* bride."

The master cleared his throat loudly and glared at Mary Jo, and she returned her eyes to her book. A moment later however, he looked away, and she turned again to Anny. "She married the boy from the next farm over—you know, the tall white house with black shutters. They were sweethearts in school before they got married. But they don't live here anymore. They moved to Kansas." Anny was looking at the top of the desk again.

"Have you ever been to Kansas? I haven't, but I'd like to go there someday. I want to go to New York too. And France. I've read about those places. Do you like to read? I do."

Anny looked up but remained silent.

"It's almost time for dinner break. We can sit together. I have some meat and bread and dried apples. What do you have? We can share."

The school master dropped his book loudly onto the desk. "*Miss Hendersen*, if you don't mind! I'm trying to teach school here, and your eternal talking is preventing me from doing my job. I'll thank you to keep your words inside your mouth until dinner time."

Mary Jo's face turned pink. She looked down at her arithmetic book.

"This is the second time this morning I've warned you. There will be no further warnings!"

Mary Jo nodded. She bent and wrote on her paper, "later." She pointed to it and smiled at Anny.

And Anny smiled back.

Finally, the morning's lessons came to an end. "Time for dinner," the master announced, and the children bowed their heads for the noon prayer.

Outside, Mary Jo introduced Anny to all the other girls.

"This is my new friend, Anny," she proudly proclaimed.

Although Anny said nothing, she did look at the girls' faces a couple of times.

Chapter Thirty Eight

Elisabeth entered the front door and strode purposefully toward the kitchen, letter in hand. "Etta? Etta, listen to this." She laid the envelope on the kitchen table. "It's from Jane." Jane wrote her sisters, the Snowburg twins, every Saturday morning, and the letter appeared in their mailbox on Tuesday afternoon.

Elisabeth skipped the preliminaries and read straight from the body of the letter.

> We have had quite an interesting week. Mr. Bergstrom, from the north side of the Island, told Ivar a couple of weeks ago that an acquaintance of his cousin's was coming here looking for work, and wondered could we care for the man's children while he went to ask about a job. Ivar said yes, that would be fine. The father brought the children on Tuesday morning and left immediately. And we have not seen him since! The father never even told us his name! He just dropped the children and left. We assumed he'd be back in an hour or two. We have no idea how to go about finding him! And Mr. Bergstrom has no idea either.
>
> Ivar is going to the cannery and maybe some lumber camps on Monday...

"So that would be yesterday," Elisabeth commented looking up. She returned to the letter.

... to see if he can find the man. We don't know what else to do.

But here is the truly interesting part—the children's names are Anny and Gibbie. Aren't these the names of the children you had living with you a few years ago? The little girl scarcely says a word. Neither child can tell us their home address. The boy tells us he is six and his sister is eight. My dear sisters, is it possible these are the same children?

Elisabeth dropped the letter on the table. "Amazing!" She laid her hand on the letter, shook her head and repeated, "Simply amazing! What do you think?"

Etta had frozen in place, a tea towel and half dried plate in her hands. "It's them," she said without a shadow of doubt in her voice. "Oh, it's them all right." She nodded, her face showing both resolve and concern. "Oh Elisabeth, what can we do? Those poor, poor children!"

*   *   *

On Wednesday morning, Anny and Gibbie walked, with Mama Jane between them, down the road on their way to school. They each carried a pail with some bread and cheese, some dried fish, and an apple in it for dinner.

We're going back to school, thought Anny. *Where we were yesterday.*

Mama Jane stopped at the crossroads and turned the children to face herself. "Now, today, I'm going to leave you here. When school's over, you need to come home along this same road and don't turn when you come to this crossroad. Understand?"

Gibbie nodded.

Anny was silent. *That girl will be there. Mary Jo. Maybe she'll talk to me again.*

Mama Jane planned on meeting the children part way home, at least today. She hugged Anny around her thin shoulders and said, "I hope you both have a wonderful day!"

Maybe she'll talk to me again. Maybe I will talk to her. I could do that.

*   *   *

Anny was at her desk before Mary Jo arrived. She had decided it was her turn to talk, and she intended to do it as soon as Mary Jo put in her appearance.

"Why do you talk to me all the time?" Anny asked, as Mary Jo slid into her place.

"I talk to you because we're friends, and that's what friends do," Mary Jo answered confidently.

Anny looked away while she thought this over. Maybe she *could* be friends with a girl like this. She had never formed a friendship with any of the other girls in the schools she'd attended. But it seemed nearly impossible to *not* be friends with Mary Jo!

Anny turned back and ventured a quiet smile, and Mary Jo burst out laughing. "I *like* your smile! I like *you*. I like you a *lot*! We are going to be very good friends. I can tell."

And Anny began to believe it herself.

*　　　*　　　*

The Harmony Saddle and Harness Shop buzzed with the lively conversation provided by Scott and Andrew Brown, neither of whom was paying much attention to the checker board balanced on an up-ended apple box between them. Mac listened with one ear as the subject progressed from politics to sheep and then to the weather. He worked in silence, but took comfort from the sounds of life around him. Still not reconciled to the loss of his children, he at least was learning to function somewhat normally. Shan, on the other hand, was struggling, though Mac didn't recognize it.

Shan placed the saddle skirt he was carving on the workbench before him. He moved deliberately and placed a hand on each side of the skirt, blowing out his breath between pursed lips. Turning to Mac he said, "I think I'm through for today. I'll be back in the morning."

Mac looked up, surprised, but just nodded as Shan removed his leather apron and headed for the door. It was only two o'clock. The shop closed at five-thirty.

Shan walked the four and a half blocks to his home with his hands in his pockets and his head down. He kicked at a couple of stones, and slowed as he approached the Baptist Church just across the street from his house. Michael and Libby would be at school. Only Grace and little Danny would be home.

What if she sees me? What will I say? Is she in the house? Over at Dacia's? In the front yard? No. As he approached closer, he could see that Grace was not in the yard. He heard a popping sound and caught a flash of white behind the house. The wash! Grace had snapped a pillow case before hanging it on the line. *She's hanging out the wash! I should have guessed. It's Monday.*

He could sneak in the front door and make his way up the stairs to his room before Grace saw him. He quickened his pace and took the front porch steps two at a time. Upstairs he entered his room and closed the door quietly. The door knob felt hot to his touch. No, it wasn't the knob, it was just him. He sat gingerly on the edge of his bed and propped his elbows on his knees, hands hanging loosely. He listened. Nothing. She must still be outside.

Okay, so I'm here. Now what?

He wanted—he had wanted desperately for some time now—to talk to Grace. To tell her how much she meant to him. How he appreciated her taking care of the children. To thank her for the new sofa covering she'd made way back at the beginning. No, actually, that's *not* what he wanted. He wanted to tell her he loved her. *That's* what he wanted!

But how? How on earth would he actually go about *doing* that?

He flopped back on the bed and stared at the ceiling. Suddenly he bolted upright, strode to the door and tore it open, and stomped down the stairs. Grace was just coming in the kitchen door, the wash basket propped on one hip.

"Oh! Shan! What are you doing here? You startled me!"

"Um ... I came home early."

"Why early? Are you sick?"

Shan put his hands in his pockets, his neck flaming red, and his face growing redder by the moment. He cleared his throat. "Yeah, that's it, I guess. I'm not feeling too good." He rubbed the back of his neck with one hand and stared at the floor.

"Well, do you want me to stay to fix supper and take care of the children?"

"No, no. That's all right. I can do it." *Shan, what are you doing? Listen to yourself! Say what you need to say!* He opened his mouth, then closed it again.

Grace nodded, unconvinced. But she certainly didn't want to argue with Shan. She hung the basket on its nail by the back door. "Okay, I guess I'll be going then. Send one of the children over if you need anything."

Shan raised his head, watched her turn to leave. *Yes I need something. I need to hold you in my arms and kiss your beautiful face!*

But she had already vanished through the back door, closing it softly behind her.

By the time a month had gone by, Gibbie and Anny had become an integral part of the class.

Anny loved playing with the girls. A couple of them were nasty—mostly Elida who seemed stuck up—but the others were friendly. Anny found she liked talking with them. At first she talked only a little, but as the days went by, she found more and more to talk about. In fact, on Friday of her third week at the Sunny Sands School, the master had scolded her for talking too much! And Anny loved it!

That night at supper she announced to Mama Jane and Granddaddy, "I was naughty at school today."

"You were ... what did you say, Anny?" Mama Jane looked at her sharply.

Anny smiled and said, "I talked too much, and Mr. Marshall made me stay in and write sentences on the board while the others went out to play."

Mama Jane and Granddaddy continued staring at her.

"'I will not talk during class.' I had to write that twenty-five times." She smiled, and continued. "I used very good handwriting, because I wanted you to be proud of me."

Both Mama Jane and Granddaddy had to turn away from Anny to hide their smiles. And Granddaddy had a very convenient coughing fit.

Then Gibbie spoke up. "*I* didn't talk too much. *I* got to go outside."

Chapter Thirty Nine

May 21, 1907

I'm sad. Tomorrow is the last day of school and I won't get to see my new friends 'til school starts again! Well, sometimes, but not every day, and I really like all of us being together! I like playing with my friends! I <u>like</u> school! I have learned SO much! I love to write like this. Mary Jo showed me how. I think it looks very elegant! (I have learned about a million new words. Elegant is one of them.)

I like living with Mama Jane and Grand-daddy too. And I really like Oslo, the dog. He is gentle and kind and REALLY BIG! His name, Oslo, is the name of the city Granddaddy comes from in Norway. He is black and white and has blue eyes and *he loves me very much. And he has <u>very floppy fur</u>! Granddaddy says he should go outside, but Mama Jane lets him stay in sometimes because he's old. And because he loves me so much.*

I talk to people now. I like to talk to people. Mama Jane and Granddaddy are very kind. Mary Jo is my best friend at school. I talk to her because we are friends, and that's what friends do. I talk to the other girls too.

And I do my school work. It is interesting. I am learning <u>so</u> many things! I like reading the stories in my reader, and I specially like singing. I don't like arithmetic, but I learned how to spell it: <u>A</u> <u>R</u>at <u>I</u>n <u>T</u>he <u>H</u>ouse <u>M</u>ight <u>E</u>at <u>T</u>he <u>I</u>ce <u>C</u>ream.

*   *   *

On the last day of school, Anny was allowed to go home with Mary Jo and spend the night at her house. She stood transfixed before the piano in Mary Jo's front room.

"Play it for me," she demanded. "Let me see how it works."

"No, that's no fun." Mary Jo wrinkled her nose. "Let's bake cookies instead."

"No. I want to hear you play the piano. I *want* to hear. *Please?*" Anny clasped her hands under her chin and put on her most hopeful face.

Mary Jo laughed. Heaving a loud sigh, she sat on the stool. She grimaced as she flipped pages in the book before her. Selecting one near the beginning, she poised her hands above the keys. Then she flopped her hands into her lap. "I'm no good," she said. "Mama wants me to play and she makes me practice." She lowered her voice to a whisper. "But I can't stand it!" Then, seeing the look of disappointment on her friend's face, she turned again to the keys and pounded out the notes as she read them from the page.

Anny watched, her eyes never leaving the fingers on the keys. "Can I try?" she asked when Mary Jo reached the end of her piece.

"Sure! Do you want me to show you the notes?"

"No, I just want to play." A smile lit up Anny's face as she lifted her left hand to the keys and played first one, then another, listening to the sound. First she played single notes. She laughed out loud. "I love it!" She tried playing several notes together using both hands. Some of them sounded good. Some were awful. She laughed at herself, spun around on the stool, and said, "What are we waiting for? I thought we were going to make cookies!"

Mary Jo's mother had the things they would need ready on the kitchen table. As they took turns adding ingredients to the bowl, the girls talked excitedly. "I can't wait for my birthday!" Mary Jo said. "Only three more weeks! When's your birthday, Anny?"

Anny didn't respond.

Mary Jo repeated the question.

Finally, Anny said, "Um, I'm not exactly sure."

"You're not exactly sure! What on earth does that mean?"

"I guess I just never thought about it," Anny answered. "A long time ago I was seven. Or maybe someone told me I was seven. But that was a long, *long* time ago. I don't remember any birthdays."

Mary Jo looked at her friend in amazement.

"I think I'm eight now," Anny said. "When Mama Jane brought me to school that first day, she told the master I was eight. That's why he put me in third grade."

"But you really don't know?" Mary Jo asked in amazement. "You really don't know how old you are or when your birthday is? How can you not know?"

Anny just shrugged and laughed. "Okay. I'm twenty. And my birthday is tomorrow. I'll be twenty-one."

The girls dissolved into laughter.

When the first tray of cookies was done, Anny opened the oven door, and Mary Jo carefully removed the tray.

As she lifted the last cookie from the baking pan and laid it carefully on the butcher paper, she waved the cookie pan in the air to cool it before placing it on the wooden table. "Well, like I was saying, my birthday is in three weeks, and I'm having a party! I'm going to be nine. And I want you to come! We'll play games and have birthday cake. Please say you'll come! You're my *very* best friend!"

Anny laughed. "Of course I'll come! Who else is coming?" Both girls used spoons to scoop lumps of cookie dough onto the pan.

"All the girls—but *no boooyyys.*" Mary Jo dragged out the word, using it to describe the lowest form of life on earth—or at least on Puget Island. She and Anny laughed.

Mrs. Henderson came into the kitchen in time to hear Mary Jo's last comment and scolded in her gentle Norwegian accent. "Now, Mary Jo, you be nice. If you can't be nice, maybe dere will be no party, ja?"

Anny looked at her with big eyes, but Mary Jo just laughed again. "Oh, Mama! You know boys aren't real people. At least not when they're eight or nine or ten years old!"

"You yust wait!" Mrs. Henderson said. "You'll see when you grow older."

Mary Jo just made a face at Anny and held the oven door open as Anny slid the next pan into place. They each took a cookie from the paper on the table, and Mary Jo's mother poured two glasses of milk.

"I like your piano," Anny said to Mrs. Hendersen. "It makes beautiful music."

"Why t'ank you, Anny. What a nice t'ing to say." Mrs. Hendersen looked pointedly at her daughter.

"Well, I don't like it." Mary Jo said. "I guess it's supposed to be fun and sound nice. But I don't think it sounds very nice at all." She shrugged. "Sorry, Mama. But it's the truth."

Mrs. Henderson sighed, and shook her head.

"Is it very hard to learn?" Anny asked Mary Jo.

"Not really. You could do it. But you just go to all that work, and all you get is a bunch of notes. Why bother?"

"Mary Jo!" Mrs. Hendersen snapped. "Don't you fill poor Anny's head with your grumps. I know you don't like it. But dat doesn't mean everybody feels dat way too. You let Anny t'ink her own mind."

"Yes, Mama." Mary Jo rolled her eyes.

"Well, I think it's lovely!" Anny giggled at the face Mary Jo made. "But I can't take lessons. Mama Jane and Granddaddy don't have a piano for me to practice on."

*   *   *

Two days later, Anny plopped on a kitchen chair and asked, "Mama Jane, when's my birthday?"

"Don't you know, Child?"

"No. Nobody ever told me. And I don't know when Gibbie's birthday is either. He's six, but when will he be seven? When will I be nine? I want to have a birthday!"

"You want a party? Is that it?" Mama Jane smiled at Anny and tossed a pie crust in the air. She caught it, letting the loose flour shake off, and placed the crust on top of one of the pies she was making— peach pies, with peaches Mama Jane had put up herself last year.

Anny was pensive as she watched Mama Jane.

"Well, a party would be a lot of fun ..." But Anny's face looked serious as she said it.

"But?"

"But ... what I really want is to know when my birthday is. All my friends know their birthdays. Why don't I know mine?"

Mama Jane rolled back the top crust of the pies, section by section, and patted water around the outside of the bottom crust. Then she laid the top crusts back in place and began crimping the edges. "Well, that seems like a reasonable request." Mama Jane spoke gently. "But I don't know when your birthday is, and I don't know how to find out. Gibbie said he was already in school when you came here," she went on. "He said he was six and you were eight. That sounded about right."

Mama Jane slid the two pies into the oven and closed the door. "What grade were you in before you came here?"

Anny shrugged. She didn't remember anything about school before she came here.

Mama Jane poured two glasses of fresh buttermilk and sat at the end of the table next to Anny.

"Truth be told, Anny, I don't know much about you at all—just that I've grown to love you and Gibbie very much." Mama Jane reached out and patted Anny's hand, giving it a squeeze. "Your father ... well, he didn't say anything about a birthday."

Anny sat silently, gazing out the window.

"He didn't come back, did he? He left us here and just ... didn't come back."

"Well, that does seem to be the truth, I'm sorry to say. That was over two months ago. We still don't understand." Mama Jane shook her head. "Granddaddy went to look for him when you'd only been here a few days. But no one seems to know anything." Mama Jane shrugged. "When you first came, Anny, you couldn't tell us anything. You didn't talk. Remember?"

Anny sat with her chin balanced on her fists. Her legs swung gently, and her eyes focused intently on Mama Jane's face. Oslo sat at Anny's side looking up at her. She reached absently to pet him.

"We asked you questions, Granddaddy and I. But you never answered. Don't you remember anything about your life before you came here, Anny? Like that mark on your eyebrow—do you remember how you got it? If we knew that, it might help us learn more about you."

Anny lifted her finger and rubbed the spot. "No. I know it's there, but I don't know where it came from."

Mama Jane nodded, disappointed. "When you first came, we asked you how old you were. You didn't answer. We asked your address and your father's full name. You didn't answer any of it. We asked if you knew where your father might have gone. No answer to that either. Apparently he left you and then just ..."

"Disappeared," Anny said.

"Well, yes. 'Disappeared' is about it, I guess. Gibbie wasn't silent like you. He talked a lot, but he couldn't answer our questions either. After a while it became obvious that your father wasn't coming back."

"And so you kept us."

"Yes. We kept you. We could have taken you to the Children's Aid Society in Portland, and they would have taken care of you. But we just couldn't do that. We were starting to love you already."

"Why would you love me if I didn't even talk to you?"

Mama Jane lifted Anny's hand to her lips and kissed it. "Love isn't about how much someone pleases you. It's something you give away because you want to. A person can't earn love."

Anny continued to gaze at Mama Jane for a moment, then lowered her eyes to the table. She moved her hands and entwined her fingers in Oslo's heavy fur. Her legs stopped swinging.

"Oh," she said softly.

*   *   *

Hair with a slight curl to it. Neither blond nor red, but somewhere in between. Well ... maybe more red than blond. Freckles across her nose.

Anny stood in front of Mama Jane's vanity gazing at her reflection in the mirror. She didn't really know the child who gazed back at her. A few hairs missing from her right eyebrow—a tiny mark. How did that get there? The eyes were kind of odd. Kind of pretty actually, she thought. Green. That was unusual. She'd noticed most people had brown or blue eyes. She liked the green.

She smiled at herself, wondering what she would look like when she was grown. Maybe her red hair would turn a beautiful dark auburn. She could always hope.

But in the meantime, she'd better get out there and hoe around her corn!

*   *   *

June 1, 1907

Mama Jane says maybe we could sit down and read the first part of my journal together. I don't know. I'll have to think about it. I don't really understand the things I wrote there. Mama Jane probably wouldn't understand either.

Chapter Forty

E ven though school was over for the year, Anny and Gibbie had not had much time to be sad about it. Mama Jane and Granddaddy were keeping them busy with gardening and chores on the small farm. Anny had even learned how to milk Daisy, the Petersen's cow. Gibbie said he wasn't interested in learning—until Granddaddy reminded him that ice cream could be made from Daisy's thick, rich cream. Then Gibbie milked willingly. And helped turn the handle on the ice cream freezer as well!

But that was last week. Today, something new was up. Anny and Gibbie didn't know what, but both Mama Jane and Granddaddy were busier than usual—getting ready for something.

Gibbie stood on a stool, looking into the bowl Mama Jane was stirring. "What is it?" he asked.

"Cake batter. It's a lemon cake."

"Can I have some?"

"*May* I have some. And the answer is no. Not now. But when I get it in the oven, you and Anny *may* lick the bowl and spoon."

"Yum!" Gibbie rubbed his tummy.

"This cake is for something special. We're going on a trip tomorrow, and we're taking the cake with us."

Anny—sunburned, sweaty, and grass-stained—banged through the back door and inhaled deeply. "Oh yum! Lemon cake—I *love* lemon cake! Can I help frost it?"

"*May* I help frost it. And yes, you may. Gibbie, do you want to help with the frosting too?"

"Do I get to lick the frosting bowl if I do?"

Mama Jane laughed. "Oh, I see how it is. If the pay is right, you're willing to work. Is that it?"

Gibbie nodded enthusiastically.

Mama Jane finished pouring the batter into the rectangular pan, set the bowl on the table for the children, and put the cake carefully in the oven.

"Oh, Anny!" Mama Jane grabbed Anny's wrist. "Wash before you stick your fingers in there. You're all covered with dirt."

"I was weeding my garden. Gibbie, don't start yet! Wait for me!" She gave her hands a quick scrub and dried them on her skirt.

Mama Jane pulled out a kitchen chair and sat with a sigh. She put her feet up on the chair opposite and stretched her back. "Tomorrow," she announced, "we are taking a trip to Oregon City."

Anny looked up in alarm. "Will we be back in time for Mary Jo's party?"

"Of course! I wouldn't let you miss the party!" Mama Jane continued, "I have two sisters who live there. Their last name is Snowburg, and they're twins. They have a boarding house, and one of the rooms is empty right now, so we'll sleep there." Mama Jane watched Anny's and Gibbie's faces for some sign of recognition, but saw none.

"How long will we stay?" Anny closed her eyes in bliss as she licked lemon cake batter from her fingers.

"Three days. But with travel time, we'll be gone longer than that. Mr. Lindner, down the way, will milk Daisy and do the chores while we're gone. We can't stay too long, but I think you'll enjoy going."

"Will Oslo come with us?" Anny asked.

Mama Jane looked at Anny tenderly. Oslo was now sleeping every night on Anny's bed. He really wasn't supposed to be in the house, much less on the bed. But Mama Jane and Granddaddy had both noticed how Anny relaxed in his presence. It was as if the dog gave her the confidence to face life. Mama Jane thought a minute, then smiled and said, "Yes, Anny, Oslo can come."

Turning back to include Gibbie she added, "My sisters have a very interesting story to tell you children."

Gibbie looked up. "They do? What kind of story?"

"It's a surprise. You'll have to wait. As soon as you've got that bowl cleaned up I want you to go get your clothes ready. Bring them down to the front room to pack in the suitcase. Tomorrow morning, we leave."

*   *   *

Breakfast on Tuesday morning was what Mama Jane called "catch as catch can." She had fixed oatmeal mush, same as usual, but then she left everyone to take care of themselves, as she hurried this way and that, attending to last-minute details. Anny sat on an empty barrel on the back porch, banging her heels rhythmically against its side. She took another bite of oatmeal as Gibbie came out to join her. He took a huge bite, and plopped down on the bottom step, nearly poking the spoon down his throat. He choked and gagged.

"You should eat politely," Anny informed him, repeating Mama Jane's frequent admonition. "Slow down and take small bites. Then you won't choke."

Gibbie responded through a mouthful of cooked oats. "You're not the boss of me. I don't hafta listen to you."

Anny made a face at him and scooped her last bite of mush into her mouth. From the corner of her eye, she spied one of the Peterson's two geese moving purposefully toward the porch where she and Gibbie sat. They had named the goose Christmas Dinner, in honor of what Granddaddy had assured them was his ultimate purpose in life.

Christmas Dinner waddled toward the porch casting a beady eye on Gibbie's bowl of mush. The goose had hatched only two months before, but was now full grown and, as Granddaddy liked to say, "all gander, and mean as any critter God efer made."

"No!" Gibbie said, lifting his bowl high above his head. But the goose's neck was long, and he stretched upward in search of a tasty morsel. Gibbie stood and pulled his bowl back even farther, but Christmas Dinner pushed against Gibbie, knocking him off his feet. Gibbie crashed to the step and, in one quick, deliberate move, smacked the goose on the head with his spoon.

The goose gave an angry squawk and ran toward the shed. Gibbie hollered after it, "Take that, you dumb ol' bird!" and went back to his breakfast.

"Oh, *Gibbie!*" Anny wailed. "Mama Jane! Gibbie hit Christmas Dinner with his spoon, and now he's eating off it again."

Anny heard Granddaddy's laugh from the far side of the shed. "Ja sure! Dis goose has oatmeal on his head, and dat's da truth!"

"Gibbie, Gibbie, Gibbie! Let me have it." Mama Jane emerged from the back door and held out her hand for the spoon. "What do you think we will eat at Christmas if you kill the goose now?" She thumped Gibbie lightly on the head with the spoon as she climbed the steps back to the kitchen.

"Blackberry pie?" said Gibbie, rubbing his head. "Pumpkin pie?"

"Here," Mama Jane said, and handed Gibbie a clean spoon. "And this time, use it to eat with, not for attacking the livestock! And besides that, if you want pumpkin pie come Christmas, you still need to hoe around your pumpkins before we leave."

"Oh!" Gibbie groaned. "I forgot."

"Well, hurry up. It won't take you but ten minutes once you get started."

Anny and Gibbie had garden plots of their own. They were learning how to plant and hoe and how to pick produce carefully so they wouldn't ruin what was left for the next picking. Gibbie had helped put up the string runners for the beans, and Anny was excited about learning to make pickles from cucumbers and beets.

Gibbie had pumpkins, radishes, strawberries, and corn-on-the-cob in his garden. Granddaddy just called it corn, but Gibbie thought corn-on-the-cob sounded better. He had to plant at least two rows, Granddaddy said, so it would pollinate and actually produce corn. Anny planted strawberries too. Also onions, turnips, beets, pie plant, and two kinds of cucumbers—some to eat fresh, and some to pickle. Granddaddy had suggested she plant spinach, but Anny turned up her nose. She did *not* like spinach.

When all the vegetables were planted, she had helped Gibbie make a scarecrow, and they planted that in the garden also. And Anny put marigolds around the outside of her garden space to set it off.

Gibbie finished off his mush in record time and ran to hoe around his baby pumpkin vines.

*   *   *

"Anny! Gibbie!" Mama Jane called out the back door. "Come on! It's time to go." Anny jumped up, eager to start the trip. She was excited about Mama Jane's sisters. She liked the idea of twins, even though Mama Jane said they looked nothing like each other.

Gibbie had expressed amazement at the thought of someone as *old* as Mama Jane having sisters. Granddaddy slapped at the side of Gibbie's head and told him to be more respectful. But he chuckled as he said it, and winked at Anny.

They rode together to the boat dock, where Granddaddy unloaded their things and then returned home with the wagon. He put the wagon in the barn, turned Chipper, the horse, out to the pasture, and walked the quarter mile back to the dock. They waited only a few minutes until there was a boatman who was willing and had a large enough boat to take them across to Westport. Gibbie loved the crossing.

Anny wasn't really convinced that being on the water was a good thing, but it was only about ten minutes. So she just sat in the very center of the boat and held on tight.

*   *   *

Mac Harmon's journey this week took him to the Washington side of the Columbia River. It was one of the longest trips he'd made. He had arrived in Portland by train two days ago; yesterday, he'd stopped at Woodland, Kalama, Carrolls, and Kelso; and then he'd spent the night at Oak Point. Today, he would go on to Cathlamet, and from there, he would cross back to the Oregon side and visit every small town or settlement along the river on his way back to Portland. Hornet, the horse he'd hired in Portland, was perfect for the trek, despite the promise—or threat—of his name. Unflappable, strong, and steady. And fairly fast as well.

Arriving in Cathlamet around eight, he asked around and was directed to Sheriff Charles Flanders, who was just walking up from the dock on the river. The sheriff was a burly man with a walrus moustache so full and long, Mac wondered if the man's mouth really was under there.

Sheriff Flanders listened as Mac related yet again the tragic story of his two youngest children, missing since the night of the flood. The sheriff shook his head. "I'm sure sorry to hear about your family. That flood was such a terrible thing! I think the whole country cried for Heppner when that happened." He patted the pocket of his shirt, then said, "Come on inside the office for a minute. I'll have to put on my eyeglasses before I can see your picture."

He led Mac into his office. Mac thought the room would be well served to have someone organize it a bit. Flanders looked all over and nearly gave up before finally finding his glasses.

"I hope you'll forgive me. I'm pretty new here. Just got elected last month."

And you made all this mess in one month? Mac was amazed, but refrained from commenting.

"Okay now, let's just see what we got here," he said, putting on the glasses and holding the picture up to the light. "This little girl, and the baby, yes?"

"Yes, those two." The family photo had been taken the summer of Lilyann's fourth birthday, Gilbert's first. "But this picture was taken about five years ago—a year before the flood, so they've grown quite a bit by now."

Flanders looked up at Mac over the top of his glasses. "Five years? That's a pretty long time, you know."

Mac nodded. "I do know. It's been a very, very long time." Mac closed his eyes for a moment. Still, four years after the flood, the pain had not lessened. If anything, it was more intense!

Flanders looked again at the children's faces and shook his head. "I'm sorry, but ... I don't recognize them. I sure do wish I could help you!"

Mac's jaw tightened, and he reached for the picture.

"Oh wait! There's the school teacher. We'll ask her." Flanders' face lit up at the sight of the young lady walking on the other side of the street. "Miss McDoodle!" he called out the door. "Can you come here for a minute, please? We have a question to ask you." He and Mac stepped back outside.

McDoodle? Mac thought. *Really?* He squelched a smile, lest he appear to be making fun of the young lady's name.

"Good morning Sheriff. It's a lovely day, isn't it?" Miss McDoodle smiled at the two men.

"Yes, yes. Lovely. But can you tell me ..." Sheriff Flanders held out the picture. "See these two children here? Do you recognize them?" He pointed. "The picture is old. They are bigger now."

Miss McDoodle looked earnestly at the photo, then shook her head. "No ... they don't look at all familiar to me. Am I supposed to know them?"

"No, no. These children turned up missing some time ago, and their father here is trying to find them. Thank you, anyway." Miss McDoodle's face registered sorrow and pity. Flanders turned back to Mac and shrugged. "I just don't know. Guess I can't help you. Sorry."

Mac took the picture and nodded his thanks. "I think I'll go across to Westport and check there."

"Good idea. Just go ask for Sven down on the dock. He'll take you, if your horse can stand the smell of fish. He was still there just a minute ago, and his barge is big enough for the horse too."

"Thanks very much for your help." Mac shook the sheriff's hand, mounted his horse, and headed for the dock.

*　　*　　*

After Granddaddy paid Sorensen, the boat owner, for their passage from the Island to the Oregon side of the river, he walked up to the livery to arrange for a team and wagon for the trip to Portland. Mama Jane took the children to Barhann's, Westport's general market, to do some shopping, while Granddaddy returned to the dock to load the luggage into the wagon.

*   *   *

When Mac arrived at the Westport dock, he paid Sven for the ride, nodded to a stocky, gray-haired man who was loading luggage into a wagon, then rode on up to the livery stable to leave the horse. He would get something to eat, check with a sheriff or whoever he could find to show his picture to, then be on his way to Portland.

He showed his picture to several men at the stable, but none of them recognized the children. They told him the sheriff of Clatsop County was located down in Astoria—25 miles away.

Mac sighed in disappointment. "Well, how about a good place to eat?" he asked.

"Right across the street, there. Best place in town." One of the men nodded his head at the hotel on the opposite corner. "Don't look like much, but the food is good. Have the Swedish meatballs. They're the best!"

*   *   *

The wagon loaded, Granddaddy walked up the street to Barhann's, where he met Mama Jane and the children. A person could find everything from string, to shovels, to fresh produce at Barhann's. It was shoes and stockings the Petersens had come for today. Mama Jane wrapped the feet of the stockings around Gibbie's and Anny's fists to find the right size and chose shoes that were a bit on the large side. She expected the children to wear them for a long time.

"And I'll thank you to take care you don't put holes in the toes," she said to Gibbie. "You're supposed to walk on the bottoms, you know."

But Gibbie was much too excited to listen to a word. In just the past three months he'd received new clothes, found friends at school, learned to take care of a garden, and to milk a cow. And now he had new shoes as well! He gazed at them in admiration.

"Did you hear me, young man?" Mama Jane stuck a finger under his chin and tilted his face up to meet hers.

"Thank you!" Gibbie said, having no idea what he was supposed to have heard, but guessing it probably had something to do with his manners.

249

Mama Jane just laughed at him and roughed up his hair. "Be careful!" she said. "Take good care of your shoes."

As they waited for their purchases to be rung up, Anny lifted the package containing her new shoes to her nose and inhaled the sweet scent of leather. *Mmmm. Nice.* She sighed in contentment. She closed her eyes and saw a picture in her mind of a small child sitting on a rough wooden floor with pieces of scrap leather arranged in a pretty geometric pattern. She inhaled the scent again.

"Anny, are you coming?" Mama Jane called from the door.

The picture vanished and Anny looked up, surprised to find herself still standing by the cash register while she could see Granddaddy and Gibbie already halfway down the street. She hurried to catch up.

*   *   *

Finally, all the purchases had been made, all the errands in Westport completed. Mama Jane, Granddaddy, the children, and Oslo made their way back to the livery and loaded themselves and their purchases into the rented wagon. Granddaddy clucked the team into motion. Gibbie lay face down in the back of the wagon, dragging a stick as they pulled out of the livery barn.

"You'd better sit up before you make yourself sick, young man," Mama Jane called to him, but Gibbie paid her no mind.

The wagon turned the corner between the stable and the hotel, and rolled out of town toward Portland ... as Mac, in the hotel dining room, showed his picture to the waiter.

Chapter Forty One

The trip to Oregon City was full of new adventures for Anny and Gibbie. They loved watching the boats on the river—especially Gibbie. And the train was just plain wonderful, even though they didn't ride on it. On the way through Portland, they saw several automobiles, something *never* seen on Puget Island. They chuffed down the street clattering and blowing smoke, amazing both children.

Finally, the wagon reached the Snowburg sisters' boarding house. Miss Elisabeth and Miss Etta appeared, to Anny's eyes, more like a hundred years old than seventy-five. Of course, she thought, she didn't know any other seventy-five-year-old people.

While Gibbie jumped down, Granddaddy lifted Anny from the wagon and set her on the walk. The two ladies came down the front steps—looking for all the world like a couple of dried apple dolls, Anny thought—and approached the children.

"Oh my!" the tall one exclaimed. "How you've grown! You both look wonderful! Just *wonderful!*"

The short, stout one held Gibbie by the shoulders so she could examine him, tip to toe. "'Oh my' is right! There's no other word for it—just wonderful!"

The two children stood quietly as the ladies looked them over, but Anny was surprised at their very enthusiastic greeting. She wondered if they were this excited about every new visitor they received.

"And how old are you now, dear?" the tall one asked Anny.

"I'm eight," she said politely—proudly. "But I'll be nine on my birthday in August." She smiled at Mama Jane. "Gibbie's six."

At this, both ladies' hands fluttered, patting their chests. The short one was blinking rapidly and the tall one pulled a hankie from her sleeve and wiped her eyes. "This is so amazing!" she warbled. "So absolutely amazing!"

Anny turned and wrinkled her nose at Mama Jane. She was very proud of having a birthday, but it didn't seem like the kind of news that would overwhelm a couple of old ladies. After all, they'd had *lots* of birthdays! Something strange was going on.

Mama Jane and Granddaddy were barely able to keep their own excitement in check. "Well den, maybe we oughta go sit on da porch and visit, ja?" Granddaddy suggested.

"Oh yes! Oh yes! Of course! Whatever are we thinking, Etta? We are so excited, we've forgotten our manners!" The two ladies began shuffling toward the porch.

"I'll bring tea and cookies," Etta said, "and lemonade for the children." She climbed the porch steps back to the house, talking to herself as she went. "Oh my, my, my! Who *ever* would have thought it? I think I'll be able to die happy now. Thank you, Lord! Thank you, Jesus!"

Anny stifled a smile and looked again at Mama Jane. These ladies were certainly ... strange, even if they were Mama Jane's sisters.

While they had lemonade and cookies on the porch, Elisabeth and Etta took turns asking the children questions—about school, the farm, their friends—and expressed amazement and delight at every answer. Finally, the cookies being gone, Mama Jane sent the children to play in the yard.

Everyone paused and looked up as an automobile chugged by. Gibbie hesitated a moment, then turned back to look at the tall sister again. He tilted his head to the side and squinted his eyes. "I've seen you before," he said.

Anny looked sharply at her brother, but said nothing. Then abruptly she tagged Gibbie on the shoulder and shouted, "You're it!" Gibbie gave chase as Anny ran down the porch steps and around toward the back of the house.

*　　　*　　　*

"Well ...?" Jane asked, as the children disappeared from sight.

"Oh, no question about it!" said Elisabeth. "It's them, all right!"

Etta nodded, "How did you do it? They are so happy, so— normal!"

"Well, I don't t'ink we can take da credit for it." Ivar shrugged his shoulders. "We was as confused as you when dey first came. We didn't know what to do. When Jane took dem to school ... well, dere was dis girl dere. She yust took a shine to our Anny, and somehow ... she started talking." He shrugged again.

"Maybe it was time," suggested Jane. "Maybe she had been just waiting to blossom, and the spring finally came for her."

"She came to you two years after she left here. Almost four years from when we first met her," Elisabeth said, thinking out loud. She looked at her sister. "I wonder where she was all that time. I wonder what happened in her life."

"God knows. We don't." Jane chuckled. "Maybe we don't need to know. Maybe we just go forward from here."

"She doesn't remember us at all," Etta said a little sadly.

"I was hoping she would." Elisabeth brushed cookie crumbs from her dress and went on. "After we discovered Anny could write, I gave her a little notebook and pencil. I remember she never, *never* let it out of her sight. I made her a pinafore with a big pocket in it so she could carry it with her all the time."

"Oh my!" It was Jane's turn to be amazed. "When she came to us, she had on a very ragged, much too small pinafore—with a big pocket in it. Muslin. With a square neck."

Elisabeth nodded. "That's the one!"

"And the notebook—she had it with her still. I remember that first night, I offered to put it on the table while she slept, but she wouldn't part with it! She didn't look at me or talk to me. She just held onto it—tight."

Elisabeth was crying again. It was too much. Just too much! "Does she still have it?"

"She does." Jane nodded. "Not with her. She's gone through two or three more these last couple of months. My, how that child does love to write things!"

"Ja, I bought her a new one when I was in town one day," Ivar said. "She hugged me so much I t'ought she might forget to let go!"

Jane laughed. "She fills them up. Once in a while she lets me read something. Some little verses, stories. She writes about things that are fun and exciting for her. Some of it is a diary—what's happening in her life. And some of her writing is very ... deep. Profound. It's hard to believe she wasn't even talking a few months ago."

"Have you read the book?" Elisabeth asked.

"That first book?" Jane shook her head. "She hasn't let me see it. It's as if it contains her very soul and she isn't ready to open that door yet. I confess, I've snooped a bit when she's not in the house. But I haven't been able to find it. And even if I did, I don't think I'd be brave enough to open it. She's made it clear, it's not available for reading."

"Well, I t'ink dat book is part of da reason she's getting better. I t'ink da writing helps her."

"What a blessing! What a great blessing!" The sisters looked at each other and nodded, tears in their eyes.

"Anny! Gibbie!" Mama Jane called. "Come here please. It's time for the story we came to hear."

*   *   *

June 15, 1907

We are in Oregon City visiting Mama Jane's two sisters. Gibbie and I used to live with them! That surprised me a lot! Gibbie even remembers one of them – at least a little bit. But I don't.

We had a father then. I don't remember him either. Well, maybe a little. He brought us to Mama Jane and Granddaddy.

Even though I don't remember my birthday, Mama Jane and I decided it would be on August 10. And Gibbie will have his birthday a week later. I'm really excited!

It's strange – I don't know what happened before we came to Puget Island. I try hard to remember. I think I do remember a few things. I remember having my book to write in. I remember a horse. Sometimes I go back and read the things I wrote a long time ago. I don't even remember most of the things I wrote about. And I didn't write when my birthday is. I just don't know.

Chapter Forty Two

The mid-summer afternoon had become overcast, even though it was still very hot. By supper time, black clouds had rolled in and were threatening rain. As Anny and Gibbie finished picking the last row of beans, huge drops of rain began to fall—at first only a few, but by the time the children had raced each other to the back door, they were drenched from the downpour. Granddaddy held the porch door open for them as they came charging through. They shook the water from their heads and arms, laughing.

"You are yust like a couple of big ol' dogs, you are! Like Oslo after a rain storm." Granddaddy laughed with them, as Mama Jane brought towels to them on the big back porch.

Suddenly the dusky sky was split by an enormous crack of lightning, followed by thunder so deep and loud it shook the house.

"Oh wow!" Gibbie's brown eyes were huge, and the smile on his face rivaled the lightning that once again split the sky into jagged segments.

Anny, however, turned white as a sheet. She grabbed the edge of the door with both hands.

"Anny! What's wrong, child?" Mama Jane reached out to hold her. Anny's jaw began shaking, then her entire body. "Oh Anny! Are you sick?"

Anny didn't speak. Her eyes were huge, unblinking.

"Here, quick, Ivar. Help me get her inside." Granddaddy scooped Anny up in his arms and carried her through the kitchen to the front room, where he laid her gently on the sofa. Mama Jane took the afghan from the back of the sofa and wrapped Anny in it, then placed her hand on Anny's brow.

"Bring me a towel. We need to get her dry," she said to Ivar.

Mama Jane rubbed Anny's hair vigorously, and rubbed her hands and cheeks as well. But the shaking continued. "Here, let me hold her." Mama Jane sat in her rocker and held out her arms as Granddaddy lifted Anny and carried her to Mama Jane.

"There, there, sweetheart," Mama Jane soothed. "It's going to be all right." She looked at her husband. "I wonder if she's just frightened." She wrapped Anny tightly in the afghan and patted her back, then her cheek.

"Gibbie, is Anny afraid of thunderstorms?"

"I don't know." He shrugged. "I think they're fun!"

"Yes, but before—has Anny ever been afraid when there's a storm?"

"Wow! Look at that!" Gibbie's face was plastered against the window as lightning once again crackled in the south.

Mama Jane turned Anny's face toward her and looked into her eyes. "Ivar, I think that's it. I think she's afraid. This is the first storm we've had since she's been here."

A low moan escaped Anny's lips. The muscles in her neck remained taut and her body rigid. Mama Jane just held her tighter and rocked her. "Sh, baby. You are safe here with us. You don't need to worry." Mama Jane rubbed Anny's back, her arm, her shoulder, cradled her head. Oslo whimpered and laid his head against Anny's leg. Lightning cracked and thunder shook the world again, and Anny stiffened even more. Mama Jane kept rubbing Anny's back and crooning to her.

The storm lasted only ten minutes before moving far enough away that the thunder was heard only faintly. Slowly, very slowly, Anny began to relax in Mama Jane's arms.

"Is Anny all better now?" Gibbie asked.

Mama Jane nodded, but continued rocking. "I think she'll be much better now that the storm has passed."

"Gibbie, haf you been in a t'understorm before?" Granddaddy asked.

"Yeah, sure! I been in lots of 'em."

"And you like dem, ja?"

"Yeah, I like 'em a lot!"

"Does Anny like them?" asked Mama Jane.

"I don't know." Gibbie shrugged. "She never noticed before. She never noticed anything 'til we came here. She just sat and stared all the time. Except she took care of me. She took *good* care of me. That was before we came. Now she does lots of things."

Granddaddy and Mama Jane just looked at each other and wondered.

* * *

August 10, 1907

Today is my birthday! For my present, Mama Jane and Granddaddy have said I can take piano lessons when school starts! I am SO *excited! Mary Jo's teacher will teach me after school on Wednesdays, and I'll practice at school every day before I come home. Mr. Marshall never plays the piano, but it's there. And now I will play it.*

Summer has been WONDERFUL! *I've been so busy I've hardly had time to write. Mama Jane has been teaching me to sew, and I made myself two new dresses for school. I've also been learning how to put up food. And on the Fourth of July (our country's birthday) we all went to a barn dance where Ole Gilbertsen played a special kind of fiddle called hardanger. And another man there played an accordion. I really liked the music. It made me want to dance! I can still hear it in my imagination.*

* * *

God, I don't even know if I believe in you! Mac was on his horse, alone, miles from Heppner. He'd skipped church this morning, figuring he needed to talk to God by himself—not in the midst of a crowd. *Where were you during the flood, God? If you're so powerful and all-knowing, why didn't you stop it?* "That's probably blasphemy," he added aloud and took a deep breath. "God, I can't help it!" He continued speaking aloud, torn between honesty and a fear of this God who could strike so unmercifully. "I can't lie to you!" he shouted. "I can't. This is the real me talking, the real me shouting at you! And you're going to hear me out! I'm tired of trying to be nice to people and always say the right thing about what a great God you are—how you are so far above us, and we just don't understand your ways. I just don't believe it!" He dismounted, ground tied the horse, climbed the nearest rise. Sobbing, he threw himself on the ground. "Oh God!" he screamed. "Are you even there?"

His body shook with anguished sobs as he poured his misery into the ground and onto God's shoulders. He was beyond words.

And he heard no answer from God.

In time, his sobbing abated. A thought entered his awareness. *I've been pretending to see you through other people's eyes, God. Shan's eyes ... Why should I look at things through* Shan's *eyes? Does he have some corner on truth that I don't?* Mac rose to a sitting position, his clothing and hair covered with dried grass and dirt. *Dacia and Johnny. Why should I try to see things their way? If you really are God, I should be paying attention to* you! He felt empty of tears and of anger.

I should be listening to YOU, *God.*

Slowly, in place of the tears, in place of the anger was only a silent knowing. Knowing that his children were alive. Knowing that God *was* good—in spite of all the evidence to the contrary.

I don't understand you God. You are too big for me! I want peace. I want my children.

He spoke aloud. "I want you."

He rose and slowly made his way back down to the patient horse. He looked up into the sky. "Amen," he added as an afterthought. Then he mounted and turned toward home.

*   *   *

September 15, 1907

We are in school again, and there's a new teacher – Miss Donlon. She's wonderful! She's a la-

dy and she's young. Last year's teacher, Mr. Marshall, was exactly the opposite – a man, and old. And he wasn't very wonderful, either.

There is a new girl at school. And her name is Annie! But she spells her name with an "ie" instead of a "y."

*   *   *

The late September day was warm and sunny. Anny came home after her piano lesson bubbling with excitement. That night, after the children were in bed, the sky turned stormy. The clouds blew fiercely in front of the moon, and lightning could be seen in the south. Then the thunder rolled—long and loud. Anny's eyes flew open, her neck arched backward. It wasn't the first time she'd heard it tonight, she knew. It had been going on for some time in her troubled sleep. She had pictures in her mind ... *darkness, a small child being pounded—by rain? Hail? Pounded! Mud. Can't breathe! The thunder rolled and she couldn't breathe. The child couldn't breathe!* Anny shot upright in her bed, gasping.

Mama Jane hurried into her room. She sat on the edge of Anny's bed and held her close.

Anny stilled. She shuddered in Mama Jane's arms, but did not cry out. She was loved, cared for. She was safe. Mama Jane held her and rocked her.

Then thunder rolled again, louder than before. *The child—the child couldn't breathe!* Suddenly Anny lunged up gasping, eyes wide, reaching higher as if trying to escape the arms that held her. "It's all right, Anny! It's all right. I'm here. Just let me hold you." Mama Jane pulled Anny down and back into her lap where she rocked her like a tiny baby. "There, there," she crooned. "It'll be all right. I'm here. Don't fret, Anny. Shhhh ..."

Oslo put his front paws up on the bed and nosed Anny, whimpering.

"That's right, Oslo. You stay with her. She always feels better with you around."

The thunder receded, and slowly, ever so slowly, Anny drifted back to sleep. As Mama Jane turned and left the room, Oslo climbed up on the bed and snuggled down next to his precious Anny.

Chapter Forty Three

Elochoman Lumber Camp, March 1908

"Kingston! Get over here or go without!" Klein looked up at the sound of the name he'd chosen for this job and sauntered slowly toward the paymaster to receive his earnings. Saturday night after work was payday in the lumber camp. This was his second week on this job. He'd worked at Simon Benson's camp out of Clatskanie on the Oregon side of the River for almost three months before getting fired. Too bad he couldn't have stayed there longer. It had been a good job. Good food, good pay.

Of course, Benson made his men work way too hard. And he had an aversion to alcohol. He said it made poor workers of them. Caused them to wake up with hangovers. Made them more likely to have accidents, he said. He was a hard taskmaster. Didn't understand a man needing to relax a bit during the middle of the day. And he insisted on absolute honesty in all things. About the only reason he could get away with such tough standards was that he was good. The best in the business, some said.

Klein hated his guts. Benson hadn't treated him right, and some day, he would get even.

The food at this place was every bit as good and plentiful as Benson's, and far better than the small gyppo outfits he'd worked for a week here and a week there. Lots of good meat here, lots of potatoes. Good food, and plenty of it. That's what Klein liked. What he didn't like was the work.

He stepped up to the pay master and watched carefully as he counted out the cash. Pocketing his take, he turned away.

"Hey Robinson!" Klein called to a surly looking lumberjack. Robinson refused to take off his hat even when he ate. He was stocky, with dark hair and an even darker look on his face. Klein strode purposefully toward the man. "What do you hear?" he asked.

"Shut up!" Robinson hissed. "You talk too much. And too loud! Anyway, I ain't heard nothin' yet. Be patient. I'll let you know when the time's right."

Klein lowered his voice. "Well, I could use some ready cash just about any time now. I don't much like this place, and I'm thinking of moving on."

"Move on then. We don't need ya." Robinson's eyes issued a challenge.

"No, no. I'm in. May as well help you out while I can."

"Help yourself out, you mean."

Klein just scratched under his beard and gazed up into the trees. He was getting impatient with this whole business.

*   *   *

By late summer, Klein's interest in moving on was even stronger. He swung his grease bucket in one hand as he walked back into camp with Robinson. The "mop" used for greasing the log skids was balanced on Klein's shoulder. He didn't like being the "grease monkey" on the job. Any twelve-year-old could have handled it. Nobody appreciated him.

The two men had fallen behind the others as they tramped down the hill for dinner break. Klein didn't like the work. He wouldn't have minded so much if he could have manned a buck saw or worked at felling trees. Instead he was stuck mopping grease onto the wooden logs of the skid road.

"Heard anything yet?" Klein asked.

"Nope. I said I'd let you know."

"Yeah, but ..."

Robinson turned aside and leaned on the fence surrounding a mama hog and her piglets. Pork chops and bacon. That's what the pigs were for. Klein followed. "Well, when *will* you know something?"

"Just shut up. You talk too much." Robinson looked disgusted.

"Well, I was just wondering ..." Klein whined. Robinson sure wasn't easy to get along with. And pretty close-mouthed too. The only reason Klein stayed was the job coming up would make it worthwhile— if they could pull it off. He wished he knew more. All Robinson had told him was that it had to do with some bank on the east side of the Cascades, and the take would be in the tens of thousands of dollars—plenty to split three ways.

Klein wasn't sure if he should even trust Robinson anymore. After their last gig in Astoria, Klein had spent six months in jail. Robinson got off scot-free.

Robinson snarled at Klein. "I've told ya and told ya. Just don't talk about it." He turned back to the mess hall, leaving Klein to catch up. Klein lifted the wire holding the gate in place and swung the gate open. He'd show 'em. He stooped and picked up a small rock. "No harm in asking, is there?" He chucked the pebble toward the hog, and watched as the animal bolted toward the open gate. People should respect him more. He turned toward the mess hall without a backward glance.

*   *   *

The two men were the last in line for dinner. The big boss, John Yeon, was there. His real name was Jean Baptiste Yeon, Klein had heard. A Frenchie—probably Canadian. He'd been there all day working in the woods alongside his men.

Yeon was an exacting taskmaster—kind of like Benson that way. He demanded the very best from his men, but he also worked alongside them, showing them what he meant by the word "work."

John Yeon

Klein and Robinson filled their plates and took the only places left in the mess tent—directly across from John Yeon.

Klein decided it was time to show Robinson a thing or two. He straightened his shoulders and took a deep breath. "Hello Mr. Yeon," he said. "It's good to see you here. Things went quite well this morning. We got six big logs out with no hang-ups." Klein's speech and demeanor seemed more appropriate for a gathering of college graduates than for a lumber camp. Robinson looked at him, surprised.

"Great! Good! That's what I like to hear." Yeon smiled. "I'm sorry, but I've forgotten your name, Mr. ..."

"Kingston. Charles Kingston," Klein said. He smiled and extended his hand across the table to shake Yeon's. "I remember the last time you were up here, we were visiting about our children. I certainly enjoyed learning about your family."

"That's right. I remember now. Nice to see you again, Mr. Kingston."

As Yeon went back to his meal, Robinson nudged Klein and muttered, "You're pretty good at that!"

Klein just looked smug and continued eating his dinner.

Chapter Forty Four

May 1908

G race stomped up the hill with such determination that if Michael had seen her coming, he would have run for his life. Professor Reid, the principal, had called, saying that Michael had been involved in yet another "disagreement" which had escalated to violence. What *was* she to do with the boy?

When Michael started second grade only a few months after the flood, Grace had already been concerned about him. He could be a charming boy, and a delight to be around, but there were other times when a deep anger seemed to motivate him. Dacia said to give him time. Shan—of course—said nothing.

Now in sixth grade, Michael had grown worse, year by year. He still seemed to have that delightfully funny, impish sparkle, but it showed less and less often because of the many incidents of aggression and vandalism.

Grace had tried talking to him, withholding privileges, sending him to stand in the corner. She couldn't spank him. She just couldn't. And besides, Shan wouldn't want her to. Michael was not her child. She was just the mother's helper—with no mother to help. That's what the boy needed—a mother! And a father! Instead he had Shan and Grace. And they barely spoke to each other—even after all this time. Michael didn't stand a chance unless something changed.

Out of breath from the steep climb, Grace pushed through the tall front door of the school building and entered the principal's office, steeling herself to address an unhappy principal and a defiant boy. But Michael was alone in the room, Professor Reid apparently called away temporarily on other business. As Grace moved a small wooden chair to sit next to Michael, he suddenly burst into tears. Grace was dumbfounded! Michael ... crying? Michael never cried! In all the time she had cared for him, he had never, *ever* cried. Not once. She sat on the chair and awkwardly put a hand on his shoulder, but Michael slapped it away.

Suddenly, Grace found the resolve she needed. "Come on," she said, standing. "We're going home." Thankfully, Michael rose and followed her meekly out the door and down the steps. She had no idea what she would have done if he'd refused to come.

They marched in silence down the hill. As they crossed the creek, Grace glared, wishing she could destroy it. And this wasn't the first time she'd felt this way. This stupid creek was the beginning of the whole problem. *If only* it hadn't wiped out a fourth of the town, *if only* it hadn't killed Michael's mother, *if only* life could go back to what it had been before.

Oh *no!* What was she wishing for? Go back? Never! At least *she* would never choose to go back. The flood had been her salvation! Her own life was split into "before" and "after."

But Michael. Michael needed help. Somehow, she must find within herself the wisdom and strength to give him what he needed. And she couldn't do it alone. It was time—yes, after five long years, it was high time for a talk with Shan. Whether he wanted it or not.

*   *   *

Grace marched back and forth in front of Shan, who was pressed up against the drain board as if bound in place by ropes of iron. Both hands were in his pockets, his gaze moved about the kitchen floor as he listened to the litany of his brother's sins.

Grace continued ticking off Michael's offenses on her fingers. She had gone through all ten of them once already and was up to number four on her second time through.

"And then last week he was tormenting the Jones's dog and her puppies. That's why he got bit. He took the jump rope from two little girls at school and was about to tie them to a tree with it when Miss Joseph rescued them." Grace started on the fingers on the other hand— again. "His teacher says he's ornery. And he sassed Mr. Gentry at the barber shop, and stole candy from the jar on the counter at The Fair— and lied about it after." Grace's voice rose to an even higher pitch. "That donnybrook down in front of the Pastime last week? Michael started it. Yesterday he hung Danny upside-down in the outhouse and threatened to let go. All the children in town are afraid of him, and the parents won't let their children play with him, and they cross to the other side of the street when they see him coming!

"Shan, I know you can't stand the sight of me. I know you wish your mother was here to do this job. But she's *not!*" Grace snatched the dish towel from her shoulder and slammed it over the back of the nearest chair. "What's past is past, and there is today—and tomorrow—to think about. You *have* to get your head out of your dreams and wishes, and take a look at what's real, because wishing will never fix anything!" She glared at Shan and lowered her voice to nearly a whisper. "Something *has* to change! *Now!* And *you* are the only one who can make it happen!" She clamped her jaws together.

Shan continued to stare at the floor.

Grace erupted again. "Shan, *say* something! Don't just ... stand there with your hands in your pockets!"

Shan withdrew his hands and gripped the drain board behind him until his knuckles turned white. For the first time in his life, he lifted his face and looked Grace in the eye. *Can't stand the sight of her? Is that what she thinks?*

Shan was consumed with anger—at Michael. Fear—of Grace. A welling within him that he couldn't name. He stepped forward, took Grace's shoulders gently in his hands.

"Grace, will you marry me?"

"Wha—? Will I—?"

He bent to kiss her. She yielded willingly, then stiffened. "What do you think you're—"

"I love you, Grace. I've loved you all along."

"Well, you certainly have a peculiar way of ..." She burst into tears.

"Grace, forgive me. Please forgive me." Tears rolled down Shan's cheeks as well, as he pulled her to himself, wrapping his long arms around her. "I've been so awful—and so ashamed of myself. Thank you for forcing me ..."

Grace felt herself sink into his big chest as sobs shook her own. She lifted her arms to embrace him, then tightened her hands into fists—each full of a good sized chunk of Shan's shirt. If he'd let go of her in that moment, she would have fallen to the floor—which was spinning around her.

*   *   *

"He did? He really asked you to marry him?" Dacia's eyes were wide with amazement, her smile tentative.

Grace nodded.

"And ...?"

"And I accepted."

"I knew it! I've known it all along! Didn't I tell you he wasn't really as bad as you thought he was? He's just so incredibly shy. So ... How? How did you get him to propose to you?"

"I yelled at him. But I wasn't trying to get him to propose to me! He just needed to be yelled at."

"About Michael?"

Grace nodded.

"So now Michael will have a mother and a father. That might be all that boy needs to turn him around—just a sense of family—a mother and father."

"Well, he *doesn't* have his father. He has Shan. And I am *not* his mother. But I do really love the children—all three of them—and I think Shan does too."

"Oh he does! It's easy to see from the way he plays with them!"

"So maybe ..."

"No. Not maybe, Grace. It's a new start for the whole family. And you are so right, so perfect to be 'Mrs. Collins.'"

"Maybe."

"*Why* maybe?"

"Maybe it won't work out. Then what? I'm scared!"

"Grace, look at me." Dacia waited until Grace lifted her reluctant eyes to meet those of her friend. "Grace ... I promise you—I guarantee you—it's *not* going to work out."

Grace was stunned. "It's not?"

Dacia laughed aloud. "You're the one who said it first!"

"Well, yes, but ..."

"A marriage doesn't just work out, Grace. It never does. It takes two people, each giving a hundred percent. It's not half and half. It's not something that just maybe happens or maybe doesn't happen. It's *work*. It's keeping a promise. That's why you say, ''til death do us part.'"

"You have to say that when you get married?"

"Haven't you been to a wedding before?"

Grace shook her head. "I never have. We ... my family lived pretty far out ..." Grace looked up at Dacia with a grim expression. "Shan doesn't really know who I am, who I was before I came here."

"I don't know either, but I don't love you any less for it. Don't you trust Shan to love you for who you are now?"

Grace said nothing.

"Grace," Dacia said, pushing her friend into a kitchen chair and sitting at the table opposite her. "I've hinted and prodded, trying to get you to talk about your past ever since you came here. You've never answered me. But I've known all along that the time would come. Maybe now is that time. You don't have to talk to me. But you *do* have to talk to Shan. If you're going to be married, there can be no secrets between you. None."

"I don't know how."

"That's what courting is for. It's a time to get to really know each other."

"Well ..."

"Grace, remember when you were talking about how little Ellie was new-born? Starting with a fresh slate—nothing had gone wrong in her life yet?"

Grace smiled. "How could I forget? Pappy told me God lets us start over again, just like being a brand new baby. We *can* start over. That means so much to me. That and the flood."

"The flood?" Dacia looked confused, aghast.

"The flood was my salvation. My new beginning."

Dacia tilted her head to the side and squinted her eyes.

"But the past didn't just go away. It's still there." Grace spoke softly.

"It will always be there, but it can't have any power over you, unless you let it. That's something else Pappy says."

"That sounds right." Grace nodded. Pappy was a wise old man, despite his odd and forgetful ways. "I just don't know how to get there."

"Go there with Shan. If you're going to marry him, he will become a part of you. And you, a part of him. It's not about the past; it's about the future. Grace, we can't kill our memories. But God can kill their power over us. Let God do it. Make that choice to let Him win, and refuse to back down!"

Chapter Forty Five

September 1908

That night, Anny dreamt. At first it was a nice dream. A mama and a papa and children. They were all playing and laughing together in the grass in front of a white house. They had no faces, but they seemed very happy. Then suddenly it grew very dark, and a loud, loud sound screamed in Anny's head. Then the family was gone. In their place was only blackness and loud crying.

Anny sobbed quietly, afraid to wake up Mama Jane, but Mama Jane sensed something wrong. When she came into the room, she found Anny sitting up in bed, her face buried in her quilt, sobbing. Oslo was licking Anny's ear, her hand, her hair.

Mama Jane didn't ask questions. She just pulled Anny's shaking body into her lap and rocked her gently, pressing her lips into Anny's hair.

After a while, Anny calmed and crawled off Mama Jane's lap. She scrunched back onto her pillow. Mama Jane pulled the covers up to her chin and stayed with her until she slept, then padded back to her own bed.

After breakfast Mama Jane asked Anny, "Did you have a good sleep?"

"Yes, thank you," Anny said. Her shoulders tightened and she reached out to grasp the kitchen counter.

Mama Jane saw, but she asked no more questions, and Anny offered no answers.

*　　*　　*

Shan wiped his forehead in the warmth of the autumn sun. He wondered if it was actually the heat, or the recent turn his life had taken. Only last week, he had asked Grace, beautiful, precious Grace to be his wife. And she had accepted! Why had he not done this years ago? He'd loved her almost since the day she began caring for his children. Yes, he thought, he considered them *his* children now. And Grace had been a wonderful mother to them. The whole thing was so right. So right ... except for Michael.

And that was as much his own fault as Michael's, Shan thought. If he had been a better "father" to the boy, perhaps all this would not have happened. But, of course, Shan had not known *how* to be a father. How could he know? His own father had died when Shan was only fourteen. He remembered his father very well. A tall man, like Shan himself. In fact, Shan was like his father in many ways. Andrew Shannon Collins had been a man in touch with beauty—an artist—even though building furniture was his job. Shan remembered.

But Michael didn't remember this father at all. He'd been only three when Pa had died. Michael had, for the most part, grown up without a father. *It's made him angry,* Shan thought. *A boy needs a father.* Well, Shan didn't really know how to go about it. But he would become the father Michael needed. And he would start today.

Shan looked back to check on Michael sitting astride Marshmallow, the palomino mare Shan had bought to replace Pretty Girl. Shan rode a horse he'd rented for the day from the livery. Michael's look was dark, defiant. He had not wanted to come and had grumbled continually about it for the first five miles or so. Finally he had settled into a miserable silence.

They'd left home early, riding along Willow Creek to a tiny lake Johnny had told Shan about. *It's beautiful!* Shan thought as he dismounted. *I don't know why I never did this before.*

Michael and Shan unsaddled the horses and hobbled them, then began to prepare their fishing tackle.

"I need to talk to you about something important," Shan began.

"I already know. You're going to marry Grace." Michael's look was defiant.

Shan choked slightly. How did Michael know that?

"I saw you hugging and kissing in the kitchen."

The redness in Shan's neck began to creep up his face. "Uh ... yeah. Yeah. So, we're going to get married." Well, it would have to come out sometime anyway. You couldn't keep an impending marriage a secret forever.

"But that isn't the thing I wanted to talk to you about. It's something else."

Michael sighed. "I'm in trouble again. I know. But you don't have to bring me on a fishing trip to tell me that. And anyway, that's not news. I'm always in trouble with somebody!"

"Well, Michael. That's not what I wanted to talk about either." The boy sure wasn't making this any easier. Couldn't he keep his mouth shut for a minute and let Shan talk?

"It's not?" Michael looked at Shan sharply. "Then what?"

Shan took a deep breath. "Michael, do you remember Pa?"

Finally Michael stopped talking. He didn't really know the answer to the question.

Shan waited—gave Michael time to think. He baited his own line and showed Michael how to do his. They cast their lines into the lake and waited.

"Do you?" Shan asked.

"I don't know for sure," Michael finally responded. "How come you're asking?"

"I thought I'd like to tell you about him, you know, what he was like and all."

"He looked kind of like you, huh?"

Shan nodded. "You too. You look even more like him than I do."

The family photo, taken less than a year before Pa died, had been hanging on the wall in the front room when the flood hit. It wasn't damaged—too high up for the flood to reach. Now it hung in the same place on the same wall. Shan realized he'd not even noticed it for a long time. But if someone took the picture down, he would have noticed the empty spot.

"Yes, I look a lot like him, and I *am* a lot like him too. He loved beautiful things. No matter what he did, he made it artistic. He was a furniture maker. His things weren't just useful, they were beautiful too. He made our sideboard with all that neat carving on it. That was all done by hand. And Ma's rocking chair and the cradle."

"He did? I didn't know that."

Shan smiled. "Yeah, he did."

Throughout the morning, Shan continued telling Michael stories of Pa, funny stories, stories of difficult times, stories of Pa making the hard choices in life, of choosing to do the right thing, the best thing, in all the little acts of daily living. He told of the time Pa had whupped him for telling Ma a lie. And the time he'd had to do all his own chores, and Pa's too, for a solid week because he sassed Pa. He told family stories going back even to the long ago times of their father's parents and grandparents in Ireland.

And Michael soaked it all in, like a frozen land when the sun begins to shine.

By the time Michael and Shan were getting hungry for dinner, they'd caught five fine trout. Along with the apples and bread and butter Grace had sent along, it was the best meal either one of them could remember for a long, long time.

*   *   *

Two days later, Shan and Grace sat on the porch swing in the late evening. Michael, Libby, and Danny had finally settled down for the night.

"Grace, I really meant it when I told you how sorry I am. It's just—I kind of got started being afraid to talk to you, and couldn't seem to get over it. The longer I waited, the worse it got!"

"Am I so bad as all that? That a person would be afraid to talk to me?" Grace smiled teasingly. "For *five years?*"

"Grace ... You are *wonderful!*"

Grace smiled, but fiddled with her fingers. "So, we've known each other for five years, and yet, we don't really know each other at all."

"I *do* know you! I've watched you, thought about you, dreamed about you, imagined having a conversation with you. Sometimes I even came home from work early and hid upstairs, just so I could be near you without you knowing."

"You did?" Grace's eyes opened wide.

"I did.

"And?"

"And it was pure torture, being so close, but ..." Shan held out his hand, tentatively. Grace looked across the street at the Burke house, but saw no one. She slowly placed her hand in Shan's and smiled as a thrill ran through her body.

"But you don't *really* know me, no matter what you think. You don't know who I was before I came here. You don't know ..." She shook her head.

Shan gave her hand a gentle squeeze and waited for her to go on.

"See ... well, I came from down south of Hardman. Came to Heppner just before the flood. Um ... I ran away from home." She looked up at Shan, but he just waited. "I ran away from home because ...

"Well, see ..." She stopped and took a deep breath.

"My mother died when I was twelve. She was wonderful. A real lady and the best mother in the world. Completely different from my pa. I was the oldest—the only girl. So I had to raise my four little brothers. I cooked and did the cleaning. Did the sewing and canning. Most everything the woman of the house does. I had to quit school so I could do it all, but we managed. And I was able to keep the boys in school.

"Then I began growing up, and ... well ... my father started telling me what a beautiful woman I was." Grace swallowed and continued staring at her hand linked with Shan's. "I didn't understand that, didn't understand why he would say that, when he'd always been so mean before." She swallowed again nervously and rushed on. "He would ... hug me and touch me. And then ...

"He said I was a grown up woman and I should learn to do what a woman does. And he showed me ..." Grace's voice cracked. She took a huge gulp of air and began sobbing quietly.

Shan gathered her into his arms without even checking to see if neighbors might be watching. He gently pulled her head against his shoulder and held her while she sobbed out the grief of an innocence lost. He just let her cry.

After a time, as her sobs slowly subsided and turned to hiccups, Shan pulled out a handkerchief that Grace had washed and folded. He offered it to her. She dried her eyes and blew her nose, then laid her head back on Shan's shoulder.

"I just—I couldn't marry you without telling you that," she whispered.

Shan swallowed his anger. Anger at a man he'd never met, who had done such an evil thing. He'd figure out later how to handle the anger. For now, it would only serve to strengthen his love.

"Grace, nothing you tell me could change my mind about wanting to marry you. *Nothing*," Shan replied. "Getting married means we're going to be one. And God help me if I don't live up to the honor of it!"

*   *   *

Anny's focus had changed perceptibly over the course of a year. Last year when Christmas had come to the little farm on Puget Island, she had dreamed of the wonderful presents she might receive— wrapped in bright paper and ribbons!

But this year she realized that she could *give.* As early as September, she began thinking about what special and wonderful things she could do for Gibbie, Mama Jane, and Granddaddy. Gibbie was easy. She was sewing him a new shirt. It was red flannel and she knew Gibbie would love it! Red was his favorite color. But more than that, Granddaddy had a red flannel shirt, and Gibbie wanted to be just like his hero. From the day the children had arrived at the Petersen's, Gibbie had followed Granddaddy around, copying everything he did, even—to some extent—his Norwegian accent.

For Mama Jane, Anny had made what she called "tickets." There were twelve of them, and each represented a night when Anny would cook supper all by herself, serve it, *and* clean up afterwards. She thought she might need just a little advice once in a while, but really, she was pretty confident she could do it. Mama Jane had been a good teacher. Now she could just sit with her feet up and relax once in a while.

But for Granddaddy ... what to do for Granddaddy?

Finally, she began to write in her journal.

GRANDDADDY

Strong and gentle,

Loving, but firm,

His presence makes me happy.

Wise, yet silly,

Guiding, teaching,

Filling our home with joy.

Hope for tomorrow,

Comfort in sorrow,

Granddaddy!

Anny closed the book and nodded in satisfaction. Tomorrow she would ask Mama Jane for some special paper to write the poem on.

Then she would decorate it with patterns like a Norwegian sweater all around the edge. Her Christmas plans were complete, and she could hardly wait for the great day!

Chapter Forty Six

March 1909

Robinson and Klein rested under a tree at the end of the day. The spring air was chilly, but tolerable. "So ..." Robinson said, "You got kids. Got a wife?"

"Nope."

"You gonna go get your kids when we leave?"

"Nah. I ain't seen 'em in a couple of years—since we dropped 'em off that day. Don't know what I'd do with 'em."

"Well, I been thinking." Robinson's eyes narrowed and he went on. "We're going to be running our operation out of The Dalles, and we need to go over there sometime in the next few months and kind of get established. A family man, living in town—you know, wife and kids—well, a family man like that probably wouldn't attract much attention. 'Specially if he was the sort of man who could fit in anywhere." Robinson glanced at Klein's face, trying not to appear too impressed. "You know how to talk and act like the boss. You could pull it off.

"Think about it. In a few more months, we move to The Dalles."

Klein nodded with interest. "Maybe," was all he said. *If it's easy, and if there's plenty of money in it,* was the part he didn't say.

*　　*　　*

Portland, July 1909

Klein leaned closer to the woman beside him at The Outpost, one of Portland's less savory bars. His move was meant to convey strength, power. She interpreted it as need. She turned to face him and tilted her head back slightly, looking down her long nose and blinking her eyelashes at him. "You're awful cute, Sweetie Pie!"

He raised one eyebrow, looking down his own nose in response. "Business," he stated. "That's why we're here—a business arrangement."

"Hmm, yes. I suppose we are. Different business than I'm used to, you said." The woman sat up straight, flipped one of her blond curls back and forth and pulled the shoulder of her dress a little lower, revealing aging skin and a desperation she didn't recognize as obvious. "So," she asked, "what kind of business? I need to know what's expected of me before I sign on."

Klein leaned his elbow on the bar and partially covered his mouth with one hand. "We would be a man and wife. We'll go to The Dalles and work with my partner there. I'll tell you, there's a lot of loot going through The Dalles, a *lot*—gold, payrolls, all kinds of loot."

"What would I have to actually *do*?"

"Different things. Depends on the gig. Mostly you would make us look respectable. You'd get a cut, of course."

"Of course," she echoed.

"Oh, and you would be a mother. Two children."

"Oh, you're going to make me a mother, are you? And just how do you plan on doing that when I can't even get you to flirt with me?" She ran a finger teasingly down one side of Klein's face and under his beard. He showed no response. She heaved a sigh of exasperation. "How am I going to come by these two children? I hate kids! I wouldn't know what to do with 'em!"

"Aw, they're not bad. Anny is seven or eight—something like that. And Gibbie's a couple years younger. You'll hardly notice them."

"'Seven or eight or something like that.' Uh-huh. How do you know these kids? Because if you're planning a kidnapping, I will have nothing to do with it. *Nothing!*" She banged her hand flat on the bar for emphasis.

"No, not kidnapping. These are my own children. Mine and El-la's—their mother's." Klein's face softened momentarily. "She's dead."

"Your own children, and you don't even know how old they are? What kind of man *are* you! What's going on here?" She rose from her stool and turned away as if to leave.

Klein reached out a hand and placed it on her shoulder. "Wait! Listen!" She sat back on the edge of her stool. "See I was ... very sick for a while and not able to take care of them. I left them with a relative—a friend's relative actually. Or a relative's friend. They have no mother, you know—except you."

The woman turned back to face Klein. "*Not* me! I'm *not* their mother!"

"Fine. I'll find someone who knows how to cooperate and wants the money." Klein stood and began to walk away.

"No! Wait! I just need a little time to get used to it." Klein settled back onto his bar stool. "So ... I would be your wife and the children's mother, and ... I just want to know for sure this is going to work out before I give up my position here. I work for a good house. There's lots of money to be made in my profession, you know."

"Yeah. I know. But you can't fool me." Klein sneered. "You're about done for. You won't last much longer in this business. How old are you anyway? Forty?"

She grimaced.

"And anyway, anything you earn here would be nothing like what we'll have in The Dalles. Not just money, but good times. There's bars galore, and gambling. And besides, the kids are old enough to take care of theirselves. You don't have to worry. You might have to cook a few meals—"

"I *hate* cooking."

Klein stood once again to walk away, but she held up her hand. "But ... if you think we'll take in enough to make it worthwhile ..."

"That's my girl," Klein said. He pulled out a roll of bills, and the woman's eyes lit up. "In the morning, we'll get the tickets for the *Bailey Gatzert*, and then we'll go get the children. You'll really like them!"

"Uh-huh," was the woman's only response.

*   *   *

The wedding was perfect. Grace wore a lovely pale blue dress she and Dacia had made, but Shan was so in love, he didn't even notice. Michael, Libby, and Danny carried flowers and rings, and even had a speaking part when Brother Mount asked them if they promised to do everything they could to support Shan and Grace in their new marriage. Libby and Danny said yes because they had been instructed to; Michael said yes because it was a vow he intended to keep.

The wedding ceremony—held in the Burke's back yard—was followed by a dance at Roberts Hall. Shan and Grace stayed long enough to dance themselves to exhaustion before adjourning to a room that had been especially prepared for them at the Palace Hotel. Shan carried his bride across the threshold into their new life together, while the dancers down the street continued to celebrate Heppner's newest family.

*   *   *

"Who's dat?" Granddaddy asked as the family walked up Sunny Sands Road. They were on their way home from the Lutheran Church located on Welcome Slough. Jane looked up and squinted her eyes against the sun's glare.

"I don't know." A man and woman were just entering the Petersen's gate. They walked up to the front door and knocked.

"Hello dere. Can I help you?" Granddaddy called, as they drew close to the house.

"Oh, hello. We didn't see you coming." The man's voice had an immediate effect. Anny didn't place it at first—only the feeling it gave her. Dread.

Mama Jane froze in place. Even though she had heard the voice only once before, she recognized it instantly.

"What do you want?" she snapped. "Why are you here?" Her voice carried no welcome, only defiance.

And suddenly Anny knew.

Father.

Book Four

Rise Above

Chapter Forty Seven

A beautiful morning in April. A perfect morning, actually. The sun was warm but not hot, a gentle breeze blew off the mighty Columbia River, birds fluttered and peeped, and crocuses poked their brave heads above the surface of the warming soil to greet another spring. Perfect, that is, until the man's voice shattered the beauty, flinging shards like broken glass.

"I've brought my new wife to meet the children," the man said, walking back through the gate and into the road. "We are going to move to San Francisco and begin a new life there."

"I hope you'll enjoy it there." Jane's voice challenged him. "The children are quite happy here, and I assume you've come to tell them good bye."

"Well no, actually ..."

"We've come to take them with us," the lady gushed. "I am *so* excited to meet them! I've never had children before. This will be so much fun!" The woman giggled slightly and she tucked her hand under Klein's arm.

"No, I'm sorry. Da children won't be able to go with you," Granddaddy said. His voice was calm. Powerful. Both Anny and Gibbie recognized his not-to-be-argued-with tone.

But Father didn't recognize it. "Well," he said, scratching his neck under his beard. "Perhaps we should all sit down and talk about this."

"Where have you been?" Mama Jane demanded, her eyes flashing. "It's been over two years. *Two years* since you left the children here and vanished into thin air! You can't just show up and decide to take them with you!"

"Well, I'm so sorry." Father lifted his chin and stiffened his shoulders. "I thought you'd be more understanding about it. You do realize, I'm sure, that as their father, I am the one who will make decisions regarding the children's future."

"You already made a decision about dere future. You abandoned dem here. From now on, dey will continue to lif with us." Granddaddy's eyes were hard as steel.

Anny stood frozen in time and space. Father—she remembered him now. The sound of him.

Klein shifted his gaze to Anny. "Anny, I've missed you," he said to her in a silky voice. "Have you been a good girl on your visit here?" She stared at the ground at his feet and said nothing.

"I thought about you—both of you—all the time. I was working in the forest. It's hard work, sawing trees. We got up every morning before dawn. The work was ..."

His voice droned on, but Anny didn't hear. Against her will, her eyes slowly rose. She saw a man—a man she didn't recognize. Long legs, long fingers, long arms and a long neck. She lifted her eyes to his face. *What is happening? I feel you calling me and I don't want to come. But how can I not?* She felt Gibbie put his hand in hers. Anny, who had never once looked this man in the face, now tried to tear her eyes away from Father, but she couldn't do it. *You have control over me, even when I don't want it. How can I stop you?*

"Anny, don't listen to him, sweetheart." Mama Jane's voice. Mama Jane's arm around her shoulder.

But Anny did listen. Not to Father's words, but to his ... his presence. His presence had flowed around her like a strong rope. Her arms were tied to her sides, she was unable to speak. Gibbie gripped her hand tighter. He felt it too. They belonged to Father. They had no strength to escape him.

"Here now, I t'ink it's time for you to move on." Granddaddy reached for Gibbie.

"Yes, it *is* time," Father said. He took one child in each hand and began walking away from the Petersens. Gibbie instantly pulled away screaming, "No!"

Mama Jane ran and put her arms around Anny, clutching her tightly, but Klein continued to pull Anny down the road. Then he put his arm around her, his bony fingers clutching her under her arm. He began to drag her, the woman following close behind.

Gibbie ran after them and grabbed Anny's free arm. "No, Anny!" he screamed. "Don't go!" He pulled, but Father's grip was too strong.

Anny was limp. Her feet simply drifted along the road with no will of their own.

Granddaddy, running up behind Gibbie, began to pry Father's grasp loose from Anny, until the man turned on him. Klein towered over Granddaddy, looking down and shouting at the top of the older man's head.

"Get out of the way, old man! These are *my* children!" He pounded a heavy boot into Granddaddy's shin, then his kneecap. Granddaddy crumpled to the ground. Klein shoved Mama Jane aside, turned, and began to run down the road, still clutching Anny to his side. The woman tagged along behind like an afterthought, an airy smile still plastered to her face.

Oslo, a streak of black and white, ran around the side of the house and through the open gate. He was on Klein before anyone realized he was there.

Klein let out a howl and kicked his leg to loosen Oslo's grip. "Get this mutt off me!" he screamed. When the dog shook loose from his leg, Klein gave him a powerful kick, turned, and ran again while Oslo fell to earth by the ditch alongside the road. He tried to get up, but fell back.

Gibbie looked from Anny to the Petersens and back again. Finally, he cast a longing glance back at Granddaddy and ran to take Anny's hand and go with her.

"*No!*" Mama Jane's angry, tortured cry followed them. She ran down the road after them.

Ivar, on his feet again, stopped her and held her in his arms as they watched the children vanish from sight. "Don't worry, Jane. He has no right. We can't stop him now, but we'll go get da Sheriff. It's all a big mistake. Da law won't let him keep dem, and we'll have dem back in no time." His face burned with anger.

Jane fell into his arms sobbing. "Let's go, Ivar. Let's go right now." They couldn't see which way Klein had turned at the crossroad, but started immediately down the road to the Cathlamet side of the Island, Ivar limping badly, to see the sheriff.

* * *

Jane and Ivar Petersen waited impatiently in front of the Cathlamet sheriff's office. The sign on the door reminded them the office would open at 8:00 a.m. Monday. But waiting was not an option. The Petersens needed the sheriff *now*! A man on horseback had been dispatched to the sheriff's home in nearby Skamokawa to bring the lawman on the double.

Jane paced frantically while Granddaddy alternately clenched the muscle in his jaw and rubbed his knee as he fretted in silence.

Finally, Sheriff Flanders rode into sight. Ivar sprang to motion, limping up to the sheriff before he'd even had a chance to dismount.

"Hello, Sheriff, and t'anks for coming so quick like. I am Ivar Petersen, and dis is my wife. We lif on da Island. Dis is pretty serious, Sheriff. Our children—well, dere fadder came after church and took dem."

"Wait." The sheriff dropped his horse's reins over the hitching rail and moved toward his office door. "Their *father* came and took them? You said they're *your* children, yes?" He pulled out a key to the office door.

"Well, the father abandoned them at our house over two years ago," Jane said. "We've been raising them since then. We've come to accept them as our own."

"Oh, I see." The sheriff made a clicking sound with his mouth and drew in his breath between his teeth. "Well, come on in and we can sit down." He held the door open and followed the Petersens into the tiny office. Pulling an extra chair from the corner, he said, "So this father, he—what? Just left the children with you and never came back?"

"Dat's right. He said he was going to check on a job at da cannery, but we nefer heard from him again. 'Til today. He was dere when we come home from church, and he took da children."

Sheriff Flanders sat on the corner of his desk and nodded to the two chairs. "So these are actually his children, not yours?" Neither Jane nor Ivar sat.

"Yes, but he *abandoned* them! How can he say they are his children? They are no more his than I am a Rhode Island red rooster! He *dumped* them at our house and just vanished. Then he comes marching in, big as you please and says he's taking them to San Francisco. Just like that!" Mama Jane snapped her fingers—nearly in the sheriff's face. "He can't do that!"

"Hmmm ... well ... if they're his children, I guess we can't stop him."

"But we *have to* stop him!" Why couldn't Jane make the man see?

"Ma'am, I understand that you're upset about—"

"Upset? It's *kidnapping!* That's what it is!"

"But if he's their father, even if he's a bad one, the children belong to him. There's nothing we can do." The sheriff spoke calmly.

"What do you mean there's noth—"

Granddaddy placed a hand on Jane's arm.

"He can't do that!" said Jane, her voice climbing up the scale. "He can't go to California. He's kidnapped two children!"

"Let me explain, Sheriff," Ivar said. "Dese two children and dere fadder came to a boarding house in Oregon City in the summer of 1903. It is owned by Jane's two sisters. Da little girl didn't talk. She acted like she was blind—nefer did anyt'ing. Da children stayed dere for a year and a half. Da fadder worked only about half da time, and didn't pay his room and board. He ignored da children—didn't get clothes for dem or anyt'ing. Finally, Jane's sisters had to evict dem so dey could take a paying boarder."

Jane picked up the story where Ivar had left off. "After they left my sisters' home, they disappeared from sight. When they came to us, they were filthy, uncared for, and starving. They did not know their former address or even their father's first name. They obviously had been neglected horribly."

Ivar put his arm around Jane's shoulder and gave it a comforting squeeze.

"He just showed up on Puget Island one day," Jane continued, "and said that a friend of his gave our name to him and would we please care for the children while he went to check out a job possibility. And that's the last we saw of him for two and a half years. Does this sound like something a father would do? How can you call this man a father?"

Sheriff Flanders nodded. "Yes, I see. It's a very difficult situation. Unfortunately, as sheriff I'm not responsible for the behavior of parents, unless they break the law. As far as I can tell, this man has not broken the law. He's irresponsible, perhaps—"

"Per*haps!*" Jane snapped.

"—but irresponsibility does not fall within our jurisdiction."

The sheriff looked intently at Ivar. "You know, anyone heading for California from this area would need to board at Astoria. I think," he continued deliberately, still holding Ivar's gaze, "that if a person wanted to try to stop someone from heading south, that's where they should go."

Ivar nodded in understanding.

"Come, Ivar," Jane said. "Let's go to Astoria. Who knows? Maybe we can figure out some way to keep them here." She hurried toward the door.

"Ja, Jane. Maybe we can. *Takk skal du ha*, Sheriff. Thank you." Ivar doffed his cap and turned to limp after Jane.

Chapter Forty Eight

The *Bailey Gatzert* with the *Charles R. Spencer* and another sternwheeler
Courtesy Alex Blendl

Anny had never felt so sick in her life. The world heaved and rolled under her feet; the sky, trees, and water wallowed all around her with relentless, unpredictable motion. The splashing sound of the huge wheel and the roar of the steam engine which turned it thundered with unbridled muscle, incredible power and fear. She closed her eyes and gripped the rail more tightly as her stomach lurched again. She couldn't wait for the trip to end.

Gibbie, on the other hand, could not get enough of this new experience. He had learned to walk like a sailor within the first two minutes of travel. Of course, both children had ridden in the little boats around the Island. But that had been completely different. This was the mighty Columbia River, in all its glory, in all its power. And a *huge* boat. Gibbie loved it.

He had put up a tremendous fuss when Father and the woman had taken him and Anny from the Island. He had yelled and pulled away from Father when they boarded the boat, and said he wasn't going and Father couldn't make him. Even now, if he'd stopped to think, he would have realized just how miserable he was. But he didn't want to think. Instead, he ran—smack into one of the biggest men he'd ever seen.

"Hey, hold it there, little guy!" The man reached out to grab Gibbie by the back of his shirt. "Just where do you think you're goin'?"

Gibbie tried to wrench himself away from the meaty paw that held him, but it was impossible. When he looked up into the face of his captor, he saw humor twinkling behind the bright blue eyes, and he suspected there was a smile as well, but it was hard to tell with the big beard and moustache.

Gibbie stopped struggling. "Wow! Are you the captain of the boat?" he asked.

This brought a roar of laughter from the huge man. "Am I the captain of the boat! Ha! Did you hear that?" He looked around at the passengers. "Am I the captain! No, I ain't the captain, I'm just John. Big John. I just do what the captain tells me. But captain or no, I'll skin the hide off a ya and throw it to the seals if you go sneakin' around where y'ain't s'pose to be!"

"Yes, sir!" Gibbie replied. "Will you show me all the stuff on the boat? I been on *little* boats before, but nothin' like this!"

"Well son, you are now standin' on the deck of the finest sternwheeler on the Columbia—and the fastest too! This," he paused and held out his hands, inviting Gibbie and the other passengers to take a good look around at the magnificent vessel, "is the *Bailey Gatzert*—one hundred and ninety-four feet of pure beauty and power. Yes, sir, the most beautiful, the fastest, the *best* boat on the mighty Columbia River. And she has the best whistle, too." He poked his huge finger into Gibbie's chest, and said softly, "And she's proud. Don'tcha let her hear you even mention your little boats in her presence. You'll break her heart."

"Oh, I'll be careful," Gibbie assured Big John, nodding. "I won't be sayin' anything to hurt her feelings."

Big John seemed satisfied with Gibbie's response. "You wanna come along with me and help out?"

Gibbie nodded, eyes big with excitement, and followed Big John around the corner to a stairway and down to the boiler room. "Stand right there and don't move!" Big John hollered over the noise of the engine, then consulted with two men who were busy heaving cordwood into the open furnace.

Big John then took Gibbie up to the top deck—the "texas," Big John called it. "Big and wide as the sky in Texas," he explained.

"Does the wind always blow like this here?" Gibbie shouted to be heard above the roar of the wind and the splashing of the turning paddle wheel. "And where are we going? And when'll we get there?"

"Yes, the wind blows. We're goin' to The Dalles. And we'll get there mighty soon."

The Dalles? Gibbie thought. Father had told Mama Jane and Granddaddy they were headed for San Francisco. But Gibbie's new friend said their destination was The Dalles. Maybe The Dalles was on the way to San Francisco?

Other than regular stops to take on more cordwood—needed to fuel the hungry furnace that produced the steam—the *Bailey* chuffed steadily upriver. Gibbie saw another steamer pull over to the side of the river in response to a fluttering handkerchief. "What's she doin'?" he asked Big John.

"Pickin' up passengers. We don't have to do that. Cap'n Aldeu says 'let the other boats belly up to the sandbars to pick up stragglers. The *Bailey*'s too good for that sort of thing.' We go Portland to The Dalles, and The Dalles to Portland. That's it. We do it good, and we do it fast. See that boat up there?" He pointed ahead to a large sternwheeler just pulling away from the Washington side of the river.

Gibbie nodded.

"Watch this," he said. "I'm gonna talk to the captain." He climbed quickly to the pilot house.

Gibbie felt the engines rev, and the boat surged forward even faster than before. He looked in amazement at Big John descending from the pilot house, and heard the *Bailey* blow two long blasts on her melodious whistle.

"That's the *Charles R. Spencer*," Big John said, his jaw set like steel. "We whupped her last week, from the Cascades up to The Dalles. Beat her by a good two boat lengths, and we're about to do it again." His eyes gleamed in anticipation.

The most dreadful sound Gibbie had ever heard shrieked from the whistle of the *Spencer*. Gibbie set his heart to prevail, to destroy. The *Spencer* would lose. She would be left in the wake of the *Bailey*, and Gibbie would be onboard to see it happen.

As the *Bailey* approached Cascade Locks, Gibbie stood at the bow, gripping the railing in excitement. The huge sternwheeler drew close to the first lock, and Gibbie leaned his body to help guide the boat through the open gates and to the left side of the enclosure. The huge paddle wheel slowed and stopped as the boat glided quietly into place and drifted up against the wooden bumpers. Gibbie ran up to the texas to watch as the *Charles R. Spencer* drifted slowly into the right side of the lock. He glared at the dreadful boat with its ghastly whistle. What a shame for a boat of the *Bailey*'s quality to have to share the lock with such an inferior vessel! He looked back to watch the huge doors swing shut, trapping the two boats in their tiny stall.

Water began flowing into the enclosure, slowly raising the level. Turning to Big John, Gibbie asked breathlessly, "How long does it take? How long 'til they open the gate again?"

"See where the water line is?" Big John pointed to an obvious mark on the stone wall. "That's how high we're going. You just keep watching. When the water gets up to that line, the front gates will open, and we'll move up into the next lock."

Gibbie glanced at the wall, and seeing the mark only a foot above the present water line, he grasped an imaginary handle and began to shut down the flow of water. "Slow down, s l o w d o w n … Stop!" he yelled triumphantly. The turbulence of the water stilled as the valves were closed off. Then slowly, the gates in front of the boat began to open. Gibbie ran to the bow, watching in fascination.

Meanwhile, his glassy-eyed, green-faced sister had all she could do to stand still at the side of the boat and keep her wits about her—and the contents of her stomach inside her.

Chapter Forty Nine

Gibbie shouted in victory as the *Bailey* drew near The Dalles, several boat-lengths ahead of the *Spencer*. This was probably the most exciting moment of his life! He did not want to leave the boat. He didn't want to leave Big John or the coils of rope or the rumbling engine.

But one look at his sister reminded Gibbie what had happened—convinced him that Anny needed him. They needed each other. Reality came crashing down around him once again. He was no longer with Mama Jane and Granddaddy. Father had taken them away. Even the best boat in the world could not change that fact or hide the hurt of it. What were they going to do?

"Oh Carl, this is going to be *so* much fun!" the woman was saying. What was her name anyway? Father had introduced her to the children as "your new mother." Gibbie hated her. This woman was *nothing* like Mama Jane. She was loud. And she giggled all the time.

"Oh, I just *love* this town already! Such *fine* people here!" Both she and Father looked mighty fine themselves, Gibbie thought. They were dressed up in the new clothes they'd bought in Portland yesterday. Gibbie and Anny still wore the clothes they'd worn to church on Sunday.

The sandbar was filled with people—some waiting to greet the *Bailey*'s passengers, some ready to load goods for the return trip to Portland, some whose job it was to buttonhole passengers and direct them to the Umatilla House or one of the other lodging establishments.

As the huge boat ground to a halt, Anny gripped the rail tightly and leaned over the edge, mouth open wide. She gagged, but nothing more happened. Maybe because she'd eaten nothing since being taken from the farm on Sunday. The moment passed and Anny gulped and closed her mouth. She sank to her knees beside the rail, still holding on for dear life.

She did not lift her head to look about her. Even the *thought* of lifting her head was more than her stomach was willing to undertake. Gibbie slipped up beside her and took her hand.

Father and the woman stood in line to disembark. Anny felt Gibbie's hand and tried to smile at him, but just couldn't manage it. Though the front end of the *Bailey* was rammed onto the sandbar, the back end still floated freely, randomly. Anny rose to her feet and tried to look around. Gibbie led her to stand with Father. As they walked down the gang plank and onto the sand, her steps were unsteady. The ground felt solid enough, but Anny didn't trust it. What she wanted most of all at this moment was Mama Jane. She wanted to sit in Mama Jane's lap and be held. She wanted Mama Jane to tell her everything was going to be all right. And she wanted it to be true. She wanted that so much!

Because things were not all right. Things were badly off-kilter and Anny didn't even know where to begin. But Mama Jane's lap seemed a pretty good place to start.

*   *   *

The Umatilla House

Anny awoke early next morning at the Umatilla House, the best hotel in The Dalles. She slipped out into the hallway where she pulled her journal from her pinafore pocket. Thankfully, it had been there on Sunday morning when Father took her and Gibbie from Puget Island.

*   *   *

July 27, 1909

Gibbie and I are in The Dalles. It's so awful I can barely write about it. I don't understand what happened. Father came for us, and I - I went with him! I don't know why I did it. I felt almost like he could make me do whatever he wanted. I don't think that's true. But it's how I felt. I don't understand.

We rode the train from Westport to Portland, and a boat to The Dalles. And now it's done. My heart is breaking! God, if you're real like Mama Jane and Granddaddy say, please help us! Mama Jane, Granddaddy, I want you so much!

*   *   *

Anny and Gibbie left the hotel room as soon as they finished the bread the woman gave them for breakfast. "Go out and discover the town," she said, gaily. "I know you'll want to find some children and make friends."

"I need to wash and put on clean clothes," Anny said to the woman. "And I need a comb." Both Anny and Gibbie had looked fine when they went to church on Sunday morning, but after two days and nights in the same clothes, they were now pretty bedraggled.

"Oh my, yes! I didn't think of that. Well, what else do you have to wear, Dear?"

"Nothing. Father didn't wait for us to get clothes to bring."

"Oh my! Well... Hmmm... We will ask your father when he wakes up. But for now, you run along and have some fun. That's what children like to do ... isn't it?" The woman pushed them in the direction of the door.

Gibbie turned away from her and rolled his eyes. Anny just took his hand and walked out into the hallway. She heard the door lock behind them.

"Those bed bugs are terrible!" Gibbie complained as soon as they got down to the street.

"They got me too!" Anny said, and rubbed her sides with her elbows, trying not to appear conspicuous.

"Anny ... who *is* that lady?"

"I don't know. Father said she was his wife."

"Is she supposed to be our mother?"

"Maybe ... I guess so. But she's not."

"What are we supposed to call her? We don't even know her name."

"I'm *not* going to call her 'Mother.' I guess we could just call her 'The Wife.'"

Gibbie nodded.

They walked slowly toward the morning sun. The Dalles was a big town—much bigger than either Cathlamet or Westport.

"We need to figure out how to get home," said Anny.

"Anny, why did we come here?" Gibbie asked.

Anny had no answer. An ache swelled up in her chest and burned her throat and eyes. She didn't understand. Why she had allowed Father to take her?

"We need to go back," she said finally in a shaky voice. "I'll write a letter to Mama Jane and Granddaddy, and tell them where we are. Did you hear Father say we were going to San Francisco?"

Gibbie nodded.

Anny continued. "But this is The Dalles. It's not even close to San Francisco!" Gibbie didn't answer, and Anny used the silence to think.

"Gibbie, do you remember Father ... from before?"

Gibbie shrugged. "Sort of. He was just there."

"Were we happy?"

"Don't you remember?"

"No." Anny shook her head. "I don't remember anything at all ... except maybe him. I remember him a little, and ... I guess mostly his voice. That's all. I don't remember anything we did or where we lived or anything." She took Gibbie's hand and began walking back the way they had come.

* * *

Finally, three days after they arrived in town, The Wife brought new clothes to Anny and Gibbie. They were cast offs, and too big, but they were clean. Now Anny could wash their other clothes. The Wife also brought them a comb.

Anny squinted into the morning sun as she walked down Front Street. She saw a general store, a tobacco shop, barber, candy store, harness shop, two hotels ... so many places. Living on the island, she was not at all accustomed to so much activity. Here, people were everywhere. Some on horseback or in wagons or buggies, some walking, and some in automobiles! She saw automobiles on nearly every street. And all in a hurry—obviously important, busy people. Ladies in fine dresses and hats paraded to and fro, carrying fancy umbrellas to keep the hot sun off. A fat, balding man with a gold chain across his ample middle and sweat dripping around his collar entered the bank just behind a man in dirty overalls and worn shirt. Turning the other direction, Anny saw a lady in a blue dress that had no front! Well, not very much front, anyway. The neckline dipped very low, showing the upper part of the lady's chest. Anny was embarrassed and looked away. The barber stood outside his shop with a smile on his face, admiring the lady in the blue dress.

Anny entered the general store and began looking around. Behind the rakes and hoes, Anny caught sight of The Wife. *Oh no!* She turned and walked quickly and quietly back toward the street. Where was the post office? Her letter to Mama Jane was in her pocket along with her journal.

The Wife caught sight of Anny's back as she neared the door. "Oh Anny!" she called. "Anny? Come here, dear!" Anny turned slowly and walked back to The Wife. "I thought you might like some new dresses, dear. What do you think of this nice calico?"

It was mustard colored. Very ugly.

"No, thank you," Anny said, and turned to go. But The Wife grabbed her shoulder and pointed to another bolt of material. "This one then?"

"No, thank you," Anny repeated. "I'm just looking for the post office."

"The post office?" The Wife looked alarmed, then smiled and said, "Oh I was just going there myself! Can I take something for you, dear?"

Anny couldn't come up with an excuse.

"Well, I have a letter." Anny spoke hesitantly and put her hand into her pocket. "But I can take it myself."

"Oh no, dear!" The Wife frowned at Anny. "I'm sure you have things to do. Here—let me take it for you." The Wife pulled Anny's hand with the letter in it from her pocket and took the letter. "It's no problem, really! I'm glad to do it for you. And anyway, you need to go find some other children to play with. How old did you say you are?"

Anny's eyes were downcast. "Ten."

"Oh that's just wonderful! Ten years old! Oh my how time does fly, doesn't it."

Anny didn't respond and kept her eyes averted.

The Wife patted her on the head. "You go make some friends and you can tell me all about it at supper tonight."

Anny turned away without responding. She walked out of the store and back down the street, looking at her feet as she walked.

Chapter Fifty

"Hello!" The Wife's voice conveyed cheerfulness, confidence, friendliness. "You must be the post mistress here."

"I am, indeed. My name is Florence. And you must be new in town. I don't think we've met." Florence was the perfect grandmotherly type. She was short and pudgy, with a smile as warm as the sunset.

The Wife didn't like her. This woman was entirely too genuine. And too happy. The Wife would have to watch her step, she could tell.

She looked around and lowered her voice. "My daughter, Anny, asked me to mail a letter for her, but there's a little problem," she began. "She is having some difficulties, my daughter is, and it's best that she not make contact with these people in her past. I can't really talk about it." The Wife waved her hand before her face and touched her fingertips to her forehead, apparently fighting back tears. She bit her lip and then continued. "It's very frightening, actually. But the sheriff has assured us that she will be safe here in The Dalles."

Florence's eyes had grown big as she considered what The Wife was telling her. What frightening thing was the child mixed up in?

"But you know how it is with children," The Wife continued. "Sometimes they don't understand everything. They tend to make decisions that are *not* in their best interest. So I thought I would bring this to you and let you see it." She held out the letter for Florence to peruse.

"You can see who it's addressed to and the return address here in the corner." The Wife took a deep breath and wiped at the corner of her eye. "We've been so worried about her! She's just a child. Only seven years old." The younger the child, the more she would need the protection of adults, The Wife reasoned. And Anny *was* pretty small.

Florence nodded as her brow furrowed with concern.

"But we can't watch her every minute. We don't know what to do. It would be a very bad thing if she actually managed to send a letter out and make contact with this person—or anyone really. The doctor in Portland said ..." The Wife stopped speaking, wiped at her other eye, and paused. "Can you help us? Can you think of anything?"

"Well, I suppose I could keep an eye out for letters like this and hold them back for you."

"Oh, you are a jewel! Would you do that? That would take such a load of concern off my heart. This has all been so hard." The Wife put her hand to her chest and patted it. Her voice shook as she spoke.

"Well," Florence glanced behind her, then back at The Wife. "It's not customary, of course, but under the circumstances ... What does the child look like?"

"She's thin. Freckles. Red-blonde hair. Usually in braids. About this tall." She held out her hand to indicate Anny's height. "Thank you so very much! I'm so glad to have met you! I think The Dalles is just a wonderful town, and I know we're going to love it here. And I'm sure, if we can just watch Anny closely so she doesn't interfere with her own destiny, she will heal in time. Thank you so much, thank you!" And The Wife swept from the post office with Anny's letter to Mama Jane safe in her pocketbook. She would read it with Klein after Anny was asleep tonight.

*   *   *

Laughing. Anny could hear laughing. A little girl giggling, and the mama and papa laughing with her. Then they were singing, and the music was beautiful. Sweet and lilting. Then there were other children too. Laughing and playing in the sunshine.

And then it was gone. Anny's eyes flew open and stared hard at the ceiling. She tried to grasp the picture in her dream. It was so real. So happy. And then, as her mind struggled to wrap up the memory to save it ... it drifted farther and farther away.

No! Come back! I want to remember!

But it was gone.

*   *   *

Anny walked into Delgado's Front Street Market, trying to display a confidence she didn't feel. She had a new letter to Mama Jane in her pocket. And she did *not* want The Wife to mail it. She had not heard back from Mama Jane, and she knew Mama Jane would write—if she got Anny's letter. Anny would mail this one herself.

Anny had been in the store twice before, but this time she was here with a purpose. She walked slowly up and down the aisles, looking to see what things the store carried. She had no idea what kind of job the Delgado's might allow her to do, but she wanted to be prepared. She noted where the back room was located, although the door was closed, and she couldn't see inside. She looked at the tools, nuts, bolts, and garden rakes; the raisins, fruits, and vegetables; the muslin, calico, and denim, as well as some really nice silk from China; flour, beans, sugar ... all the time thinking of what kind of job she could offer to do.

She saw Mr. Delgado back by the garden tools and plumbing things. He was busy helping a man with some pipe fittings.

But Mrs. Delgado—the *formidable* Mrs. Delgado with one eye that looked straight at Anny while the other wandered off to the side—was standing guard at the till. She had a grim face—almost like she expected a person to filch some penny candy or an apple. And she appeared to have excellent eyesight—in the eye that seemed to be in working order. Kind of like the hawks Anny saw soaring above the hills around The Dalles.

Mrs. Delgado looked Italian. And her name sounded Italian. But Mr. Delgado? In spite of the man's pride in carrying his father's name, there must also have been an Irishman or Scotsman somewhere in his family tree. He had brilliant orange hair! Definitely not Italian. He was bald and shiny on top, but his baldness was more than compensated for by the robust, carrot-colored fringe extending from one ear, around the back of his head to the other. His eyes were large, blue, and friendly looking. And his ears, which lay tight against his head, would have looked fine if it weren't for the fact that his neck was larger than his head, forcing the bottom half of each ear to point outward at an angle.

Anny thought she would like working for the man. His wife, however, was one of the grumpiest people she'd ever seen. Anny hoped she would be able to wait to speak to Mr. Delgado, but unfortunately he was still helping the customer. Mrs. Delgado, however, had nothing to do at the moment but stare at Anny. Finally, Anny decided she'd better state her business before she got thrown out as a potential thief.

She summoned up her most confident demeanor and approached the front counter. "Hello Ma'am, my name is Anny Klein, and I would like to earn some money," she told Mrs. Delgado. "I have a letter to mail and I need to earn money for a stamp. Maybe you have some work I could do for you?"

The woman looked straight at Anny—with the eye that knew how to look straight. A young child. Probably not more than 7 or 8 years old. What reason would she have to be writing letters to people?

"Where do you live?" she asked, casting a suspicious look at Anny.

"At the Umatilla House for now," Anny said. "We just got here this week. We'll be finding a permanent place to live soon. I've been looking around the store, to learn where things are. I'd be able to help people who come in looking for something."

Mrs. Delgado nodded. "Huh." The woman glared at Anny. "Can you sweep?"

Anny nodded. "Oh yes, I'm quite good at sweeping."

Mrs. Delgado again said, "Huh." And then, "Well, I don't usually hire help, but maybe just this once. Would you be willing to sweep out the store at closing time tonight?"

Anny nodded. "Oh yes, I'd be happy to do that. What time should I come?"

"Six o'clock. And you better be on time!"

"Thank you." Anny tried to smile. "I'll be here at six." She turned and walked quickly toward the door.

On the street again, Anny glanced up at the courthouse clock. Three-thirty. She would come back in two hours. And her letter would go out to Mama Jane tomorrow morning. And then ... somehow, then everything would be all right. Mama Jane and Granddaddy would take care of it.

*   *   *

August 8, 1909

We live in a horrible place. Father says we should be glad to live here and save our money for more important things, but The Wife hates it. She is mad at Father because he lost all his money gambling and drinking. She yells at him about it. Downstairs is a market. Not Delgado's – another market. Upstairs is where we live. We are right next to The Cosmopolitan. It is a really old and run-down hotel. The weather is very hot, and inside our apartment is very, VERY hot! There are just two rooms in our apartment. One is a bedroom for Father and The Wife. The other is the front room where I sleep on the sofa and Gibbie sleeps on a little rug on the floor. The kitchen is part of the front room. But I don't think we really need the kitchen. Except for boiling coffee, The Wife doesn't cook. But we do have an ice box. Sometimes there is ice in it, usually not. We mostly just eat bread and leftovers she brings home. I don't know what The Wife does all day, but she's not around much.

Gibbie has three new friends. He seems to be having fun with them, but I'm not sure they are the kind of friends Mama Jane and Granddaddy would want him to have. I haven't really met them, but I've seen them.

We don't have a garden, but sometimes we get vegetables at Delgado's Market. I sweep at the end of the day, three days a week, and they let us take some things that are too old to sell. That's how they pay me for sweeping. But today she paid me in money so I could buy two stamps. She also gave me some spinach. Yuck! But it's not so bad if you eat it raw.

Chapter Fifty One

Gibbie stood close by the Umatilla House, watching as the *Bailey Gatzert* nosed into the landing. His fists were clenched, and his body swayed slightly as he mimicked the movement of the boat. His eyes were on Captain Aldeu in the pilot house. Rain poured down— an unusual event in The Dalles. But the rain made Gibbie's plan even more likely to succeed, he thought. He watched as passengers, many of them under umbrellas, began walking quickly down the ramped walkway and up to the shelter of the Umatilla House. When about half the people had offloaded, he ventured from his soggy post and started up the walkway, squeezing between startled passengers as he made his way onto the boat. Once aboard, he headed straight for the texas where he hoped to find Captain Aldeu.

As he rounded the corner by the stairway, a hand reached out and grabbed his arm. "Hey!" Gibbie complained, trying to pull away, but then saw that it was Big John, his friend.

"Hey, yourself! What are you doing here? Hmmm ... ain't you that kid who followed me all around the boat when you rode up from Portland? Gib, aint it?" He looked Gibbie up and down.

"Yeah." Gibbie pulled his arm away from Big John. "Gib." He liked the sound of it. More grown up. "And I'm gonna ask Captain Aldeu if I can work on the boat."

"Ha! You? You're about as big as a grasshopper! You ain't even close to big enough to work on the boat. Look at you! You're just a little rat of a thing!" He shoved Gibbie on one shoulder, but Gibbie stood firm.

"But I'm strong, really I am! I can do almost anything!"

"Um hm. And how old are you?"

"Don't matter how old I am." Gibbie clamped his jaw and looked straight into Big John's eyes. "What matters, is—can I do the job. And I can. I'm strong and I'm smart."

"Six? Seven?"

"No—eight! But I'm almost nine, and I really need a job!"

"Why would a little runt like you need a job? Your job is to grow up. You don't need a real job!"

"Yeah, I do!" Gibbie's eyes pleaded with his friend.

Finally realizing the boy was in earnest, Big John pulled the boy inside the shelter of the cabin. He tilted his head to the side and squinted his eyes. "Come to think of it, you are looking a mite scrawny. Are you getting enough to eat?"

Gibbie nodded. "Mostly."

"I ain't so sure about that. You got folks, right? Don't I remember you had a mama and daddy?"

Gibbie just shrugged.

"Hmmm." Big John's face gentled. "Well, come help me for a couple of minutes, and we'll see what we can do."

He took Gibbie to the stern of the boat and showed him how to coil the ropes lying on the deck. When Gibbie finished, Big John said, "Okay, come on. You've earned yourself a dinner, I guess."

Gibbie marched along proudly beside his friend off the boat and up to the dining hall at the Umatilla House.

"The grub here's okay, but don't ever sleep here if you don't have to. They have more bed bugs than any place west of the Mississippi!"

"Yeah, I know," Gibbie told him. "We stayed here a couple of nights when we first came."

Big John ordered dinner for them both. It was in front of them almost immediately, and they ate in silence.

"So what happened?" Big John asked as he leaned back and patted his full belly. "You got no home anymore?"

"Oh yeah sure, I got a home."

"But yer starvin'." Big John looked pointedly at the nearly empty plate before Gibbie.

"Naw. I just got a big appetite." Gibbie grinned. "Now can I go talk to the Captain?"

"I guess I'm not going to get rid of you any other way. Sure, come on. I know what he'll tell you, but I s'pose you can at least ask." He led Gibbie to the far end of the dining room, where Captain Aldeu sat with a group of men.

He said no. Just as Big John had predicted. Gibbie was disappointed, but at least his stomach was full. Life seemed much more manageable with a full stomach.

*   *   *

Wood scow on the Columbia

Anny and Gibbie sat overlooking the mouth of Chenoweth Creek. "That's Squally Point down that way," Gibbie said, pointing. "You can see the boats as they come around the Point. Every day the *Bailey* comes through, and the *Charles R. Spencer*. They are mag-ni-fi-cent!" He spoke the word slowly, as if he'd just learned it.

Anny nodded. Yes, it was impressive, but the very thought of boats traveling over the water turned her stomach.

A barge with tall sails and a huge load of wood rounded the Point. Gibbie watched in excitement. "See Anny? It's a wood scow! That's the *Honker Bill*. It can haul one hundred, sixteen cords of wood at a time! Anny, they're amazing! They have those big sails on 'em, and no engine at all. The men have to know how to use the sails to get where they're going, and going upriver against the current is really hard—it's hard to steer. They know where the dangerous places are and they have to be sure not to go there."

Anny only nodded. It was an impressive load of wood to be sure. And the sails looked kind of pretty. But the water! Rolling and wallowing. She gulped and closed her eyes, then lifted them to the land on the opposite side of the river. "Gibbie, look! There are houses across the river. I never noticed them before."

"Yeah, I know, and Anny, guess what? That big tall mast in the center of the boat? It's over one hundred feet high! And it's made out of the trunk of a fir tree. And those poles across the bottoms of the sails? Those are called the 'booms.'"

"Gibbie, how did you learn all this stuff? You really like the boats, don't you?"

"I *love* 'em! I'm gonna be the captain of the *Bailey Gatzert* when I grow up. But I'll probably work on a wood scow first. You know—to learn how to sail and to learn the river better. I can learn all about the sand bars and hidden rocks and everything. Then I can hire on the *Bailey* when I'm fifteen."

Anny smiled at her brother. She felt as if she was just beginning to know him. During their years on Puget Island she and Gibbie had gone their separate ways much of the time—each had their own friends. Now they had no one but each other. In spite of the misery Anny felt anew every morning when she woke to find that it was not a nightmare after all, but real life, she liked getting to know her little brother. All of a sudden, he didn't seem so little any more. He seemed more like a real person.

But why—why on *earth*—did he have to like boats so much?

*   *   *

Anny walked slowly up Union Street, looking and listening. Everything at this time in the morning seemed sleepy, quiet. The businesses weren't open yet; people were not out; the wind was still at this time in the morning; even the dogs seemed to be at home sleeping. Her legs began to ache as she climbed higher and higher up the hill behind town—a place she'd not been before. Finally, far above the tops of the highest buildings, she stopped and looked back down on the town, nestled up against the river like a baby, sleeping against its mother's breast. The Dalles had built itself up along the riverfront and was gradually stretching farther and farther up the hill toward the place where Anny stood.

The land was barren. The few trees Anny could see from her perch on this hillside were small and scrubby. There were no thick forests where a person would have to cut their way through the underbrush. Instead, lots of wide open spaces, lots of rock—big cliffs, in fact. When Anny allowed her eyes to take in the big picture, she saw the beauty of this raw and ragged land.

She pulled some thin leaves off a dried up plant near where she sat and smelled them. Nice. Smelled like Thanksgiving turkey at home.

She tried a handful of grass. Not so nice. Really, it just smelled like dust. Almost everything in The Dalles smelled like dust.

There were wild flowers, but Anny didn't know their names. Maybe she could learn at school. If Father let her go to school. She hoped he would. Or maybe she would be gone from here before school started. That's what she really wanted!

She tried to think back to life with Father before Mama Jane and Granddaddy. She couldn't think; she couldn't remember. She knew he was there. But that was just about the end of it. She thought of the things she'd written in her first journal. She had read through from start to finish one day, and had been amazed. She felt as if she had been reading about the life of a child she did not know. Now, she just felt sad and lonely. Afraid. And she didn't really know why.

She took her journal and pencil from her pocket and began to write.

August 10, 1909

Today is my birthday. I am 11 years old.
Father does not know it is my birthday. Last year I
had a party. And the year before. My very best present
at my first birthday party was piano lessons. I wish I
could play a piano now.

Anny set the notebook aside and clutched her knees to herself. *But I would gladly give up the piano lessons if only I could go back to Mama Jane and Granddaddy. I would be happy even if I never got any new clothes. Even if I never had another birthday party. Even if I never knew when my birthday was. I don't care about those things any more.*

She picked up the book and pencil again.

"I want to go home," she wrote. And then she cried.

Chapter Fifty Two

The next day, Anny stood on the sand bar, watching the men un-
load wood from the *Honker Bill*. She held tightly to the piling beside her. It gave her a sense of security, hanging onto something
that wasn't moving. She could only watch the boat for a minute or two at
a time. She lifted her eyes to the other side of the river whenever she
began to feel queasy.

Finally all the wood was unloaded, and the men began walking
up to the Umatilla House. *Courage,* Anny told herself. *Be brave. You can
do this!* She walked toward the one who was obviously the boss, the one
Gibbie had pointed out as Bill, the man the scow was named after. He
brushed past without even noticing her. Determined, she followed in his
steps. She would have to stop him before he reached the saloon at the
Umatilla house.

Hurrying past him, she turned and planted herself right in front
of him. "Ex—excuse me," she stammered. "Could I speak with you for a
moment, please?"

If she hadn't been so nervous, she would have laughed at herself—trying to sound like a grownup. *Think Anny! Remember what you
need to say.*

"Well, well, what have we here?" The man looked at his friend
and added, "a little young, don't you think?" They both laughed.

Anny continued to walk backward as she talked to the man. "I'd
like to talk to you about my brother, you see he really likes the boats,
and I was thinking, maybe, if it wouldn't be too much trouble, well, I was
wondering if there's any way that he could, I mean, you know, ride on
the boat with you sometime, and he wouldn't be any bother at all, and he
would really love it, and I'm wondering how much it would cost and if

you might accept some service rather than actual money, because I'm a little short on cash just now, and ..."

Honker Bill finally stopped walking. 'Wait! Wait up there, Girl! Slow down! I can't understand a word you're sayin'! Now, start that again. At the beginning."

Anny took a deep breath. "Can my brother ride on your boat?"

"Now, *that* I can understand," he thundered. "And the answer is no! Absolutely not! Too dangerous."

"Oh, but ..."

The three men brushed by her and entered the saloon at the Umatilla House, laughing over the strange encounter.

Anny stopped at the door and stood looking after them. *Well, that didn't work. What next?*

She sat on a bench by the door and settled down to wait for the men to come out.

* * *

A half hour later, the three boatmen exited the Umatilla House, and Anny fell into step behind them. At first they didn't notice her. But her deliberate steps behind him finally caught Bill's attention. He stopped abruptly—causing Anny to run smack into the back of him.

He turned and leaned his big frame over Anny. "What do you want now?" he roared.

Anny didn't flinch. She tilted her head up to look him in the eyes. "I wanted to let you know that I'm very good at putting up food." Bill blinked, confused by this blunt statement. Anny went on. "I've canned beans and peaches—'course the peaches aren't ready yet—but I can do beans and beets, and I can make pickles, and I was thinking maybe your wife would like someone to help her with the canning, seeing as how you're too busy to help—with your very important job—hauling the wood, you know."

"Yes, I *know*." His voice boomed, but Anny didn't flinch. She took a breath.

"Well, I'm thinking maybe your wife would appreciate some help. Canning is pretty hard work, you know. And I can see that you're pretty old, so you probably don't have children living at home anymore, so your wife will probably need some help. I am also very good at washing windows and other cleaning."

"What makes you think I even have a wife?"

"You do ... don't you? If you tell me where you live," Anny said, "I'll go talk to your wife."

Bill slapped his hand to his forehead. "Okay, I give up. Tell me what it is you want."

"I want for my brother to spend a day on your boat." She smiled hopefully. "He *loves* the boats! It's all he talks about—how he's going to be a river pilot when he grows up. I'll pay whatever you ask. I'm a good worker, really I am."

"Huh! Determined little critter, ain't ya?" He sighed. "Okay, so when is this boat ride going to happen?"

"Next Tuesday."

"Tuesday, huh?" Bill looked at his two companions and shook his head. "Goin' soft in my old age, I am."

He turned back to Anny and blew out a huge breath—his cheeks puffed wide. "Alright, Girl. You have him down at the landing at seven o'clock Tuesday morning, and I'll take him along. Seven o'clock—not a minute after. You hear?"

Anny could hardly contain her excitement, but tried to appear business-like. "Thank you very much! And now, if you tell me where you live, I'll go discuss with your wife the work I'm to do for her."

Bill put his hand on Anny's head. "Little Girl," he said. "This one's on me. No charge. But I'll tell you what ... if I ever need someone to do some salesmanship for me, I'll know where to look!"

"Oh thank you so much! He's going to be so very happy!" Anny turned and began skipping down the hill.

"Hey! Wait a minute!" Bill called after her. "How old is this brother?"

"Eight. But he'll be nine on Tuesday."

"NINE! What have I got myself into?" He slapped his head and turned back toward home, as Anny watched him go.

*   *   *

The banjo twanged. Both Mac and Shan looked up from their work. Pappy entered the shop without Will—using only his shillelagh for support. And today was Friday, not Wednesday when Pappy usually came to the shop. He marched unsteadily toward Mac, stopping only inches from the man.

"Go find them," he said. "Go get them. They need you."

Shan shook his head and rolled his eyes, as if to say, "He's off his rocker!"

Mac, heart pounding, hung his apron on the hook, nodded at Shan, and followed Pappy out the door.

Michael Collins stood on the board walk outside The Fair running through his confession in his mind. He wanted it to be right. Tell him what you did, tell him you're sorry, and ask him what you can do to make it right, Grace had told him. One, two, three. Simple as that.

This was not Michael's first confession since Shan and Grace had married last summer. He had been methodically working through the list of people he had wronged, admitting his fault and doing what he could to make things right. It had been hard—very hard—at first. But now, he was actually beginning to enjoy it. Oh, it was still hard, but it felt so good to come clean!

Finally, exhausting himself of excuses, Michael entered the store and looked around for Mr. Marquardson. He must be in the back. Good. A confession in private was much more appealing than one with everyone in the store listening in. He walked to the back corner of the store and knocked on the wooden door.

Mr. Marquardson pulled it open and looked at Michael with cautious optimism. He'd heard the boy had changed. He hoped so. He *certainly* hoped so.

"Could I come in and talk to you?" Michael asked. Mr. Marquardson stepped back from the door and opened it wider.

Michael entered and shuffled his feet for a moment trying to remember how he planned to begin.

"I did a bad thing, and I want to make it right," he began. And before Mr. Marquardson had time to say anything, he went on. "I sneaked under the store at night and drilled a hole in the floor under the peanut barrel. And through the barrel too. So I could get peanuts. I didn't pay for 'em, so that means I stole 'em. And I also damaged your floor. And I want to know what ... no." He shook his head, reminding himself of numbers one, two, and three. "First, I'm sorry. And then, I want to know what I can do to make it right.

Mr. Marquardson's smile began with the words, "I did a bad thing," and kept growing even past the end of Michael's speech. *This* was a new Michael entirely! Maybe what he'd heard about the boy was true.

*   *   *

"Gibbie! Gibbie, wake up!" Anny shook Gibbie's shoulder.

"Mmnff."

"Gibbie!" She shook him harder, whispering louder. "Get up, right now!" She'd slept longer than she intended and needed to hurry.

"Go away! I wanna sleep!" Gibbie rolled to his other side and moaned.

"Gibbie—come on! It's your birthday! I have a surprise for you!"

He sat up abruptly—eyes huge. "It's my birthday? Really?"

"Yes! And I have a really great surprise for you, but you have to be out of bed and have your clothes on. Now!"

Gibbie was on his feet almost before Anny had finished talking. "What? What's my surprise?"

"Shhh!" she warned him, glancing at the bedroom door. "Get dressed." Anny took a knife from the counter and began slicing bread. By the time she had two thick slices cut, Gibbie was ready. Anny grabbed some carrots and a big piece of cheese from the icebox, and wrapping it all in a small towel, she put it in a pail. "Come on. Let's go."

She led him out the door and down the stairs to the street. "Come on! Hurry!"

"Where are we going?"

"You'll see. Just hurry."

Anny led the way down to the sandbar where the *Honker Bill* was tied up. Bill and his two helpers were there, and they appeared to be just about ready to sail.

"Hello!" Anny called with more confidence than she felt, as she waved at Bill. "We're here!"

Bill raised his head and looked hard at Anny. He inhaled and blew out his breath with puffed cheeks. "She did it," he muttered. "She actually brought him. Ho boy! I wonder what his mother will have to say about this!"

Anny turned Gibbie to herself and put a hand on his shoulder. "You are going to ride the *Honker Bill* today. Here's your lunch." Her smile rivaled Gibbie's as she pushed the pail into his hand. "Be good. Do whatever Bill tells you, and *don't* get into things you're not supposed to. Make me proud of you, Gibbie. I'll be waiting for you when you get back tonight." She turned him and gave him a push in the direction of the scow.

"Oh wow!" Gibbie fairly flew down the sand bar and onto the barge. "Hi!" he said as he jumped aboard. "My name's Gibbie. What can I do? I want to help!"

Anny smiled and turned to climb the hill to the house where she'd seen Honker Bill go after agreeing to take Gibbie along today. She was pretty sure his wife would be happy to have help of some kind.

*   *   *

Anny tossed restlessly in her sleep. Her blanket, which had been lying loosely at her side, wrapped itself tightly around her as she rolled over. Thunder rattled the open windows of the apartment and wind blew in, its voice haunting, screaming.

Anny rolled over again, the blanket wrapping her even tighter. She tried to put her arm over her head, but it was stuck in the blanket. With the other arm, she flailed upward—reaching.

Another crack of lightning, and almost instantly, thunder, louder than before.

Anny groaned, then her mouth opened wide in a scream. She thrashed frantically, trying to release her arm, her body. She screamed again.

Gibbie jumped to his feet, staring at his sister. Klein and The Wife both flew out of the bedroom.

"Stop it! Stop it!" The Wife shouted. "Carl, *do* something."

"She's scared," Gibbie said. "She's scared of thunderstorms."

"Anny!" Klein shook her. "Wake up, Anny! It's just a storm."

Anny screamed even louder. *People shouting! Rain! Hail! The sound of it!* She was trapped! She struggled to reach upward again, but couldn't get her other arm free.

"Good heavens, Carl! Stop her! She's giving me a headache!"

Klein slapped Anny across the face. "Stop!" he shouted.

Gibbie pulled the blanket from Anny, freeing her body. Jumping to her feet, Anny's scream turned to a moan, but still she stood rigid—shaking. Her eyes were wide open, but focused on nothing. Gibbie put his arms around his sister and squeezed tight.

"It's okay, Anny. I'm right here. You'll be okay." He sat on the sofa, pulling her down beside him. "Anny, it's a storm. It'll be okay. Just relax." He held her close as he'd seen Mama Jane do, and little by little, Anny began to quiet down. Her rigid muscles softened and she drew a long, shuddering breath.

"Well, *that* was just about enough to ruin the night," The Wife said. She swore and stomped off toward the bedroom. Klein just scratched his head and followed.

Gibbie and Anny sat together on the sofa for a long time after that. When Anny finally came to herself, she looked curiously at Gibbie. "You can go to bed now," she told him. And he did.

*   *   *

"How's it coming?" Mr. Marquardson looked over Michael's shoulder at the new copper patch on the wooden floor. The patch was square, but it had a spiral shape scratched into it. "What's the design for?" he asked.

"It's to remind me of the drill. Every time I come in the store I'll see it and remember. Grace says 'what's the use in making mistakes if we don't learn from them.' So this is to help me learn. I'm almost done. You can check the barrel and see if it's okay. I'm about ready to start moving stuff to its new place."

Mr. Marquardson tipped the barrel to its side and admired the new, peanut-shaped piece of copper tacked neatly in place. Michael had also marked the copper, making it look like the outside of a real peanut. Mr. Marquardson nodded. The bottom of the peanut barrel would not even show, and yet, Michael had taken the time to make it look good. "You did a good job. Nice and neat. Maybe there's some artist in you."

Michael smiled. "I dunno. But there's got to be something better than just being a trouble-maker!"

The boy and man exchanged knowing smiles. In addition to assigning Michael to repair the damage he had done and work off the cost of a couple handfuls of peanuts—*and* the pouch of Beech-Nut chewing tobacco the boy had also confessed to stealing—Mr. Marquardson had shared with Michael a few of the less admirable shenanigans from his own boyhood in Chicago. "I promise you, it's possible to change," He told Michael. And Michael believed him.

*   *   *

September 1909

    Father was gone for four days. He didn't tell us he was going, so we didn't know if he would come back. But he did. We didn't see The Wife much while Father was gone. She was at the Umatilla House a lot. Father had a job while he was gone. Now that he is home, we have money!

    Father's hand is all wrapped up in a handkerchief. He says he got injured on his job.

The Wife took Gibbie and me shopping and we got lots of things – cans of salmon, and lots of beans and oats and a bag of rice and a bag of potatoes, and some cabbage, and some other vegetables. Also cherries. They are yummy! And a jar of honey!

The Wife bought a new chair for the front room and a mirror to hang on the wall in the bedroom. The chair is covered with deep red velvet and it has fringe around the bottom of it. It's beautiful! The mirror has a gold frame. It's very fancy. She offered to buy me a new pinafore, but it didn't have a pocket, so I told her "no thank you." I need a pocket, because I need to keep my journal with me. Granddaddy gave it to me. It has a beautiful dark blue cover. All my other books had brown covers. I had to leave them at Mama Jane and Granddaddy's house. I hope I can get them back some day.

Chapter Fifty Three

The school wasn't far—only six blocks up the hill, right below the reservoir that supplied the town with water. Anny and Gibbie walked in the front door and looked around. Anny's heart was beating a tattoo against her ribs, but she was determined. Neither Father nor The Wife had said a word about school. Anny only knew it was starting because she had overheard a lady in the store talking about school starting on Monday. So here it was Monday, and she and Gibbie had come.

She had pried Gibbie out of his bed early and made sure they were both as clean and neat as possible. They each had two complete sets of clothes now, and each dressed in their nicest. The Wife sent her own clothes and Father's out to the laundry, but she never mentioned washing the children's things. And Anny never asked her to. She washed her own and Gibbie's clothes herself.

Anny was amazed. This school had a large hallway with many rooms leading off it. Nothing like Sunny Sands! She looked around the hallway and saw a number of girls about her age. They were all talking to friends, chatting happily. Anny wanted to be included, and smiled tentatively, but no one spoke to her. Gibbie saw one of the many friends he'd already made and went to him. They walked together to the fourth grade room.

Anny stood, undecided for a moment. She could still leave. No one knew her. No one expected her to show up for school today. She could just go home and forget about it. If she had a home. No. She would not go back to the apartment.

She took a deep breath and went in search of the sixth grade classroom. She found it without too much trouble and took a seat near the back.

The teacher, a pretty, dark haired young woman, entered and busied herself with papers at her desk while other students came into the room and found seats. Anny said nothing. She just watched quietly.

When the bell rang, the teacher stood and faced the class. "The class will come to order," she said. Her voice quavered a bit as she said it. The girls came to order and looked expectantly toward the lovely teacher. Fair skin, dark hair, and rosy pink cheeks. She was beautiful!

The boys however, at least so far, were not interested in either her beauty or her authority. They discontinued the loudest of their talking, but continued to fidget in their seats and poke at one another.

"My name is Miss Valentine," she said, as she wrote her name on the board. "And this is the sixth grade class. If you are in the wrong room by mistake, please raise your hand."

No hands went up.

"Good," she said. "I will call the roll now, so I can begin to know you all." She cleared her throat. The boys were still restless, but she did nothing to stop them. Maybe this was her first year teaching, Anny thought.

As Miss Valentine read the names on her roll sheet, she gazed at each child in turn as if memorizing their faces. When she had finished, three children remained whose names had not been called. Two boys and Anny.

She addressed Anny first. "And what is your name, dear?"

"Anny Klein."

"And are you in the sixth grade?"

Anny only nodded.

"How old are you?"

"Ten."

"Ten-year-olds should be in the fifth grade. Maybe you got in the wrong room by mistake."

"I'm eleven," Anny shook her head as she corrected herself. "My birthday was August 10th, and I'm eleven now."

"Hmmm," said Miss Valentine, with a skeptical look on her face.

Anny knew it was her small size Miss Valentine was really thinking about, rather than her age. "I already did fifth grade," she said. "Last year."

"Hmmm," Miss Valentine said again. "Well, maybe we'll let you start in the sixth grade and see how it goes." She smiled with her lips, but Anny didn't like the smile.

She saw two of the girls near the front of the room whispering. They looked back at Anny and whispered some more—then laughed. Anny just gritted her teeth and said nothing.

After getting the necessary information from the two new boys, Miss Valentine gave each child in the class a piece of paper and asked them to write about what they had done through the summer. Then she set about assigning books.

At first, Anny sat and did nothing. She had nothing to tell about her summer. She couldn't write that she had been stolen away from her family on Puget Island; that she'd been sick on the *Bailey Gatzert*; that Father and The Wife pretty much ignored her and Gibbie; that she often didn't know where the next meal would come from; that they lived in a stinky, miserable apartment; that she rarely got a full night's sleep because Father and The Wife came in loud and drunk in the middle of the night; that she only owned two dresses and no nightclothes. She had *nothing* to write about her summer!

Miss Valentine called Anny's name, the last on the girls' list, to come to the desk and receive her books. As she placed the books before Anny, she said, "Now, these may be too hard for you, dear. And if they are, you just let me know, and I can get you moved to the fifth grade." Miss Valentine patted Anny's hand and called the first name on the boys' list.

Anny returned to her desk and opened the history book. Easy. No problem here. Reading? She could read just about anything written in the English language. Arithmetic—now that could be a problem. Gingerly, she opened the book to the first page. Not too bad ... She leafed through the rest of the book, stopping here and there to read and look at diagrams. Well, it looked hard. But she vowed right then and there to learn it so well, the beautiful teacher would be forced to eat her words. Anny would be the best in the class.

She took her paper—the one she was using to *not* write about her summer—and began writing of the wonders of Puget Island in the Columbia River. She wrote about Lewis and Clark and about the Wahkiakum Indians, about the first white settlers to the area, the fish cannery and the lumber industry. She was careful to make a new paragraph for each subject and checked her spelling and punctuation. By the time all the books were handed out, Anny had looked over her work and decided that she had written well. She hadn't done as she was told, but she was satisfied.

*   *   *

319

September, 1909

Today was our first day of school. Gibbie goes to fourth grade. I go to sixth. My teacher is Miss Valentine. There are thirty-eight children in my class, but I don't like them. I'm smarter than they are. They're not very nice.

Father's hand got blood poisoning or something. It swelled up big and got very red – and even green and white in some places. He said he might die, but he didn't. The Wife wasn't here, and Father poured whiskey on it and made me put on a new bandage.

Chapter Fifty Four

Although Esmerelda had returned to Heppner after nearly a year in Baker City, Grace Collins hadn't seen her friend often since her marriage to Shan and the birth of their first child. What with caring for four active children, she hadn't even noticed she'd been missing her friend—until they bumped into each other at The Fair. Now, six and a half years after the flood, it was still the biggest and best store in town.

Grace had left Michael and Danny at the front of the store to admire the candy while she took Libby in search of material for new tea towels. Grace followed nine-year-old Libby back to the dry goods. She was just moving baby Benjamin from one hip to the other when she rounded a corner by a tall display of clocks and almost ran right into Esmerelda.

"Oops! Sorry!" she said, smiling.

"Grace! I'm glad I ran into you—well, almost ran into you!" They both laughed and looked around them to see if anyone might be viewing their accidental meeting. They stepped a little farther back where they were not so easily visible from the front of the store.

Grace turned to Libby. "Go look at the material and see if you find what you want, Libby. I'll be along in a minute."

*　　*　　*

Mabel Dupont entered The Fair wearing a new dress. She stood a little taller, held her head a little more erect than usual. The crispness of autumn was in the air, and she had filled her lungs and spirit with the freshness. She had always loved the fall. On top of that, she was having a late dinner with Mac at the Palace this evening. Everything about her spoke of happiness, self-confidence, hope in the future. She greeted the owner warmly. "Good morning, Mr. Marquardson. Isn't it a lovely day out? I surely do love this Indian summer!"

"I'm feeling pretty good myself, today." Marquardson smiled in response. "I hope it makes a person feel like spending money too!"

They both laughed as Mabel responded, "That's exactly why I'm here. I need ... let's see, where did I put that list ... Here we go. I need a dress length each of two different calicos. I'm looking for something dark, but still cheerful looking—for Christmas time. I hope you have some pretty ones in stock. And I'm also looking for a nice black voile, and some notions."

"Well, I think I can help you with most of it, anyway."

"Oh and some soda and beans and flour. I almost forgot!"

"Can't forget the food! You'd starve! Go ahead and take a look at the fabric. I have some new ones just in last week. Let me know when you find what you want. I'll get the beans and flour for you. Ten pounds of each, same as usual?"

Mabel nodded and walked toward the dry goods shelves to look over the calico. As she walked past the aisle stocked with soap and other toiletries, she noted the presence of one of the "girls" from Mollie Reid's *Chateau de Joie*. Mabel's bearing changed immediately. She still held herself tall and erect, but her demeanor was no longer prompted by the beautiful weather. Instead of light-hearted and joyful, she became strict, righteous, offended. She said nothing, but noted with shock that the girl was talking to Grace, the young woman who had married Shan Collins.

Well, of all the ... What business does that girl have talking to a fine young lady like Grace? Mabel continued on to the dry goods, but walked only halfway down the aisle, putting herself in a position to overhear the conversation in the next aisle over.

"Grace, ever since you left us, I've been thinking about what you said."

Ever since you left us? The words shouted themselves in Mabel's mind. What was that supposed to mean? Ever since Grace had left— what, Mollie's? Had Grace ever been there? She wasn't one of ...

Oh, surely not! But what else could those words mean—*ever since you left us?*

Mabel gazed without seeing the fabrics before her eyes. She fingered them without feeling them. The rest of the conversation in the next aisle was lost to her, as her mind and emotions swirled around those words. *Ever since you left us.*

"I would really like to talk to you sometime ..." Esmerelda said.

"Tonight? Same place?"

"Sure. Around seven?"

Grace nodded and moved on down the aisle as Esmerelda walked to the front of the store to pay for the soap she held in her hand.

*   *   *

Heppner's cemetery showing just a few of the flood victims' headstones

When the supper dishes were done, Grace grabbed her shawl, gave Shan a quick kiss, and headed up Cemetery Hill. The evening was cool, but not cold, and with only a gentle breeze—perfect. October was a wonderful month, maybe Grace's favorite. The trees all around Heppner—cottonwoods, willows, locusts—were losing their leaves. She loved the sound of the dry leaves crunching underfoot as she walked toward the south end of town. She kicked at the leaves enjoying the crisp sound of them.

Climbing the hill, she strolled slowly through the graveyard, looking at the stones.

> Perished in the Flood, June 14, 1903
> Drowned in the Flood, June 14, 1903
> Died, June 14, 1903
> All perished in the flood, June 14, 1903
> Passed Away, June 14, 1903
> With the Angels, June 14, 1903

And I was saved. Why? Why me? I did nothing to deserve this! It was by grace alone. Mama named me well!

The thought frightened her. *If I didn't do anything to deserve this, then could it be taken from me as easily as it came?* She hugged her shawl tighter around herself and shuddered at the thought. *No,* she thought. *No. I could fail, but grace doesn't depend on me.*

She walked to the far end of the cemetery and stood gazing over the Willow Creek Valley. So peaceful. She looked back at the grave stones behind her. *How is it possible ... this little stream ...*

Then she saw Esmerelda approaching along the far side of the cemetery. Grace turned and walked down the hill to a stunted tree growing alone. She sat beneath the tree.

Esmerelda joined Grace. She sat in silence for a moment and then said, "I'm leaving again."

"Leaving! When?"

"Next week. Mollie's sending me to The Dalles."

"She sent you to Baker City a few years ago. And before that, Redmond. Why?"

"Well, in this business, you work in one place for a few years, and then they move you around. The men like to see new faces now and then." Esmerelda drew her knees up close to her body and wrapped her shawl around them. "They like a little variety. I'd only been here a week or two when you came to town. Anyway, now it's time for me to move again."

She turned to gaze back over the cemetery. The two of them were still alone. "I'll miss you, Grace. You are the first real friend I've ever had. Well, a friend who's not a whore."

"I'll miss you too. Truly, I will," Grace said. "You and Mollie were my first friends here. I've always felt that I could trust you to help me if I needed it. That's really precious to me. I just wish we'd been able to spend more time together."

Esmerelda folded her arms around her knees and looked intently at Grace. "I wish I had what you have."

"What do you mean?"

"Not just your life, but ... whatever it is inside you. You're brave and confident. I'm scared. I'm sick of this life, but I don't know how to get out of it. I don't even know how I got into it!" She wiped at one eye and turned to stare off into the distance.

Grace looked at Esmerelda in amazement. This was a side of her friend she'd never seen before. "Pappy—Johnny Burke's grandfather—says why bother making mistakes if they don't make you a better person? He says we're called to rise above our past."

"Well ... that *sounds* really good ... but I just don't know how to do it. How to get a new life." Esmerelda shrugged her shoulders.

"I don't know how you can do it either. Does anyone ever leave your ... profession?"

"Sometimes. Sometimes a girl will find the right man and get married."

Grace looked confused.

Esmerelda laughed, almost bitterly. "Yeah, I know—what kind of man would want a cast-off hooker? But there are some. I feel like there's no hope for me, though. I'll be old by the time I'm thirty-five. No good for anything."

"I didn't know you wanted out." Grace spoke softly.

Esmerelda just nodded, and said nothing. "It's like being in a prison without bars. I didn't ask for this, you know. Becoming a whore isn't something you choose. It's something that happens *to* you."

Grace took a deep breath. "I remember when Dacia's baby was born."

"The leap year baby?"

"Yeah," Grace said with a smile. "She's five years old, and she's only had one birthday!"

"That's one way to stay young, I guess!"

Grace laughed. "Anyway, that night, after little Ellie was born, I said something to Dacia about how a new baby was such a wonderful thing. Nothing has gone wrong in her little life. I was wishing I could go back and be like a new baby—get rid of all the bad stuff in my life and start all over again. A couple days later, Pappy told me that's what God does for us if we let him into our lives. When we decide to trust him completely, a whole new life starts for us somehow. I don't understand it very well, but I decided right then—yes. Yes, that's what I want. To be able to start all over—like a new baby."

Esmerelda looked intently at Grace but said nothing.

"So," Grace continued. "I decided to give God my life—to really and truly trust him in everything. It hasn't always been easy, but ... Well, it's always been good!"

Esmerelda nodded slightly. "I need to think about that. It kind of makes sense."

Grace just smiled. "I'm sure sorry you're leaving."

"It's okay." Esmerelda shook her head as if to shake away the cloud of gloom she had called down upon herself. "It'll be fun! Come up to The Dalles and see me sometime. We can go stand around the waterfront and pretend we don't know each other." She laughed.

Grace felt like crying instead. Esmerelda, a prostitute plain and simple. But a real person! With real feelings. With dreams of a different life—a good life. And Grace was powerless to help. She could only point her to the One who truly *could* change her life.

Esmerelda rose and brushed her skirt. "I'll never forget you, Grace."

Grace was on her feet instantly, hugging her friend, and she didn't even check to see who might be watching before she did it. "I'll pray for you," she said. "Take care!

"And go with God!" she shouted as Esmerelda's form faded into the distance.

Chapter Fifty Five

"I know what I saw and I know what I heard," Mabel insisted. She sat across from Mac in the Palace Hotel dining room. Why couldn't Mac just believe her? Why did he have to be so aggravatingly calm and deliberate?

Mac took another bite of his steak. It was excellent.

"And I think somebody needs to do something about it!"

Mac finished chewing and swallowed. "Do what?" he asked thoughtfully, taking another bite.

"Well, do something to get her out of there! She's got herself married to Shan! She's raising his children! Who knows what kind of evil ideas she's putting into those children's heads? Why is a woman of that character even allowed to move among the fine citizens of this town as if she were one of us? It's about *propriety*, Mac. It's just not right!"

"What's not right about it?" Mac's face was as calm as ever.

"What's not—" She laid her palms carefully on the table on either side of her plate. "Mac! Think!"

"I am thinking. I'm thinking very carefully." Mac deliberately took a bite of his fried potatoes. "I'm thinking more clearly than I have in a long time, as a matter of fact."

"Well, you certainly have a funny way of ..." Mabel took her napkin from her lap and laid it decisively on the table. "All right," she said. "I think I understand. I was wrong about you. I thought you were a man of good character. I thought you were an upstanding citizen. I thought you and I agreed about things like this. I guess I was wrong. Forgive me for taking up your precious time. Forgive me for caring about you. But you don't need to worry, because I don't care anymore. This is over."

She stood and marched toward the door of the dining room, head high. As she stepped through the doorway into the lobby of the hotel, she nodded royally to Les Matlock, just before her heel caught on the threshold and she nearly fell. She grasped at the umbrella stand— the nearest thing to her—which in turn created a loud clatter as the lone umbrella rattled in its brass enclosure.

Mac looked down at his dinner and tried to hide a smile.

Les Matlock stepped up to Mac's table, chuckling. "Little misunderstanding?"

Mac looked up and nodded his head to the chair opposite him. "Have a seat, Les. The lady seems not to need it anymore." He didn't try to hide his smile now.

"Don't mind if I do." Les sat and moved the unfinished dinner to one side. "Ah yes. Women. They'll be the death of us for sure!"

"Aw, it's okay," said Mac. "I think maybe she sees things a little more clearly now. I know for sure that I have a whole new perspective. And ... I think I'm going to like it!"

"You mean she might give up on her campaign to get you to the altar?"

"Mm ... Looks like rain," Mac responded with a wry smile.

Matlock ordered the lamb, then turned back to his friend. "Well, I guess I'm not the one to be giving you advice on such matters, seeing as how I've never married." He gazed around at the few people remaining in the dining room. "So what else shall we talk about?" Sobering, he asked, "How's the search for your children coming along?"

Mac put down his fork and sighed. The smile faded from his face. "Can't say I'm having any luck. I had hoped this would all be resolved long ago. After all this time, it seems less likely than ever that I'll find them." He shook his head. "But I won't stop. I won't."

Matlock just nodded.

"I'd like to take one last trip before the winter weather sets in— over to Boise. In fact, I wish I could go farther—clear over to the eastern side of Idaho. I just don't know what else to do except keep searching. I *know* they are alive. The thing that tears me up is the time going by. One more day, one more week, one more year they are lost to me. They need their father."

Matlock looked deeply into Mac's eyes and saw determination. And something else—love. "I think you're right, Mac. I think they need you. And I think I believe you. They are alive." He leaned to the side asMatlock laid his fork down. "You ever heard of William Butler Yeats?"

Mac shook his head.

"Irish poet," Les said. "Here's something he wrote:

'I have spread my dreams under your feet;
Tread softly because you tread on my dreams.'

"Thanks for sharing your dream with me Mac. I'm honored."

Chapter Fifty Six

November 16, 1909

I am doing a good job on my school work, except for Arithmetic. But I'm way better than I was at Sunny Sands, because I'm working <u>very</u> hard on it. My other studies are really easy, so I'm spending extra time on my Arithmetic. I'm improving, but I'm not very fast. Yet.

I don't like Miss Valentine at all. She is not nice to me. I don't talk to her – unless I have to answer a question. And none of the girls will talk to me. So I don't talk to them. Even Amanda, who is poor too, is not nice to me. She wants the other girls to like her, so she tries to stay close to them and far away from me. They don't like her anyway. They laugh at her behind her back. She doesn't even realize it.

Miss Valentine hates me even more than she did at first. One day she said nobody lived on any of the islands in the Columbia River. I said I did. I told her I lived on Puget Island. She said I was wrong – that Puget Island was up by Seattle. I said no, it is between Westport, Oregon and Cathlamet, Washington. She got mad at me and told me not to sass her. But I'm right. I know I am. She may be the teacher, but she's not very smart.

Father hasn't gone anywhere lately, and we don't have any money again. The Wife doesn't like it. She yells at Father a lot. He just leaves and goes to the Umatilla House or one of the other saloons. But she goes after him. At least then Gibbie and I can be alone.

I have written eight letters to Mama Jane and one to Mary Jo, but have not had an answer. I don't know what's wrong. The first letter, The Wife took from me. She said she would mail it, but I don't think she did. But I sent the other letters myself. I took them to the post office and gave them to the lady with my own hand. But I never get a letter back. I don't understand why.

I am trying to save up money so Gibbie and I can go home. But we will go by train. I will NOT get on that boat again! Well ... that's not really true. If it was the only way to get back to Mama Jane and Granddaddy, I would do it. But I think we can go by train. I hope.

*   *   *

Esmerelda descended from the train in The Dalles and looked around. The town had changed a lot since she'd been here last. A couple of businesses in her line of sight looked different, and new buildings had sprung up in many places. Leaving her trunk to be delivered later, she flagged a cab and lifted her small bag up onto the seat. The driver offered his hand to Esmerelda as she climbed to the passenger seat.

"Where to, Miss?"

"Um, I think I'd like to go to the Delgado's Market. It's still there, isn't it?" Delgado's was just across the way from the largest brothel in town. "I'll need to pick up a few things there," Esmerelda went on. She sat back to enjoy the ride. "I haven't been here for quite a while. I've always liked The Dalles! It's good to be back. The town is lovely," she said with a smile.

The driver clucked the horse into motion and answered. "Yes, it is a pretty nice place, I guess." The driver's tone of voice made it clear that he recognized Esmerelda's profession, and probably wasn't in favor of it.

"Do you like living here?" she asked the driver.

"Yes, Miss. It's fine."

"Do you have family?"

"Yes, Miss. I have a wonderful wife and six children."

Esmerelda nodded and stopped questioning the man. She could take a hint.

*   *   *

Gibbie walked into Delgado's as close as he dared on the heels of a woman wearing a dark brown dress and carrying a basket on her arm. He was hoping to be mistaken for her son, but he didn't want her to turn around and ask him what he thought he was doing, tagging after her like that. He had to get the timing right. Gibbie had noticed when he entered a store without an adult, the storekeeper kept a closer eye on him. But if he was "with" someone, things usually went pretty smoothly. He didn't want to look at Mrs. Delgado, but he could hear her talking with a customer, so she probably didn't notice him at all.

Gibbie hated going to Delgado's. After all, these people had given Anny a job. But he'd been run out of the market on Fourth Street when the storekeeper saw him put an apple in his pocket. And the man behind the counter at the little market on Liberty kept looking at him suspiciously every time he entered the store. That left only Delgado's in this part of town. He knew he was risking Anny's job, but his stomach was hungry. Now.

Gibbie followed the woman back toward the canned foods and plucked a tin of salmon from the shelf. He kept the woman between himself and Mrs. Delgado as he pocketed a can of peaches. He then moved to several other places in the store, sometimes near the woman, sometimes not. He worked his way toward the door, then walked out just in front of a mother and her three children while Mrs. Delgado was tallying up the brown dress woman's purchases.

No one had noticed. He started to run.

*　　*　　*

As Esmerelda stepped from the cab, she paid the driver and thanked him. Turning, she saw a scraggly boy pop out the door of the market, obviously intent on escape. He was wearing a ragged pair of overalls and clutched something stuffed inside the front. Both pockets bulged as well. He took off at a dead run in her direction. Curious, she stepped directly in front of him, forcing him to stop. He dodged, trying to slip by her, but she put out her foot to prevent him.

"Excuse me. I'm just wondering if you can tell me where I can find the post office?"

The boy looked over his shoulder, then turned and bolted down the sidewalk.

Esmerelda narrowed her eyes and nodded. She recognized desperation when she saw it.

Chapter Fifty Seven

Anny rolled to her back, then to her left side, then back again on the sofa that served as her bed. Images flashed in the picture window of her mind and faded again just before she was able to grasp them. A family at the supper table. A mama and papa and children. A big boy, a little boy. The girl in the middle.

Another picture. The girl in her nightgown and bare feet. The papa swinging her high in the air as she giggled.

The girl outside, climbing a rose trellis, walking barefoot in the grass ...

Moving chickens out of the way to grab their eggs ...

Walking hand in hand with the papa. The sound of a banjo and a familiar smell—leather?

She could see only the backs of the people. No faces. The papa swinging the girl around and around until she was dizzy. And the girl laughed! Her laugh sounded like tinkling bells.

But Anny felt dizzy. Oh! She felt sick! Clutching at her stomach, she sat up abruptly. She was sweating, though the room was cold. Her mind grabbed at the images she had just seen, but they dissolved into nothingness. Gone. She closed her eyes and tried to think. People ... something about people. Who were they? The harder she tried to remember, the farther away the memory moved. It was there, and then ... it was gone.

She threw back her blanket and rose from the sofa. Going to the kitchen sink, she took a glass from the shelf and pumped herself a drink of water.

She didn't know what to feel. The dream had made her happy. But at the same time it frustrated her because she couldn't remember it. She couldn't make it come back.

Setting her empty glass on the table, she walked slowly to where Gibbie lay curled up in his blanket on the small rug in the corner. He had the blanket wrapped tightly around him with only his face sticking out. Anny watched his deep, measured breathing. So peaceful. She wondered about the food he'd brought home this afternoon. In response to her questioning, he had insisted that he hadn't stolen it. If he had, then he'd added lying to the sin of stealing. Tears sprang to Anny's eyes, but she ignored them, watching Gibbie, matching her breathing to his. Only a few days until Christmas. What could she do to make his Christmas special? He was all she had now. How could she take care of him? How could she continue what Mama Jane and Granddaddy had begun? How could she save her brother?

God, please help us! We can't help ourselves.

*　　　*　　　*

Klein was drunk. Not falling down, forget everything about this night drunk—just a good distance the other side of sober. In other words, normal.

The wife had stomped out mad a few minutes ago. Klein kind of enjoyed the reprieve from her annoying voice. He was plenty tired of the kids too. Not that he saw them all that often, but it seemed like they were always hanging around. They weren't his kids, after all. Why should he have to take care of them? Why should he have to spend his hard earned money to feed them? He'd like to lose them. Maybe he could give them to someone else. Maybe he could just send them away.

In a rare moment of remorse, he even considered returning them to where he got them—taking them back to Heppner.

Klein looked up just as Robinson entered through the swinging saloon doors. Klein caught his eye and raised his eyebrows in question. Robinson ignored him.

Disgusted, Klein rose and walked, only a bit unsteadily, to the door and out onto the street. He could find a friendlier place to drink his beer.

*　　　*　　　*

December 25, 1909

Anny woke to a beautiful world on Saturday morning. Christmas day. The soft, rounded contours of a white blanket covered the hillside above town. It covered the buildings and hitching rails and made little white hats on the pilings at the edge of the river. It slithered from the steep-pitched roofs to land below in soft white puddles of fluff.

There was no tree to celebrate Christmas. No gifts. Nothing to make it a merry season. But this morning—snow!

Anny shivered and pulled her thin blanket tighter around her shoulders. She left the window and got back on the sofa so her bare feet would not freeze on the cold floor. Even though she was wide awake, she would snuggle under her blanket for a while longer. It felt good.

Her tummy was not crying for something to eat like it often did. Last night Father and The Wife had taken the children with them to The Umatilla House for a late dinner. Roasted chicken, mashed potatoes, green beans, even apple pie ... oh, it had been heavenly!

Gibbie still slept on his mat in the corner of the front room. He would wake before long and want to go out in the snow. Anny wanted to go herself, but her shoes had pretty big holes in the bottom, and the thought of freezing her toes didn't sound too appealing. She would let Gibbie go and tell her about it after. She had not been able to think of a gift she could buy or make for Gibbie. But now—there was snow! A gift from God himself.

*   *   *

By the time Gibbie came in from playing in the snow, he was a sloppy, soupy mess. Anny made him change into his other clothes, and hung the wet ones to dry. The Wife made hot soup for the children for dinner. She had to ask Anny how to do it, but Anny helped, and it was good. And hot. And filling!

Father woke up when he smelled the aroma of potato soup. The four of them ate at the tiny table, Father and The Wife sitting on the only two chairs, Anny and Gibbie standing.

Father said nothing—just slurped his soup. Anny began to wonder if this Christmas day could be the beginning of something new. Maybe Father and The Wife would like to do good things for her and Gibbie. Maybe The Wife would like to learn how to cook. Maybe she would bring home some more food for the children. And maybe Anny could get some new shoes—without holes in them. She didn't know how to suggest these things to Father and The Wife, so she said nothing. But when the soup was finished, Father spoke to her.

"You don't remember your mother, do you?" he asked Anny.

She shook her head and waited. *I had a mother? Why did I not know?* She wished it could be true. She wished she had Mama Jane.

"She was really something, your mama was." Father looked at The Wife. "Beautiful figure, beautiful lips. She could really kiss. She loved to kiss me." The Wife got up and left the table.

"Really something!" Father nodded and continued. "She died in childbirth, you know. Having babies is hard on a woman. She almost died having you. Don't know as how you're worth it." Anny winced, but said nothing and continued to stare at the floor. This was not how she had hoped this conversation would go.

"She loved me, you know. She married me and had us some kids. You look a lot like her." Father reached out and tweaked one of Anny's light red braids. She steeled herself, didn't flinch. Her eyes gazed blankly at the ugly scar on Father's hand without seeing it. "She was beautiful, your mother was, and she loved me better than she loved anybody in the whole world. She didn't have time for those other men— only me. I was the only one she ever really loved."

Father seemed to be talking to himself. His face carried a faint shadow of a smile. The Wife slammed the bedroom door. Gibbie put his soup bowl on the table and moved closer to Anny. She was biting the inside of her cheek and refused to look up.

"Yeah, we were married in a big wedding—lots of people there to see her marry me. Then they knew—knew she loved me the best. No one else, just me. I was the best! And I kissed her after the preacher said we were all done—officially married. And we lived together in a little house ..."

He gazed out the window—seemed to have forgotten the children's presence. "I never had a father, you know. He ran off before I was even born. Hardly had a mother either. She was so drunk most of the time it didn't matter if she was there or not. I have a sister—older'n me. We pretty much raised ourselfs."

He noticed Anny again and said to her, "You're lucky, you know. You got a father. You got me. I'm a good father to you, huh?" He looked out the window again. "Your mama was so beautiful, and she loved me so much."

Chapter Fifty Eight

School started again the second week of January, and both Anny and Gibbie were glad to go back. The school rooms were nice and warm. Miss Valentine didn't like Anny any more than she had before Christmas, but Anny was happy in spite of her. She was doing well with her studies and was helping Gibbie with his reading and arithmetic at home in the evenings. Gibbie said he didn't care to learn, but Anny told him he should try, to make her proud. So he tried.

On Friday, at the end of the first week back in school, Gibbie had stayed outside to play with some of his friends before coming home. When he burst through the door of the apartment later, he shouted, "Anny! Guess what!" He held out his hands, a large red apple in each one. "Apples!"

"Gibbie?" Anny's voice was cautious. "Where did you get them? Did you ..."

"No, Anny. Honest! A lady gave them to me! She stopped me on the sidewalk, and she said, 'Here—maybe you and your sister would like an apple.' Really she did! Cross my heart and hope to die. That's exactly what she said!"

Anny looked at her brother with interest. "Huh!" she said. "Who was she?"

"I don't know. She didn't say what her name was, and she was in a hurry. She was a fancy lady with a big hat. And she gave me a note." He fished in his pocket and pulled out a crumpled piece of paper. He took it over to the window to read it.

Hello, I cannot really be your friend. I am not a good person, and it would be bad for you if people thought you were my friends. So please don't talk to me if you see me on the street. I hope you like the apples.

"We've seen her before, Anny. I'll show you who she is next time we see her." Anny just looked at Gibbie with questioning eyes.

*   *   *

January 17, 1910

Father went away again. He was only gone three days this time. I guess he didn't work while he was gone, because we don't have any money. The Wife wasn't here last night or the night before. Not that we need her. Gibbie and I do just fine on our own – in fact better than when she's here. But still, it seems a little odd. I wonder where she was.

*   *   *

Klein sat at a corner table in the Umatilla House Saloon. Robinson, across from him, looked around warily, then addressed Klein.

"Monday. You'll head out at night. There's a chestnut mare in the pasture behind the Anderson place just out of town. Tack's in the little shed. Nobody will notice it's missing for a few days. Take it. Me and the other guy will leave the next two nights."

"Who's the other guy?"

"Never mind. You can just call him Smith. The less you know, the less you can tell."

"Who would I tell?"

Robinson ignored him. "Mention to some people around town here that you have to go to Portland for a few days. Then tomorrow night, you head over to Five Mile Canyon." Robinson drew a map on the table top with his finger. "Hole up there all the next day. Then head east, and stay on the Oregon side of the Columbia. Go around the big bend of the river and head for Walla Walla." Robinson's finger showed the route. "And then come in like you're comin' from Boise."

"Why Boise?" Klein asked.

"Don't ask questions. Just do what I tell ya."

Klein looked down at his drink. Why couldn't Robinson treat him with a little respect? He didn't seem to realize what a fine man Klein was. Ella had loved him. He had her kids to prove it. Of course, The Wife wasn't all that great, but at least he was doing okay at the family man charade. And Klein was the one who could impersonate a "quality" citizen. He could make them look respectable. Robinson ought to treat him better.

"Once you're there, get yourself cleaned up, put on your fancy duds, and rent a nice hotel room."

This was to Klein's liking.

"Make yourself known a bit. And do that thing you know how to do—real educated like, you know." Robinson glanced around, but no one was close enough to overhear the conversation. "Let people know you're only there for a short time—that you'll be leavin' town come Saturday mornin'. That way, no one will give it a second thought when the bank goes down Friday night, and you're gone on Saturday." Robinson raised his eyebrows in question, and Klein nodded.

Robinson continued. "Go into the bank on Thursday to do some kind of business. Look it over real careful. And be friendly! When we show up at closing time on Friday, you're our ticket inside."

At this, Klein narrowed his eyes suspiciously. "They'll know what I look like if I go in ahead of time and make friends with them. I don't want to go to all this trouble just to get thrown in the clink." Klein glared suspiciously at Robinson.

Robinson waved off Klein's concern. "They'd recognize us—maybe—if they ever got a chance to see us again. But they won't. You'll shave after." Robinson rocked his chair back on its hind legs, crossed his arms over his chest, and nodded in approval of his plan. "And anyway, they won't be looking in The Dalles. They'll probably be looking in Boise. Maybe even Spokane or Pendleton.

"Afterwards—" he banged his chair back into an upright position "—you head out east fast as you can and ditch the fancy duds. As soon as it's dark, double back. Do your traveling at night and overland, but get back here to The Dalles just as fast as you possibly can. And don't forget to shave. The other guy and me will take it slower—prob'ly separate and go someplace else for a while. We won't be together—won't get back to here at the same time."

"And the take?" asked Klein.

"It'll set us up for the next year at least. Maybe more."

Klein nodded. He didn't really understand all of it. It sounded more complicated than the other jobs they'd pulled recently. But he could do one thing at a time. He could do what he was told. "The wife will like the money. She's been griping at me lately."

"Meet me at the Watering Hole Saloon Thursday evening at nine o'clock sharp. We'll take it from there. And that's all you need to know for now. Got it?"

Chapter Fifty Nine

The thick potato soup on Christmas had been wonderful, but it was the last good meal the children had eaten. And it was over a month ago. The food Anny brought home from the store three days a week provided meals for the children. Father and The Wife usually ate at the Umatilla House or at one of the saloons, but they never brought anything back for the children. It was as if they weren't aware that the children needed food. The Wife occasionally said to Anny, "You are such a wonderful big girl. I'm sure you won't mind fixing some supper for yourself and your brother."

And Anny wouldn't have minded—if there had been some food in the apartment to fix. But so often, there was nothing.

Today was one of those days. Supper last night had been meager, and this morning Anny could find nothing at all to eat for breakfast. She hurried Gibbie along, wanting to be dressed and out the door before Father or The Wife woke up.

"But I haven't had any breakfast yet!" Gibbie didn't sense the same urgency to leave.

"I'm sorry, Gibbie, but there just isn't anything. I'll figure out a way to get something by supper time tonight. I promise!"

"But I'm hungry now!"

"I know. I do know, Gibbie. But there's nothing I can do about it. I wish I could."

Gibbie looked as if he could cry at any moment. "Anny, I want to go back—back to Mama Jane and Granddaddy. When are they going to write to you?"

"I wish I knew, Gibbie." She took his hand and pulled him out the door and down the stairs, into the biting wind. "I've written a bunch of letters to them, but there's been no answer. I go to the post office nearly every day to check, but we haven't had a letter back. I don't understand why."

"Write another one." At the bottom of the stairs, Gibbie stopped. "Wait! I know!" he said, and disappeared around the back side of the building. He returned only a moment later with part of a loaf of very stale bread. He beckoned Anny, and she slipped back with him to the darkness between the buildings.

The children began tearing at the bread's tough crust, pulling off enough to fill them at least for now. "How did you know it was there?" Anny asked.

"Saw a man from the restaurant throw it out last night. I remembered."

Anny thought a moment. "Gibbie, I want you to go on to school," Anny said around a mouthful of bread. "I'm not coming. I'm going to go in and see if Mr. Delgado will let me work extra during the day today. If I get some money, I'll buy food and bring it to you at school. If I don't, then you come to the store when school's out, and I should be able to help you by then. Understand?"

"Yeah. Anny?"

"What?"

"Remember that time when Father left us outside and didn't come back to get us?"

Anny said nothing, her face a mask.

"He told us to stay there 'til he came back to get us, but he didn't come back."

Anny frowned and waited for Gibbie to go on.

"It was before Mama Jane and Granddaddy. I was really little. It was cold. And I cried and cried, but you took care of me. We didn't have any food. And you took me ... I don't remember. You took me someplace, and told a lady that I was hungry, and she yelled at us. Then a boy gave us a roll. You let me eat the whole thing." He looked startled. "You let me have it all, Anny. And none for you. We slept under some bushes. You tried to wrap me up inside your coat with you, but I wouldn't fit. Then we woke up in the morning and ... and—"

"Gibbie, are you sure? I don't remember any of that." Anny looked hard at Gibbie. She did remember reading it in her journal. So it was real. It had really happened. When she had read it in her book ... well, she thought it might have been a story she'd made up. Like a fairy tale.

"I'm sure. I remember."

Anny and Gibbie just looked at each other, each thinking their own thoughts.

"Go to school," Anny said, finally. "I'll come if I can bring you something to eat."

*　　　*　　　*

"It would be just for today, Mr. Delgado. It's for something special."

The storekeeper stuck a finger in one ear and wiggled it while he thought. It made the ear lobe stick out even farther than usual. If Anny hadn't been so desperate, she would have laughed.

"I've been coming here on Mondays, Wednesdays, and Fridays ever since August," she reminded him. "I've never missed a day. And you've always told me I am doing a good job. I promise—I can do other jobs just as well as I can sweep. I will do anything you want me to, and I'll do it very well."

Mr. Delgado still said nothing, but his face said he was thinking.

"And you wouldn't have to pay me very much," Anny added. "I can take produce, same as usual, or money if you'd rather. Either way works fine." *Why don't you answer me? You're making me nervous just staring at me.*

"All right," Mr. Delgado finally said. "I really do have a lot of work that needs doing. I'm behind, so ... all right. And we will pay you in money this time. That way you can decide what you want to buy." He nodded, as if to assure himself he was making the right decision.

"First thing," Mr. Delgado continued, "there are some boxes in the back room that came in yesterday afternoon. You open them and put the things where they go on the shelves. When you're finished there, come see me and I'll show you what to do next."

Anny wanted to jump for joy. Instead she walked quickly to the back room and got to work.

*　　　*　　　*

Anny saw Gibbie come in the front door of the store after school, but ignored him until she had finished dusting the shelf which held mittens, gloves, and scarves. They were so soft and warm! She could tell Gibbie was trying to summon her with his eyes, but she refused to look. Mr. Delgado saw Gibbie waiting and called Anny to him.

"Anny." He laid one hand on each of Anny's shoulders. "I'm not happy about you skipping school today. I was glad to let you work this one day, because it seemed really important to you—and because I really needed the help. But I don't want you to ever do this again, you hear? You can come in after school, like always, but no more skipping, understand?"

Anny nodded solemnly. "I won't do it again, Mr. Delgado. Today was just a special case."

"All right. As long as we understand each other." The stern look vanished as Mr. Delgado smiled at both children. "You're a good worker, Anny, and that's the truth. But you need to go to school! You know ... my brother is on the school board. I don't want him to accuse me of keeping kids out of school."

"I understand, Mr. Delgado. I won't do it again." *Now will you just pay me? Please, please!*

"Go on up to Mrs. Delgado then. She'll pay you for your work."

Anny collected her pay from a grumpy Mrs. Delgado, while Gibbie looked over the food at the front of the store. He'd already selected two apples, a can of salmon, and a handful of penny candy when Anny joined him. She made him put the candy back and told him they would buy only good wholesome food. Then she measured out three pounds each of navy beans and rice, and two pounds of oats. She looked longingly at the raisins, but used some of her newly acquired arithmetic skills to figure the cost, and decided she didn't have enough money for them. Mrs. Delgado cocked her head to the side and looked quizzically at Anny as she took her money and made change. She glanced at the candy jar on the counter ... but then pressed her lips hard together and shoved Anny's items toward her.

"Thank you," Anny said quietly.

Mrs. Delgado just crossed her arms and scowled as Anny gathered her purchases and turned to leave the store.

Chapter Sixty

On Friday, Anny put the broom back in its place and accepted the five potatoes and two onions Mrs. Delgado handed her. The potatoes had sprouts already, and they were mushy feeling. But Anny took them gladly.

As she walked out of the store, the lady Gibbie had pointed out to her stepped into Anny's way. Quickly she shoved a cloth bag into Anny's hand. "Take it home with you," she said quietly, as she walked on.

At home, Anny pulled two small pork chops from the bag. Gibbie gaped at her with hungry eyes. "Did Mr. Delgado give you the meat?" he asked.

"No," Anny replied. "The apple lady. She just gave me the bag and told me to bring it home with me."

Gibbie grabbed the bag to be sure Anny had not missed anything.

"There's a letter!" he said, and pulled out a folded sheet of paper. He unfolded it and read aloud.

Hello,

I don't know your name, but I have seen you sweeping at the store. And I've seen your brother. I just had some extra pork chops and I thought you might like them. You can fry them in a skillet for about ten minutes on each side. Be sure they are cooked all the way through. Put a little grease in the skillet first if you have some. And if you don't have grease, put in just a little water so the meat won't stick.

If you give the bag back to me (but don't let anyone see) I will help you again sometime.

Esmerelda

Anny's eyes grew large, and she took the paper to read it herself. "Wow!" she breathed softly. "She's nice!"

"Cook it, Anny! Hurry up!" Gibbie was already pulling the skillet from under the sink.

Anny got out their one kettle and lit the single gas burner. "Let me start some potatoes first." She quickly broke off the sprouts with her thumbnail, cut the potatoes in pieces, and set them to boil. While supper cooked, Anny re-read the letter. "Esmerelda ... I've never heard that name before. Have you?"

"Huh-uh." Gibbie got out the first note Esmerelda had written them and re-read it. "Well, she's a really nice lady. That's for sure! Who do you think she is?"

"An angel, maybe?" Anny was speaking only half in jest. She sent Gibbie down to the alley to find some more wood for the fire and built it up enough that it not only cooked the potatoes, it warmed the room.

Gibbie stared at the pot. "Is it ready yet?"

Anny poked at a potato with the fork. "Yes, take it off and set it on the table. The meat will only take a few minutes." Anny set the skillet in place and put in the two pork chops and some sliced onions. The apartment smelled wonderful.

"She says she's a bad person." Anny said to Gibbie. "How can that be true? She's so nice to us! We should think of some way to thank her."

"She's not a bad person! She gives us food!"

"I know. I don't understand it either. And I don't know how to thank her."

"I think it's ready, Anny. Let's eat!"

*　　　*　　　*

February 14, 1910

Today is Oregon's birthday. I still haven't heard from Mama Jane. I sent another letter today – handed it to the lady at the post office myself, so it should get there okay. I saw Esmerelda on my way home from the market. She didn't look at me, but she gave me her bag with a loaf of bread and some cheese in it as she walked by. I like her.

*   *   *

After school on Monday, Anny took Esmerelda's bag with her to the store when she went there to sweep. Esmerelda came in to do some shopping, and Anny got the bag from the back room and laid it near the counter where Esmerelda would be sure to see it. In it was the letter Anny had written.

Dear Esmerelda,

I am Anny, and my brother is Gibbie. He is 9, and I am 11. We used to live on Puget Island down by Westport, but now we live in The Dalles. I work at the store on Monday, Wednesday, and Friday.

Thank you very much for being such a good friend to us! When we lived on the Island, Granddaddy butchered a hog and we had lots of pork chops. We both really like them. We each had a garden of our own there so we *could grow all kinds of wonderful food. But we don't have a garden here in The Dalles. If I had a garden, I would give you some good things to eat.*

Anny

*　　*　　*

March 1910

Anny and Gibbie each had new clothes. They had dinner at the Umatilla House two nights in a row. There was lots of food in the cupboards, new blankets, a new journal for Anny, and a whole bag of marbles and a new pocket knife for Gibbie. The Wife had returned, and she had lots of new clothes and jewels she'd not had before and a parasol to keep the sun off her head. Father also had new clothes, including a very spiffy looking derby hat. But the biggest difference was that Father had shaved. He had been gone for a week and a half. But now he was back—with money!

The same thing had happened before, in small ways. Father would be gone for a while—working, he said—and then when he came back, he had money. But *this!* This was like nothing Anny had ever experienced before. How could she be so happy and so miserable at the same time? She really liked her new things, but somehow ... it made her uneasy.

Her new clothes were very nice. She had picked out the dark red dress herself from the dry goods store. It was ready-made and fit her perfectly. The first day she wore the dress to school, the other girls had gathered around admiring it. Even Harriet, who had been so nasty all along, was impressed. She had used it as an excuse to taunt Anny, but at least she'd noticed.

"Oh look! The little ragamuffin has a new dress. Isn't that just precious?" Harriet said. "Did your daddy rob a bank or something?"

Anny chose not to answer. Instead, she took out her New Mental Arithmetic book to review. She was determined to be the last one standing in the drill today.

As the day progressed, and Anny thought of the arithmetic drill coming up, her stomach grew tighter and tighter. At least she assumed that was why she felt as if she were tied in knots.

"Did your daddy rob a bank or something?" The words bounced around in Anny's head, while she tried hard to focus on arithmetic.

In truth, Anny wondered herself! How else could a person suddenly become so wealthy? Father had never shown any inclination to actually *work*, as far as Anny knew. So how *did* he get his money? She wished she could talk to someone about it. But who?

*   *   *

"Samantha," said Miss Valentine. "What number is that which, being increased by the difference between its one-fourth and one-fifth, equals 42?"

Samantha grimaced. She was still standing—the longest she'd ever been on her feet for math drill. Anny stood beside her, and George stood opposite them on the boys' side of the room. George was usually the last one standing on the boys' side. But neither Samantha nor Anny had ever made it this far before. Suzanne, who usually remained on her feet the longest of all the girls, had been eliminated early on when she answered a simple question without thinking. She was so embarrassed by it, she was still wiping her eyes and sniffling.

"... Number increased by the difference between ... Could you repeat the question please, Miss Valentine?" Samantha said.

Miss Valentine read the question again.

"Let's see, it's probably a number divisible by 5 ... *and* 4." Her fingers moved against her thumbs as she counted silently. "Thirty?" she finally guessed.

"No, I'm sorry, Samantha. You may sit down." Anny was thinking hard, trying to find the answer as Miss Valentine turned to the boys' side. "George, what number is that which, being increased by the difference between its one-fourth and one-fifth, equals 42?"

George spoke confidently. "Thirty two."

"No, George. That's incorrect."

George's mouth opened in surprise. "Wrong? Let's see ... A fourth of 32 is 8 ... Oh no! A fifth of 32—?" He slapped his forehead. "I wasn't thinking!" he said.

Miss Valentine looked at Anny. Anny thought the look said, "I know you can't do it, but I have to give you a chance." If Anny failed to answer correctly, all three students, Samantha, George and Anny would be given another question.

"All right, Anny, what number is that which—"

"Forty," Anny said.

Miss Valentine looked up. "Excuse me, Anny. Allow me to read the question, please."

Most of the girls in class snickered behind their hands, and Anny's face burned.

"What number is that which, being increased by the difference between its one-fourth and one-fifth, equals 42?"

"Forty."

"That's correct. You may sit down now."

That's all? I may sit down now? Whenever Suzanne or George wins you tell them how smart they are, and you tell the rest of us to try to be more like them. But if I win ... I may sit down now?

Tears choked Anny's throat. Finally, she was the last one standing for the weekly math drill—a goal she'd sought since the first week of school. And she could sit down now! She opened her eyes wide in an attempt to keep the tears from forming there, then quietly sat and stared at the top of her desk.

*   *   *

Anny stood rooted in place, staring at the poster in the post office. She'd come to see if there was a letter for her, but now this.

Anny felt dizzy. Finally she tore her eyes away from the notice and moved slowly toward home. The scar on Father's hand was it his left hand? Yes, the left. But he didn't have a beard any more. And he wasn't in Spokane or Boise.

Chapter Sixty One

March 18, 1910

I was the last one standing at Math Drill today. But Miss Valentine was not proud of me. She doesn't like me.

In my class, I am first in spelling, first in geography, first in history. I write well and read well. But I don't care. Father doesn't love us. The Wife doesn't love us. I don't talk to Father. I don't want to. I don't talk to The Wife either. Even Esmerelda loves us more than they do, but she has to hide it for some reason. I want Mama Jane and Granddaddy so much! And I really miss Mary Jo and the other girls!

I heard a man talking about God. He was standing up on a big box in the street. And he said God was our Father. I think that's wrong. I think God is like Granddaddy.

*   *   *

March 29, 1910

The Wife left. We don't know where she went, but it's just Father and Gibbie and me now.

*   *   *

April 12, 1910

We've been in The Dalles for eight months. I still have not heard from Mama Jane. I hope she and Granddaddy are okay! Sometimes Father goes away for a while. The longest time was almost two weeks. Esmerelda is such a good friend! She won't act like she knows me, and I don't understand why, but she keeps watching out for us. She still gives us food sometimes. Yesterday I was at the back of the store and she carried in a big bag and set it down on the floor right next to me. She leaned over to look at some things on the shelf, and when she did, she whispered that I should take the bag home with me. Then she went away. So I took the bag and put it in the back room until it was time to go home.

When we opened it, there were two peppermints ... <u>AND</u> a new dress for me ~ a pretty green one! And it has a pinafore ~ with a big pocket! I guess she's noticed I always wear my pinafore. Maybe someday I will show her this journal. Maybe. And for Gibbie, there was a pair of trousers and a new shirt! Esmerelda is <u>so</u> nice to us. I wish I knew how to thank her! And I wish I could understand why she pretends like she doesn't know us.

*   *   *

Anny's heart was full and her pencil ready to write. But no words would come. How could she possibly thank Esmerelda for all she had done? Anny thought first of all the things she could not give—the material things she had no way of getting. She thought of the friendship Esmerelda seemed afraid of. Anny could think of only one way to let Esmerelda know how greatly she and Gibbie appreciated her.

*   *   *

Dear Friend, Esmerelda,
*   Thank you for being so kind to us! I still don't understand why you say you can't be our friend. You ARE our friend! You've done so much for us! I don't know how to thank you. I hope you like this poem about <u>you.</u>*

Friend

A friend is a rare and precious treasure

Far beyond measure

Friendship tip-toes in

When it's least expected

Riding on the tail winds of disappointment

Or heartache or tragedy.

That's when a friend shines

like a light in the sky

Like a fire in the cold darkness of night.

Sometimes life tries to pull a person down.

But a friend helps a friend to rise above.

You are a true friend!

Love, Anny
(and Gibbie)

*　　　*　　　*

Anny stood with her back to the wall, looking at the floor across the room. She'd been wakened from a sound sleep as Father and The Wife came in late—the first time Anny had seen The Wife in over three weeks. The sour smell of whiskey was strong, and Anny knew it would be a long night. Gibbie cowered on the floor in the corner. Anny dared not lift her eyes as The Wife slammed the pile of letters onto the table and shouted at her.

"Look what I picked up from the post mistress today, my dear." The woman's voice was harsh, sarcastic. "And just what do you mean by this, may I ask? You've been writing letters to these ... *people* ever since we got here, and you haven't told me about it. Sneaking around, thinking you're so smart." The Wife swayed a little and sat down abruptly on the beautiful red velvet chair. "Yeah, you think you can fool me. But you can't. You can't fool me because I'm smarter than you think." She pried herself up out of the chair and turned on Father.

"You see? You see now? What I said is true. She's just a little sneak, that's all she is. Let's just leave them here and go. They're big enough to take care of theirselves. That's what you said when I agreed to help you on this crazy idea of yours. And where's all the go-o-old and jew-w-wels and money you talked about? Huh? Where?"

Anny's eyes were riveted on the letters. *Her* letters. To Mama Jane and Mary Jo. How? How had The Wife gotten them?

Klein said nothing. He was uncharacteristically silent as The Wife stormed on and on.

"I gave up a perfectly good career to do what—tolerate your miserable ways and your miserable children. Well, I'm through! Finished! Good-bye!

"I can't take any more of this," she shouted at Klein. "I told you when I signed on, I hate children. Well, I hate them even more now. And you're not far behind! Father of these dreadful, wretched, miserable ..."

Klein opened the door to the apartment and stood, swaying, with his hand on the knob.

"Out!" he roared at her, "I don't need ya, and I don't want ya. And I don't ever wanna see your ugly face around here again!"

When The Wife finally stomped out the door, neither Anny nor Gibbie watched. They simply attempted to appear invisible.

Father slammed the door so hard the whole building rattled, then stomped into the bedroom, slamming that door too behind him.

Anny waited a few moments, then walked quietly over to her brother and straightened his blanket for him. "Go back to sleep," she told him, pulling the blanket up to his chin like Mama Jane used to do. "Sweet dreams, little boy. I'll see you in the morning." That's what Mama Jane and Granddaddy always said to Gibbie at night. And to her they said, "Sleep well, sweet girl."

Anny had hoped for so long that Mama Jane and Granddaddy would come and get them. Now she realized they couldn't. They had no idea where she and Gibbie were. Anny's letters had never reached them. Father had said they were going to San Francisco.

Anny walked to the table and picked up the letters. She counted them. Eighteen letters to Mama Jane and Granddaddy. Six letters to Mary Jo. Every single one she had written. Anny sat on the edge of her sofa and cried.

Chapter Sixty Two

Nickelsen's Book Store in The Dalles
Photo from the website for Klindt's Booksellers and Stationers

L es Matlock arrived in The Dalles in the early afternoon. He would
be traveling on to Portland on the 7:00 p.m. train, but first he
would enjoy his few hours here. He cut a fine figure as he strode
purposefully toward Nickelsen's Book and Music Store on Second
Street—hair combed, mustache waxed, wearing a three piece suit and
carrying his gold-headed cane. Matlock swung the cane jauntily as he
strode down the street.

The town of The Dalles was humming. With the return of spring
weather, the water was filled with boats toting passengers and goods up

and down the river. The *Bailey Gatzert*, still first in its class, would arrive later this afternoon, as would the *Charles R. Spencer.* The wooden sidewalks in town were crowded with men and women from all walks of life—sheep shearers, boatmen, lumberjacks headed west, and prospectors headed east. And of course, a full complement of bankers, merchants, farmers, ranchers, and horse thieves. There were Indians too, clad in their native dress.

Matlock tipped his hat to a number of ladies—he seemed to know most of them—and stopped to visit with gentlemen friends as well. He hadn't been in The Dalles since last summer and enjoyed reacquainting himself with the town and its citizens.

Arriving at Nickelsen's Bookstore, he visited awhile, browsed awhile, and ended up purchasing a copy of Robert Service's *The Spell of the Yukon.* The book looked like a good one. He would enjoy reading it on the train that evening.

Back on the street, he nodded and tipped his hat as he approached Esmerelda in front of the Umatilla House. "Good afternoon, Miss Esmerelda. It's good to see you."

Esmerelda smiled back, surprised to see Matlock in The Dalles. He was a friend, not a customer. He had always treated her—and all of Mollie's girls—with the greatest respect. Matlock seemed to be a gentleman in every sense of the word. A gambler and a dandy, yes, but still very much the gentleman. Esmerelda was pleased to see him.

"What brings you to The Dalles?" she asked him. "Business, or just looking for a change of scenery, now that spring's in the air?"

"Maybe a little of both," Matlock smiled. "Actually, I'm on my way to Portland. I'll be on the seven o'clock, headed west."

"Well, I hope your trip is successful on both counts." Esmerelda smiled and prepared to go on her way.

But Matlock held out his hand to stop her. "Before I head out tonight," he said, "would you care to have an early dinner with me?"

Esmerelda looked sharply at him. No, he wasn't joking. And there seemed to be nothing more to his invitation than the invitation itself. "Well, yes, sure. That would be mighty fine. I would enjoy hearing how the home town is doing. I really like Heppner, and I miss it."

Imagine that! A man inviting Esmerelda to dinner! Not buying her a drink before he turned tables and bought what she was selling. Just an ordinary man, a human being, offering to share dinner with her.

*   *   *

Matlock had finished his salmon dinner and was patting his stomach with obvious pleasure. Esmerelda was only half done. It was a huge plate of food. More than she could hold. She took a cloth from her bag and began wrapping the rest of her meal.

"I have some friends who will be glad enough to have the rest of this," she said to Matlock. "They're children." She stopped and looked into Matlock's eyes, wondering if she should tell him about Anny and Gibbie.

"Children?" he asked, smiling.

Esmerelda nodded and continued packing up the food. "Well, they've stolen my heart. A little girl and her brother." Esmerelda placed the wrapped package in her bag. "They are about the same size, but the girl is two years older. They are such sweet children, but their parents neglect them just terribly. They rarely have enough to eat. And they're so raggedy." Esmerelda's eyes became sad at the thought of the children's struggle. "But hard working? That girl will work like the dickens just to get food for herself and her brother. She works at Delgado's Market three afternoons a week stocking shelves, cleaning ... whatever they will let her do. And for pay, they give her leftover produce—usually just short of rotten. But she takes it, politely. And she's intelligent. Gifted, actually. You should see the poem she wrote me!"

Matlock smiled. "A budding poet, huh? I like poetry. How did you meet these children?"

Esmerelda laughed at the memory. "The first day I arrived here in town, the boy nearly ran me down. He was sneaking out of the store with something hidden in the bib of his overalls. So I began noticing him, and then his sister."

"Huh." Matlock shook his head. "It makes you wonder what some people have ever done to deserve children. How old are they?"

"Anny's eleven. Gibbie's nine." She stopped as Matlock's eyes focused sharply on her face. "What?" she asked.

"Eleven and nine years old ... names Anny and Gibbie ..." He spoke the names slowly. "What do these children look like?" Matlock had become suddenly and intensely interested.

"Well, Anny is small, delicate. Very serious looking. And very thin ... *too* thin, actually."

"Her hair?"

"She has light red hair ..."

Matlock's look became even more intense.

"Braids. Freckles. Her eyes are green or blue—or maybe kind of in between. Gibbie is skinny but muscular, 'wiry' I guess you'd say.

Brown eyes, kind of curly dark blond hair ..." Esmerelda tilted her head to look at Matlock. "All of a sudden, you're *very* interested ... what is it?"

Matlock blew out his breath, almost whistling. "You remember the flood ... of course you remember the flood. Two children, a boy and a girl, were not among the living when it was over. But their bodies were never found either."

Esmerelda nodded. "That does sound vaguely familiar." Was Matlock suggesting ...? Was such a thing possible? "But I remember that there were quite a few bodies that were never found." Esmerelda looked doubtful.

"True. But the children's father doesn't believe they died. Mac Harmon. Do you know him?"

Esmerelda shook her head.

Matlock continued. "He still thinks of them as missing—alive somewhere."

"And you think Anny and Gibbie are his missing children?"

"Well, I sure think it's a possibility!" Matlock stared hard at Esmerelda. "Listen, I have to be in Portland tonight. I *have* to. Wish I didn't, but I do." He glanced at his watch. "My train leaves in half an hour. I'll go, but I'll be back here ... I can leave early and get here by Friday. Can you arrange for me to meet these children?"

Esmerelda nodded. "I've told Anny not to talk to me when she sees me, but I'll get a note to her. I'm sure we can make it work."

"You told her not to talk to you ...?" Matlock's eyes pierced hers. "Esmerelda, you're a good woman. Has anyone ever told you that?"

No. No one had ever told her that. She just shrugged. "I just want to help her rise above her circumstances. I want her to have a better life than I've had. It's something I learned from a friend in Heppner. I can't help Anny if she's known to be a friend of someone like me."

Matlock smiled and nodded. "I need to really think about this. I'm tempted to wire the father right now, but I'd better not. I'd really hate to disappoint him if this all turns out to be nothing." He looked intently at Esmerelda. "Friday night then. Bring them here, to the Umatilla House, about seven o'clock." Esmerelda nodded.

Ten minutes later, in front of the bordello, Esmerelda's head was spinning with thoughts of the children. Matlock tipped his hat, thanked her for dining with him, and wished her well. Something she had never experienced before in her life.

Chapter Sixty Three

Anny didn't know what time it was when she awakened, but she'd been sound asleep. Father was in the apartment and had the oil lamp lit. He was stumbling around the room, cursing loudly. Was he looking for something? Her letters maybe? She had put them under the cushions of the sofa. He couldn't get them while she was lying right on top of them.

"HEY!" Father spoke so sharply that Anny jumped, even though she was awake.

Gibbie sat up suddenly and said, "Huh?"

Father's words were slurred, angry as he accused Anny. "Why did you write letters? You don't trust me?"

No, she didn't trust him. Why would she?

"I bet you wondered why you never got an answer." He hiccupped and took a drink from the bottle in his hand. "You never got an answer because they never got the letters." Father giggled drunkenly.

He picked up something from the table beside him and held it up. "See here? See what I got? I got your book!" He held in his hand Anny's precious journal.

Her heart stopped.

"You hid it, didn't you, you little sneak. I pulled it out from under your pillow while you were sleeping." No longer laughing, Father snarled at Anny. "She was right. You're more trouble than you're worth!" He tried to slam the bottle onto the table, but missed, and it shattered on the floor. He swore and kicked at the shards.

"No!" Anny screamed. "No! You stole it! That's mine!" Her eyes flashed fire as she lunged up off the sofa and charged him, reaching for the book. She didn't even notice the sharp pain in her foot as a piece of broken glass cut into it. She wrested the journal from Klein's hand and ran back to the sofa.

Suddenly his face and voice hardened. "You better respect me."

"No!" Anny shouted. *"I won't!"*

"You *will*! I'll see you do! I'm your father!"

Anny stood and heard herself scream at him. "You are NOT my father! I don't even know you! *Who are you? And where's my Papa?"*

Anny gasped as she heard her own words.

They were true.

She did *not* know this man. He was *not* her father. Where was her real father? Her papa?

Klein looked stunned. "I took you, and now you're *mine!*" Then his eyes narrowed to arrows of steel. He picked up the oil lamp from the table and flung it, with all his strength, across the room at Anny. Had he been sober, it would have hit her. Instead, it crashed against the ledge of the window behind the sofa, breaking both the lamp and the window glass. Fire leaped instantly up the limp, dusty curtains and began eating at the tattered wall paper.

"NO! Gibbie! Gibbie, come!" Anny grabbed her brother's hand, and fled through the door to the stairway, bloody footprints trailing behind her. Klein charged drunkenly after them, his lips curled back in a sneer.

Papa! Oh, Papa, help me!

The fire spread, searing the peeling paint and consuming the tinder-dry wood of the building's exterior.

"Fire! Get water!" a voice shouted from below, as flames spread quickly over the outside of the building.

Anny dragged Gibbie down the stairs with Klein right behind them. Both the children jumped the last few steps to the ground and ran for the street.

*   *   *

Klein clattered to the bottom of the stairs, but was stopped by the bulky figure of Robinson, his partner in crime, who stepped in front of him, halting his drunken dash after the children.

"There you are, Klein," Robinson said in a silky voice. "We was just coming up to pay you a little visit. I see you've saved us the trouble of climbing the stairs."

Klein backed away, but heard the click of a pistol being cocked behind him. He stopped.

"What do you want?" he whined. "I don't have anything. I don't know what she told you, but I don't have anything."

"We think different. We think you have a little extra something from our gig Thursday night."

"I don't even have *my* share! She took it. That woman took it all."

"Yeah. Of course." Robinson tickled the end of Klein's clean-shaven chin with his pistol. "Why don't we just empty your pockets and let us be the judge of that?"

"The kids. They took it." Klein reached as if to show his pocket, then broke into a run. He made it to the intersection of Front and Washington when two shots rang out. He fell face down in the street.

The sound of the fire alarm and the crackling of the flames competed with the shouts of men rushing from both the Umatilla House and the Cosmopolitan Hotel to watch or fight the fire. But Klein made no sound at all.

*   *   *

Anny and Gibbie dashed around the corner at Front and Court, where they ducked into a recessed doorway. Gibbie crept slowly back and looked around the side of the building. Klein lay face down in the dried mud ruts of the street.

Anny peeked over her brother's shoulder, waiting to see movement. She stepped around Gibbie and stood still in the street, in a moment of indecision, then began walking—slowly, as if in a trance—toward the prostrate figure only a short block away.

"Anny, come back!" Gibbie hissed at his sister. "Anny, what are you doing?"

Anny's steps slowed even more as she drew near. The saloons of both buildings had emptied at the first cry of "Fire!" and while many of the men were working at extinguishing the flames, a small crowd now stood in a circle, gazing down on the man in the street. Anny was only vaguely aware of men running, shouting, the attempt to keep the fire from spreading to the Cosmopolitan.

As Anny stepped into the circle of men surrounding Klein, Esmerelda appeared out of the shadows and put her hands on the child's shoulders.

Klein groaned as two men rolled him to his back. The bigger one planted a foot firmly on one of Klein's wrists and rifled through his pockets. "Where is it?" the other man demanded.

"My kids! They stole it from me. They have it!" Klein could barely talk. The two men began backing away into the darkness, both of them surveying the crowd. Esmerelda turned Anny, blocking her from the men's view. One of the onlookers reached out to check the flow of blood from a gunshot wound in the side of Klein's neck. Anny pulled against Esmerelda's hands, stepping back to Klein's side.

Klein looked up, saw Anny's face and struggled to speak. "Anny, I'm sorry." He gasped for breath. "I done wrong. Go back where I found you. Go back to Heppner."

Klein exhaled one last time, and his body lay still.

*   *   *

Anny felt herself being pulled backward by strong arms. She struggled to free herself, but then heard a woman's voice.

"Anny, Anny, it's okay. It's me, Esmerelda." She turned the girl, gazing into her very white face. "Come on. Let's get you out of here." She took Anny's hand and pulled her away. She hurried Anny back toward the corner of Front and Court.

"It's okay, honey. Don't cry. It'll be okay."

But Anny *was* crying—and couldn't stop. Rounding the corner of Court Street, Esmerelda pulled Anny with her into the bordello and drew her into a hug. She patted her shoulder and the back of her head. "There, there ... Don't worry. You'll be fine." She sat on a bench inside the door, holding Anny on her lap like a small child.

Finally, Anny's sobs subsided. "He's dead," she said with a hiccup. "He's dead."

A man clattered down the stairs and out the door, ignoring Esmerelda and Anny.

"That's right, honey. He's dead. But this isn't the end for you. *You* are still alive. Where's Gibbie?"

"Gibbie!" Anny eyes widened. How could she have forgotten him? She struggled up from Esmerelda's lap, but was pulled back.

"What's this?" Esmerelda asked, noticing for the first time the blood on the floor under Anny. She lifted Anny's foot and looked at it. Through the mud, she could see a deep cut.

"I have to find Gibbie!" Anny struggled to pull herself out of Esmerelda's arms.

"Let's both go," Esmerelda said. "Can you walk? We'll find Gibbie first, then fix your foot."

Anny rushed to the door, keeping her left heel off the floor.

But Gibbie was nowhere to be found. He wasn't where Anny had left him. He wasn't among the men fighting the fire. "By the river!"

Anny said, and she pulled Esmerelda with her down Court Street to the water's edge. They glimpsed a movement near the pilings at the back of the Umatilla House, but when Esmerelda checked more carefully, Gibbie was not there.

Finally, Esmerelda insisted on returning to the brothel to clean and bandage Anny's foot. Esmerelda took Anny up the stairs to the bedroom where she spent her off-duty days and hours, and laid her gently on her own bed. She cleaned the cut on Anny's heel the best she could and wrapped it in strips of a torn sheet.

"Don't be afraid," she said, brushing loose hair from Anny's eyes. "I'm going to leave you here for a little while. I'm going to go find Gibbie. Just stay here and stay quiet. Don't leave this room. Go to sleep if you can—you'll be safe here. I'll bring Gibbie back as soon as I can."

Anny nodded, her eyes huge in the moonlight streaming through the window. Esmerelda turned and faded into the shadows of the hallway, closing the door behind her.

*   *   *

Despite the efforts of the fire-fighters, the Cosmopolitan was fully engulfed in flames. Even though it was late at night, the fire had drawn a huge crowd of onlookers. Amid the chaos, Sheriff Chrisman and a small group of men were standing around Klein's body. The doctor rose and stuffed his stethoscope into his bag. "Yup. He's dead, all right," he said. "Gunshot wound. Pure and simple."

"Anybody know who was firing shots?" the sheriff asked. He surveyed the ring of faces. No one answered.

"Doesn't matter, I guess," said Sheriff Chrisman. "He was wanted dead or alive. Here he is—dead."

Chapter Sixty Four

A s daylight began to filter through the small window, Esmerelda sat on the edge of the bed, watching Anny sleep. Long lashes, a graceful ballet of pin-point freckles across her delicate nose, her cheeks tear-stained, hair pulled loose from her braids. Anny was a mess. She'd had only a few hours' sleep since last night. Not enough. Sensing Esmerelda's presence, her green eyes flickered, then opened to gaze into Esmerelda's blue ones.

Anny said nothing. Where was she? Her eyes burned. Her foot throbbed. Her head was swimming. She looked up at her friend, trying to bring her eyes and her mind into focus.

And then she remembered. It all came rushing back, and tears filled Anny's eyes.

She sat bolt upright. "Where's Gibbie?"

"I haven't found him yet, but please don't worry about him! I *will* find him. I promise." She handed Anny a wet washrag for her face.

Tears dripped from Anny's eyes as she squeezed them shut.

Esmerelda took Anny's shoulders gently in her hands and looked directly into her face. "I will find him," she repeated. "Understand? Do you trust me?"

Anny opened her eyes and nodded slowly, miserably. She wiped at her eyes with the washrag.

"Who do you know in The Dalles, Anny? Anyone? Friends at school?"

No. Anny had no friends at school. Not even the teacher. *Especially* not the teacher.

"What about the Delgados?"

"Well, *Mr.* Delgado is nice to us sometimes, but ..." Anny shrugged. "*You* are the only friend we have here."

Esmerelda blew out her breath. She had been afraid it would come to this.

"Anny, you can't stay here. It's not safe for you here." She didn't know if Anny had heard her father's comment last night about the kids having it—whatever "it" was. But it made her feel very uneasy. Esmerelda hated to send the child off alone. She had tried to think of something else. Keep Anny here at the brothel with her? Impossible. Let the Delgados take care of her? Knowing Mrs. Delgado as she did, Esmerelda dismissed this idea too. What then? The only reasonable thing left was to send her to Heppner, where her father had told her to go. No matter how bad he was, Esmerelda believed he had a reason for his parting words to Anny—especially in light of Les Matlock's questions about the children. Esmerelda would wire Grace to meet Anny at the station. Grace would know what to do. At least Anny would be safe.

"Anny, the train for Heppner leaves in half an hour. We need to get you on that train."

"I don't want to go on a train," Anny sobbed. "I don't want to go!"

"Do you remember what happened last night? Do you remember what your father said to those two men?

Anny looked into Esmerelda's face. "He's not ... What? What did he say?"

"You know, Anny. You heard him."

"He said his kids took it."

Esmerelda nodded. "It's not safe for you here in The Dalles. Whatever it is, those men think you have it. They will be looking for you."

He said more. Think of his words. What did he tell you?"

Anny spoke in a tiny voice. "He said to go back to Heppner." She sniffed and wiped at her nose with the back of her forearm. "He's *not* my father. And I've never been to Heppner. I don't even know where it is. And I don't know where Gibbie is either," she wailed.

"He's not your father?"

Anny shook her head.

Shivers ran down Esmerelda's arms and back. Les Matlock was right! These had to be the missing children!

"Anny, look at me." She waited until Anny's eyes met hers. "I *will* find Gibbie. And *you* need to get on the train to Heppner. Trust me, it's a real place. I used to live there."

Anny's teary eyes opened wide in amazement. Esmerelda stroked Anny's shoulder and brushed a strand of hair from her face. "You know, when someone knows they are dying, the words they say can be very important. If you were about to die, and you had a chance to say something, wouldn't you say the most important thing in the world?"

Anny thought for a moment, then nodded.

"You need to go," Esmerelda said quietly.

"Why can't I stay here 'til we find Gibbie? We can stay here with you, and I would take good care of Gibbie, so you wouldn't have to worry about us, and we wouldn't be any bother at all."

"No." Esmerelda shook her head sadly. I'm sorry Anny. You can't stay here with me." She gestured to the room they were in. "This is a bordello."

Anny's shoulders slumped. She wasn't surprised, only sad. Nothing. Nowhere to go. Maybe Heppner was the right choice.

Anny sniffed again. She felt like a little child. She didn't know what to do or where to go. She didn't know where Gibbie was, and she was afraid for him. She had never wanted Mama Jane as badly as she did at this moment. Her body shook with sobs. Her own words from last night came back to her. *Where's my papa? My papa!* Anny continued crying softly while Esmerelda just held her and rocked her.

"I won't go without Gibbie," Anny finally said.

"Anny, listen. You can't stay here. If you are safely on the train out of town, I'll know you are okay, and I can go look for Gibbie. I know where to look—along the waterfront. We both know he'll be somewhere near the boats. I know I'll find him. I know I will."

Anny breathed out a shuddering sigh. Finally she nodded slightly.

"Let's get you ready to go, then." Esmerelda pulled the ties from Anny's braids and combed through her hair, pulling gently at the snarls. "You braid one; I'll braid the other," she said to Anny. "I have a friend in Heppner who will take care of you. Her name is Grace. I'll send her a wire and she'll be there waiting for you."

Anny looked up at Esmerelda, a flicker of hope in her eyes, as she tied the limp ribbon on her braid.

"Here's money for your ticket." Esmerelda placed some coins in Anny's hand. "I'm sorry I don't have any clothes that will fit you. But I did find you some shoes and stockings." Esmerelda didn't mention they were from the things the girls of the bordello had collected to help the poor. "The shoes are a little big, but that will actually be good with your one foot all swollen and wrapped like it is." She bent to help Anny get the shoes on and tied.

Then Esmerelda pinned a scrap of paper to Anny's chest. *Heppner,* it said. She held out a small cloth bag to Anny. "This is for you. I put a comb and a washrag in there. And this" she said, handing Anny a newspaper wrapped package, "is your lunch. And your book," she added. "It's in the bag too."

"What do I do when I get there?" Anny asked, then sniffed and wiped at her nose.

"I don't know exactly. But my friend will help you. Just go there. Then see what's next." Anny's face showed absolutely no confidence in the arrangement. Esmerelda placed her finger gently under Anny's chin and looked into her eyes. "Are you afraid?"

Anny nodded. Esmerelda pulled her into an embrace.

"Don't be. Be brave. Remember, my friend will meet you there. She is someone you can trust. She's a good person." Esmerelda drew back and looked deep into Anny's eyes. "It's time now, Anny. Time to go."

Esmerelda led Anny to the back door of the bordello, down the stairway, and out into the alley.

Anny looked somberly at Esmerelda one last time before turning and limping slowly toward the train.

This train is heading west from The Dalles (in front of the Umatilla House).
Anny's train went east toward Arlington, and then on south to
Heppner.

Chapter Sixty Five

"Heppner," the conductor sang out. "End of the line."
As the train chugged to a stop, Anny gazed about herself in wonder. This? This was a town? The only building in sight was the train depot! What on earth was she doing here? Why had she even come? Because Father—that man—had told her she should come here. "Go back to Heppner," he had said. She had never been here in her life! And she didn't want to be here now. She had left Gibbie behind, and what did she have to show for it? Nothing. She should have at least tried to return to Puget Island instead of coming here! Anny blinked tears from her eyes, and then remembered. *Grace. Esmerelda's friend. She will be here.*

The few other passengers began moving down the aisle and descending the steps to the platform. They juggled their belongings, their children. Anny just sat, thinking. Maybe they would take her back without charge. She would tell them it was all a mistake.

A tall, thin man on his way out of the car hesitated and said to Anny, "Are you coming, miss? Do you need help?"

Anny looked up with a start. She grabbed the bag Esmerelda had given her and scampered off the train ahead of the man. The afternoon sun warmed her shoulders, but Anny saw no one on the platform who might be Esmerelda's friend. Only a couple of families greeting one another. *Where is Grace?* Anny stepped into the building, but no one waited for her inside either. She stood for a moment, undecided, and finally took a seat. She looked around at the wainscoted walls, the long oak benches, the ticket agent's window at one end of the room. *Maybe she was too busy to come. I'll wait a few minutes.* The other passengers all claimed their luggage and started off to their destinations. Still no one came for Anny.

I shouldn't have come. Anny felt tears rising to her eyes, and her throat began to constrict. Just as the muscles of her mouth tightened and she almost dissolved in sobs, she gulped and controlled herself again. *Maybe the friend came and saw how ugly and dirty I am and decided to just leave me here.* Anny brushed at her dress, trying to erase some of the wrinkles. She sat up straight and tried to smile, but the smile dissolved and tears filled her eyes as a new thought entered her mind. *Esmerelda lied to me! There is no Grace! I trusted her! She doesn't care about me at all or she wouldn't have sent me here. Oh Gibbie! I'm so sorry I left you! Mama Jane! I need you! Papa! Where are you, Papa!*

Jumping to her feet, Anny determined to stop crying and *do* something. The ticket master sat watching her from his little cage. She walked directly to him, took a deep breath, and explained that she'd gotten on the wrong train by accident, and could she possibly go back to The Dalles, because Portland was where she really intended to go, and she didn't mean to cause any trouble, but you see, it was all a mistake.

At first the gentle, gray haired man looked confused, but finally he told Anny he would allow her to make the return trip to The Dalles without charge. "But," he said, "you'll have to wait 'til tomorrow. No more trains today."

Anny gulped. She thanked the man, turned, and limped out of the station. If Esmerelda's friend was not going to come for her, Anny would have to take care of herself. *Who needs Esmerelda and her imaginary friend?*

She spotted the edge of the town a short distance down the road and began walking. *Go back to Heppner.* What had Father meant, go *back* to Heppner? Had she been here before? She peered curiously into the faces of the few people she passed on the road. None of them looked the least bit familiar. Had she misunderstood Father's dying words? No. Esmerelda had heard them too. *Go back to Heppner.*

Well, here she was. Now what? Should she ask someone if they could help her find Grace? No! If there was a Grace and she didn't care enough to come for Anny, Anny would not go in search of her. What, then? What should an almost twelve-year-old girl do in a strange town with no money and no friends? *Think, Anny!*

She suddenly realized she had left her paper-wrapped lunch on the train. But she wasn't hungry. Her stomach was too tied in knots to care about food. But she would need someplace to stay tonight. Where would she sleep? And even if she found a place, she would be expected to pay. She had no money. Anny thought of the forty-six cents she had saved up, intending to buy passage for herself and Gibbie back to Puget Island. It was gone now. Buried deep in the rubble of last night's fire. She had not one penny. Nothing.

Maybe there would be a store. Her countenance brightened at the thought. She knew how to work in a store. Maybe there would be a kind storekeeper who would let her work in exchange for a place to sleep.

She could see, now that she was closer, that this really was a town, even though it was small. The train station had been just at the edge of it. Several stores lined the main street. A barber, jeweler, blacksmith, butcher, a furniture store, another barber—there! A general store. She would talk to the storekeeper—just as soon as she plucked up her courage.

Seeing a bench in front of the jewelry store, she perched herself on the edge of it and gazed across the street at the general store—The Fair, it was called.

A brown-haired boy in overalls approached, following the biggest yellow dog Anny had ever seen. The dog stopped to sniff at Anny. "Come on, Sport," the boy said.

Anny reached out and petted the animal. What wonderful silky ears! Just being close to the dog was comforting to her. "I don't mind," she said softly, looking up at the boy. He had a scar that cut through his eyebrow—like Anny's, only longer, and he had a pleasant smile. Anny sank her fingers into the long fur on the dog's neck. She scratched as the dog stretched his neck and rolled his head from side to side. "Oh, you're a good dog, aren't you? Yes, you are." Anny rubbed her face on the dog's head, letting the comfort wash over her.

"Yeah, he's a good one, alright," the boy said. "Purt' near the best dog in the whole town!"

"The biggest anyway, I bet!" Anny smiled, wondering just how many dogs there could be in a town this size. Not many, she thought.

"You new here?" the boy asked, tilting his head as he looked at Anny.

The happiness faded from Anny's eyes as quickly as it had come. "Sort of, but I'm not staying. I'm going to The Dalles tomorrow."

The boy nodded.

"Hey, Will! Come on! What's takin' ya so long?" The call came from a younger boy down the street at the blacksmith's shop.

"Gotta go," said Will. "I hope you enjoy The Dalles!" And he was gone, his dog galumphing along behind him.

Anny took a deep breath. There was nothing to keep her from crossing the street now. She swallowed hard and rose from the bench. Walking reluctantly, slowly, she made her way across the street and in through the front door of The Fair. A woman holding a baby approached the counter with some muslin. Anny glanced at the storekeeper. He looked like a friendly man. Maybe this would work after all. She turned and walked past the buckets, brooms, mops, scrub brushes. A table at the back held bolts of muslin and calico. Her fingers stroked a delicate blue calico, then a bright yellow. Pretty, she thought.

She walked around the store, becoming familiar with the layout. She wanted to impress the storekeeper that she was intelligent enough to do any job that might be required of her.

Finally, she marched resolutely to the front of the store, where the storekeeper was cutting a length of muslin. Anny smiled at the baby sitting on the counter, while the man finished his cutting and folded the fabric.

"Anything else, my dear?" he asked the woman.

"I think that's it," the woman said. "Oh wait!" She called back to her friend who was just coming from the back of the store. "Do we need buttons?"

"No, I saved the old ones." This woman too, was carrying a young child.

"I'll be with you in just a moment," the man said to Anny. The woman turned and glanced at Anny, then counted out the money for the fabric. She looked back at Anny, a question in her eyes.

"Hello," she said, smiling.

"Hello," Anny answered.

The woman closed her eyes, took a breath, then looked down at the counter and back at Anny again, her eyebrows furrowed.

What? I know I look awful, but don't stare at me! Anny hung her head and hunched her shoulders, shamed by her appearance.

The woman accepted her wrapped bundle from the storekeeper and thanked him. She looked back at Anny, narrowing her eyes, then picked up the little one from the counter and joined her friend and several more children at the door.

"Now then, Little Miss, how can I help you?" asked the storekeeper, turning to smile at Anny. His face looked friendly, kind.

"Hello." She could hear her voice trembling, but continued. "My name is Anny Klein, and I'm wondering if you need help in the store. I've looked around and I see that your stock is pretty much the same as the store where I worked in The Dalles, so I think I could do a good job for you." Anny's words picked up speed like a train rolling out of town. "I noticed that your tinware and dry goods sections could use a bit of tidying up. I could do that. I can sweep and clean. I know how to restock the shelves and I can even wait on customers. I've had experience. Or I can clean or make signs—most anything you might need, I can do for you."

The man looked surprised and shook his head. "Well, we don't really need any help right now. You're a bit young to be out looking for a job, aren't you?"

Anny could hardly speak. They didn't need her. Even though he seemed like a nice man, he didn't need her.

"Actually," her voice broke. She struggled to gain control of it, then started again, this time speaking more slowly. "I—I just need a job for one day and a place to sleep tonight. I don't want any money—just a place to sleep."

"Wait, wait, wait!" the storekeeper held up his hands, smiling and shaking his head. "Let me get this straight. You want to work for one day in exchange for a bed for one night. Is that it?"

"Yes, that's it." Anny wanted to act confident, mature. Instead she felt about two inches high, and her voice was shaking. "I've worked at a store in The Dalles. I really am quite a good worker." *Oh please, just think of something I can do! I need to get back to The Dalles—to Puget Island. I want this nightmare to end!*

*   *   *

The woman who had bought the muslin was still standing at the door, watching. Now she moved back to Anny's side.

"Maybe I can help," she said. Anny looked up at her. A beautiful woman with dark hair and light blue eyes. The eyes were smiling. Anny felt a breath of hope.

"Can you care for children?" the woman asked.

"Oh yes. I can do almost anything that needs doing. I'm very good with children!" *Well, actually, I've never cared for any children other than except Gibbie, but I'll do anything—anything!*

The dark-haired woman smiled and took a deep breath. "Come with me," she said. "I think we can work something out." She smiled and nodded at the storekeeper, who shrugged his shoulders in return.

Anny walked down the street between the dark haired woman and her younger friend. "My name is Dacia Burke," the woman told her, "and this is my friend, Grace Collins."

Grace! Anny turned to her with big eyes. "Your name is Grace?"

The young woman smiled. "Yes. And what's your name?" she asked.

"Anny. Um ... I came in on the afternoon train ..."

Neither Grace nor Dacia responded.

"... and someone was supposed to meet me there, but she didn't."

"Do you know who this person was?" Dacia asked.

"Well, her name is Grace." Anny did not take her eyes from Grace as she said it.

"Oh my goodness! What a coincidence!" Grace truly seemed to know nothing about meeting the train. "I don't know of another Grace in town. Do you, Dacia?"

Dacia shook her head and asked Anny, "How do you know this person?"

Anny hung her head again. "A friend told me she would meet me. I guess she forgot. But it's okay. It'll all work out." *Maybe Grace has moved away and Esmerelda doesn't know it.*

What was this friend of Esmerelda's supposed to look like, Anny wondered. Esmerelda hadn't said. She had told Anny nothing except Grace's first name. This woman was young and pretty, had brown hair. And she was friendly. But she obviously knew nothing about meeting the train.

"Well, don't worry about a place to sleep tonight. We will be sure you are taken care of." Dacia said. "Did I hear you say you are from The Dalles?"

"Well, sort of. Most recently. I used to live down near Westport—on Puget Island."

"I see." Dacia smiled pleasantly. "And do you mind if I ask why you have come to Heppner?"

Anny felt trapped. Honestly, she didn't know why. "Well, someone told me I ought to come here. But it was all a mistake. I shouldn't have come."

"Is that why you are only going to stay here for one day?" asked Grace.

"Mm-hm. I have to go back to The Dalles tomorrow." *She seems like a nice lady. Maybe this is Esmerelda's friend. Maybe Esmerelda forgot to send the wire.* They turned a corner and continued walking.

"Do you have many children?" Anny asked. She should at least try to be polite to Mrs. Burke, show some interest.

"Six, now," said Dacia. "The boy with the dog is one of mine. His name is Will. And that was his younger brother, Walter, who called him away from you."

Noticing Anny's puzzled expression, she added, "I saw you sitting on the bench before you came into the store."

Dacia continued. "I also have these four little girls. Sarah, Ellie, Abigail, and Lucy." She nodded to the children with her—black haired every one of them, just like their mother. Baby Lucy reached her arms toward Anny, opening and closing her fat little fists. Anny laughed and reached for the baby. She came willingly into Anny's arms, but immediately turned back to her mother with the same gesture. The woman took her back, laughing.

Anny smiled, or at least tried to smile at each of the children, then looked back at Grace. *Grace Collins. Can she help me? Is she the one?*

"I have four children," Grace said in response to Anny's questioning look. "This is Ben, my youngest." She bounced the child in her arms and tickled his chin until he smiled. "He'll be two next month."

Only two blocks from the store, they stopped at a tall house with a picket fence around it. "This is where I live," Grace said to Anny, opening the gate. "Dacia ... I'm not sure what you have in mind..."

Anny realized that it had been only Mrs. Burke who had made the offer to her and that Grace had no more idea what was going on than she, herself, did. Anny needed to talk to Grace. Later. First, she would go with Mrs. Burke. After all, she was the one who was offering her work in exchange for a bed.

"Grace, could I leave the children with you for a little bit?" Mrs. Burke asked.

"Of course ..." Grace looked confused, but seemed quite willing to watch Dacia's children. She closed the gate and began herding them toward the back yard to play.

"Anny, let's put your bag at my house, and we can visit a little bit." Dacia smiled.

Anny felt confused. She was exhausted, she was worried about her brother, her foot was throbbing, she was hungry—now that she had time to notice—and she had absolutely no idea what was going on. Mrs. Burke had wanted Anny to care for the children, but then she left them with Grace instead. And now she wanted to visit!

Dacia led the way across the street to her house and showed Anny where she could freshen up a bit. Then she poured two glasses of lemonade. Anny came back into the kitchen, still confused and overwhelmed, but looking and feeling a bit better. She thanked Mrs. Burke for the lemonade, sat on the edge of a kitchen chair, and sipped slowly.

"Would you like something to eat?" Dacia asked. But Anny, unsure if she would be expected to pay for the food, shook her head no.

Dacia glanced at the rag sticking out of Anny's shoe. "Looks like you're limping a bit. Would you like me to take a look at your foot?"

Again Anny shook her head.

Dacia took a deep breath and tried a completely different kind of question. "Anny, would you be willing to tell me a little about yourself?"

Anny didn't know how to answer. "Um, I've only lived in The Dalles less than a year. Before that, I lived on Puget Island in the Columbia."

"Mm ... and how old are you?"

"Almost twelve."

Mrs. Burke smiled. "You must think I'm being horribly snoopy! It's just that you remind me very much of someone I used to know. Do you have any brothers or sisters?"

Suddenly, Grace burst through the front door, carrying Ben in her arms. "Dacia! I just got this telegram! It was tucked in my screen door – must've come while I was gone all morning. Read this!" She thrust the yellow paper into Dacia's hand.

Dacia read the telegram quickly.

Form No. 1.

THE WESTERN UNION TELEGRAPH COMPANY.

INCORPORATED

23,000 OFFICES IN AMERICA.   CABLE SERVICE TO ALL THE WORLD.

ROBERT C. CLOWRY, President and General Manager.

NUMBER	SENT BY	REC'D BY	CHECK

RECEIVED at _____ 9:16 AM   APRIL 21, 1960

Dated _____

To_____ GRACE COLLINS

MEET ANNY KLEIN 2:15 TRAIN

MAC HARMON'S DAUGHTER?

ESM

Goose bumps covered Dacia's arms. She felt dizzy. She put her hand on her mouth and looked at Anny, then nodded at Grace. "I think so. But I don't think she knows it." Her eyes burned into Grace's. "We need to find out for sure." She remembered Mac's anguish all the times

378

his hopes were raised, then dashed again. "I can't talk to him until I'm positive."

She thought a moment, then turned to Anny. "Anny, I'd like to show you something. Come with me."

Anny's forehead furrowed in confusion. "I thought you wanted me to take care of the children."

Dacia smiled at her. "I'm sorry. I know this must be confusing for you. Can you be patient for just a bit longer? We'll take the buggy so you won't have to walk on your sore foot. Okay?" Taking Anny outside, she quickly harnessed the horse to the buggy, and she and Anny started back the way they had come, then continued down the length of Main Street away from the railroad station. As they reached the far end of town—and it wasn't very far at all—they turned left, then right and followed the road up a steep hill. At the top was a cemetery.

A cemetery? What are we doing here?

Dacia asked Anny, "Do you know where we are?"

"At a cemetery." Anybody could see that.

Dacia nodded as she and Anny got out of the buggy. "This is Heppner's cemetery. Come over here. I'd like to show you something." She reached out and took Anny's hand.

A short distance away stood a group of gravestones, obviously a family. The plot was well cared for, trimmed and neat.

"Start here," Dacia said. She pointed to a marker with a lamb carved on it.

Ada Louise Harmon

Anny read in a soft voice.

Born September 26, 1897
Died March 3, 1898

Only a few months old. It was always sad to think of a little baby dying. Anny uttered a quiet "Mmmm," and shook her head slightly.

"Then this one," Dacia prompted.

Anny read aloud.

Ella Louise Harmon
Born July 5, 1874
And Unborn Baby
Perished in the Flood
June 14, 1903

Anny looked up at Dacia. "What flood?" she asked.

"It was almost seven years ago. She was my best friend." Dacia bit her lower lip.

Anny swallowed and stared hard at Dacia. She felt a tightness in her chest as she turned to the next stone. She read aloud, her voice shaking.

Charles MacKennon Harmon
Born January 27, 1895
Died in the Flood, June 14, 1903

Charlie?

Dacia said nothing.

"He was only eight." Anny said. She thought of Gibbie, now nine years old. Her stomach had tightened into a hard knot.

"Ella had four children," Dacia said. "This was her oldest, Charlie. Her next baby was the little girl, Ada, but she died several years before the flood."

Anny couldn't speak. She could barely think. Mostly, she could just feel. Baby Ada. Charlie. Ella? Was that the Mama's name? Perished in the Flood. *Her* mama?

Dacia continued, watching Anny carefully. "Ella's next two children disappeared on the night of the flood. Most people think they were drowned and their bodies never recovered. I don't believe that. I think they are alive—somewhere."

"What ... what are their names?" Anny's voice was choked; tears ran down her face.

"Gilbert and ... Lilyann."

Anny nodded and began sobbing uncontrollably. Between sobs, she choked out the words, "Lilyann. Yes. Yes! I remember. I do remember. Lilyann—that's me!" She looked up at Dacia again, sobs still shaking her small body. "Mrs. Burke, that's me! And Gibbie ... yes! His name was really Gilbert!"

She looked back at the gravestone labeled "Ella Harmon."

"The mama ... *my* mama. She died?" Tears filled her eyes afresh. Tears for the mama she'd never mourned. Dacia put her arms around her and held her close. Finally Anny pulled away, and looked again at the gravestones. No stone for the papa.

"What happened to the ... father, the papa?" Anny's words were soft, almost silent. But Dacia heard.

"Come with me. I'll show you." Dacia took Anny's hand again and returned to the buggy.

*   *   *

Pappy sat in his usual chair at the Harmony Saddle Shop, regaling three other men with tales of the old country. At the sound of the banjo, he looked up to see Dacia entering with a child in tow.

Anny looked up at the banjo and took a deep breath, inhaling the scent of leather as she entered the shop. For only an instant, she saw a picture—Papa, in a leather apron, the banjo needed to be tuned, the saddle shop—and then the picture was gone. But her heart felt comforted, secure. Anny closed her eyes and shook her head. Was she dreaming again? She reached out and took Dacia's hand.

Pappy stopped talking mid-sentence and slowly stood to his feet, both hands on the top of his shillelagh. He nodded, satisfied. His voice cracked, but his message was strong. "She's come back."

Dacia nodded slowly, tears streaming down her face. She stood behind Anny, one hand on the girl's shoulder.

Pappy's eyes shone with tears as well. He muttered to himself, "I knew it. I knew they'd come back." He reached out his hand to her, assuring his mind that the sweet little fairy girl he'd seen taken almost seven years ago was finally home.

Dacia, still holding Anny's shoulder, walked her back to the bench where Mac was working. The men in the shop were silent, watching. Mac continued making holes for the splice he was working on, as even Shan paused to look up.

Finally, Mac sensed the silence and raised his eyes to Dacia. Saying nothing, she turned her head and looked at Anny's face, then back at Mac.

Mac lowered his eyes to the girl. His face softened. "Lily," he whispered. "Lily." The mallet dropped to the floor. He opened his arms and Lilyann melted into them. She knew. This was her Papa. She knew.

Chapter Sixty Six

L es Matlock stood by the door fidgeting as the train pulled into The Dalles. He hadn't been able to concentrate on his business in Portland, and had finally made his excuses and returned to The Dalles. He was almost positive Esmerelda's young friends were Mac Harmon's children. And the more time passed, the more positive he became.

As the train slowed to a stop, Matlock gave only a quick glance of surprise to the burned-out shell of the Cosmopolitan Hotel down the street, then swung to the platform and headed directly to the Umatilla House. As he rounded the corner, he saw Esmerelda walking up the sandbar, a young boy following not far behind.

"Esmerelda!" Matlock called.

She looked up and waved, then turned and spoke to the boy. They hurried up the incline to Matlock.

"I couldn't stand it. I came back early," Matlock explained.

"I'm glad! I sent Anny on ahead this morning." In response to Matlock's questioning look, she said, "It's a long story. I'll fill you in later. Here's Gibbie." she added. "I just found him." She turned and indicated the boy. "Gibbie, this is my friend I was telling you about, Mr. Matlock. Mr. Matlock, Gibbie Klein."

Matlock found himself looking into a smaller version of Mac Harmon's face. He smiled, nodding slightly. Les reached out to shake Gibbie's hand. Gibbie's chin jutted out and he narrowed his eyes, as he surveyed Les Matlock coldly. He finally sighed and allowed the man to shake his hand.

As the trio moved toward the entrance of the Umatilla House, Matlock stopped to send off a quick message. "I'm wiring Shan Collins—Mac's business partner," he said to Esmerelda. "If they track him down quickly, we should hear back right away." He handed her his copy of the message.

Western Union
Tuesday, April 21, 1910 7:30 p.m.

Shan Collins
Girl arrived Heppner this afternoon. Who is she?
Matlock

Esmerelda smiled, her eyes twinkling in barely suppressed excitement.

Matlock turned back to Esmerelda and Gibbie. "May I buy dinner for the two of you?" he inquired with a formal air. Gibbie squinted even more, but the mention of dinner was a hard one to pass up. And he needed to find out what had happened to Anny. He nodded, and the three of them walked back to the Umatilla House entrance.

They found a table and Matlock ordered for all three of them, then sat back to survey Gibbie. Yes, this was very definitely Mac Harmon's son. No question. But Matlock had no idea how to connect with the boy. It was obvious he was not off to a good start.

Before their meal came, a waiter approached with a telegram.

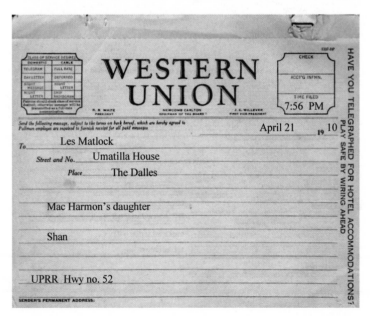

Les scrawled a response, sent it off with the waiter, and lifted the telegram he'd just received for Esmerelda and Gibbie to read.

Esmerelda's face lit up. Gibbie was baffled.

As soon as they had eaten their meal, Matlock ordered pie for Gibbie, then sat back and said, "Gibbie, I'd like to tell you a story."

Starting at the beginning, he told Gibbie of the flood, the missing children, the father's determined search. Gibbie listened, but appeared to take more interest in his pie than in the man's words.

"So," Matlock finished up. "You and I will take the early train to Heppner tomorrow, and you'll be back with your sister by afternoon."

Gibbie put down his fork and crossed his arms. "I'm not going."

Esmerelda took a deep breath. "Gibbie, I sent Anny this morning. She's waiting for you in Heppner. I *promised* her I would find you and send you to her there."

"I'll go with *you*," Gibbie said. "I don't want to go with him."

Esmerelda looked at Matlock and pursed her lips. This was certainly a young man with a mind of his own! "Gibbie, do you remember when I first gave you some apples? I gave you a note, too. Remember that?"

Gibbie nodded. "You said we should not talk to you in public— that you were not a good person."

"Do you understand what I meant by that?"

"I think so."

When Gibbie hesitated, Esmerelda simply waited. He turned pink, looked down at the table, and nodded. "I think you're a whore."

Esmerelda nodded miserably.

"But we're *eating* together in public!" Gibbie almost shouted

She had no answer for him and looked to Matlock for help.

Les folded his napkin and dropped it on his empty plate. He sucked on his teeth for a moment, then said, "Gibbie, Esmerelda doesn't want people to see you coming into town *with* her. She thinks it wouldn't be good for you. So—what about this? Since I'm going anyway, you and I can ride together, and Esmerelda can ride in the same car where you can see her and feel comfortable that she's there. Would that be alright?"

Finally, Gibbie looked at Esmerelda and asked, "Anny's in Heppner, now?"

"She is. And she can't wait for you to come!"

Gibbie's resistance melted away.

"So it's settled," Matlock said. "I'll get an extra cot in my room for tonight, and you can stay with me. We'll be on our way first thing in the morning."

Gibbie sighed. He didn't know what to feel.

*   *   *

According to Pappy, the ceilidh was fine and the craic was oh so grand at the Burke house that evening.

It was a pretty big gathering. Dacia and Johnny Burke with their six children and Pappy, Shan and Grace Collins with their four, and of course, Mac and Lilyann. The children—those who were tall enough—had eaten standing around the kitchen table, while the adults held their plates in their laps in the front room.

Supper had been a chaotic event, with the people of Heppner stopping in to see with their own eyes the child "returned from the dead." The ladies gushed over her, crying freely, and the men patted her gruffly on the shoulder welcoming her back in voices hoarse with tears. The many children *each* wanted to be her best friend. After all, she was famous!

There were too many people for her to remember all their names, but she knew she would learn them before long. First though, she just wanted just to be with Papa. *Her papa!* She left the table and sat on the arm of Mac's chair.

She gazed at Papa's face. Just like she remembered. And his voice. All of it—just like she remembered. Only she *hadn't* remembered. It was all too much to think about. She was exhausted, confused, and at the same time, more alive than she'd been in—well, in seven years. She felt as if life was just beginning.

"When will we leave?" she asked Papa. "I'm so worried about Gibbie."

"As soon as the train leaves, first thing in the morning." Mac touched the scar on her right eyebrow with his thumb, then put his arm around Lilyann's shoulders and gave her another hug—one of many in the past few hours. "I'm as anxious about him as you are, Lily. I know we'll find him."

Lilyann leaned her head against Papa's shoulder. "I want to find Mama Jane and Granddaddy too. But first Gibbie."

"We'll do it. We'll do it all." Mac looked up. "Shan, I guess the shop's going to be your baby for a while."

Shan smiled. "Looks like you have more exciting things to do."

Everyone looked up as they heard a loud banging at the front door.

The boy from the telegraph office opened the door and entered, not waiting to be let in. He was grinning from ear to ear as he slapped the telegram into Shan's outstretched hand.

Shan read it as everyone watched in silence. He looked up smiling at Mac and handed him the telegram.

Mac read aloud.

Form No. 1.

THE WESTERN UNION TELEGRAPH COMPANY.

INCORPORATED

23,000 OFFICES IN AMERICA. CABLE SERVICE TO ALL THE WORLD.

This Company TRANSMITS and DELIVERS messages only on conditions limiting its liability, which have been assumed to by the sender of the following message. Errors can be guarded against only by repeating a message back to the originating station for comparison, and the Company will not hold itself liable for errors or delays in transmission or delivery of Unrepeated Messages, beyond the amount of tolls paid thereon, nor in any case where the claim is not presented in writing within sixty days after the message is filed with the Company for transmission.

This is an UNREPEATED MESSAGE, and is delivered by request of the sender, under the conditions named above.

ROBERT C. CLOWRY, President and General Manager.

NUMBER	SENT BY	REC'D BY		CHECK

RECEIVED at HEPPNER STATION   APRIL 21   19☓10

Dated   8:10 PM

To   SHAN COLLINS

BRINGING GILBERT TOMORROW

2:15 TRAIN

MATLOCK

Shan slipped behind Grace, his arms encircling her. She sensed a peace, a rightness with the world she'd never known before. "Penny for your thoughts," Shan whispered in her ear.

Grace drew a deep breath and exhaled slowly. "Papa, father. A true father is a mighty wonderful thing." And the rest she treasured in her heart.

*   *   *

April 21, 1910

I am home! I've discovered so much these past two days – most of all WHO I AM! *I am not Anny Klein at all. I am Lilyann*

Harmon. Now I have my REAL papa! Gibbie is here too. We are a family!

Epilogue

There's more to the story, of course. We wrote letters to Mama Jane and Granddaddy. Papa took Gibbie and me to visit them only a few weeks after we returned to Heppner. Papa loved them as much as we did – more, he said, because of what they did for us – how they had loved and cared for us when he couldn't find us. Papa had a house built in the same place where we lived before the flood, next door to Shan and Grace and across the street from the Burkes. We went to see Mama Jane and Granddaddy at least once every year, and they came often to visit us too.

A year after we returned to our home, Papa married Lou Lundquist. She had two older children, Tommy and Claire, that she had adopted after the flood, so there were four of us children in the family. Esmerelda stayed in Heppner. Papa built a nice little apartment on the side of our house where she lived and started a sewing business. She always said she was born into a new life – because of Grace.

A lot of my character – the way I think, my views on life, the person I've become – can be traced back to things I learned during those early years following the flood. I learned that bad things can happen to anybody – not just to bad people. I learned that the world is not fair and that righteousness is often found in unexpected places. And most of all, I've learned to live today and trust tomorrow to the Maker of Life.

Lilyann Harmon Burke

Discussion Guide

1. Aside from the ending, what is the most powerful part of the story to you? Why?

2. Is it possible to live a fairly happy, comfortable life even before knowing our true Father and identity?

3. What factors, other than the head injury, would have worked together to cause Lilyann to forget her former life? Identify similar factors at work in the world we live in.

4. What things contributed to Michael's bad behavior after the flood? Do you know children whose behavior is affected by negative circumstances in life? Is there anything you can do to improve their situation?

5. Why could Will not walk after the flood? Has guilt—either real or imagined—ever paralyzed you in any way?

6. If you had been Dacia, what might you have said or done to help Grace overcome her past?

7. Have you known someone who, like Pappy, doesn't seem to fit into "normal" life and culture much of the time, and yet has a greater knowledge or insight in some ways than most people?

8. Why did Anny allow herself to be taken by Klein when he returned to the Island for her and Gibbie? Can something similar happen in our lives? What gave Anny the courage to finally stand against Klein?

9. How did living in the presence of evil affect Anny's outlook on life?

10. What, if anything, in this book revealed a truth in your own life?

11. Why *do* bad things happen to good people?

12.   An allegory is never perfect. It only serves as an example of a Truth. What parts of this story might be considered allegorical?

13.   Even though it was Mac who desperately wanted his children returned to him, in the end, it was others who shared his heart and vision who actually did the job. Think about that!

Cast of Characters

Names in bold type are real historical characters. Ages of the children are at the beginning of the story.

- The Harmon family: Mac, Ella, Charlie, 8; Lilyann, 4; Gilbert, 2
  Lilyann and Gilbert are just about to turn 5 and 3.
- The Burke family: Johnny, Dacia, Josie, 12; Martin, 10; Will, 7; Walter, 5; Sarah, 3.
  Dacia is pronounced "DAYsha." And for those who are interested, Dacia (pronounced DAH chee a) is the ancient name of Romania.
- Pappy (Burke): Johnny's grandfather who lives with the family.
- The Collins family: Kitty (Ma), Shan, 17; two teenage girls, Dennis, 12; Aiden, 9; Michael, 6; Libby, 4; Danny, 1½.
- Grace: a young lady who ran away from home and arrived in Heppner the morning of June 14, 1903, the day before her sixteenth birthday.
- Esmerelda: a prostitute at Heppner's *Chateau de Joie* (House of Joy)
- **Mollie Reed:** Madam at the *Chateau de Joie*
- **Les Matlock:** well-known gambler in Heppner, 30 years old, loved poetry, was known for always dressing sharply and for helping people financially. His involvement with Mac Harmon (a fictional character) is, of course, entirely fictional.
- **Bruce Kelley:** good friend of Matlock, 30 years old.
- **Sheriff Shutt:** Morrow County Sheriff in 1903.
- **Frank Gilliam** (pronounced "GIL um): Heppner's mayor and Johnny's boss.
- **James Yeager:** the town's furniture dealer and undertaker.
- **Jim Carr:** local builder and musician, lost a daughter in the flood.
- Karl Klein (also goes by Kingston): spurned by Ella in the past, he gets his way by taking her children. Mentally unbalanced.
- Mabel Dupont: young widow who, after the flood, has her eye on Mac Harmon.

- Lou Lundquist: local youngish spinster, Not well-liked at the beginning of the story.
- Etta and Elisabeth Snowburg: elderly twin sisters who keep a boarding house in Oregon City.
- Ivar and Jane (Snowburg) Petersen (Mama Jane and Granddaddy): They live on Puget Island in the Columbia River. (Puget is pronounced PYOU j't.)
- Mary Jo: Anny's first real friend after the flood.
- The Wife: the woman Klein has talked into helping with his family charade in The Dalles.
- Mr. and Mrs. Delgado: store-keepers in The Dalles.
- Miss Valentine: Anny's 6th grade teacher in The Dalles.

Some additional minor, but real, historic characters and places in the story

- **Frederick Krug** and his steam laundry
- **Dr. McSwords**
- **Alvin C. Giger**, owner of The Fair before the flood
- **J. A. Woolery**, mayor of Ione
- **Guy Boyer**, **Dave McAtee**, and **Frank Spaulding** who rode for help immediately after the flood when all outside communication was cut off
- **J. E. Gibson** and his barber/tonsorial shop
- **Katie Currin**
- **Guy Boyd** and **George Kinzley**, owners of the Liberty Meat Market
- **Dr. Kistner**
- **Fred Warnock**, editor of the Heppner Gazette
- **Mr. Marquardson**, owner of The Fair after the flood
- **Tommie Brennan**, ferrier
- **Noble's Saddlery**
- **George** and **Lillie Conser**

- **Cora May Ashbaugh** and **children**
- **Ed Ashbaugh,** owner of **The Pastime**
- **Scott** and **Andrew Brown**
- **The window** given to All Saints' Memorial Episcopal Church in memory of their daughter by the Carrs.
- **Sheriff Til Taylor**, Umatilla County, Oregon (Pendleton)
- **Police Chief Reddy** (Spokane)
- **Pap Simmons**, blacksmith
- **The Welcome Slough** and **Sunny Sands, schools** on Puget Island
- **Ole Gilbertsen**, hardanger fiddle player
- Wahkiakam County Sheriff, **Flanders**
- **Miss McDoodle**, Cathlamet school teacher
- **Simon Benson** and **John Yeon**, timber barons
- The *Bailey Gatzert* and the *Charles R. Spencer*
- **The Honker Bill**
- **Nickelsen's Book and Music Store** in The Dalles (now Klindt's Booksellers and Stationers, the oldest bookstore in Oregon)

The Real History

Yes, the Heppner Flood really happened. The final number of dead will probably never be determined, due in part to the large number of unidentified bodies that were buried in a common grave. In the midst of the horror, those working in the make-shift morgue did the best they could to record every body prepared for burial, but the list stops at number 177. Some of the well-known citizens of the town who would have been easily identified were never found. And there are many other known deaths—probably about 247, total.

Les Matlock and Bruce Kelly did make their famous ride the night of the flood. Mick Doherty of Portland, OR has written a song about the event called "Heppner's Washed Away." You can enjoy the song here: https://www.facebook.com/CascadiaFolkQuartet (See post from July 5, 2012.) Les Matlock was *not* involved in the return of Mac Harmon's children, as Mac and the children are *fictional* characters.

Fred Warnock was the editor of The Heppner Gazette, one of Heppner's two newspapers. The words from his story on the flood are quoted (abridged) from the June 17, 1903 newspaper.

The letter from the three little girls to Mayor Gilliam was real, as was his response (presented here in an abridged form).

The area called Valby is real. It was peopled mostly by hard working Swedish farmers. The Valby Church is still in existence and in regular use.

Puget Island was settled in the late 1800s, primarily by Norwegians and, to a lesser degree, Swedes and Irish. Most islanders were either fishermen or farmers. Although Cathlamet, on the Washington side of the river, was also readily available to them, most of the island's inhabitants did their business in Westport, Oregon. Puget Island is actually part of Washington State. It is currently linked to Washington by a bridge and to Oregon by ferry.

The Dalles was one of those "wild west" towns—wide open and ready for any adventure. It is still a thriving community—and considerably better behaved than it was back then.

Heppner's cemetery now has a large monument listing the names of all the known victims of the flood. It is located over the area used as a common grave for the unidentified bodies.

For an excellent, definitive work on the Heppner Flood of 1903, read *Calamity* by Joann Green Byrd.